©COPYRIGHT 2023

All rights reserved. This ____ ty of the author and may not be cc____ other than brief quotes for revie____ support the rights of authors by buying or borrowing books from authorized sources. Book piracy is not harmless. It's theft and hurts authors in many ways.

Thank you for respecting an author's hard work.

If you enjoy this book, please consider leaving a review. It truly helps indie authors succeed in bringing you more stories.

Cover design: Haelah Rice Covers.

Join DD's Chickadees on Facebook for fun, teasers, sales, and freebies as well as giveaways, fun chat about book boyfriends, and most of all... shenanigans. http://facebook.com/groups/ddprincefangroup

Subscribe to The Scoop, DD Prince's free email newsletter to get notified of new releases, sales and other news: http://ddprince.com/newsletter-signup/

Wicked
A savage alpha shifters romance
Book 3

BY DD PRINCE

Dedication:

For My Mister, who will most likely never read this book, but it's my twenty-fifth book and you should know that pieces of you and our love are in every single hero and story I write.

Peas and carrots, Hubbalicious.

Author's Note

This is book three of my Savage Alpha Shifters series. While each story is about a different couple, they're intended to be read in order. Book one is called Wild. Book two is called Twisted.

Please note: This is a steamy paranormal romance series with lots of carnal behavior and over-the-top wolf shifter heroes who claim, bite, and knot their fated mates.

This isn't categorized under dark romance but does have some darker elements.

This story contains mature language and open-door love scenes. My wolf shifters are also alpha, primal, and when it comes to their fated mates... sometimes quite feral.

My website, http://ddprince.com, has more information about elements found in my books.

Riley Savage thought his fated mate was lost in the river almost seven years ago. But when it's revealed that not only is she alive, but also that she's a witch who's been hiding from him, fury doesn't begin to describe how Riley feels. He's determined to get answers and hits nothing but dead ends.

And then she shows up.

Despite how angry he is, the desire to claim, bite, and knot her is stronger.

Come back to Arcana Falls and the Savage Alpha Shifters, wolf shifters who identify their fated mate and chase, claim, bite, knot, and purr for them. These stories are best experienced in order, starting with Wild.

"REGARDLESS OF TRYING to work against it, fate will always work harder than you. Fate has aces up its sleeve that you have no hope of comprehending." – Lyrica Young

1

ERICA YOUNG

The door to my hippie bus flies open with enough force to make everything inside rattle, not the least of which is me.

Everything in me has been coiled tight since I parked. Heck, since I decided to drive here. And now the moment I've been both dreaming of and dreading for seven years happens, and seeing him? I'm rattled to the core.

The look on his unbelievably handsome face? The furious, accusing eyes touching me? Together they make pain radiate through every single shaking cell in my body.

Barely leashed fury crackles as his eyes give me a once over from head to toe. Urges war within me. Run toward him? Hide?

I can't run to him. Absolutely not.

This is going to be agony. More anguish. Part of the price; it's time to pay. Though really, it feels like I've already been paying for nearly seven years. My entire body is a heartbeat, thumping, aching to touch – no, aching to fuse with him.

The cozy interior of this van suddenly feels even smaller. He can only stand in here because the overhead bunk is popped up and he takes up a lot of space with his height, his muscle. His presence. His fury.

He's pulling the door shut, towering over me as I sit on the bench seat that takes up the majority of the back of the van. I clench the patchwork quilt that covers it. Coincidentally, I'm gripping the piece of fabric from the shirt he wore the last time I saw him.

He doesn't know how important this quilt is to me. How important *he* is to me. How my sisters found that shirt dangling from a tree branch days after it all went wrong and brought it to me. I slept with it for months until I put it in this quilt and have slept with it nearly every night since. He doesn't know I've kept him close to me in the only ways I could for the past seven years, despite the fact that my mistakes cost us both so much.

He's even more handsome than I remember. And I never forgot just how easy Riley Savage is on the eyes. But the handsomeness I saw back then looks hard now. And it's down to me that there's no light in his green eyes at this moment.

The set of his more-than stubbled squared jaw is hard. He hasn't shaved in at least a week, maybe two. His dark hair is a mess, long enough there's a curl to it. It looks like he's been raking his fingers through it in frustration. And I can feel the rage shuddering inside him, as if rattling his rib cage, ready to burst out.

He's even more muscled, even more deliciously built. He's got a few sexy crinkles around his eyes. Has he laughed much? Or have I given him those faint crow's feet due to stress? It was a given he'd mourn the perceived loss of me, but has he held others, gotten pleasure from others? Sought comfort? Because I haven't. I wouldn't. I have so many questions and no right to ask any of them.

There's something strange in my chest, something elusive. It feels like I can almost reach out and touch the soul of him with mine, but his is caged by an invisible wall. A wall I built. My aches and fears shift into need. Stark need. Vivid desire. The need to feel him. The desire to be touched by him. The pulsing ache not only in my heart and my soul, but also in that forbidden place I've been saving for him. To show him how much I love him, to have him understand that I never meant for any of this to happen.

I wish I could touch him. I'll never forget the way it felt when we had that first kiss. The last one, too.

I don't even get to make a move toward him. It's like he senses the intent before I've done more than flex a muscle in my foot and his hand flies up to halt me.

"Do not take one step toward me, witch," he shouts, his voice coming out guttural, filled with emotion so raw, so visceral, it can only be described as loathingly. The way he says *witch* is as if it's the gravest insult he can hurl at me.

Danica told me when he smelled me in the Drowsy Hollow covenstead, there was significant fall-out. And I knew it was coming, knew last Fall when I dug deeper than ever to help Holden and Isabella with their problem that this could come at any moment. I knew I had no control over when it would happen. I gave it to fate. And now I guess fate is showing me that I reap what I sow. I fucked up so epically.

I've had a couple important occasions requiring me to step into the area and have been careful with masking my scent as well as traveling with a hat and glasses, I'd managed to avoid him up until then and still don't know how he caught my scent. But I guess it had to happen.

Is it better that he's had time to digest things rather than catching him off-guard? I don't know, won't ever get to know. This is how it is. And the day the coven helped with Amelia and Mason's problem, I knew my time had run out. Tyson Savage wanted to drag me here to answer for my crimes. His mate Ivy talked him out of it, believing me when I swore I was heading this way.

And now... here I am.

Of course I knew things would be amped today. Vivi saw that things were crazed, knew major events were underway with the first two couples as well as that a third couple was about to come together. But she wasn't sure if it'd be me and Riley. Suspected there would be a change in mating order and that if that happened, it could throw things off kilter.

I knew, we all knew, that I couldn't leave this any longer. A foreboding bell tolled inside me letting me know it was time.

I needed to face this. Begin the mission of fixing things. I've always known it'd be difficult. I knew it would hurt. As the days have gone by I've become more and more sure I'll lose something I never got to have.

But I doubt anything could have prepared me for the loathing that's coming at me from the man I love. The man I've wanted to connect with, with an unrelenting ache since just days after I turned eighteen. The loathing isn't just coming from my remorse. *His* loathing is weaving its way through me, showing me that we truly do have a connection with depth to it that I don't yet comprehend. I don't understand this bond we would've shared, but it hurts to know I've destroyed what could've been. I had to wait until my coven knew it was time. They told me it'd be about seven years. And we're less than two weeks away from that seven-year mark.

I've wanted him for ten years but have been punished for nearly seven. Because of my crime of using witchcraft to make him mine. The way I went about it, too. The kick in the gut being he would've been mine had I waited on fate. It's felt like one long punishment so far, feeling how I feel and knowing that he's likely been mourning me all this time.

But maybe now is when the real punishment begins. Seeing the results of my fuck-up. *Feeling* the consequences.

I don't even know where to begin with him. I haven't even allowed myself to play out scenarios in my mind of what this might be like. Wouldn't dare to hope it'd be okay somehow. I've done things to try to atone, to build goodwill. To give way more than I take. But the bottom line is that I'm now powerless to do anything but face what I did.

They told me that when this time came, I would come here and tell him the truth. That using magic would be forbidden while I'm in the village of Arcana Falls. I have to wait until he makes his decision before I attempt magic.

So, here I am. I'll do my best to make peace with the man I love, the man who I've known for seven years would think of me as his greatest enemy when he found out the truth.

He continues glaring at me as I do my best to not wither into a heap of emotion. My body trembles and I know my eyes must be oozing with my feelings.

His fists clench and unclench. When he growls low, with warning, like I've done something, like he's reading my thoughts, his eyes coast over my body again as my underwear become saturated. It's as if that growl called it forth. And this throws me for a loop, and I press my knees together.

Riley's nostrils flare and suddenly, he lunges, caging me on the bench seat. It's not big enough for this, but that means nothing, because I'm on my back and he's on me, my wrists painfully pinned over my head.

Another rumbling growl rolls up from deep within him, this one angrier. His eyes flame with fury. His exceptionally strong sense of smell coupled with this reaction shows me he knows what's just happened in my underwear.

His chest heaves up and down as his eyes bore into mine. His jaw muscles clench and unclench before he buries his nose in my throat. I melt as he inhales me deeply. I'm about to burst into flames of desire as his scent fills my senses. He pulls back and his eyes move up to the roof. He's looking at the pop-top bed up there.

Our eyes meet again and his glow a luminescent green for an instant.

"I can explain," I whisper, wanting to drink that scent, fill myself with it. "I still come off looking like the bad guy, but..."

His head jerks slightly, like I've shocked him, knocked him out of a trance, something.

"I do have an explanation," I continue. "I didn't mean it, Riley. I screwed up, it all went wrong, and then it was too late and-"

He knifes off me, making the camper van shake with the action. One of my glass jars of herbs smashes to the floor and books from my little shelf fall as well. If it weren't for the fact my bed is popped up, he'd have hit his head on the roof.

He roars, "Are you out of your fuckin' mind?"

I cower at the rage coming at me.

He continues shouting at me and three more jars smash to the floor. "Nothing you could say... fuckin' nothing!" He grinds his teeth and then shakes his head before he drops his voice an octave. "Go back wherever you came from, Rikki."

I flinch at the name; the nickname Dad gave me. Rikki-button, cute as a button. It's the name I told him was mine that day, the name I haven't let anyone use since.

Because of how right it sounded on his lips back then. Because of how wrong it was to do what I did. Because what I did meant I ceased to be Rikki. I became someone else after I had to face the music of my actions. I knew I'd never hear my dad say it again and suspected I'd never hear Riley, either.

"I'm here to explain, Riley. I-"

"I don't fuckin' care!" he roars.

"But..."

"Do you think there's anything you could say to me to make up for what you did to me? Anything? You know what you did. What it'd do to me. Right?"

I swallow.

"Right?" he bellows his question.

I nod. "I do know what I did." My voice trembles. "And no. Nothing's going to make up for it. Nothing."

"So you knew. You knew what it'd do." Somehow, the hatred intensifies.

"No."

"You didn't know?"

"Not exactly. I found out after."

"And you didn't put me out of my misery?"

"I couldn't. I wasn't allowed to."

"Fuck your excuses and fuck you."

"Please let me explain."

"Why? It's not gonna change what it did to me, how it changed me, what it took from me. From my pack. Go, witch. Let me finally have some..." his voice goes gruff, "some fuckin' peace."

Ouch. Ouch times a thousand.

I choke on a sob.

"Don't you dare," he snarls, pointing at me accusingly.

He doesn't want my tears. He's right, I don't deserve to have an emotional meltdown right now.

I try to hold my shit together. "I'm not leaving until I expl–"

"What, confess? So I can absolve you of your sins?" His eyes travel over me with disgust in them. "I don't think so."

The look on his face makes my chest feel like it's caving in.

"Go," he says coldly. "Crawl back under your rock, witch."

"I'll wait until you're ready to talk," I whisper.

"Go!" he roars.

I tremble, arms cradling myself.

"Then I'll fuckin' go," he states icily, then he leaves, slamming the door behind him.

All this time and now he's just... gone.

I don't deserve to meltdown and let it all out, but I can't help it.

I somehow manage to crawl up into the bunk. And as soon as I fall face-first into the pillows, I fall to pieces. It pours out. All of it. Finally. Flooding rivers of pain. Crying so long and so hard it's as if seven years of grief tsunamically surges straight out of my soul.

And while it happens, something digs in deep, weaves its way in, settling within my chest. Something strange and new. And I'm pretty sure it's got something to do with him and the bond we could have developed if I hadn't fucked up.

2

RILEY SAVAGE

My wolf form runs faster than my human form, so to get the fuck away from the sensations chasing me, sensations from her, fur bursts from my skin the minute the night air hits and I'm on all fours.

I'm gone. Gone, but being chased by pain coming at me through that new, odd place in my chest that hurts so much it's got me in some sort of chokehold that means I can barely breathe with it.

I vaguely sense my pack brothers nearby, along with knowledge that something has tweaked somebody on the council. But I can't linger on that or any other thought whatsoever because my paws are pounding the ground and I'm running, full speed toward the forest to get away from what she's feeling. Because I can't process any of it. I don't have the capacity.

But her emotions chase me all night long, clawing for me, nipping at my ankles, trying to pull me to the ground and drag me back to her.

No. Not happening.

Instead, I rip shit up.

3

ERICA
Ten Years Ago

The mystery surrounding my Great Aunt Lyrica drove me half-crazy through my teens. But when I found out the truth, it fit like a glove. Whenever someone questions my magic, I tell them I've been told my entire life my gift is spell-writing. The truth is, the day I found out I'm a spell-writer, it felt like my life finally began. I finally knew who I was. Why I was the way I was. The truth about my family, about my gifts, was unveiled for me on my eighteenth birthday, when it was finally my turn to take the trip - the infamous, secretive Young sister eighteenth birthday trip to Drowsy Hollow, the town where we were born.

I woke up fraught with worry, certain I messed everything up by being stubborn and digging my heels in.

I hadn't even packed. Danica and Jessica packed a week early. But me? Nope. I told them all last week not to bother with presents or a cake because I wasn't taking part in any of it.

You could say I'd carried some bitterness since Danica's eighteenth birthday thirteen months before and had been kind of hard to get along with ever since.

This trip was something I'd been anticipating since shortly after my oldest sister Vivica turned eighteen. With each sister turning that age, my curiosity grew while my patience waned. Because going on that trip changed whoever went.

Yes, it changed them.

They came back different, *very* different. But the kicker was that they weren't allowed to talk about the trip with anyone who hadn't already taken it.

Being the youngest of the five of us, with a little over or under a year between each of us in age meant that as every one of them turned eighteen, I was more and more left out. Because my sisters all got to be in a club I wasn't yet welcome in. They had secrets I wasn't allowed to know. I was the last sister standing alone.

And waiting isn't my strong suit. But they were all adept at following the rules and telling me nothing.

I've felt my sisters' excitement for me the week leading up to my eighteenth birthday, despite the way I've behaved.

The smiles. The nudges and eyebrow wiggles? I have not handled it well.

But, they ignored my brattiness and woke me today with Veronica's cream cheese frosting-filled carrot muffins, singing, and excitement anyway.

It was finally here. I didn't feel relief, though, because Aunt Lyrica who was normally here on a Young girl's birthday morning was absent. So I spent the morning of my birthday on the verge of tears, basking in regret.

I'd pretended my heart hadn't skipped a beat when I'd gotten the handmade invitation in the mail a month ago. I pretended I no longer had any interest in going. So, I didn't call or write to Aunt Lyrica to accept her invite and the last forty-eight hours was fraught with worry that she wouldn't come, that not answering her invite meant I'd ruined everything. That I'd never get to join the club my entire family, save me, was a part of.

But early afternoon while I was curled up on the big chair by the window with my sketchbook, doodling dying flowers to match my mood, I heard, "Happy birthday, beautiful birthday girl!" in that familiar raspy voice. My heart skipped a beat and then excitement spiked. She'd let me sweat it out. And I *so* deserved it.

Aunt Lyrica came; I hadn't even heard her pull up, but there she was... doing a slow bridal walk toward me carrying a pink cake with a lit candle on top of it. My sisters and Aunt Mimi were behind her.

Today, she wore her long, dyed black hair in *Bo Derek style* braids and had a black and green scarf holding it back. She was decked out in her trademark jangly bracelets, big chandelier earrings, and she wore a long broomstick dress with a bustier that pushed her ample boobs up high. As usual, she had her signature green eyeshadow and rouged lips.

Though Aunt Lyrica was in her late seventies, her fashion sense was a cross between Captain Jack Sparrow and Elvira, Mistress of the Dark.

She gave me a knowing look as she set the cake down in front of me, proclaiming, "Someone should be served some humble pie instead of pink cake, but I'm a forgiving type."

"No, you're not," Aunt Mimi corrected.

Aunt Mimi and Aunt Lyrica looked alike. Aunt Mimi was ten years younger than her sister, not nearly as flamboyant – more Cher than Elvira.

"True, I'm not," Aunt Lyrica admitted cheekily. "But I'm not the one who's had to put up with your hijinks lately, so blow out your candle, birthday girl; we need to hit the road."

I looked down at the baby pink cake with the big, rose shaped swirls of frosting and blew out the black candle knowing I didn't need to make a wish; my wish was coming true. I was finally part of things. I wanted to kick my heels up in the air. Instead, I sheepishly admitted, "I haven't packed."

"We packed for you," my sisters Jessie and Ronnie piped up in unison. They were all in the doorway watching. Smiling.

"And your presents are tucked into your bag. Open them later," Vivi added.

My reaction was to burst into tears.

My sisters took turns hugging me, cooing and comforting me, and then Ronnie accidentally spilled some beans by blurting, "We can't wait until you come back so we can have the very first full Young coven meeting."

"Young *what* meeting?" I asked.

"Ronnie!" Danica admonished at the same time as Vivi shouted, "Veronica!"

It was written all over their faces. The cat was out of the bag.

Coven.

Things snapped into place for me like the last few pieces of the puzzle I'd been working on. I'd suspected I'd known what it'd look like. I wasn't surprised. I was ready. Very.

"Oh," Ronnie went as pink as my cake but still waved her hand dismissively. "Well, she's eighteen now. She's waited long enough. And she had her suspicions."

I very much had. And I very much *did*.

"Save the questions for the road. We've a long drive ahead," Aunt Lyrica decreed.

"Okay," I agreed readily and stared at my cake, a big smile spreading across my face as the facts sank in.

Coven. I knew it! Well, I suspected it. I mean, my aunts looked the part. Aunt Lyrica refused to hide who she was. I knew she told fortunes and did tarot card readings in the back of her tailor and drycleaning shop in Drowsy Hollow. Aunt Mimi's boutique went along with the same look because of the goods she sold, lots of household goods, but also crystals, essential oils, boho clothes, old books, hand-made jewelry, and antiques along with tarot card decks. But still... I suspected it wasn't just a gimmick.

Dani and I exchanged glances. Her eyes were bright with emotion.

I smiled wide and then we embraced, swaying back and forth and giggling.

"Stop being mad at me now?" she demanded.

"Okay," I readily agreed and then we giggled some more.

"I can't wait to eat this," I said, looking at my cake.

"Do we want to sit here and eat cake, or do we want to go have an adventure?" Aunt Lyrica asked.

"Can we take some cake *on* our adventure?" I asked.

She threw her head back and laughed loud before she tossed me a set of keys. I caught them and examined them.

She said, "Drive me home, stay a week, then you can drive it back."

"And then you may start working in the shop," Aunt Mimi added.

The rest of them took turns running the boutique with the fortune teller tent in the back. I'd been bugging for years to work there, but none of us got to do that until after our eighteenth birthday.

My jaw dropped as I examined the black metal keychain holding the key to her van. "Really?" I managed. "I get to drive the hippie bus back? But why?"

"It's yours now. I'm getting something compact. It'll be delivered this week. This is your reward for waiting so patiently for today." She gave me an exaggerated wink. "Pack up some cake for us, will you, Vivi-darling?"

"Absolutely!" Vivi hopped to it. "Erica, do your cut first."

I did a happy dance, pulled the knife through the cake and then licked frosting off the tip.

My sisters' eyes were on me and full of joy. Full, too, to bursting with secrets they couldn't wait to share. Because when I got back, they could finally share them.

Laughter bubbled up in me and I didn't hold it back as my sisters all piled on me with more hugs and kisses.

Aunt Mimi, often serious and stoic, gave me a warm hug. And she wasn't the touchy-feely type.

"Enjoy it, girl," she whispered. "Your patience has paid off."

"A smile and a joke from you, Aunt Mimi? What is it, my birthday or something?"

We all laughed, including Aunt Mimi. Because I've been the opposite of patient. In my defense, it's not easy to feel, for eight years straight, like you're further and further disconnected from your family.

First, we lose Mom and Dad. And then year by year I've lost a piece of each of my sisters as their secrets created distance between us.

I've been sulky, and downright bitchy at times about it. Especially since Danica's birthday, when I became the last Young sister standing alone, left out of *the club* as she and Aunt Lyrica drove away. I didn't even wave her off, just stared from the bedroom window watching my other three sisters stand together, arms around one another as they waved at the departing duo.

"It's important. You'll understand after," Vivica, my oldest sister told me that day when she found me sulking.

I hadn't really figured out that the birthday trip was all about secrets until shortly after Jessica's birthday because though Vivi and Ronnie (Veronica) were always super close, after Jessie's birthday, it became very apparent there was a strange club of three. Me and Dani weren't part of it, but we had one another. And then when she turned eighteen and disappeared for her trip with Aunt Lyrica, and came back giving me the same speech Jessie had given us, I felt forsaken. I was determined to uncover the secrets. I didn't want to wait the thirteen long months.

Nobody would tell me a thing. Dani and I had tried to guess after Jessica. And it turned out we pretty much had it figured out, but nobody would confirm or deny or give us any details. And I had no idea what any of it meant.

After Dani came back, I'd find out the four of them were doing things without me. I didn't know what those things were, but I knew I wasn't invited, and got caught spying. I never figured much out.

Our family has always been strange. All five of us were born on the eighteenth of our birth month, so our special enlightenment birthday, as Great Aunt Mimi called it, included the special trip with Aunt Lyrica along with admittance into what I'd first dubbed The *Secret Young Club*, then when I was the only one not in it, I started calling it The Erica Young Haters Club. And I was very vocal about it.

They encouraged me to be patient, but as the youngest of five, I was tired of always hearing those words. Be patient. Wait. Wait until I was older. Until I was taller. Until, until, until. It drove me half-mad sometimes.

But now I was in the club. No more waiting.

AUNT LYRICA'S CAMPER van made me think of the gypsies in their caravans with colorful decorations, stocked to the brim with stuff. But now I was looking at it with fresh eyes and could see she traveled with a sort of apothecary. Plants, crystals, jars. The van had many nooks and crannies filled with not just stuff, filled with things she might need.

It didn't have running water, but it had a pop-top tent and fold out bed on top. The back had a bench large enough to sleep on. Running from behind the driver's seat to the bench was a long counter with shelves underneath. I opened doors and hatches in the past and got reprimanded for snooping.

Now, I could snoop if I wanted to. She was gifting me this van.

"You're the youngest Young, the last to be admitted into the coven from your generation, and my job is now nearly done." Aunt Lyrica took a dramatic bow. "I'm going to settle in and get ready for retirement. You'll be trained by me and by Mimi."

"Trained?" That was exciting. "But retire? You? As if," I scoffed.

"I'm ready," she said.

I frowned. Aunt Lyrica was looking tired and older all of a sudden.

"Almost done. We'll get you trained first." She smiled and the years melted away. "Let's go."

"Where to?" I asked. "To Drowsy Hollow?"

"To Drowsy Hollow," she confirmed, gesturing toward the road with a wave of her bejeweled hand.

Aunt Lyrica had stayed in the town where we were born. She lived in the apartment above the shop. I knew it was four hours away, but hadn't been there since we moved away when I was little. It was a place that I often thought about, sketching what I remembered of the main street. I remember it being small, quaint, and being surrounded by what felt like an enchanted forest. I wondered if it would feel the same.

We went years without seeing any members of Dad's family until my parents' untimely death, three months before Vivi turned eighteen.

Vivi and Ronnie used to talk about hearing them fight about home and Dad's family who he wanted to visit. After our parents perished in that awful freak accident, we moved in with Great Aunt Mimi.

When Vivi turned eighteen and took her trip, the first change I noted in her was her refusal to discuss Drowsy Hollow with us with anything other than vagueness.

And then Ronnie's tune also changed eleven months later after her trip. Subjects got changed and the rest of us wondered why. But one by one, we were divided. Divided into two groups until it was just me being left in the dark for thirteen long months.

I was finally on the cusp of getting answers. I wiped sweaty palms on my jeans, regretting that I'd rebelled this morning and refused to wear a party dress. Aunt Lyrica loved it when I would mirror her gypsy style with my own little bohemian twist. I loved shopping for dresses at Aunt Mimi's shop.

Aunt Lyrica settled into her seat and gestured toward the road. "While you drive, I'll talk. There are things to know. A lot of things to know."

Excitement bubbled up. I started the van and off we went.

And she told me a lot of things and answered a lot of my questions over what felt like a quick four-hour trip until I made it to the main street of Drowsy Hollow. I was still shaking with the truth of the Young coven as I took in the main street that I'd captured in my sketches. I'd left when I was five, but turned out I remembered it very well.

I'm a witch.

My sisters are witches. Dad should've been a warlock, but never exhibited gifts. Sometimes the gifts skipped a generation for some of the children. And when they did, the rest of the coven would brace because the generation that would spawn off the ungifted individual would be one to watch. No one in the family born on any day other than the eighteenth of a month exhibited gifts.

I was warned that sometimes those with strong gifts fell victim to the dark side of magic, that we had such witches in our family, in Dad's generation. She'd been excommunicated because of her actions. Her magic had been stripped, too. It sounded terrible and I knew I'd never do anything to risk that.

She said the Young sisters were the generation to watch. Five girls. Our coven is important to this area and that's why I've felt so drawn to come back. And she also told me my parents' death is the direct result of their attempts to keep us from fulfilling our destiny of becoming what we are.

Mom wanted nothing to do with it and was furious with my father for not telling her about any of it until she had five daughters who were all born on the eighteenth of their birth month.

Upon learning the truth, she moved us away to try to keep us shielded, but fate evidently intervened. Aunt Lyrica drove it home to me that regardless of trying to work against it, fate will always work harder than you. Fate has aces up its sleeve that you have no hope of comprehending.

I would see firsthand how true this was over the coming years.

4

RILEY

Now

The chattering of squirrels rouses me from a deep sleep. I've slept for a few hours in the forest, just feet away from the river. I rise, my tongue mopping drool from my muzzle. It's mixed with dried blood.

I hunted last night. I ate until I threw up. I wasn't part man, part wolf last night. Feels like I was *all* wolf. And like I haven't had nearly enough sleep.

I slide into the river, doing whatever I do when I have to swim it, blank my mind as much as possible before shifting to man underneath the water, swimming for a moment until coming up for air on the other side of the waterfall, inside the cave. Because of her, I try to only swim the river as wolf, because it somehow hurt slightly less over these last years.

I'm not alone. And it's no surprise.

Mason, Ty, and Jase are here. All three sets of eyes hit me. They're nude, ending their morning run here as we often do when we want somewhere private to talk pack matters. I know by their expressions that I've been a topic of conversation, know they have questions, and I'd rather not linger and deal, so I lift the lid off the big blue tote in the corner to fetch a bottle of water. I decide maybe I'll avoid shifting next time I dive into the river. Time to make amends with it. Because the river didn't steal my mate from me. My mate was the one who stole from me. Stole nearly seven years.

Savage House, Tyson and his mate Ivy's place, is a sprawling place on the shore not far from the other side of the waterfall, so he keeps the tote in this cave stocked with drinks, protein bars, fruit leather, and swim trunks in case we need them. He swims the tote back and forth when it needs a refill.

When we end runs at my place, my garage also has a similar stock. I have a stocked fridge in the garage, which is also the shop for Savage Construction.

I bought my childhood home from my parents who wanted to downsize two years ago when my sister went off to school. It made sense with running the business from here and it's an easy five-minute walk from the riverbank, which ends by the bridge between Aunt Cat's medical clinic and Roxy's bar. Less than five minutes in the other direction is our town hall along with the general store and gas bar, also known as the four corners of the Village of Arcana Falls.

Mason's got a stash of clothes of ours in his basement, and his drink stock is much better than Tyson's selection of warm sports drinks and water. Good that I'm here and not at Mason's or I might be tempted to day drink.

Unless we're in a coded situation, we come and go from runs without worrying about clothing. Though, I don't know what the code situation is today after yesterday's events. And I should find out.

I'm struck by how odd it feels to be out of touch with my pack, especially after the past six years of being at the core of everything going on. When she disappeared into that river and I thought she was lost to me, I left. I hit the road to get away from everything. I got called back for the change of the council and threw myself into that.

I've always figured they called us to it early, hoping it'd help with my healing. And it did. Throwing myself into caring for my pack saved me. Being called to the council definitely helped; not to mention coming back for that and soon after getting hit with the scent of Tyson marking around the village, letting us know he wasn't dead. Between the council appointment and Tyson, I had new focus.

"How'd last night go?" Jase interrupts my thoughts, eyes hard.

"It didn't." I know they already know this. They would've felt the change if it'd gone differently. They'd smell it and wouldn't see me for days as I'd be otherwise occupied. But I don't want to talk about this, can't wrap my head around it, need to not think about it to keep myself level-headed. I need to be able to function, so that if there's anything I need to do for the pack after yesterday, I've got the capacity for it.

Though I feel like 'level' isn't gonna be something I am for a while.

I'd never mated her, never got the chance to give her my mark almost seven years ago. It would've happened if she hadn't disappeared into the river. The river I'd always loved but have had a strained relationship with since.

I've always felt like the river took her from me. Because I scared her into her death by revealing my nature and insisting I was about to make her mine. She fell in and I couldn't find her.

My chest is hollowed out now where the aching grief was. I told myself I had to ignore the pain, push past it to function for my pack, my family. But at night, alone in my bed, I knew what I was missing.

I grieved a lie.

Anger fills that space now. Anger and bitterness that form a Molotov cocktail verging on rage, threatening to bubble over at the reminder of all I've been through and all I haven't had because of her deception.

The chances at connection I've turned away because I couldn't stomach the idea of anyone that wasn't her. I've walked around for almost seven years with a gaping hole in me. Living with her fear-filled face inked inside my eyelids. And my pack has suffered for it, too.

The song she sang that day I met her still worms its way through my mind at times. On the rare occasion it pops on the radio, I'm a shell of a man for the rest of that day.

I felt guilt the night Roxy kissed me. She was drunk, sad things weren't going anywhere with Mase, who she's carried a torch for since forever. I stopped her because it felt like I'd be cheating on Rikki.

But Rikki doesn't exist. She's Erica Young. A witch who lies.

"You'd rather spend your life alone?" Roxy asked, unable to grasp why I wouldn't let myself have a night of carnal pleasure with no strings a couple years after losing a mate. "What a waste, Riley. Would she want that for you? I bet she wouldn't."

Seeing her face again last night after not believing for all this time that I'd ever see it other than in my watery nightmares? Hearing her voice? Catching the scent of the slickness she made for me when I growled at her...

Where would I be now if she hadn't fucked with me? Tyson and Mason have their mates, so I guess it'd be my turn now. But what she did stole that from me. Stole seven years from me where I could've been whole, could've lived differently. Could've anticipated meeting my mate instead of mourning her. Though, what good would it have done if she was my destiny anyway?

When I found out she's a witch, my first thought was that she'd faked our connection. Cast a spell. But I'm told she's my true mate. Maybe I couldn't bring myself to move on because she wasn't really gone.

Fuck me now or fuck me then; I guess it would've been the same. She's here now because why? Because it's my turn to mate? If she hadn't shown up seven years early, I'd have had the past seven years to enjoy my life before being saddled with her, I guess.

Lorenzo moved on with Kathleen Brennan because he knows his wife is gone. He held her as she died.

Graydon moved on with Carrie because his first wife did things so heinous he had their connection severed. We don't know what those things were but severing rarely happens with an alpha's connection. As far as I know, it was a first for a council alpha in our pack. While Graydon hasn't said what she did, clearly it was extreme enough to sever their connection while Grey was an infant.

I figured the first thing out of my mouth at seeing her would be a demand that our bond is severed. Instead, I wanted to grab her by those copper curls and bury myself so deep in her that I'd never find my way out.

And that's probably why I want to put my fists through the walls of this cave right now.

"Talk to us," Tyson requests, likely sensing my frustration through our pack connection.

I down a long drink of the tepid water. All eyes are on me.

Finally, I dig deep, dig where I've never truly shared from and say, "It happened in a field of wildflowers. Saw her the day before and was curious. But the next day, seeing her, catching her scent, I knew she was mine."

I haul air into my lungs then expel it slowly before continuing, finding it difficult to not simply shift and go on another rampage. "We only spent a few hours together and it was..." I shrug. "Felt like everything you hear it'll be when you find her. Dug everything about her. I wanted to seal it. I knew it didn't make sense, that it shouldn't have been my turn since Mase hadn't mated. Didn't know you were alive then either, Ty; didn't catch your scent until almost half a year later. But that day? I felt it and knew it was real, that she was *it*. She was this tiny, beautiful thing surrounded by flowers. She got timid when I told her the truth. What I am. How I knew I wanted to take her home and keep her. Explained things to her, knowing she wasn't shifter and wouldn't know otherwise. Thought she was human; didn't smell the magic on her. Told her I'd show her my wolf to prove I wasn't batshit crazy. But she ran, fell off a cliff and disappeared into the river. It... it gutted me. I tried to get to her, but she was just ... just..." I snapped my fingers. "Gone. Vanished. Blamed myself." My nostrils flare and my voice goes guttural, "And then I find out she's a witch who's been hiding from me. Hiding, masking her scent, and knowing what it did to me?" I shake my head.

"You didn't spend very long in her van," Jase states.

"No." I keep shaking my head.

"Didn't like what she had to say?" Jase pushes.

"Didn't give her a chance to spew lies," I state.

Jase's jaw flexes.

"I spoke to her late last night," Tyson tells me.

I flinch. And avoid the strange urge to grab my cousin's throat.

He goes on, "She's here to explain."

"Stop. Don't wanna talk about this."

I'm feeling too much. I feel like I'm about to lose it. I can't do this.

Ty's mate already told me the witch had given her a message when they all got back from Marblehead.

"She didn't mean it, Riley," Ivy told me. *"She didn't mean to stay away, but she had no choice. It's haunted her every day since."*

Empty words that meant nothing to me.

Mase takes a breath, about to speak, so I lift a hand.

"At all. Don't wanna talk about it at all, brothers. I need to go. But first, what's happening? Where are Grey, Linc, and Joel? What else? I've got the sense there's more going on than my bullshit. You're okay?" I ask Tyson. He was shot yesterday. And here he sits looking absolutely fine, thankfully.

"I'm good," Ty assures. "But Riley..."

"No. Anything but me. Tell me what's happening around here. I know there's things happening."

"Amie's pregnant," Mase announces.

A smile cracks my otherwise stone-cold face. Despite all I'm feeling, Mase looks ecstatic. I feel it from him as well as see it on him and I'm stoked for him. I approach and he stands. As we embrace, I say, "Congratulations, my brother."

"Thanks, Rye," Mason slaps my back. "Found out last night. Over the fuckin' moon."

"Over the strawberry moon," Jase puts in. "Sure there's other babies on the way, too. How's your mate taking it?"

Mason laughs. "She's on cloud nine. She thought she was infertile. Was convinced of it. She just hadn't met me yet." He looks proud.

"Thrilled for you, man," I thump my chest with my fist. I am. As thrilled as I can be given my current state.

"It's a boy," Mase adds with an emotional look in his eyes. "Just the size of a seed right now but it's a boy. I smelled him on her. I already have a bond with him. Can't explain it, but I do. I can't..." Mason's voice has gone gruff. "I can't wait to meet him."

"Great news. Could be the start of the next gen council," I say.

I wanted kids. A lot of kids. I've given up on the idea of that.

Her face flashes in my mind. Her wild copper-colored hair that seems to twirl down her back to nearly her waist. Half a foot longer than last time I saw her. More of it. Begging to be fisted.

I see the way she twirled in the field of flowers that day so long ago with her head thrown back, a smile on her face, hands upturned, like she was summoning something as she twirled barefoot in those flowers, singing with joy. Wildflower bouquets in her hands. Summoning all right. Summoning me.

Now I see her face last night. Her almond-shaped clay-colored eyes with copper flecks in them. Her full mouth. Her high cheekbones. The emotion all over her face as I stepped inside her van. Something ugly uncurls, spreading through my gut as I ponder the fact that she's as beautiful as she was then. More. I remember how she felt under me. More curves than back then. Full tits. The scent of her arousal. Arousal instead of the fear scent I smelled on her the last time I touched her.

My cock hardens at the same instant as the urge to smash something returns.

Something slides through my mind, through the connection with my pack and we all exchange glances. I know their glances are at least partly about me and the thoughts that are seeping through the shield I'm trying to put up.

"What's happening with Grey?" I change the subject, feeling with certainty that something's up with him. "Where is he?"

A scent suddenly hits my nostrils. And my council co-alphas' noses, too, by their faces.

"The diner waitress that shot me is Greyson's mate," Ty informs. "I think they've just mated. The pack connection sensation is familiar." Ty turns to Mase. "I think it's what I felt when you and Amelia mated."

"Yep. Feel it. I smell it too. That's Grey. Surprised he held out all night," Mase states. "Though his mate has some explaining to do, too."

"Bring me up to speed," I request.

"Supposed to be you," Jase says. "You should've mated last night. Is this gonna fuck with things?"

"Don't know," I shrug. "What happened with Grey?"

The alpha's mating scent spreads the first time an alpha knots his mate. The fragrance spreads for at least a mile and it lingers a couple days letting any other shifters in the area know it's happened. When it happened with Tyson and Ivy, it could be smelled for ten miles instead.

Jase says, "Right after you headed for your witch's van, Grey went back inside the town hall, telling Joel she was his. Must've been whatever she was masking her shifter scent with finally wore off."

"Don't think it was cat grass. I think it was something stronger," Ty says. "Something from witchcraft. But something about her smell... I know it. Or someone related to her. Can't put my finger on it."

"Where are Joel and Linc?" I ask.

Ty replies. "Linc's watching your mate. Making sure she doesn't leave, though she says she won't until you two speak properly."

"Joel?" I ask.

Mase answers with, "Joel messaged and said he was diggin' in to help with research. I got the sense it had to do with Grey's mate more than yours for the moment. Joel's got his investigator hat on."

They keep referring to her as my mate. My gut sours.

"Any of the rest of you gonna have uncomplicated matings?" Mase muses.

Ty scoffs.

"Fuck, please," Jase mutters to the ceiling of the cave, folding his hands in prayer position.

"From the man next in line," Mase puts in.

Jase pales.

I pipe up, "I'm gonna go home. Shower. Go to work and finish that basement reno."

Mase says, "I already called the client. Goin' back over there in a few hours. Not much left to do; Ty's gonna help me wrap it up."

"I'll come," I tell him.

"You should go speak to your mate," Tyson suggests. "I'll help Mason out today."

My eyes meet his. "I'd rather work. Get this job done. Besides, what do you know about construction?" I mean for it to come across like a light-hearted jab, but I know this fails and I come across like an asshole instead.

"I can learn," Ty replies, unfazed.

"She could have reasons for what she did, Rye," Jase offers.

Done with the dancing around this, I bark, "That witch fucked me over and left me thinkin' she's dead for seven years." I shrug. "She can sit there in that van if she wants to. She can go take that swim and never come up like I thought she did. Couldn't care less."

"Bullshit," Ty clips. "Talk to her."

"You feel drawn to her?" Jase asks.

I don't answer. And that's obviously an answer. And it's a stupid question. She's my intended mate; Of course I'm drawn to her. She was made for me.

"Riley?" Ty pushes.

"Back off," I demand.

"He's right, you know?" Mase tells me. "You need to talk."

I lift a shoulder like I couldn't care less. "Maybe I'll talk to her in seven years. Maybe fifty."

The three of them exchange looks and look ready to push me some more.

"Don't," I warn.

"Gonna head out. See what Joel's up to, if he needs my help," Jase says, getting to his feet, obviously bowing out for now. He shakes Mase's hand. "Congrats again, brother."

"Thanks, brother." Mase slaps Jase's back.

"Later, boys." Jase says, shooting me a look loaded with concern. "Here for you, Rye. Okay?"

"I know you are."

I shake his hand. He pulls me in for a hug.

I break away after a second, feeling like I'm about to spin-out. There's too much to wade through right now. I don't have the bandwidth for any of it. "Meet you at the job site, boys."

"Meet us at Roxy's for breakfast at eight and then we'll head to the client together," Mase amends.

I shake my head. "I'll just meet you there. Need to get my head down, focus on something else." Anything else.

"You should focus on your mate," Tyson presses.

"Fuck off, Ty," I tell him, glaring.

He holds my gaze, still unfazed.

"If you're sure about the job," Mase says slowly, offering me an out. "We could just-"

"I'm sure," I state.

"Comin' anyway," Ty advises. "I wanna learn."

"Whatever." I shrug.

INSTEAD OF GOING TO my place, I find myself at the store up the road from it. Her van is still parked there. The same van from all those years ago. I feel her presence in my chest, catch her scent in my nostrils and as it spreads through me, my gut churns and I have warring urges that I refuse to dissect.

Visions from seven years ago flash through my brain.

She's dripping wet standing outside this van; we both are. She's embarrassed, hiding her chest under her transparent dress. The next day, I saw her again in a field of flowers.

I shake the vision off and turn my attention to Lincoln, who's on a bench outside the store, eyes and hands on his phone. At my approach, he looks up and is about to speak.

"You don't need to guard her," I speak first.

His brows crinkle. "Why haven't you taken her home?"

I rear back at his pissed-off attitude.

"Even Grey took his mate home. Mated her already. You're gonna risk her slipping through your fingers again? Covering her scent again?"

I flex my jaw muscles. "This is *my* shit."

My shit that's too close to me right now. I'm suddenly nauseous. My body wants to shift, to let my wolf burst forward. So I can run and run. Like that'd protect me from everything else trying to permeate. Take me away from here so I don't go in there and do something stupid.

My cock goes hard again. Like a fucking traitor.

"It's *our* shit and you know it. Deal with it." He gestures to the van. "You should've mated her last night. Grey mated his this morning. The mating birth order's all fucked up now."

"So?"

Lincoln grinds his teeth.

"You got more to say?" I demand.

He stares without answering.

"I'll deal with it when I'm ready. Or not, Linc. Stand down."

My insides are disjointed. She's too close. Her scent. Her emotions. I'm not supposed to feel her emotions until after the first mating. I push the sensations, the odd urges away, refusing to acknowledge them. But her emotional state claws into me like barbs. Magnets pull at me. Pull me in the direction of that camper van that I'm just fifty feet away from. Why does she have to smell so fuckin' good?

I'm hanging on by a thread. Wanting to go to her. Rip her clothes off. Take her. Bite her. Knot her. Rip her to fuckin' shreds and then explode in a storm of the blood and guts and pain that I've held in for all this time. Weep. Scream. Roar. Set everything ablaze and burn with it.

Linc's nostrils flare. "What if she takes off again and you don't get your answers?"

I say nothing.

Rage bubbles just below my rim. I need to vacate, otherwise it'll boil over and who knows what it'd take to get me back on level ground?

I hear the door creak open. Her scent gets stronger. Before I have to set eyes on her again, before I take the chance I'll do what Ty did to his mate, knowing I could easily rut her publicly in the gravel right now, I shift to wolf and bolt toward my place.

5

ERICA

Ten Years Ago

Drowsy Hollow had been a big mystery most of my life. But as I pulled into the parking lot behind the dry cleaners it struck me that I could *feel* things there. It was penetrating that the town that was such a big mystery to me for all this time felt like home. It was small, quaint, and it felt very magical. It wasn't something I could decipher, but I somehow just knew it.

I felt a pull. And I'd felt strange and similar pulls toward places in the past. Forests. Gardens. The water. Old trees. Aunt Lyrica had been telling me this was all natural. That I love windy days. That I prefer being barefoot. That I adore the smell of rain. Earth. Touching nature. Listening to leaves rustle.

She explained that to the north of Drowsy Hollow was a wolf shifter settlement. A town to the east had once been heavily populated by vampires but now it was a little bedroom community with just one or two. To the west, it was rumored to have once been a stomping ground for visiting fairies from a parallel universe. On the fringe of the town there was a haunted section of woods that Aunt Lyrica told me I'd learn about later, because we were stewards and needed to keep the entity haunting the woods confined.

It was a whole lot to absorb but I was taking it all in. And she was observing me closely as I did.

The Young coven had overseen the area for generations, striving to keep things in balance because of how much magic was present. Aunt Lyrica told me that when there's a high concentration of magic in an area such as this, it has to be carefully managed.

She explained that the sheer number of supernaturals that settled here, lived, loved, and died here over the past two and a half centuries meant that this area had a very high concentration of supernatural energy. I would learn a lot about energy in my study of our craft.

I wasn't shocked to learn that there were supernatural forces at work. Or that our family was deeply entwined with it. I'd always believed in magic. As little girls, me, Dani, and Jessie would play games with magical themes. Though I was the youngest, I seemed to have the biggest thirst for magical roleplaying games. But we had to do it in secret, or it would send our mother into a tizzy.

Now I knew why.

Aunt Lyrica broke it to me that though Mom and Dad's death came as a shock, it was not a surprise. The family had warned them against taking us away, about keeping our nature from us. Aunt Lyrica swore that neither herself nor Aunt Mimi had anything to do with their deaths, that they had resigned themselves to the fact that maybe the Young coven would cease to exist after they were gone, that maybe times were changing. That perhaps they should look to another coven nearby to take on our region. They were nervous about that, but said they hadn't intervened beyond trying to talk sense into our mother and father, warning them that nature could intervene.

Mom was adamant; Dad was her simp. Mom didn't think you should dabble with anything magical; that it was blasphemous. And she was determined to protect us from it.

The coven's numbers were dwindling as neither Aunt Mimi nor Aunt Lyrica had children. Aunt Mimi was a twin and her twin sister died giving birth to a daughter. That daughter gave birth to just one son who was raised not knowing our family. Their oldest brother, my grandfather, had died young and the remaining Young coven family members were sprinkled throughout Europe with work of their own to be concerned with.

It was a big responsibility looking after this region and a lot of work between Aunt Lyrica and Aunt Mimi, who was drawn to live on the coast for reasons of her own. The universe just wouldn't allow it to stop there. Our family's calling was too important to the other supernatural beings in the area, so that's likely why when we were at that county fair that day just three months before Vivica's eighteenth birthday, we saw our parents die.

Mom and Dad were on the rented pedalboat on a pond on the perfectly sunny and cloudless day. Me and my sisters sat on a blanket with ice cream cones, watching them pedal around, looking happy. And then we watched with utter horror when lightning struck that boat. It immediately burst into a fireball and sank, taking my parents with it. There weren't even any remains to bury.

We went to live with Dad's Aunt Mimi, who I hadn't remembered, not having seen her since I was a toddler.

Aunt Mimi seemed very serious and no-nonsense, but she had a free-range parenting style, letting us live our lives the way we wanted, within reason, which was a stark contrast to the way Mom was raising us. With her came Aunt Lyrica, who I only remembered vaguely, having met her once when she visited, and Mom got home and hurried her out.

Mom told us she was eccentric. A bit of a kook. In the past six years, Aunt Lyrica visited every few months, and we all adored her quirky, colorful personality.

"They died just before Vivi was to turn eighteen," I muttered.

"Yes," Aunt Lyrica replied softly.

"Meaning we got brought to Aunt Mimi and Vivica was given a few months to mourn before she was allowed to learn about everything."

"Yes," Aunt Lyrica told me, patting my knee while continued to drive despite the tears brimming in my eyes.

"Magic took them from us," I said, brokenly.

"Magic ensured you weren't taken away from your true path," Aunt Lyrica corrected. "Don't be angry with magic. And don't be angry with your parents. Anger serves nothing. Magic needs you to be a vessel for it. To help direct it. Your mother couldn't understand the importance of your role. Your father couldn't fully comprehend it either. He didn't have the gifts; didn't have the understanding. They thought they were keeping you girls safe from things she feared because of her lack of understanding, and I can't blame him either, because things happen as they're supposed to do. What they did only kept you segregated from it for eighteen years each. They weren't able to wrap their minds around the fact that it was simply their role to bring you girls into the world. That was served. I knew you'd all need to know the truth at the age you're at now. My gifts told me this. I believe they're both at peace now. So does Jessica. Jessica's gift assures her they are."

My head felt like it was swimming with all the information. Not only was our heritage revealed to each of us on our eighteenth birthday, along with the reason why our parents were taken from us, also part of the trip was designed around spending time in the area learning about our history, our heritage, and our craft. And time together there would allow Aunt Lyrica to determine our strengths, so it could be documented for the coven as well as the supernatural council collective for future needs.

The supernatural council collective, which she referred to as the SCC, consisted of supernatural beings who oversaw beings with or from magic and intervened where necessary. They had codes of conduct established for each supernatural classification. Laws. Rules. Consequences if the rules were broken.

Aunt Lyrica told me that Vivica, Vivi, is a clairvoyant with strong precognition skills. She had visions of varying degrees. Always accurate, not always detailed or easily discernible straight away.

Veronica, Ronnie, has skills in psychometry which meant she could gather information from people and objects by touching them. If she touched you, she'd glean information about you. If she touched something of yours, the same.

Jessica, Jessie, was classified as a medium with powerful skills to tap into other dimensions. She could also connect with the dead. She had some precognition skills, too.

Danica, Dani, was developing exceptional healing skills. Not only healing the body but also spiritual healing. It had only been just over a year since she started to tap into her skills.

This trip would reveal what my strength was, but Aunt Lyrica told me she suspected my strengths would make all of us stronger together.

And this made me feel special. It took the bitter sting of being last out of things just a little. Like they needed to wait for me to fully experience things. Knowing they were waiting for me after all the waiting I did felt special.

Aunt Lyrica said she and Aunt Mimi had many strengths. She wouldn't list them for me. She said they began their journeys much like me. She did tell me she's a reincarnation of the original Lyrica Young, born over two-hundred years ago, though she only has select memories from that time.

They've gathered new strengths over the years via a variety of methods and we'll all continually hone our craft for the rest of our lives. We're stronger together but also strong alone. Aunt Lyrica also told me we'd be occasionally called on to help with matters that could be regional or even global. She made sure to drive home that witchcraft isn't a set course where you can graduate with honors from the highest learning degree. There are so many facets and it's ever-changing with the world and other witches, warlocks, and supernatural beings contributing to it, so it's a never-ending quest for knowledge, skills, and balance.

Depending on what my skills were determined to be, the five of us together could be stronger than what's been seen for at least a few generations in the Young coven.

I couldn't wait to learn all about magic. I couldn't wait to be part of the coven, their secret club, and in hindsight I knew by my sister's faces that morning that they were just as excited about bringing me into this fold as I was.

AS SHE SHOWED ME THINGS in the covenstead hidden in the back of the drycleaners, I was filled with a strange combination of wonder, rightness, and remorse over how much of a brat I've been. I couldn't even count how many times my sisters asked me to trust them. Even when Dani, who was almost as frustrated as me just over a year ago pleaded with me to trust her, said this while holding my hands and staring deep into my eyes, I couldn't get past my anger to trust her. I thought for sure she'd tell me everything and couldn't understand why after all our talks, she would leave me out.

Aunt Lyrica picked up on my mood, consoled me, and assured me that my sisters understood and that I hadn't done irreparable damage with my brattiness.

They've all been anxious for the day when the secrets no longer had to be kept. Aunt Lyrica told me there would be many good things to look forward to now that all five of us were of age. But she cautioned me that it'd be a long and winding road. Not an easy one. That with these gifts we'd been given, we had a tremendous amount of responsibility as well.

"I don't want to delve into darkness here on your birthday, on day one, but there are pitfalls to be wary of. Dark magic. Things that will crop up that you'll need to wade into. Things that will put you and your sisters at risk. Tolls you'll need to pay. Punishments you'll have to dole out, too, even if you don't want to. There's heartbreak on the road ahead, Erica Young. Heed what I say to you so you can be safe and so that you can do what you were intended to do in life. It won't always be easy. You girls may put yourselves in danger and some of you might even one day be lost to it. You have purpose that will help many. But you must do your best to follow the rules. And if there are times when you cannot, you must do your best to always repay your debts. Build and bank goodwill always so that you'll never be without it. Good energy is the essential ingredient for our work and for your magic. Save it up. Don't spend it all in one place or you might run out of it when you need it most. And even if you're sure you have more than enough, conserve it. Make your actions matter, girl. Always try to serve the greater good."

While her words and the gravity permeated, unfortunately, I was impatient and had far too much confidence in my abilities.

6

ERICA
Now

A big brown blur of fur runs away as I step out of my bus. My gaze hits a large, lumber-snack of a man who rises from a bench outside the gas station door. He looks me over, disdain written all over his handsome, bearded face as I move in his direction.

"Was that Riley?" I ask when I'm about ten feet away. I know Riley's wolf is brown and look to where the wolf was. No sign of him now.

"Don't even think about trying to leave," the lumber-snack warns instead of answering.

"Guess I don't need to tell you I'm Erica." I extend my hand anyway.

He crosses his arms over his broad, grey t-shirt-covered chest and gives me a once-over perusal that's not remotely carnal. A switch from normal male interactions, but shifter guys are clearly different from regular ones.

I'm wearing a long A-line blue with green paisley maxi dress with pockets and brown leather gladiator sandals with a manicure and pedicure in a soft peach with a pearl finish. My long, curly, gingery corkscrew curls are everywhere, in desperate need of attention after tossing and turning on it all night long.

I pull my hand back. "I'm gonna guess you're Lincoln."

I recall from Aunt Lyrica's ledgers that Lincoln's wolf changes colors. It's suggested he does it to be chameleon-like, blending into his surroundings. The seven top alphas in this pack all have strong shifter traits as well as some anomalies. In Aunt Lyrica's ledgers it's listed that Greyson Blackwood's eyes change color, alternating from brown to silver, silver when he's got heightened emotions. Silver like most of the Young clan. My eyes are a cross between brown and gray, a bit of my mom, and bit of my dad, so obviously Greyson's silver eyes come from Soleil Young. Although Greyson is a Young family member, only Dani and Aunt Mimi have technically met him so far. We've all talked to him on the phone.

"Right," Lincoln mutters.

Lincoln hates me. I can hardly blame him.

"I'm not planning to leave. I need a bathroom, if that's not too big of an ask. What time does this place open?"

"Anything out of your mouth is too big of an ask. There's a can in there. It's open." He jerks his thumb backwards at the store. I see a dark-haired, piercing light blue-eyed beauty watching us through the window. She steps outside.

"You can use this bathroom. But it'll cost you."

"Cost me?"

"Your story," she advises, shrewdly looking me over. She's tall, though most girls seem tall to me as I'm just five-foot-one. She's fit, dressed in jean cutoff shorts and a tight black t-shirt. She's gorgeous. And a little intimidating.

"I can't give my story to anybody before I've given it to Riley. But I'll buy something if you let me use the bathroom."

She crosses her arms over her chest. "Did you cast a fake spell to make him think you're his mate?"

"Fake?" I muse for a minute, then shake my head. "That's not the right word for it. More like wishful. Though I didn't know enough back then. Didn't understand the..." Their eyes are on me, earnestly. I shake my head sharply. "Sorry, but I really can't say anything until I explain it to Riley. It wouldn't be fair."

"Oh, you're being fair to Riley, are you?" Lincoln snaps. "That's rich."

"Can I possibly use the facilities in there before you all rip me a new one? I've been holding it for so long I'm about to embarrass myself."

"Are you his true mate?" she asks.

I nod. "Unfortunately for him."

She gestures inside, holding the door open for me.

When I come out of the bathroom, she's on the phone behind the counter.

"I don't have those answers," she says, "but the council knows about the visitor and it's all in hand. No. Code yellow still as far as I know. Feel free to spread the word. Okay, bye." She hangs up, eyes on me.

This is more than a gas station. Though it's no bigger than the average convenience store, there's a decent selection of food, toiletries, and even a little coffee station with fresh coffee, muffins, and other pastries.

"Thank you," I say and examine the full pot of coffee. "Smells like fresh coffee."

I have a little French press in my van, a small generator, but always try to buy something when I use a store's facilities.

"Made fifteen minutes ago," she replies.

I pour a large one and grab a carrot muffin before placing it on the counter separating us. "Just a minute. I need a couple things."

I browse the aisles and cart over two gallon-jugs of water. She's staring at me, stone-faced as I grab an orange from a fruit basket beside the cash register along with a bag of trail mix from a rack.

"All this, please." I unzip the brown suede belt bag I've got on crossbody.

The door chimes jingle as a blonde and a brunette burst in, both wearing stylish tracksuits. Ivy Brennan, the blonde with a purple tracksuit and her sister Amelia, the brunette in the pink tracksuit.

Not only did I meet them briefly in Marblehead, I'd know them anyway. Their photographs are in Aunt Lyrica's ledger, which I've spent hours upon hours reading and re-reading since she died a couple years ago. And then of course intervening to make sure things happened the way they were intended with their matings.

Me, Vivi, and Jess were all quite busy during both those matings. Vivi got visions that meant more intervening was done than usual with the shifter-human pairing, making sure that Mason was out of the way for Tyson and Ivy's mating. And then Jess and Ronnie had to get involved more recently with the mess between Amelia's ex and Mason. I was involved in both cases with the spell-writing.

The Brennan sisters both smile brightly at me.

"Erica," Ivy greets. "I knew you'd come."

Amelia waves but concern is in her eyes. "Hi," she says softly. "Saw your van last night, then saw Riley head your way, so figured we'd see you eventually, but not this soon."

"Yeah, hi," I say, knowing my eyes betray my feelings on the subject. "Things okay with you and Mason?"

"Better than okay. Hope it's gonna be okay for you and Riley too," Amelia says.

"Have faith," Ivy says softly.

I try to smile but it probably comes across as fake.

They turn and Ivy greets the cashier with, "Mornin' Cicely," as Amelia waves, then they move to the coffee pot while she rings me up.

"I'm not having one, I can't," Amelia says, pouting. "You go ahead."

"If you want one, it probably wouldn't hurt this early. I kinda don't want one. The smell is making me a little... ugh." Ivy's face twists with distaste. "Maybe orange juice instead."

"But you're a coffee fiend. Maybe you're up the duff, too," Amelia whispers.

"I'm due for Aunt Flo today, so we'll know soon enough," Ivy whispers. They both give one another bright smiles that shows that not only are the two of them bursting with happiness, but that also shows their incredibly strong bond.

I don't always get to see the effects of our work, but seeing this right now, I get a rare moment of warmth through my whole body. And I know I need to add a note about these two to the jar I've been saving to show Riley. *If* I get the chance. Though based on how he reacted to me last night – that may not happen.

"I heard that," Cicely says, and squeals. "Yay. You're pregnant!"

"I am," Amelia announces. "Just found out last night."

"Congratulations," I say as Cicely squeals and runs out from behind her counter to hug Amelia.

All eyes move to me again.

"You okay?" Ivy asks, touching my shoulder.

"No," I reply frankly.

"How can we help?" she asks, genuine concern on her face.

"Seventeen forty-five," Cicely states loudly, going back behind the counter and seeming like she's giving these women a message. A message that I'm the enemy. "Cash only. ATM there if you need it," she tacks on, gesturing to the bank machine beside the bathroom door.

I fish a twenty out of my bag, thinking that she's probably charging me double for what I've bought. I guess I'm lucky she served me at all.

"Is there a motel around here somewhere?" I ask as she hands me my change, dropping it in my palm without touching me.

"Drowsy Hollow is the closest town with a motel. Why?" Cicely kind of snaps.

"My camper van has what I need for eating and sleeping, but there's no bathroom and I left in a hurry, forgetting to bring my camping toilet and outdoor shower. I could really use a hot shower, so I figured I'd see if there's a motel or a bed and breakfast here."

"Neither. Those are conducive to visitors, and we don't appreciate those," Cicely states. "There's a truck stop the other side of The Hollow that rents showers to truckers."

"You don't mince words at all," I observe.

"You can shower at our house," Amelia offers.

"Or ours," Ivy chimes in.

"Mine's a little closer," Amelia tells me.

"I don't think it is," Ivy counters. "You're up that road." She points toward the door. "And we're up two blocks and then another road over, but you're further down your road than we are ours, and-"

Cicely speaks up, eyes on me. "I suppose you can use my shower upstairs. Which will save you the hassle of Linc preventing you from going anywhere. But it'll cost you."

"As I said, I can't tell you anything until I've talked to Riley."

"Gimme something," Cicely says. She slaps the counter and repeats herself, "Some. Thing."

I'm about to reply when she adds, "I've watched Rye grieve for years. Do you have any idea what you've done to him? Do-"

"Yes!" I thrust my hands through my hair. "I do have some idea because I've been living it, too. I screwed up. I screwed up when I was turning twenty-one and broken-hearted and not knowing what'd happen with a little love potion I put together when I was under the influence of something powerful. Not knowing that the fall-out would affect not only my life but his, too. I've paid, believe me I've paid. I sat in a prison cell on my twenty-first birthday because of it, stood trial for it, and I've been extensively punished for it and couldn't do a damn thing about it until now. So now I'm here. I'm here and I'm not going anywhere until I talk to Riley and do my best to explain what's happened and how I've tried to- " I shake my head. "I can't say anymore. I've said too much. Was it enough to buy me a shower? Please? If not, can I take a hooker bath in that bathroom?"

"Yeah," Cicely rasps out, her voice thick with emotion, like she feels my pain or something. Ivy and Amelia's faces mirror hers. "Around the back and upstairs. It's not locked."

"Thank you," I rasp as I gather up the things I've bought.

"I'll give you a hand," Ivy offers, grabbing a water jug.

"Me, too," Amelia says taking the other one. "But once again, it'll cost you something."

I tilt my head to the side in question.

"After your shower, let us take you to breakfast at Roxy's."

"That's probably not a good idea, Amelia," I reply, hoping she reads the gratitude in my eyes.

"It's probably a *great* idea," Amelia corrects. "Seems like you could use some friends. And a big ole order of crepes or waffles or something."

Ivy nods. "Definitely a carb moment."

I bite my lip in contemplation.

"We'll talk to Lincoln for you. And we're not gonna push you to talk before you're ready," Amelia states, "But we have some stuff in common, I think. These Arcana Falls shifters, they..." She seems to go into a mini daze. A smile creeps across her face. I think she's probably remembering when her journey with Mason started, which wasn't long ago.

"They're a lot," Ivy puts in.

"Yeah," Amelia nods. "To put it mildly. Mason and I met right outside this place. And he carried me away kicking and screaming."

If only Riley did the same with me.

She goes on, "I maced him. But it didn't deter him. I tried to be a raging bitch and he didn't give up."

My stomach twists.

She keeps going. "I was so determined to not let him get in. I was a walking disaster because of pain and trauma with relationships. I know it's probably different for you, but when you're going through something major, you need people to lean on. And you and your sisters helped me out big time. So did some of the women in this pack, and I'm a pay-it-forward type."

I blow out a slow breath and nod. "Breakfast sounds... good."

"You?" Ivy asks Cicely. "Can you get away for a bit? That's why we came in – to invite you to breakfast."

"Yeah," Cicely says quietly.

The Brennan sisters are freshly mated, so they probably think I'm going to be part of the pack like they are. That I'm about to be initiated into the club they've recently joined.

But that's not a given. In fact, I'm pretty sure it's not even possible.

I don't need a welcoming committee right now; I need to talk to Riley. And once he tells me how unforgiveable what I've done is, how much he loathes me, I'll tell him he can request a severing. Just the thought of that hurts. Though, I know it's what's coming after the way he looked at me last night.

When he severs our connection, he'll be free of the pain of ending things with me. But I'll never be free of the feelings I have. Not ever. I could magic my way out of it, but I'm saving that card for someone else. Someone who *does* deserve it.

My sisters can help with the severing, but they can't help me through this, not in person anyway. They're not allowed to use magic to interfere. All they can do is let me bend their ears, though that's not my style. Never has been. As the baby of the family, as the one who was last to know everything, I've always been fiercely independent and tried to solve all my problems on my own, tried to prove I was just as capable as everybody else. And it was my pride, stubbornness, and carelessness that thrust me and Riley into this situation in the first place.

CICELY'S APARTMENT above the store is adorable. And surprising. It's more *girlie girl* than I'd have expected. It's a bit reminiscent of the inside of the *I Dream of Jeannie* lamp; a big room done in pastels, a pale pink sectional couch filled with purple and champagne-colored pillows on one end, a rice paper divider and then a bedroom space with a double bed covered by plush bedding and dozens of pillows in a variety of shapes and sizes.

There's a tiny kitchen space in one corner with cream cupboards, a purple countertop and 1950s style fridge and stove. I go into her spacious bathroom with a large lion-footed tub, pedestal sink, and a washer and dryer in the corner and set down my shower gear before I undress. After I've pulled the white shower curtain with the happy-looking dolphins all over it around the perimeter of the tub and am safely drowned out by running water, I can't help myself; I burst into tears.

7

CICELY OAKES

It's been a crazy half-hour since the village started waking up and word got around. Lots going on around here. In addition to Amie and Ivy coming in, plenty of others have popped in to look around and see what sort of gossip they can catch.

Because Tyson got shot yesterday. Thankfully with no lasting damage. This pack has waited years for his return, so it's had everyone in an uproar. And while everyone smelled that Greyson mated, it's not getting around that she's not only the woman that shot Ty but also that she was the one poisoning our pack members.

And on top of all that, there's a mysterious camping van parked in the far corner of my parking lot that had a tent popped up on top overnight, so of course people want to know who it is and why they're here. Those who've come close enough can smell the stranger, and I've told them not to worry about her, that the council is aware of her presence and haven't implemented any code alerts. A few of the alphas have made noise about the fact that she's a witch. They can smell it. I smelled it, too, though didn't know that was the nuance in her scent until Linc told me the background he knew about the situation.

We don't deal with many outsiders here. People who stop here for gas, convenience items, or to use the bathroom are generally only here because they took a wrong turn. We're north of Drowsy Hollow, but our village leads nowhere else; it's all dead-end streets or circles that take you back to this intersection, the town's four corners. We have surveillance equipment recording everyone who comes, and the council runs their plates to make sure there are no concerns. And if they don't use cash to pay for their purchases and instead use our ATM machine, the council uses that transaction to trace them and run a deeper risk analysis check.

Anyone in our village for longer than the time it takes to pump gas or buy something in the store results in an alert going out to everyone to let them know there's a stranger in town, to be on alert and cautious. No alert went out because of who this stranger is.

I'm sure it won't take long for word to travel through the pack that this is the woman who fucked Riley Savage up royally.

Two strangers here. One she-wolf. One witch. Both are women who've hurt our council alphas.

I saw Riley's exchange with Linc this morning. And while Linc was spitting nails, that was nothing compared to the look of murder on Riley's face when he walked up and spoke to Linc, then shifted and took off like his ass was on fire. I've known Riley Savage my entire life and have never seen that look on his face.

Amie, Ivy, and me are in conversation, though it's mostly the two of them talking about what happened with Grey last night, how that girl is now going to be part of our pack after trying to kill Tyson, after poisoning several of our pack members. I'm thinking about the fact that these first two additions to our pack have worked out well, but the following two council alpha matings aren't looking so good for us.

Then it'll be Jason Creed and I know Bailey's hoping it's her and dreading the notion it isn't. She's been mooning after him since we were kids. Before her first training bra. And then Linc before Joel. And Linc's mating will gut me, because I've carried a torch for him for years and I somehow know, deep down, that it won't be me he identifies as his, even though he's had me more times than he can probably count. Though I've counted. Twenty-seven times. The last dozen times I've told myself it'll be the last.

A lot has happened around here lately. And we've got three more matings to go.

We waited six years for Tyson to come back to us after finding out he was alive. We were overjoyed when he did. In fact, I wept uncontrollably with absolute joy the first time I saw the large black wolf and felt his connection to us. And I'm not a crier.

That's how much it means to us to have him back. And Greyson's mate tried to take him from us? Poisoned my dad, Cade, and Gus along with who knows who else?

Most probably wouldn't be sure who they're angrier at... Greyson's new mate or the witch, Erica Young.

I think I'm angrier at Grey's new mate after seeing the look of pain in Erica Young's eyes.

I ponder this while quickly texting my father to ask if he can come man the store so I can go to breakfast with these guys when the witch comes back down, not because I want to go for breakfast with her, but instead because I need to be there to be eyes and ears for our council since the sisters are still so new to our pack, not shifter, and have no skills to deal with any sort of DEFCON situation, should one arise. Besides, I feel like I need more information about Erica.

But then my ears prick because I hear through the ceiling the sound of absolute anguish coming from my bathroom up there. The girls don't hear it, don't have the hearing a shifter does, but that girl upstairs is in absolute agony. And I'm betting that Linc can hear her from outside, too.

It's a difficult thing to listen to when you want to despise someone, but can tell that they're obviously in a whole lot of pain.

Since Linc filled me in on last night's happenings, I haven't been able to stop wondering what might possess some she-shifter from another pack to attempt to kill Tyson after poisoning some of our people.

I also can't fathom why anyone would hide from everything that is Riley Savage, especially knowing the way a super-alpha shifter would grieve their lost mate. And witches would know that, wouldn't they? Bailey believes so.

Yeah, some people move on after losing a mate, my father included. He mourned my mom for a long time. It hurt to see him feel that pain, but Dad eventually found it within him to move on. And now he's freshly mated to Amie and Ivy's mother, which he was worried would upset us, but it made me happy after watching him suffer with losing her.

My older sister Candy was another story, but she'll eventually come around. My younger sister Colleen is away at school, but I know she'll feel the same as I do when she meets Kathleen. It's a great match.

Mom died after a battle with a long illness. Shifter illnesses are rare but when they happen they tend to be treacherous. The only thing that plagued her more than her chronic pain was the worrying she did about my father living the rest of his life grieving her. I know she'd be happy; she'd love Kathleen. She'd love Kathleen's girls, too.

When I hear the water turn off upstairs, Erica is no longer audibly crying.

Why did she hide? Why did she disguise her scent, letting him believe she was dead? I do know that one look at her and it's obvious – though not as obvious as it is now after the sounds I heard. That girl in my apartment is in tremendous emotional pain.

I'd better message Bailey to meet us for breakfast. If she finds out I went out with Amie, Ivy, and Riley's mate and didn't invite her, I'd never hear the end of it.

8

RILEY

Showered and dressed, I head out the door with a rumbling stomach. Hunger, despite the fact I feasted all night as wolf.

I swing left to Roxy's instead of right to leave the village, also giving me an extra couple minutes before I need to drive past her van, the notion of which makes me want to grind my teeth to dust. I'll grab one of Roxy's breakfast wraps to wolf down on the way to the job site, focusing on food instead of the magnetic force trying to pull me to that van and what's inside.

Mine.

I growl at the intrusive thought and shove it away.

Though I was haunted by the aroma I thought was her when I left the clinic last night, I wasn't convinced it was real until I saw the van. Suffice it to say my head has been fucked since all this started that day in the drycleaners. After catching her scent, I went half out of my mind because my nose couldn't find her. Kept waking whenever I did get some actual sleep wondering if I caught her scent again. If it was on the wind, out of reach and evading me, demanding I shift and chase it down.

I even hired Jared, a lone wolf that lives on the other side of Drowsy Hollow, to help track her down when our usual channels brought us nothing. Even him with his skills didn't help. She was not only hiding, she was disguising her scent again. And her family were no help.

My days and nights were haunted with the dregs of faint scent that was still in my nose. That's why it took until I was steps away from the four corners last night, looking at that van, that I knew the spike of it hitting me in the face was real. My senses weren't playing tricks on me.

Because I've had that scent in my lungs since then and the entire village smells like Grey right now, I'm again thrown when I catch the sight of her long, copper curls inside Roxy's.

And now that her scent has hit me again with a strength that overpowers Grey's, I know I shouldn't question my nose again. But as this thought occurs, I realize I have no choice but to question everything after all I've been through.

Correction: after all *she's* put me through.

And I'm feeling like inside me are two wolves. One wants to ring her neck. The other wants to spank, bite and knot her sixty-nine ways to Sunday.

It's infuriating.

She's at a table with Ivy Savage, Amelia Quinn, Bailey Blackwood, and Cicely Oakes. And the restaurant is full, as it would be with the hullabaloo of the last twelve hours. A newcomer in town that hasn't resulted in a code color change. Tyson getting shot. Greyson taking a mate, his mate being the one that shot Tyson and poisoned several pack members.

As if sensing my presence, her head turns and our gazes lock.

And suddenly, I'm growling and all eyes in the joint are on me, though I'm focused on her.

Cade moves in my direction, concern in his gaze. My eyes snap his way for two seconds, then he submits, picking up on my energy, showing me his neck. My eyes scan the perimeter and every other male in the place is also showing his neck.

My gaze cuts back to her and her eyes are wide. Not only that, she's wet for me. It's in my lungs and it's absolutely infuriating. Because I'm split in two over what to do about the best scent that's ever hit me. Like the day on that old hiking trail, then in the meadow when I knew. It's stronger than then and it's crashed into me like a freight train. Even more than last night, and I'm feeling like I might need to do something about it.

There's movement behind me. I know the scents as well as the vibrations in my gut. Those vibrations used to be in my chest, where my council co-alpha bond existed, but they've moved and something else resides in my chest instead.

Mase and Ty are behind me.

Now that Ty and Mase have mates, now is when I should've smelled her. Is that why these sensations are hitting so hard?

"Everybody out!" Mason hollers, like he knows what I'm about to do.

Am I about to do that?

Roxy quickly rounds the bar and flings the patio doors open. I'm only vaguely aware of the place emptying as my eyes continue to hold the witch's. Or maybe her eyes are holding mine. I don't even know.

She shakily rises and her long dress twirls as she turns to leave, but Ty commands, "Not you. You stay."

I bare my teeth and growl again, this time at him, feeling a sensation I've never felt, like I'm about to shift against my will and like I want him the fuck away from her. Like I'm about to make sure he's away from her. Ty shakes his head curtly and I realize what's happening and pull it back.

He's the last to go; the doors slam and it's just her and I.

Her chest rises and falls rapidly and without realizing I've moved across the space and grabbed her, I'm on her, pinning her back to the table.

"Riley," she whispers as stuff crashes to the floor around us.

I roar in her face with all the anger I feel. The room shakes with my fury.

The look in her eyes isn't the fear I'd expect at my show of absolute rage. It's something else. And I can't fuckin' bear it. Deep, undiluted sorrow oozes from every pore of her being and the force of it affects me in ways I can't fathom.

I can't bear to touch her, smell her, can't handle the sound of my name on her tongue and the emotions pulsing from her, the feelings filling me with the vilest sensation I've felt in my life. Like my nearly seven years of pain, but magnified multiple times – as if her pain quadruples mine.

I stagger backwards at the profound intensity and vault away, shifting to wolf form in mid-air and bursting through the now exploding glass of the front window of the restaurant.

9

ERICA
Ten Years Ago

Aunt Lyrica and I were on a blanket under a magnolia tree full of blooms. I had them in my hair, on my lap, and in my hands as I was trying to weave myself a wreath with the beautiful flowers that she told me never stopped blooming on this tree. Even in winter! A tree full-to-bursting with magic, and I swear I felt it tingling in me, connecting with me. A few others existed in this area, and she said that while all trees contain energy, many of the older trees in this area were full of important energy that we can easily harness. Especially me. Before we sat down, she asked me a lot of questions about how the tree made me feel, how the grass felt between my toes.

I didn't pluck the blooms; they rained on me as soon as we sat, which made Aunt Lyrica happy. She told me the tree accepted me and was happy to share gifts with me. That today I saw the permission but in future I would feel it instead. *If* I practiced my magic in the right way.

She sat cross-legged (it always amazed me how dexterous she was for a woman in her upper seventies) and was animatedly sharing details of the eccentric woman who had come into the shop that morning and pleaded with me to break the spell she'd paid Aunt Lyrica to have put on a man.

Though the business operated as a drycleaning and tailor service, Aunt Lyrica also did readings and in some cases, provided additional magic services. She read my concern as she'd already told me to guard our family secrets when this contradicted that. She explained she did things in a way that kept most people in a safe place in terms of knowledge about what she's capable of. Most people were either skeptics or held some level of skepticism. Some thought she was a complete fraud. Others looked to her as a kind of spiritual guide or their own personal psychic and tried to glean wisdom from her to help them make decisions about their lives.

She ran her business in a way that gave some folks a little of what they wanted - belief in the mystical. And fostering her reputation as a quirky town fortuneteller meant that most people regarded her oddities as quirks, which often just threw them off the trail of figuring out anything that could harm our coven.

But she had clients that she provided deeper services for, too, and this lady was one of them. Aunt Lyrica told me she was careful about who she took on as clients and said some people were drawn to her for reasons. Sometimes she took them on because she needed to, because of her magical responsibilities, even if she wanted nothing to do with them. I didn't understand what that meant, but would later learn a whole lot about that kind of thing when ledgers were handed over giving me a long list of dates and events to ready myself for, to prepare for and in many cases intervene for.

Beyond that, I would often see Vivica go into a sort-of trance as facts would come to her and we would often help her get them down. We'd go through those notes together to help us anticipate future or current events that needed our intervention.

Aunt Lyrica said sometimes her clients got exactly what they asked for. Other times they got something they needed instead. She admitted that sometimes she threw people off the scent of the truth because of the danger it or they represented. And for some, she gave them enough to believe in to keep them working to put themselves in a better mental place.

She'd been practicing for nearly six decades with strong intuition - knowing what people were truly about as well as often getting an inkling of what they needed. She was considered a very powerful witch. Sometimes people were directed into her path for reasons that served the greater good and she had the sight for the gifts people had, such as psychic abilities and supernatural bloodlines. I counted myself beyond lucky to have her as my teacher.

SO, THERE I WAS, COVERED in flowers, laughing at the tale of the lonely legal assistant who went to Aunt Lyrica for a love potion to make her grouchy boss fall in love with her. Aunt Lyrica told me how she weighed it all out, how she found a way to do it safely with no risk of harm, so made the potion and handed it over. And the lawyer boss did fall, but the secretary had buyer's remorse. She's been trying to talk Aunt Lyrica into reversing it, but had already agreed to Aunt Lyrica's *no cancellation, zero reversals* policy. Aunt Lyrica was a stickler.

The woman regaled me with her tales of woe that morning after finding out I was Lyrica's great niece as I was manning the cash while Aunt Lyrica was busy in the back getting something ready for today's lesson. The woman pleaded with me to talk my aunt into making a reversal potion as she couldn't handle his lovesickness any longer. He was driving her crazy. He was much hotter as the broody boss than as the lovesick puppy.

I told the lady I couldn't help, and she offered me money. I said I still couldn't help, so she skulked out of the shop throwing her arms up in exasperation. Not five seconds later, I saw a handsome man in a three-piece suit rush along after her with a bouquet of flowers in his hand and a goofy grin on his face.

"Be careful what you wish for, baby witch," Aunt Lyrica warned. "Sometimes when your wishes come true, you realize they weren't what you expected."

WE'D BEEN SITTING HERE under the tree for a while, and I was getting impatient about what today's lesson was going to be, but I tried not to show it because I knew she'd make me wait even longer.

But then she pulled out a frosted glass bottle and squeezed its sparkled pink atomizer and a pungent loam-like scent hit my nose as a dusty haze swirled around me.

"What are you-" I started to ask.

"Hush," she commanded in a sharp whisper. "They'll be unable to see you, but this won't mask our voices." She spritzed again in front of her own face, and I watched as the dusty vapor wrapped around her before shimmering and then disappearing, taking her with it.

She instantly blanked out of my view.

I clamped my mouth shut and held my breath, unsure of what was about to happen. And then I lifted my hand in front of my face and saw nothing, so I stretched to grab a blossom from about two feet away and could only see a blossom, not my own hand, so dropped it and swallowed a gasp. I couldn't see the blossoms on my lap but felt for them and they were still there. *Whoa.*

It was day three with her and I was thinking *yes, we were finally getting somewhere*. Up until this point it had been a lot of her talking and me listening. Talking about how I can harness energy from the earth, the sky, from water, and trees. Telling me about how energy begets more energy, so I'll have to think about where energy comes from and learn how to wield it. She told me intention counted for a lot, but that didn't mean you couldn't screw something up royally even if you had the right intention going into it. You could gather energy and spend it in the wrong place, finding yourself tapped out when you most needed it. She told me I'd learn to communicate with my surroundings to see where energy might be available, where there might be a deficit and talked about practicing as part of my daily regimen so that I could bank energy and goodwill. I'd learn to read signs in the sky, the stars, the sun, the surroundings. I'd work with my sisters, particularly Vivi who would get new assignments for us outside the scope of the already active roster in the coven's ledgers. There were rules and guidelines for us on how to conduct our work. I'd learn about directing energy, using ingredients, and crafting safe spells and potions to help with our work.

And I couldn't wait for all of it, which was a problem, because Aunt Lyrica told me patience was an essential ingredient. I had to meditate on what needed to be done and the best way to go about doing it. And then I'd need to be careful, meticulous, because lives, love, and futures could depend on me.

My sisters' birthday gifts to me had been a mortar and pestle, a set of glass jars that I'd be able to fill from Aunt Lyrica's greenhouse, a ledger and grimoire set with an assortment of quills and inks, some pretty crystals, candles, a small cast iron cauldron, a deck of tarot cards, and a stack of botanical reference materials. And Aunt Lyrica told me I'd learn things that couldn't be written down, that could never be shared with anyone outside a select few, but said I'd have to be religious about notations in my ledgers. Where I cast spells, where I interfere. I had to secure my ledgers and grimoires as well. I was responsible for the contents.

She had all sorts of crystals, potions, and herbs in her back room at the drycleaning shop. She was also well-stocked upstairs in her apartment, along with her van. She drove it home that you had to be prepared.

She had a greenhouse on the roof terrace, and it was a beautiful jungle of plants that were essential to the coven, and I couldn't wait to take my fill. I'd spent a lot of time touching things, explaining how things made me feel. Asking and answering questions. No, I couldn't have a broom yet and though I couldn't ride it through the sky, but I could use it to sweep away bad energy and old spells. Yes, I'd need a wand but not yet. I had a lot to learn first.

When she finally told me yesterday that she believed I'd be a spellwriter at minimum and that she suspected I had further gifts, too, that she's believed this all my life, I was practically busting to try it out. It felt like the truth to me, like I'd always known it, too, which was strange, but that's how I felt. I felt like my life was finally beginning.

I was beyond disappointed when she advised I needed at minimum five years of study, before beginning to write spells. She read my reaction and drilled home that my gift is special. That it's dangerous to simply tap into it, to wield what could be a dangerous weapon without training.

More waiting didn't sound like my jam whatsoever, and I initially had a little internal tantrum about it, but told myself to try to be more patient. She warned my lack of fortitude in that arena could be my downfall if I wasn't careful.

Pondering all this while being wowed at my invisibility, I heard male voices.

Excitement kicked my heart rate up as I reminded myself we were actually invisible. I held my breath as rustling indicated the voices were moving closer. The clouds parted and the sun shone down on three men walking in our direction. Three absolutely delicious shirtless, shoeless male specimens of rugged good looks wearing a light sheen of sweat on all their muscled bodies.

My belly dipped as my eyes locked on one of them and I couldn't tear my gaze away. He was on the right and he was laughing. He had sexy cheek dents, beautiful green eyes, and dark, slightly curly hair. The sound of his laughter blended with the light in his eyes made my belly swoop. For some reason, my hands started to tremble.

I didn't know why my hands shook, whether it was the way he looked or if it was about the fact that we were invisible.

Were we? Were we really? I couldn't help myself. I threw a magnolia blossom and it hit him on the shoulder before I held my breath.

He looked right through me as his eyes scanned the space and then he resumed talking to the other guys with him. The one in the middle had dirty-blond hair, light brown eyes, and tattoos. The other was extra-tall, dark-haired and had piercing peacock blue eyes. I'd put them all in their mid-twenties.

"I say we build it here," the guy I had my eye on said, pulling a folded piece of paper out of his back pocket. "Me and Mase worked on this last night. Picture it up there." He pointed to the tree we were under.

The other two guys huddled with him and examined the piece of paper.

"Why here?" The tattooed one asked.

"Climb this tree and you'll see why I picked this spot," the guy holding the paper mused. "Good vantage point of our village in one direction, The Hollow the other way. This tree is the biggest of its kind around here, so it'll give us a bird's eye view and the flowers'll help shield the platform from view."

"Could build a shelter with one of those shed kits?" The tallest, dark-haired guy suggested. "Save ourselves some time."

My guy scratched his jaw thoughtfully, "Can build it from scratch just as easily. And it'll be better."

"Riley!" a shout came from a distance. The three heads swung that way, as did mine.

"Yeah?" my guy answered.

"Grey's old man says since this tree contains a shitload of magic, it's a bad idea."

Riley shimmered. Sun glinted, sending a prism of beautiful light off his smile with a ping I was sure only I could hear. The world stood still for two beats where his name echoed in my heart.

Riley.

I then saw who the smile was aimed at. Another gorgeous guy with light brown hair and dark eyes. He carried a gym bag, which he tossed to the ground kind of close to where we were. He wasn't dressed for a day at the beach like the rest of them; he was in jeans, a t-shirt, and work boots.

I held my breath, thinking we were in danger of having our invisible bubble breached, but Aunt Lyrica whispered something that I didn't catch and then I felt a little whoosh in my ears. It was as if air sucked us backward a few feet.

I gasped, but nobody looked my way. And now the tree we'd been under was in front of us and though pink mist now hung in mid-air in front of us where we'd been, it dissipated.

The four men talked about the thing they wanted to build in the tree, and I didn't make out much because I was mesmerized by the one called Riley who then climbed the magnolia tree and talked from a big trunk-sized branch that he stood on.

It was as if a spotlight was on him while I took in his body language, examined the way his lips moved. He oozed charisma; it was addictive to watch. The four friends were clearly very close. The late arriver opened the backpack, pulled out beers, and passed them to everyone, tossing one up to Riley. They continued to shoot the breeze, talking about finding another tree to build their security tree house so they could use it to see what was happening all around the area. I wasn't even fully aware of the contents of their conversation because not only was it tool and building supply talk, mostly because I was so fascinated with watching Riley move, watching how his throat bobbed while he drank his beer, and thinking on the fact that my great aunt had cast a spell, an actual spell that allowed us to watch these men while unseen.

I wondered if their arrival was part of the lesson or if it was by chance. My head turned in her direction, and I was surprised to see her. She was jotting something down in a notebook and not paying much mind to the four men.

"I can see you," I whispered.

She nodded and shushed me by putting her index finger to her lips while continuing to jot things down. I could see my hands, the magnolias in my skirt and this startled me.

I figured she had to do a second spell, that this one was different, and it made me wonder how many invisibility spells there were. I then wondered how long the spell would last and if she'd need to spray more of whatever her potion was that let us sit here like this undetected. Did she have enough of it? What was in it? Would I get that recipe as part of my training? I was giddy at that notion but not giddy about waiting five long years.

What if I needed to use the bathroom? At that thought, the power of suggestion took over and my bladder nudged me a teensy bit.

And then something crazy happened. Riley and the tattooed guy went from standing together laughing to dropping their shorts. But before I could fully take *that* magnificence in, their arms and legs stretched into fur-covered limbs as their faces morphed from men to animals. Wolves. Big ones. Very big ones.

I gasped out of reflex and immediately covered my mouth.

Riley was a massive chocolate brown wolf, though at least twice the size of any wolf I'd ever seen. His fur looked as soft as a mink's. The tatted guy was a light brown colored wolf, equally as large. They were running. The other two men were quickly in the same form, one pure white and one black and white. The four of them were sprinting away from us, leaving their clothes, the bag, and the empty beer cans behind.

I couldn't help the audible gasp that escaped my lips.

"Quickly, let's go. I can't do it again without leaving myself short," Aunt Lyrica said, grabbing my hand.

I was in awe as we quickly moved back the way we'd come in.

We were a short drive away from town; we'd parked in a thick part of the woods and walked in.

I didn't see the bus until I was just about to ask where it was. It suddenly came into view as if reverse-dissolving.

"Cloaked it. Good timing," Aunt Lyrica muttered and then got into the driver's side.

I slid into the passenger seat and the minute the door was closed, I couldn't hold my excitement any longer. I was bursting at the seams.

"Holy horses! Oh my word! Those were werewolves! Beautiful, strong, men who... oh my God, Aunt Lyrica, did you see that?"

"Wolf shifters," she corrected. "They shift at will, no full moon requirement. Nobody turned them into that with a bite like you've seen in the movies; that's what they are, what they were born to be. They change from men to wolves at will."

"Wow. Wow wow whoa." I clasped my hair on either side of my head and gave myself a shake.

"Indeed. There are a number of things you'll learn about and learn *from* going forward, baby witch. We look after the pack they're in as well. It's a unique pack, contains a lot of magic. And they're important to this area, to our family, our coven for many reasons. We do it from a distance nowadays."

"Do they know of our existence like we know of theirs? And what was the thing that whooshed us? Was that something else you sprayed? How many invisibility potions are there and when can I use one? Please don't tell me I have to wait five years, because oh my word!"

"They know of witches. I have a working relationship with one of their council alphas. They have six. Their next generation will have seven. Those men you saw will be on the next council. First, I used a potion. Then, when we were at risk, I used some banked energy to move us and put us behind a cloak. That second move was advanced. Not something many witches can do."

"Seven alphas? Wow. Not just one alpha like in the movies?"

"Generally, wolf shifter packs have just one. This one has seven alphas each generation. This area once became a haven for displaced wolf shifters escaping tyranny of lone alpha packs, and things transpired. They decided to do things differently. We helped them form bonds to keep things harmonious with a combination of a government-like structure coupled with leadership from the best candidates of each generation."

"That one called Riley? He was absolutely dreamy."

She snickered. "Third-born alpha of his council, which hasn't been appointed yet. But they're all exquisite, aren't they, baby witch?"

"I don't know about the others, didn't pay much attention to them, because Riley?" I sighed heavily with a dramatic shoulder scrunch and drop. "Oh my goodness. I've never seen such a beautiful specimen of a man in my entire life. I could've sat and watched him talk, watched him move for a dozen years and not gotten bored." I stretched my fingers and toes languidly.

"Hm," she said without inflection.

I should've noted that *hm* as odd because Aunt Lyrica was very animated most of the time, it was more Aunt Mimi to *hm* her way through a conversation, but I was too preoccupied by all that had just happened.

I was busy pondering the possibilities that would open up if I could do what she'd just done. I was also pondering that I had confirmation of the existence of men that could shift to and from a wolf form. I had so many questions. I had so many I didn't even know what to ask first. I was lost in thought for the short drive back.

Later, I'd reacquaint myself with everything about that encounter and Aunt Lyrica's reaction to it – on an excruciating loop and wonder if it'd been a set-up to introduce me to the Arcana Falls wolf shifter pack and specifically, to Riley.

"DO I REALLY NEED TO study for five whole years, or could I dabble a little?" I asked again.

She gave me a shrewd look.

"A teeny dabbling?" I tried, holding my thumb and forefinger aloft an inch.

She clasped both my hands in hers. "Darling... this is an important gift you have. But it's one you have to be extremely careful with. You need to study. You need to learn. You can't rush into it. It's going to take years of study. I recommend at least five, preferably seven."

"Seven?" My face fell. "You said five. No changing it now!"

She nodded. "Five at minimum."

"No changing it unless it's less than five," I amended.

"Erica, *if* you work very hard it could be five. There are too many things that could go wrong. An inexperienced spell-writer can wreak havoc. You must wait until you're ready."

"I feel like I've been ready my whole life. Waiting my whole life. And I'm so bad at waiting. How about a teeny one with a proven spell. One of yours!"

"I know you feel like you've waited forever, but waiting for some fruit to ripen before you take a bite means readiness."

"Maybe I prefer green bananas," I volleyed.

I really didn't.

She pinched the bridge of her nose in exasperation.

"Sorry," I whispered.

"Girl, this is part of maturing. You have to mature to be ready for the power you wield. There is so much you and your sisters need to learn to be able to take over for me after my time is up. Things our ancestors put in motion that you have to oversee. New things that will come up. So much. It's a great responsibility, my girl."

"Teach me everything." *And hurry up about it* is what I was thinking, and I had the feeling she knew it, too.

"You need to return home the day after tomorrow. And I'm going to give you lots of reading to do."

"That's not enough time. I need more time. I should move here with you so I can learn. I-"

"Should go home and let your sisters guide you. Should take the opportunity to also let Mimi guide you."

"I could help at the shop. I could learn full-time. I could-" *see more of Riley the wolf shifter...*

"No, dear one. There's a plan for you. You must follow it. I'll be around. I'll visit often to teach you. We all have so much to teach you."

I sighed. "I'll come back here and visit too. A lot," I said.

She smiled. "You absolutely should."

I didn't want to read about the magic. I wanted to *be* the magic.

One Year Later

IT WAS MY THIRD DAY here and finally, I saw them stroll by the magnolia tree. This time, there were six of them and they'd arrived as wolves and then transformed to men right before my eyes. And Riley was even more ruggedly handsome than I'd remembered. Though his hair was shorter, curls chopped off, he was still a dreamboat. He was laughing. He was tanned. And he was naked. And whoa. Holy broomsticks.

I only saw them for about three minutes before the six of them walked off in all their naked glory. And it was a good thing, too, because my cloaking potion was wearing off. I was about to pack up and head back to Aunt Lyrica's, when I heard, "Look who's here."

Aunt Lyrica had followed me. And was cloaking herself. So I could hear her but couldn't see her.

"And you nearly got yourself caught," she said from somewhere to my left.

"I just wanted a peek," I defended sheepishly.

"You're sweet on that one. And you're playing a dangerous game, baby witch."

I shrugged and didn't even try to hide my amusement. "It's fun to look."

All of them were deliciously handsome and built. But I only had eyes for one of them.

She shimmered into visibility right where I suspected she'd been. She wore a stern look on her face.

Needless to say the last year had been one of discovery. I hadn't spent nearly enough time in Drowsy Hollow, but I'd spent a lot of time learning. And dabbling. And getting wrist slaps for it.

I still wasn't allowed to write my own spells, but I had performed a few simple and proven beginner spells. And I'd played with a few simple potions and had created this one, though mine didn't last very long and it took a lot of effort to grow, cultivate, and activate one of the herbs that was essential in the mix. I'd been growing things like crazy. Plants. Flowers. Vegetables.

And I'd seen my sisters' gifts for myself and though I had nothing to compare us to, I had to say... we *were* a powerful coven. Vivi was all-knowing, all-seeing, or so it seemed. It was astounding to hear her talk of coming events and then witness those events with your own eyes.

If you handed Ronnie something that belonged to somebody, she was often overcome with their personal stories, particularly if they were deceased. Sometimes it was painful to watch as she'd be overcome with emotion after learning someone's truth. Sometimes she'd shake someone's hand and have to fight to stop her face from showing them everything she felt. Her gifts had recently meant finding an abducted child just in time, because the clock was about to run out.

Jessica was still working hard at perfecting her skills as a medium, but she was already damn good at it. And Danica hadn't had a whole lot of opportunity yet to use her skills as a healer, but she'd dazzled us a couple times and also held a skill she was just starting to tap into – one that Aunt Mimi was terrified of.

It was the opposite of healing. Dani and Ronnie could work together to siphon certain types of energy from objects and from people, making someone's health, emotional capacity, or their memory wither. As far as healing went, though, they were able to get an old man at the nursing home Dani volunteered at, to remember his wife for a brief time the other day and he hadn't remembered her in a decade. She was terminally ill, and her time was coming to an end. The woman's greatest wish was to have one more afternoon with the man she'd loved for fifty-five years. Dani was elated to be able to give that to her.

Collectively, we were getting stronger. And it felt like we were gearing up for things that were important, things our great aunts didn't want to talk about, so it was easy to surmise it was because they were preparing us so that we could function without them some day.

Aunt Mimi was in her sixties, Aunt Lyrica seventy-nine, so this made sense, though it didn't make any of us happy. We'd all become even closer in the past year and the ability to draw from their knowledge was priceless to us. They encouraged us to learn, to study, to connect with one another so we could leverage one another's strengths while building upon our own strengths and knowledge. They were all excited about my supposed skills – skills I wasn't really allowed to dabble much with since I was still in the early phases of learning. I was so entrenched the past year in learning about herbs, crystals, about energy, learning to listen to the earth, the environment, growing things, and poring over old grimoires and ledgers that I'd had plenty to keep me so busy that I wasn't too tempted to write spells. Though I did dabble a little more than I should've.

A Month Before My 20th Birthday

I SAW RILEY AGAIN, but not because I'd spritzed myself with a potion. I spotted him in the supermarket in Drowsy Hollow when me and Vivi were picking up supplies for Aunt Lyrica's eightieth birthday dinner.

I went into a mini trance when I saw him pushing a cart of groceries while two women who I suspected were relatives filled it. He looked amused as they talked amongst themselves. Dressed in worn and faded jeans, construction boots, and a faded soft yellow t-shirt, he made my mouth water. He had a baseball cap on and when he made what was clearly a smartass remark, one of the two ladies pulled his baseball cap off and walloped him on the behind with it before he threw his head back and laughed heartily.

He put the hat back on his head backwards and I walked my shopping cart into a wall. I didn't dare look to see if he'd noticed. Couldn't make eye contact; it felt like it'd be breaking some rule or something, even though I knew of no such rule.

"Rikki!" Vivica exclaimed and grabbed my hand.

"I'm okay. Just a klutz." I waved it off.

"No. I..." Her eyes flashed with something that made my scalp prickle. I knew her eyes were on him, but I was afraid to look, afraid he'd be looking in our direction.

My cheeks flamed as she shook her head and hurried me the other way.

"What?" I asked when we were down the cereal aisle.

"There's something between you and him. The hot guy with the yellow t-shirt."

My back straightened. "What?"

"Something." She gave her head a shake, her dark curls bouncing.

"Something what?"

"I don't know. It's murky. I can't bring it into focus. But..." She let that hang.

"Think, Vivi, think," I pleaded.

"I'm trying."

I offered context, "I saw him two years ago. He was there when Aunt Lyrica did the first cloak on us under a big magnolia tree. He's beautiful, isn't he? And Vivi... dibs." I smirked.

Not that the gorgeous wolf shifter would have any reason to know I exist. Unless the fact that the last six shooting stars I'd seen and wished upon granted me what I wanted.

"I need to see that tree," she interrupted my thoughts. "We'll go there tomorrow. We'll bring Ronnie. Have her lay hands on it."

ALL FIVE OF US WERE under the magnolia tree, but there was a complete block from Vivi. She could only feel the immense magic of the area, but couldn't explain what she'd felt the day before and was unable to elaborate on it.

"Maybe we should come back tomorrow, cloak ourselves and wait and see if he shows," I suggested.

"We have to leave today," Vivi said. "I have to open the store tomorrow."

"Why don't Dani and Jessie open the store tomorrow and Vivi and I will stay here? Maybe Ronnie, too."

"No," Vivi denied. "I don't know why, but we can't be here tomorrow."

"Then we'll-" I was about to suggest we come back the following weekend, but I was cut off.

Vivi waved off whatever had happened the day before, saying she couldn't pinpoint it and didn't think it was significant enough for her to waste time coming back here. But I didn't quite believe her. Though I was kind of pissed off about it, I had no choice but to let it go.

It wasn't until the next summer, just before my twenty-first birthday, that I'd fuck not only my life but Riley's life up royally.

And I often wondered who or what had blocked Vivica's visions. Because if she'd seen, or if we'd known, could I have prevented the shitstorm that followed?

10

ERICA
Now

    I gasp as glass explodes around Riley's giant, brown wolf body. It doesn't slow him down; he's gone. Can't get away from me fast enough. Before my broken heart sinks, it immediately sprints forward in panic because my first thought is *he could be hurt*. My second thought is that I want his irresistible scent in my nose all the time.

    Ugly emotion twists at that.

    We hadn't even been in Roxy's long enough to get served our drinks. Coming in, I'd taken note of the sign indicating *Private Event, Closed to the Public* which is obviously permanent signage for any non-pack visitors who happen upon the area.

    Myself, the Brennan sisters, and Cicely walked in to be greeted by a light-brown haired, bespeckled twenty-something half human, half she-shifter staring at me with unconcealed interest at a table for six. I already knew who she was. Bailey Blackwood, the half-sister of my cousin Greyson Blackwood, though no blood relation to me.

    By the time introductions were made and congratulations given to Amelia on her pregnancy, I knew Bailey was trying to suss me out. Cicely, showing intuitiveness, spoke up first saying, "She can't tell us anything until she tells it all to Riley. Amie and Ivy wanted to bring her out for breakfast as part of the welcoming committee."

    "That's a little..." I started to say. Premature? No, impossible. "Um, I'm just here to talk to Riley."

    "We have so much to talk about," Bailey had said to Cicely with urgency, as her eyes took me in.

"Lots goin' on, girlfriend," Cicely agreed. "But not sure now's the time." Cicely's head tipped slightly in my direction, and I knew she didn't want Bailey giving me access to more information than necessary.

"Greyson's-" Bailey started and stopped just as a frisson of heat trilled up the back of my neck.

I looked over my shoulder and saw Riley's eyes on me. Then everything happened really fast. Growling, neck-baring by one of the staff, then a few more, plus council alphas coming in before Tyson ordered the place emptied, which happened quickly and then Riley was on me like a bull seeing red, pinning me to the table, with a prominent erection pressed against me.

And now left on this table in a restaurant full of half-eaten meals, I'm alone. He wanted away from me so badly, he exploded through the window to expedite his exit.

Infuriated glowing eyes, loud and terrifying growling, pinning, hardness against me, and then gone.

"ERICA?" BAILEY POKES her head in, interrupting nothing but me being alone with my thoughts. "Are you okay?" she asks.

I must look so pathetic lying on the table.

I get to my feet and look around. "Yeah, I'm... uh..." I try to swallow down the lump in my throat as I smooth out my dress, "just dandy." I squat to lift the fallen sugar packets, salt and pepper shakers, and the napkin holder.

Bailey helps.

Promptly, I burst into tears. She reaches out a hand and I'm about to take it when she pulls it back.

"Um..." She looks torn.

I search her face.

"Sorry. Uh... my first instinct is to give you a hug, but my father told me never to let a witch touch me."

Not a surprise.

"He's drilled it into me my whole life. But... come to my house. I'll make you breakfast. We'll talk."

"If you're that unsure about me, you really shouldn't have me to your home." I wipe my eyes with my sleeves.

"Are you going to be a problem?" she asks.

"I'm trying to fix the problem," I advise then whisper, "I fucked everything up, so god knows what it'll take." Or what'll be left of me when he cuts me out of his life permanently. "He won't even talk to me. If he just talked to me, I could explain and then give him his options."

"Let's just get you out of here for now. You can figure the rest out later."

WE MAKE OUR WAY ON foot down the main street back the way I walked up earlier with the Brennan sisters and Cicely. We pass a few curious-looking people who greet Bailey and smile at me with curiosity. Some were probably in the restaurant when it got cleared out. Some people are now on front lawns and porches in little groups, obviously discussing what happened.

They're trying to figure out who I am. If they knew who I was, I'm guessing they'd have different expressions on their faces. The kind of expression Lincoln and Cicely both wore first thing this morning.

I feel solidarity from Bailey, though we don't talk while we walk toward the store. Once we pass the group of a half dozen or so people outside it, Cicely included, Bailey says, "I'm just down there. Still living with my parents."

Cicely gives me a curious look with a chin jerk. I give her a tight smile and we keep going.

"Call me," Cicely calls out to Bailey.

"Okay," Bailey answers with a wave.

A handful of houses away from the store, the road begins to loop into a large circle of around thirty or forty cute family homes.

"This way," Bailey says and leads me down the driveway of the second house on the right of the cul-de-sac. It's a Cape Cod style home done in white and blue with meticulous landscaping.

"Wow. This is pretty," I say.

"Mom loves working in the garden. She's home. I'll introduce you."

"Oh... uh..." I nervously tuck my (probably wild) hair behind my ears. "I'm not sure I'm in a position to make a good impression on anyone's mom."

Bailey dismisses this with a wave of her hand. "Don't sweat it. You'll have to meet everyone eventually, right?"

We're at the door and she's reaching for the knob.

"Not necessarily," I say.

"You're Rye's mate. This is home now. No?"

"Not if he requests to sever our connection," I mutter.

Her body locks tight and she's in frozen animation for a moment, her hand on the doorknob. "Do *you* want it severed?"

She looks into my eyes, and I know she knows the answer is no. But I answer with, "It's complicated."

Something prickles at the back of my neck, and I turn in time to see a giant wolf running toward us. It's pretty startling seeing what looks like a super-sized wild animal running toward you, even if you know they're supernatural. He's suddenly, as if in slow motion, rising from four legs to two as the fur evaporates and the face morphs and tattoos appear on his arms. Jason Creed. A very naked, very large (all over) Jason Creed.

I try to work down a swallow and avoid the temptation of gawking at his crotch. He's angry.

"Bay!" he clips. "What's goin' on?"

"Tried going for breakfast but Riley showed and went all... you know... so we left, but he took off on her and left her in Roxy's alone. I've got her."

"She doesn't leave," he warns.

"I'm not leaving your village until I talk to Riley. Just like I told Tyson and Lincoln," I say.

Tyson made a point of showing up last night to let me know I needed to fix things with Riley. I made it clear that it's what I'm here for.

Jason doesn't address me. He gives her a meaningful look.

"We're just having breakfast and then I'll bring her back to her van," she defends herself. "Unless you want to come to the library with me, Erica?"

I stare blankly. "Um..."

"It's here in the village. I have a corner of our town hall as our library," she explains. "It's just across the street from your van."

I give her a non-committal smile. Of course Bailey Blackwood would want me at the library. She wants to pump me for information. I already know she's the town librarian in a way that means more than checking out book club picks to the residents of the village. She's recordkeeping.

"You might want to go check on Rye," she suggests to Jason.

"Did that. I'm makin' sure this one doesn't take off again."

"I'm not going anywhere, Jason. Not until Riley and I straighten things out."

"You know who I am?"

"I do."

"How much do you know about us? How much have you fucked around with our lives?"

"No offence, but I can't talk to you about anything like that. But I'm not planning on leaving the village until Riley and I have an important conversation."

Jason stares at me with hate. It's a stare that'd make anyone wither. If they hadn't already withered inside long ago.

"I'll wait here and just make sure," he says, crossing his arms over his fabulous chest.

"Go on, Jase. I believe her," Bailey says.

"If you try to leave town before Riley says it's all right, we'll find you," he warns, finger pointed at my face.

"I'm here until Riley and I figure it out," I say, hoping that's before Halloween. That I've got closure by then. Because there are people that I need to check in on, who will need our coven's help then.

"So, let me get this straight," Jason leans forward.

"Here we go," Bailey sighs.

He shoots her an annoyed look and then turns his ire to me. "You took one look at him and decided you wanted him, right? Because he's big, strong, good lookin'?"

It was a lot more than that. Jason is big, strong and good-looking too, and he was there the day I first saw Riley. It's not like I can even articulate just what it was. Because it was everything about him. And even if I were in my regular state of mind right now I'd have trouble with articulation, because this big, strong, good-looking guy is addressing me on the street while he's naked.

"Well, let me tell you somethin'," Jason goes on, pointing his finger in my face, "Riley Savage is more than meets the eye. That's a man who'd put his life on the line for his family, his pack, for a stranger even. He'd give anybody the shirt off his back. He puts himself last in every fucking thing he does. Everyone else is first. He's loyal. Strong. He's got a heart bigger than anyone's. And I'm not convinced you deserve him, so if he gives this thing a go with you, you're gonna have a lot of work ahead of you to convince me and most of us that you deserve that shot with him. Because I wanna know my boy's got a woman who will deserve all he's gonna break his back to give her and I sure as shit don't think it's someone who'd fuck him over for seven years."

"Jase," Bailey tries to chastise, but I doubt he even hears it. He turns, shifts to his wolf form again, and runs the other way.

"Don't listen to that. He doesn't know you and he's got no right to tear a strip off you when he hasn't a clue what your side of the story is."

I shrug. "He kinda does. It's good that Riley has such good friends. But anyway, where did Amelia and Ivy go?" I need to change this subject.

"Their men sent them home when the restaurant emptied out."

She opens the door to her house, and we're greeted by a hesitantly smiling blonde woman and a tall, built, angry-looking salt and pepper-haired man who has to be Graydon Blackwood.

"Dad, Mom, this is Erica Young. Erica: Carrie and Graydon."

"What's she doing here?" Graydon demands as I'm extending my hand to shake Carrie's hand. Before she can accept my hand, he's putting himself between her and I. Protectively.

"Do not let her touch you, Care." He points, finger close to my face. "You don't touch my mate. Have you touched my daughter?"

I don't have a chance to reply before Bailey answers for me. "She hasn't touched me, Dad."

"What's your designation in the coven?" he demands.

"Spell-writer," I answer.

He looks me over with scrutiny.

I know this man knows our coven; he was mated to Soleil over thirty-four years ago. Their mating was severed just months after Greyson was born. This was just a short while before Cornelius Savage poisoned his brother Tiberius and abducted Tyson.

I also know Graydon sought Aunt Lyrica and Soleil's help in locating him, in finding out the truth about whether Tyson was alive or not, but Soleil had been stripped of her magic and Aunt Lyrica couldn't give Graydon any information without breaking our rules, so refused to answer questions and after that, the relationship between this pack and our coven was strained. Graydon then only dealt with us when he felt he absolutely had to. And he refused to let anyone named Young near his son.

"Why are you here?" he demands.

"I'm here to deal with something between Riley Savage and myself. I'm under sanctions and I won't use any powers while I'm within the village of Arcana Falls."

"No powers?" he checks.

"Not for the forseeable."

"I'll check," he warns.

"Feel free to do that," I invite. "The only way I'm allowed to use power here is if Riley invites me to stay."

And that won't happen.

"There was drama at Roxy's," Bailey speaks up. "So I've brought Erica here for breakfast. We'll eat, have a gab, and then I'm taking her to the library with me for the day."

"Where's Rye?" Graydon demands. "I'm not sure I want this one in our house."

"Maybe talk to someone on the council, Dad. Erica needs a minute to regroup, and I'd like to help her with that. She could wind up being a member of our pack and there's no reason not to be hospitable."

"That's not what I heard," Graydon grumbles.

"I'm okay," I insist. "The walk over here helped a little. I'll just go back to my bus and-" I take a step backwards.

"You're not okay; I can tell," Bailey says, clasping my hand and giving it a squeeze.

My heart squeezes, too, at the affection in her touch and in her eyes.

Graydon growls, eyes on our joined hands.

"It's fine, Dad," she insists. "Do we have eggs, Mom?"

"We do. Bacon, too. Or ham or sausage. I've been cooking up a storm for your brother and his new mate, but I can whip something up for you both."

"I'll do it," Bailey declares.

"Maybe I should do it while you girls have a chat. Go ahead in. I'll bring it," Carrie offers.

"Sunroom only. Enter through the back door. No letting her in the house," Graydon declares.

"I really don't want anyone to go to any trouble," I protest.

"It'll only be trouble if our daughter cooks it," Carrie says lightheartedly, humor sparking in her eyes.

Bailey rolls her eyes. "I'd defend myself and say I can cook something as simple as breakfast, but my mom's right."

"Water burner," Graydon puts in with a touch of humor.

"I got distracted."

"Nose always in a book," Carrie says affectionately.

"When there's a plot twist, sometimes you just gotta keep reading to find out what happens."

Carrie snickers. "Go ahead girls," she invites, "I'll brew some fresh coffee."

Graydon's eyes are still on me and hard as nails.

"I'm not here to cause any trouble, Mr. Blackwood. I'm here to fix things."

One way or another.

He says nothing, but his eyes continue to bore into me with warning.

He might be retired from the alpha council, but though you can take the alpha off the council, he'll still see his pack as his responsibility.

CARRIE BLACKWOOD DELIVERED clubhouse sandwiches, fried potatoes, coffees, and a pitcher of orange juice to us in the sunroom on the back of the house, a pretty space overlooking lush flowerbeds and fruit trees in their big backyard. We're seated at a rattan with smoked glass dining set, flowers in the center.

I've forced myself to eat more than half, despite lack of appetite, because the effort was made, and these folks are being hospitable. But I'm finding myself more upset now than even earlier.

"So... you and Riley?" Bailey says.

I set my fork down and wait for her to ask whatever she's going to ask. And then I'll repeat myself. Again.

"I know you can't tell me much, but can you tell me this?"

I wait.

"Are you here because you're forced to be here?"

I moisten my lips and consider my words carefully for a moment.

"Do you want to be with Riley?" she asks before I've had a chance to answer.

And then her face changes and I know she can see my answer on my face.

"I fucked everything up," I whisper brokenly. "He's not gonna want me."

"Maybe after you-"

I shake my head and she stops talking. "The look in his eyes just now and last night? No. I need to say what I have to say and then give him his options."

"And those are?"

"I won't talk about this with anyone until I've talked to him."

She nods slowly, pushing food around her plate. "Do you know much about shifters? About our pack?"

"Yes, I know quite a lot."

"So, you know what your 'death' did to him." She uses air quotes over the word death.

And though I didn't really die, it felt like part of me did when I realized how Riley would be punished for my sins.

I nod, knowing agony is twisting in my features.

"And you've hurt because of it?"

"Every single fucking day." My voice cracks on the word *day*.

She says nothing, but she looks like she's trying to empathize with the weight of that.

"Thank you for breakfast. For getting me out of view for a while. It's really good, but I really should get back. I need to be where he can find me if he wants to."

"If he wants to find you, he'll find you. So long as you're not using magic to hide yourself again."

"I'm done hiding."

"Please don't rush back to your van to sit by yourself. Come to the library with me. I'd like to ask you some questions."

"I can't divulge anything, Bailey. I'm sorry."

"Not about magic, more about our early family trees that we don't have records for. I'm wondering if your coven might."

"We do. We have records of every birth and death up until the last thirty-odd years at least. After that, we haven't been involved in the same way."

"That information would be a big help."

"I'll have a look at what you've got, and I can ask my sisters if those records can be sent to fill in some gaps."

"Awesome," she says and sips her coffee. "Greyson wants information too," she adds. "He's busy, obviously, with his mating or I'm sure he'd be here to ask them himself."

"I'll be here until further notice," I say. "And Greyson now knows how to reach me and my sisters after that."

I sip my orange juice and then put my napkin down. "Please thank your mother for me. It was delicious. It's just that my belly isn't cooperative at the moment."

"I understand. She will, too."

Everything about Riley made me melt from the minute I saw him. But meeting these people, *his people* here so far? I'm now like a vat of liquified butter. To be part of *this* community? I've barely scratched the surface of seeing what this village has to offer, but between the flora, the fauna, the tight-knit community and family-atmosphere so far?

I know that not only have I obliterated my chance at a life with Riley, I've also fucked up the opportunity to have that life here. With all that I feel this is. The pack mentality I've craved my entire life.

When I finally saw Drowsy Hollow again on my eighteenth birthday, I felt drawn to that area.

But the nearby village of Arcana Falls? It actually feels like *home*.

I don't excel alone. I've always called myself a pack animal, long before I knew about shifters and their pack mentality. And I've long suspected that this is likely part of why Riley and I were considered a match.

11

RILEY

We're in the town hall for a meeting called by pack alphas. When shit's going down, it's our habit to keep everyone informed. But with the shitstorm of the past eighteen or so hours, several non-council alphas put in the request for a meeting. The only council alpha not here is Greyson as he hasn't emerged from his house since he took his mate home last night. Nobody has talked to him, but his scent floods the village.

Though that's in my nose, it's not as strong as the little witch's scent. It's getting stronger by the minute, it seems, and to say it's fucking with me is an understatement.

Ty has quickly fit in despite his short time with us so far. Right now he's standing up with Mason while the rest of us are seated in a soundproof meeting room in the basement, near the holding cells.

Ty and Mase have just updated everyone with all they know so far about the Drowsy Hollow Diner waitress who poisoned pack members. We only know that she then shot Tyson while under some sort of scent cloak. It wore off and Grey identified her as his. Her true scent lingers down here in the basement, likely due to her adrenalin spikes once Grey identified her before taking her home.

That he hasn't surfaced yet is the norm, particularly since he mated her this morning. The only men asking questions about Grey's wisdom right now are unmated ones.

Mase and Ty along with Lorenzo from the retired council are doing their best to drive the message home that they have no idea what it's like to be in Greyson's shoes because they haven't met their fated mate. It doesn't matter who she is or what she's done, he'd need to claim her.

And I know they're also saying that for my benefit.

Bruce, retired council alpha, fifth in birth order, just suggested someone go over there and make sure she hasn't murdered him.

"Our council link with Grey feels intact," Jase reasons.

"It does," Joel confirms.

I can't say I feel it; my senses are all clouded by my proximity to the witch.

"We should check anyway," I state.

All eyes swing to me because I'm sure they're curious about why I'm here when my unclaimed mate's vehicle is parked across the street.

I'm further discombobulated because I smell her here, too. Graydon caught my nostrils flaring when I walked in and muttered to me that my witch was here with Bailey earlier, that Bailey has been in mother-hen mode, which Bailey is known for.

"Could it be she found a way to fake the connection to get close?" Someone asks.

I don't even clock who, which isn't like me.

"Doubtful," Ty puts in. "Though you never know with witchcraft. These masking potions usually come from working with witches."

"Agree," Graydon speaks up.

"Maybe we should ask Riley's mate some questions," Mase says, looking to me.

Everyone else's eyes are on me, still, and my lip is curling in response to Mase's phrasing.

My mate.

"Or you'd ask her, I mean," Mase amends.

There's a long silence.

"Speaking of witchcraft... run that down for us?" Lorenzo requests.

I huff out a breath, dozens of sets of eyes on me making me feel unsettled. And I don't like the warring emotions in me. My pack should come first; I should've been the one to call this meeting and I should've done it earlier.

That two alphas had to request it for an update shows just how disjointed things are right now. Tyson is new. Mason just got news of his mate's pregnancy and he's still early on in his marriage, so he's preoccupied. Grey's not here. The rest of the council is capable, but I've always taken lead on pack-facing shit. My head's not in the game, so things are slipping around here.

They all wait for me to answer, so I manage to pull myself together enough to speak.

"I met her about seven years ago. Saw her the next day, felt she was mine and when I was about to claim her, she got scared and ran. Of course, I chased. She fell off a cliff and disappeared into the river. You all know I went off alone for a few months after that, to process, and came back when we took over the council. Threw myself into the council and thought she was dead until I smelled her in the Young's covenstead. Looked for her for answers but she stayed hidden until last night."

"And she's your fated mate? She didn't fake it?" Lorenzo asks.

"So I'm told," I say.

"But you haven't mated yet," Robert Creed, Jase's father and another retired council alpha asks.

"No."

"Because?" he pushes.

"He's conflicted," Tyson answers after I don't. "Infuriated. As he should be. He's probably protecting her from his anger by keeping his distance."

"*He's* right here," I mumble.

"But you should go to her. Deal with it and hash it all out," Robert offers.

I bare my teeth at him and say nothing.

Grey's father Graydon mutters, "Poor fucker."

The room goes wired. My eyes meet his and I bare my teeth.

It doesn't faze him. "Finding yourself mated to a witch is a disaster."

No fuckin' kidding.

"Why is that?" Linc asks.

"A complete disaster," Graydon mutters dolefully.

My posture relaxes, realizing it wasn't a jab at me. "You would know."

He nods, looking wrecked for a minute, even though it's been over thirty-two years since his bond to Greyson's mother was severed. I still don't know what happened with them. Neither does Greyson.

"Why do you say that, Graydon?" Tyson asks.

"They're dangerous," Graydon mutters.

"No shit," I fire back.

Graydon's expression tells me I have no idea. "For more reasons than you'd think. Though your mate was at my house this morning with my daughter, stating she can't use her magic in the village."

"If that's the truth," Linc mumbles. "Is she choosing not to or is it disabled?"

"She was vague," Graydon states. "But I'm not talking about witchcraft being dangerous, though it is. Very. I know that from personal experience. I'm talking about how they get. Addicted to your knot. My witch ex-mate got high on her own juices; she was wild with it. Couldn't get enough of me. You'll find yourself with a vixen doing her best to get your cock as many times a day as she can. An alpha I know in Alaska has the same problem with his witch mate."

"Sounds terrible," Cade stage-whispers, grinning wide.

"Awful," Gus chimes in.

"I'm sure not all witches are evil," Mase says.

"Maybe, maybe not. But…" Graydon throws me a dark look, "be cautious you don't get so caught up enjoying her you miss signs she's doing evil shit behind your back."

I don't need this shit and I know my body language illustrates this, but I'm in a room full of alpha males, many of them unmated.

"What's your plan, Riley?" Andy Quinn, Mase's father asks.

"Don't know yet," I state, honestly. Because I haven't a fuckin' clue.

Everything inside me wars with itself. I've been in a state of torment since I caught her scent. I was desperate to hunt her down, nothing in my head but a predatory instinct. Now that she's here, every time I get close, I malfunction.

"Talk to her. Hear her out. Go from there," Ty advises.

I say nothing. I don't want advice on this. And I've made that clear.

"I'll go out and check on Grey. Hey Linc, come with? After this?" Joel jerks his chin up, saving me from telling Tyson to fuck off. Again.

"Yeah. Right after this," Linc agrees.

"I'll come too," Jase says.

"Jase is the one to watch now," Lorenzo puts in.

"Riley's mating isn't solidified. Might be that I've got a breather until that happens. Take your time, Rye," Jase teases.

His expression drops when our eyes meet.

"Or do what you need to do. Don't worry about me."

I look away. "If I'm not needed here, I'm gonna dip."

I need time to myself. All they're doing is talking shit over that they can't resolve.

"You're not all right, man. What can we do?" Jase offers.

"Nothin'. I wanted to find her to get answers and now she's here. I don't… I don't want the answers. What difference would it make? She knows what she did."

"Do you want it severed?" Graydon asks.

"I don't know what the fuck I want. I just know you all need to let me figure that out. I need space."

When nobody speaks for a minute, I go on, "You're meeting about me and about Grey. Grey will figure out what his mate is all about and tell us when he gets the chance. We've gotta trust him. And as for me… I got nothin', boys. You wanna make sure she stays at that corner and doesn't go anywhere, feel free. You don't? Whatever."

"You'll talk to her?" Tyson asks.

My eyes roll. "You wanna let her go, do it. I'll find her if I decide I'm ready to listen. Unless she masks her scent again."

"I think you should go now. Don't put it off," Ty advises.

"You've been heard."

"Are you gonna listen?"

I huff out a small fraction of my increasing impatience.

He leans in. "Did I listen to you when you asked me to give you a chance to show me what I was missing not being part of our pack? Do you know what *you're* missing by not claiming your female?"

I scowl. "Two very different situations, Ty. This pack did nothing wrong to earn your absence. This witch has only been sittin' there not even twenty-four hours. You think she deserves me droppin' everything when she left me and hid for seven fuckin' years?"

Mase answers, "I think you need to listen to her and then make a decision. We all feel your headspace. We all feel the rift, the disconnect, Riley. The sooner you hear her out, the sooner you can move forward."

"And sad to say," Ty contributes, "the disconnect doesn't feel right. I've only had this connection with you for a short time and I don't want it broken like this."

"Best deal with it, Riley," my father speaks up from the wall by the door, where he stands with a few more male pack members that I hadn't clocked. He's here likely because I'm on the agenda. "Listen to what she has to say, son, then process how it all makes you feel. Do it soon. Don't put it off."

He wouldn't want me putting anything off. One of the values he raised me with was that procrastination was always a downhill slope.

After I lost my shit this morning and ran off not even a sliver of my rage, Mase and Ty caught up with me and I went to the job site with them. I was next to useless. Ty's a natural. He helped me and Mase wrap the job up. After that, Mase invited me to go for a beer to get me talking. I wanted no part of it. Before we were back, the alphas of our pack had requested this meeting. But I've had enough. I need time to get my head together. That I didn't even clock my father in this room feels odd to me.

"You think I'm not thinking about going over there? Her van's a hundred feet from me right now. You think I can't feel it in every cell in my fuckin' body?"

"What's stopping you?" Tyson asks.

"Fuckin' leave me be, you guys. I'll deal when I'm good and ready."

Twenty-one alphas and four betas watch me storm out.

When I get outside, I see her van lit up. I smell her. She's in my lungs. She's somewhere in that hole in my chest that I've felt for seven years and she's trying to take residence there, but it feels like she's using an ice pick around the edges to dig her way in, and I don't know if I should let her wreak more havoc or find a way to expel her.

I get into my truck and peel off in the opposite direction of my house. Tonight, I'm grabbing a motel room.

IT'S LAST CALL IN THE Stagecoach Tavern at the edge of Drowsy Hollow that's farthest away from Arcana Falls. And the foxy waitress I've been flirting with all night stretches across the bar to get two inches from my face, giving me a view straight down her loose blouse.

"I'll be done here in twenty, so if you wanna sip that drink slowly, I can walk you home," she offers, breath tickling my ear.

She already knows from small talk that I'm staying in the HoJo motel about fifteen paces away. She doesn't know me; she's new to town so hasn't seen me around. Most locals who know me do so because of Savage Construction. Despite the way she fills out that blouse and those skintight lowrider jeans, my cock hasn't even stirred.

I give her a lazy smile and I'm about to agree, had already decided I was doin' this tonight, shaking the seven years' worth of cobwebs off my game, but something hits my nose and makes my gaze snap to the right.

My eyes meet the piercing gray eyes of a woman at the far end of the bar. She has red hair and a familiar mouth. I take a deeper pull of the air and over the scent of beer, the bowls of peanuts all along the bar top and the scents of the patrons in here, I know she's related to the witch. She's leveling me with a look of disapproval. Her hair is almost the same, though hers is straight, not as long, and she has bangs where Rikki's is curly and one length.

"Riley?" the bartender tries to get my attention and for the first time, touches me.

And her hand on my forearm feels wrong.

I pull back while I force my eyes forward. "Excuse me, darlin'." I down my drink as her expression drops. She looks toward the redhead as it's obvious she and I were in an eye lock. I drop cash to cover my tab and a tip before I jerk my chin toward the door with my eyes on the redhead.

She hops down off the barstool and follows me outside.

As soon as the night air hits, I spin around for a face-off, knowing my glare shows her just what I think about her showing up here.

"Who are you and what the fuck are you doin' here?"

"I'm Jessica. Erica's sister. I have some records for your library, as requested by Bailey Blackwood."

"Excuse me?"

"My sister called this afternoon and asked me to send them over for your librarian. She requested I not visit your village, so I had planned to leave them with Kathleen."

"Kathleen?"

"Brennan, or now Oakes, I suppose. Ivy and Amelia's mother. She was renting the apartment above our-"

"Right."

"She'll be back tomorrow to pack, so she said she'd bring what I've photocopied to Bailey Blackwood."

"Why were you in there gunnin' me?" I'm not stupid enough to believe she just happened to come into the same bar as me at the same time.

"Because I know who you are. I know what you're about to do. Furthermore, I know who waits for you at home."

I scoff.

She reaches for my shoulder. I step back, not wanting her hands on me. She drops her hand.

"But bigger question, Riley. Why were you in there getting ready to leave with a woman who isn't yours? I thought people of your…" She looks around before continuing, "upbringing didn't flirt in bars with women when your unclaimed mate sits right now in your village waiting for you."

I grind my teeth. The nerve of this bitch.

"Nothing I do is any of your business. Or your sister's."

"You do this, you won't be able to take it back."

I fold my arms over my chest. "Meaning?"

"I'm assuming you haven't heard my sister's side of things."

"So? I owe her nothing. Less than that after what she did to me."

"If you knew the whole story, maybe you'd have no need of being in bars trying to make up for lost time with women who won't matter to you."

"I don't need to answer to you or anyone else about who I choose to fuck."

"If you do this, you'll regret it."

"Are you threatening me, witch?"

She shakes her head. There's no animosity coming at me from this woman. Sadness, maybe. Concern, definitely. Not that I give a shit.

"I'm not threatening you. I'm educating you before you do something you'll regret. It'll sicken you to your core if you do this once you have all the answers. When you realize what you've done. So please, don't do this tonight. Talk to Erica. Give her a chance to explain."

I sear her with a glare. "After what she's done to me, what makes you think I have any desire to hear a thing she has to say?"

"I shouldn't tell you this, but I'm going to anyway."

She takes a big breath, then says, "Erica hasn't let anyone lay a hand on her. Ever. If you catch my drift."

I flinch; I'm knocked for six.

Jessica goes on, "She's saved herself. For you. She's not going to tell you that with the state of things between you right now, so I'm telling you. I'm telling you so you have that information before you go giving something to someone that you can't take away when it should be for just my sister. Whatever you've done before knowing she was alive and that you belong together doesn't count. But if you do it now while she waits there for you, believe me, it'll count. Maybe not to her as she'll forgive you for anything, but you might not be able to forgive yourself."

She moistens her lips, and her expression reminds me of the girl I saw in that field of flowers seven years ago. So much so, it feels like a blade sinking into my chest.

"Can I give all these records to you since you're here? Can you take them back to your village and give them to Bailey to save Kathleen the trouble?"

I stare blankly as what she's just said to me tries to penetrate the shield I've built over the past several days.

My chest is on fire. My hands shake and I'm sure she notices.

When I don't answer, she pops her trunk and reaches in, pulling out a banker's box.

I see a brunette sitting in the passenger seat. A brunette that looks an awful lot like Erica Young, too. She gives me a look loaded with meaning but says nothing as Jessica sets a box on the ground before reaching in and pulling out another, which she passes to me. I stare blankly at the box in my arms.

She lifts the first from the ground and walks it to my pickup truck, three spaces from her vehicle.

"Going home?" she asks.

"None of your business," I manage, putting the boxes in the truck.

"She suffers, Riley," Jessica says softly, setting the box on concrete. "She's suffered as long as you have. Hear her out. Her answers aren't good ones, but she's grown up a lot since then; she had no choice but to do so when faced with the consequences of her actions, which came from the longing of her heart rather than from something nefarious. Her punishment was much harsher than it needed to be. She's got the most beautiful heart I've ever known."

She gives me a look loaded with meaning before she walks away from me and gets into her car.

I immediately turn away.

What she's said makes no sense to me.

Why the fuck would the witch hide from me for all this time if she's suffering for it? Why save herself for me? What? Hope that I'll forgive her when she knew she left me thinking she was dead for all this time? I don't get it. Any of it.

Inside, I know there's only one way to find out.

I also know I'm not going there.

Every fiber of my being tells me I need to keep my distance from the witch who shattered me. The witch oozing with so much pain that I can't handle how it makes me feel. Is Tyson right? That I stay away to protect her from my anger? I don't even know. It feels more like I need to protect myself from her pain, which I can't wrap my mind around. Which I can't stand. I can't stand that she hurts this much. I can't understand how she hurts this much yet did nothing about it. None of it makes sense.

I glance over my shoulder and then look away knowing Jessica and the other sister watch me walk to my motel.

THERE'S A KNOCK ON my door as I shut the shower off. And I'm pissed off as I pull on my boxers, thinking it might be Jessica again. As I open the door, my nose tells me before I see her that it's the bartender. Though she told me it, I can't remember her name.

She smiles, jiggling a bottle of whisky as her eyes travel across my chest, which is still wet.

"Sorry, babe. Not gonna happen tonight."

Her expression drops before she breathes out, "Oh."

And then she pouts. And I'd find it very fuckin' cute if this were seven years back.

"I'm tryin' to get over someone who fucked me over pretty bad. Thought I was ready. I'm not."

She waits a beat, then says, "I see. You know where to find me if you change your mind some other night. Have a good one." She turns but then stops and looks over her shoulder. "You sure? Sometimes the best way to get someone out of your system is to let another someone in."

That's what I'd been thinking before Jessica Young talked to me tonight. "Have a good night, babe."

"Okay, well, goodnight then." Her eyes travel my body and I know she's disappointed. I smell her arousal and it's doing nothing for me. Part of me wishes that wasn't true. The other part of me is dominant right now because I'm taking Jessica Young's advice by not doing something I might regret. And I'm not sure how to feel about it as I watch the bartender wander off.

I'm about to shut the door when something hits my nose that has me bristling. I take a deeper pull of the humid night air. Two shifters. Two shifters I don't know.

They're not within fifty feet of me, the scent is too faint, but I suspect they're here at this motel. My nose is weak right now and I don't like that.

Since I smell them, they might also smell me, depending on how strong their noses are. I don't have backup here and everything inside me warns that I shouldn't track down that scent and ask questions without my pack brothers at my back.

I quickly throw my clothes on and get the fuck out, driving toward my village while calling Joel who answers on the first ring.

"Hey Rye."

"Joel. Any reason you know of that there's shifters visiting the area from another pack?"

"No."

"Gut's telling me it might have something to do with Grey's mate. My head's fucked, so I can't be sure, but the scent of one… might be related to the scent I caught in that meeting tonight."

I don't have an accurate sense of that waitress's scent, as it was just vague remnants of it. Not to mention how my senses are muddled because of my own mate.

My own mate?

The phrase bounces around in my chest, feeling like a ball covered in spikes.

"Might be?" Joel asks.

"Think so, not a hundred per cent."

"The way shit's been goin' for us lately, me and the others made a decision tonight after you left."

"What's that?" I ask.

"We're in the orange zone for now with one council alpha, one pack alpha or strong beta on surveillance watch here at my place around the clock."

Joel's house isn't far from the village's four corners; he has our surveillance setup in his basement with a separate entrance so the team can access the room without disturbing him when he's not on shift.

"Good idea. Who's downstairs now?'

"Me and Sean."

"You sendin' me the schedule?"

"You and Grey aren't on the schedule."

"Why?" I demand.

"Riley," Joel says, and he means *you know why*.

"Fuck," I mutter. "I'm headin' home from town. You call me if you need anything."

"Will do, bro."

12

JOEL

Ten minutes after I hang up with Riley, I see his truck come up on the screen mounted on the wall in front of me. He idles at the intersection of the four corners. And I know why he sits so long. He's watching the dark van on the corner with the pop-top tent.

Sean snores in the chair beside me. He's been at it half an hour, but I've left him be. The guy has an infant at home that doesn't like sleep and loves exercising his lungs. I figure Sean's offering to do as many nightshifts here as he can knowing he'll get a chance to catch twenty winks at a time instead of five. I'll only wake him up if I need to. Partly because we've got another set of eyes on the corner as well. Linc's.

Right now Linc is wolf, hunkered down at the back of the store, low and out of sight. He's likely using his clothes as a pillow for his chin as he keeps one ear on Riley's mate. Making sure she's not going anywhere. He has his phone there, too; if I phone him, he'll shift so he can answer.

There's been major traffic at this corner today anyway. After the scene I heard about in Roxy's this morning, word traveled that Riley's mate isn't dead, she's in town, and a witch who's been in hiding. There are a lot of people asking questions and unhappy that they're not getting detailed answers. There are also a lot of busybodies finding reasons to go to the store, drive by or walk past it hoping to catch sight of the mystery woman that broke Riley Savage's heart.

Rye finally pulls over into the corner of the parking lot and sits idling there for a few more minutes before his truck door opens. I lean forward in my chair, feeling like I'm watching a movie, waiting for the *big thing* to happen.

I'm sure he's about to step out and stride to that van, kick the door down, and claim his woman. If he does, Linc will give them privacy.

But the truck door shuts without him first getting out, and a good five minutes go by with no movement from his truck, no lights. And then I mutter a cussword when his headlights go on and he backs out and drives through the intersection. Fast. He's going home without her.

I lean back with a disappointed shake of my head and then I dial Linc's number. It takes three rings before he answers.

"Yeah?"

"See that?"

"Yeah. He was warring with himself."

"Yeah," I agree. And then I cock my head and frown. "Strange. Feels like I can't sense him in our pack connection. Something feels... missing. It's been a little fucked since he found out she's alive, but it's... fading or some shit."

"I agree," Linc says. "This ain't good. Witchcraft?"

"Might be but more likely it's his state of mind. We all know what can happen to an alpha who rejects his mate."

Nothing good, that's for sure. He can go feral as a wolf and stay that way. He can lose his ability to shift. He can lose his mind. Riley knows all this, too.

"Fuck, I know it. Not good if he shuts everyone out. Also not good if that witch is doin' something to disconnect him from us."

"Nope," I agree. "Either way it's not good. What's your sense after watching her all day?"

He takes a minute before he speaks. "I don't know a hundred per cent yet, Joel, but maybe 75 percent sure Riley should get his ass back here and claim his woman."

"Hm."

"Riley Savage is a good fucking guy," Linc grunts.

"The best," I agree.

"And after what he's been put through, I can't help but think he's got a sweet reward coming. Maybe she's that reward."

"Could be he gets the pain and reward in the same package," I say.

I probably can't compare what I know about this pain to Riley Savage, though in my mind I feel like I know more about it than most. Used to think I didn't know what was worse: thinking the woman I loved was dead or knowing she was living her life with another guy.

It's been said repeatedly that Susan wasn't meant to be mine. I haven't kept close tabs, but do know she's now got four kids with him. Word is she's happy. But I haven't ever fully been able to wrap my head around that. I've dreamt a hundred times of the night I watched that bastard carry her away from me, fear in her eyes.

And it's made this whole situation of watching my council alpha brothers find their mates strange. I haven't spent a whole lot of time around the two that mated with their mates, but what little I have has had me in a state of reflection about Susan and me.

Was our bond as strong as theirs? Pack lore says it wouldn't be, and it's said that young love feels so intense because of hormones mixed with infatuation. We all had girlfriends. Some serious. Some not so much. I thought Susan and me were serious. I figured one day I'd know we were forever, that she'd be mine. And when I found out she wasn't, I didn't think I'd ever feel anything as strong as what I felt about her. Time will tell.

13

ERICA

"What do I do, Aunt Lyrica?" I plead, gripping handfuls of my hair as I once again plummet toward the river. The angry river that can't wait to swallow me whole. "How do I survive this?"

"Beautiful girl..." her voice, a comforting whisper inside my head, encourages, "I'm sure you know, deep down, that you have to wait. Wait. Endure. And then finally reap your rewards. So many are coming..."

Rewards? I haven't earned any where Riley Savage is concerned. I know by the hatred in Riley's eyes that nothing I could do would make up for what I did to him.

So I drown. I drown in my dreams again. And just like the other thousand times it happened, it feels real. It's terrifying. Even though I know it's not real, even though I know I deserve it, my every instinct tells me to fight it as my lungs fill with gallons of water.

THROBBING PAIN BEHIND my eyes is palpable as I open them and squint at the too-bright sun. Sometimes I wake up just before plunging into the angry water. Not today. I struggle to catch my breath as I pull the quilt over my head, my sleep-terror state fading, giving way to my bleak reality. Another morning here on my bus. Another day in the village of Arcana Falls, the place where my deepest fantasies as well as my most vivid regrets live, breathe, and ache.

I often talk to my deceased aunt in my dreams, hearing her voice like a narrator over the vivid images, sometimes images like this morning with the sensation of falling and drowning. Other times, it's a psychedelic-looking kaleidoscope I see behind my eyelids in those few minutes somewhere between asleep and awake. I ask questions. She answers in non-answers, politely imploring me to search within myself, to summon my own wisdom.

Wait? Endure?

If only I'd had some wisdom seven years ago.

Do I throw myself at his feet, hook my arms around his ankles and beg him to listen to me, enduring the contempt in his eyes?

Wait for him to tire of ignoring me, finally demanding what I'm sure he must be itching for?

A severing. A permanent separation from the mate bond he would've felt and grieved for the last several years.

He'd finally be free of the pain I caused him.

I dash away the moisture leaking from my eyes as I throw the covers back and crane my neck to look out the netting surrounding my bed. I watch the wolf beside the store get up and stretch, before shifting back to his male form.

Lincoln. Keeping watch for his friend and pack mate, Riley.

Lincoln squats to pick up a steaming mug on the pavement by the door.

Most women would languidly take in the absolute male beauty of a naked Lincoln Fowler, but I don't. I avert my eyes, then I climb down and change out of my nightgown, clip on a clean bra, then pull on a clean dress and panties. As I'm pushing my arms through armholes, there's a soft knock on the side window. I pull the curtain across and see Cicely holding a steaming mug. She's not smiling; she's also not frowning.

I open the door and tentatively greet, slash ask, "Hi?"

"Here's a cup of coffee for you. If you need to use my bathroom, feel free."

"Oh, thank you. I appreciate that."

"In fact," she goes on, "a spare key that you can use while you're here." She hands me the mug and key, hooking her thumb toward the building with her free hand. "In case you need to use it and I'm busy in the store or not here or whatever. But it's usually unlocked."

"That's kind of you. But, why are you being so kind?"

I feel self-conscious as she takes a good five seconds giving me a once over before answering.

She finally says, "Bailey has strong intuition. Mine's not bad either. We don't know why you did what you did or how it's going to turn out, but you're fated to be part of our pack, and we take care of our own."

A lump forms in my throat.

She must see it by the panicked look creeping across her face. "It's just access to some plumbing." She raises her hands like I'm about to shoot.

"It means a lot. Particularly since you don't have much information. I appreciate it."

"Yeah, well, there's a reason your coven has been part of our pack since the beginning, despite whatever happened with Graydon Blackwood and Grey's birth mom. You also made sure things worked out with Tyson and Ivy and with Mase and Amie, so…"

"Those things probably would've worked themselves out eventually," I reason, "but we might have worked to smooth out some of the wrinkles in the journey. After all Tyson Savage has been through, he didn't need wrinkles."

She nods. "And Mase and Amie are strong enough for the wrinkles."

She *does* have intuition. But I say nothing. I sniff the coffee. It smells heavenly. I blow on it, anxious to get it cool enough for a mouthful.

She goes on, "And yet nobody is allowed to iron out the wrinkles for you and Riley?"

I shake my head. "No. Because I'm the one who wrinkled things, so I get to do things the hard way and Riley gets to suffer." My defeat is evident in my body language.

I straighten up. I don't deserve to act like a martyr.

"Then I hope the reward will be all the sweeter," she rasps, looking emotional as our eyes meet.

I bite my lip.

God, I hope that's true. But it's not like I deserve it.

"But if you wind up hurting him more…" She stops.

"I'll do my best not to," I vow before she has to deliver her threat.

Her eyes rove my face for a beat. "Anyway…" She takes a step back. "I've got to open up. Don't hesitate to use the bathroom. The kitchen upstairs. Whatever you need. I'm here all day today. Linc tasked me with babysitting you. He was desperate for a run."

"I won't make your job hard," I vow, empty hand over my heart. "Thank you so much, Cicely." I sip from the mug. "Mm. That's good."

She gives me a tight smile and heads to the store.

I gather a few toiletries and a towel and carry the mug to her place with me.

IT'S THE EARLY AFTERNOON and I have my nose in one of Aunt Lyrica's notebooks when Bailey approaches, a bag in hand.

"Lunch?" She holds the bag out.

I straighten up in my folding lawn chair with the footrest, while arranging the ribbon bookmark and closing the old leather book.

"Um… I hadn't thought much about lunch yet." There haven't been as many curious people looking me over today. My guess is that they now know who I am and have no desire to breathe the same air as me.

I should count myself lucky they haven't publicly stoned me.

"Food is my love language," Bailey advises. "Though I can't cook, so it's complicated. But I brought chicken wraps from Roxy's."

"Why are you speaking your love language to me?" I inquire with a frown.

Cicely. Bailey. These people are good people. I have no clue what's in store for Cicely, but Bailey will definitely have her reward. Though my sister Vivi wouldn't tell me who she'd end up with, she said it'll be an angsty journey. I find curiosity niggling at me about Cicely. I'd love to have Ronnie lay hands on her to see what she can glean.

"Because your sister dropped off those records already. They arrived this morning and I've had a great morning compiling data. I'm a spreadsheet geek. And I figured lunch would be a good way to say thank you. So… thank you." She extends a foil-wrapped tube and after I take it, she unearths two cans of pop from the bag.

"Mind if I sit here and eat with you? Probably just a half an hour. I'm also anxious to get back and dig through data."

"Sure," I say. "C'mon in if you want. I only have this one outdoor chair, but we can both fit comfortably inside."

She follows me in.

I pull the footlocker out from under my back bench seat and slide the notebook into it, then lock it.

Bailey is taking in the space. "This is really cute."

"I came in a hurry. Forgot my outdoor shower and camping toilet."

"You should come stay at my place. We have a guest room."

"Somehow, I don't think your father would appreciate that. Besides..." I trail off and say nothing.

"You're making a statement," she whispers.

I stare at her.

She continues. "You're exactly where you arrived, waiting like you said you would, even if it's less than comfortable. You're letting your mate see that you're willing to be less than comfortable. But, you're probably punishing yourself needlessly."

I guess I *am* punishing myself. Though I wouldn't agree with the part about it being needless.

"When he's ready, he'll find you. And he will get there. He has to. It's biologically inevitable."

I say nothing for a minute and then I ask, "How did one of my sisters get the documents to you?"

They're not allowed to come to Arcana Falls until they're invited as part of my punishment.

"Riley brought them." She says, eyes widening as she opens her mouth to take a bite of her wrap.

"Riley brought them?" I whisper in shock.

"Don't know how that came about because he refused to discuss it; just dumped two boxes of paperwork on my desk this morning and grumbled that he didn't have time to answer questions and left."

Wait. What? How? Who gave them to Riley?

Heat floods my face. I need to get ahold of my sisters.

"Um... if you're not allowed to practice magic here, why do you have so many..." she gestures to the cabinet that's open a little. It's filled with jars.

"Herbs, lotions, and potions?" I finish for her.

"Yeah." She lifts a jar out of my fake, decoration only, apothecary. It reads "love potion number ninety-six" and is filled with dried lavender and sparkly red heart confetti in it. The fake apothecary was a joke gift from Ronnie on Christmas the year I turned eighteen.

"That's not real. It was a gag gift. But I don't travel light," I say. "Besides, I might have to perform magic the minute I'm out of here." I take a bite of the wrap, pushing away the thoughts of the severing ceremony that'll likely happen as soon as I step outside the village. "Mm. This is good," I lie, not because it's not good, but because I can't even taste it. "Thanks again."

14

RILEY

Five of my council pack brothers are in my garage. Years ago, my father converted it to the Savage Construction office. Everyone's here but Greyson, and the air is thick with their combined concern. It's nighttime and I've spent the day here, trying to bury myself in work. Trying to bury myself in something so I don't go to that witch and bury myself in her.

I can smell her from here. Clean, hungry, virgin pussy with a hint of lilac.

Hungry? More like ravenous. Beckoning to me like a siren. A siren in the depths of the deep, dark blue water, wanting to drag me to the bottom.

Virgin. That's the kicker. Saving herself for me after what she did to me? It makes no sense. Despite how I've tried to push it all out of my head, it's playing on a loop. What she did. That she's here. What her sister said. *If* it's true.

I'm pissed off. These guys need to leave me be. I can't handle the lectures.

Ty and Mase are pushing me to hear her out.

Joel and Jase aren't saying much, but look concerned.

Lincoln seems like he's waffling between the two sects.

And I'm pushing back.

> *"Leave me alone. Give me space."*

> *"She can sit there and wait for more than a couple days since I've been here seven goddamn years."*

I'm tired of repeating myself and am ready to leave, ready to hit the fuckin' road if they don't lay off warning me about what might happen to me if I reject her, if I reject my instincts.

Beyond seeing where I'm at where she's concerned, they wanted to update me on the fact that three of them went to check in on Grey and said the air is thick with mating scents. Grey poked his head out to good-naturedly tell them to fuck off. That he'll see them in a few days. Ish.

"So this means we have zero answers about his new mate so far? Not why she shot Tyson. Not why she targeted our pack?" I demand.

"Nope. Nothing," Jase responds.

Greyson Blackwood loves nothing more than this pack, but if I were in my right head I'd have pushed for at least a few answers before now. I'm not in my right head. Not about that; not about anything.

"We're disconnected, brother," Mase says, putting his hand on my shoulder.

Though I feel my connection with him, it's like the volume is turned down low. And I know it's because of whatever is going on with *her*. Mason didn't feel right from the time Ivy neared the village the night Ty claimed her. He was right again after he mated with Amelia.

"I need you guys to give me space, leave me be. Please guys," I try.

"Claim your woman and we'll do that," Ty volleys.

This fucker has certainly taken his place as firstborn alpha of our pack's council. And I should find it irritating to the nth degree right now, but instead, I get him. Despite the muted connection, I feel a stronger connection to Tyson Savage than anyone. My father tells me he's a lot like Uncle Tiberius. And I'd never hurt my council brothers by saying it, but from the moment we met I knew he wasn't just perfect to fill the missing piece of our council, our pack, but also that he was deeply connected to me. Our fathers were two sides of the same coin. I know this not because I had a chance to get to know Uncle, but because I've grown up learning who he was to our pack, learning who he was to my father. Who he was to my Aunt Cat. Everyone who knew Uncle Tiberius does their best to keep his memory alive.

And though Tyson is a blood relative, related to me on both sides of my family since our fathers were brothers and our mothers are sisters, he feels like family. *This* soon.

Despite my anger at the situation with the witch, my feelings for Ty aren't dulled. I do like that he's fallen naturally into step with us, and it gives me some peace of mind that though I'm giving the pack very little attention right now, these guys can handle things and they've got Tyson to help pick up my slack.

But I've got half a mind to draw their attention to the fact that we need more intel about Grey's mate. I know that'd be taken as me deflecting from my own situation. The fact is that she's there, under his care, smelling like him, and if he felt there was still risk, he'd deal with it. Maybe he's still getting answers. Maybe she's hostile. New mates can sometimes put up a fight. I know these guys are watching for threats, that all members of our pack are on alert.

"Rye, I told these guys you scented shifters in The Hollow last night," Joel says. "And you're thinking it might have to do with Grey's mate."

"Yeah," I reply. "Maybe some of you should scour The Hollow. Make sure nothing else is afoot. I can't be sure, but one scent might have been related to Grey's mate's scent I caught in the town hall yesterday."

Mase speaks up. "Already had a couple guys scour The Hollow this morning. Nobody caught any scents."

"Maybe this needs stronger noses." I look to Linc.

"Good idea," Mase agrees.

"*We* can do that," Jase says. "Right, Linc?"

"Cicely says she'll keep an eye on Erica," Linc says, looking at me.

"Yeah. Let's go. Comin' Rye?" Joel pushes.

"We should leave an alpha to watch Erica Young," Ty states.

"We've got surveillance on the corner," I mutter.

"You comin'?" Linc asks.

I shake my head. "Negative. Told you already. Need space."

"It'd help since you know the scent," Joel presses.

Our eyes meet.

Shit.

"The more you distance yourself from us, the worse you're gonna feel," Mase advises.

Ty adds, "Unless you do what you were born to do. Take her."

I grind my teeth so hard they squeak. "Change the fuckin' record, Tyson."

"I know you want space but I want to understand, cousin. What is it? Is it that you're pissed? You don't want the truth? Don't want her?" Ty asks. "Are you rejecting your mate and just not telling us?"

"There's two issues at hand here, boys. Let's deal with one issue at a fuckin' time," I state.

"Which issue then?" Mase asks. "Your mate or these unknown shifters?"

"Fuck sakes," I mutter. "Let's go to The Hollow."

I catch them giving one another concerned looks. Yeah, they think I'm picking the wrong area to focus on right now. But I pretend not to notice.

"IT'S THERE, IN MY HEAD, but…" I shake it off. "Can't find it."

"Should be there somewhere," Linc mutters, looking at me with concern. "Let's do another loop."

"We've already done two," I bite off.

I bite because he's right. I should be picking it up where I found it last night, even a trace of it and I'm not finding it at all. And if I caught a bit of it and could get on the trail, Linc could help. He's got the best nose of anyone I know.

"They must be using the scent masking agent she used," Jase offers.

There's nothing here. And the motel had a nearly full house last night according to the clerk, so he couldn't tell us much, didn't remember two males traveling together who would've checked out this morning.

Since there's not much to go on, we decide to head back. We're in Linc's SUV. Jase is in the passenger seat; Joel and me are in the back.

Linc speaks up. "Know you're sick of hearin' it, know Ty hasn't figured out about boundaries yet because he's new to the pack, but brother: gotta say I agree with him. If you take care of business, your head'll clear. You're off your game."

I flex my jaw muscles and stare out the window.

"Rye?" he pushes. "Maybe you didn't smell anybody. Maybe your senses are even more *off* than we think."

"Turn the music up," is my answer.

I catch sight of his judgmental gaze in the rearview mirror. It should infuriate me to have my senses questioned, but the fact of the matter is, I'm questioning them, too.

The stereo is cranking out AC/DC's *Shoot to Thrill* when Joel calls out, "Turn it down, man," and as the song halts, Joel answers his ringing phone.

The energy in Linc's SUV shifts and I watch Joel's body lock tight.

"Fuck. Fuck! There in five. Cat been called? Right. Is Cicely okay? Call Mase and Ty. Yeah? Okay." He's looking at me as he ends the call. I'm beside him and yet I couldn't hear the person on the phone, which is alarming.

"It was Peter," Joel says, "He was on security cameras with Gus. Unknown wolf shifters turned up at the four corners and Gus ran to check it out but didn't get there fast enough. Cicely got knocked unconscious when she tried to intervene."

"With what? What happened?" I demand.

"Pete watched two unknown shifters approach the four corners as wolves. One ran into Riley's Erica. She was getting out of her van, heading for Cicely's door when he shifted to man and..." Joel looks me in the eyes and finishes with, "Cicely ran out. One hit her, knocking her out. Camera shows the other took off with your woman."

Took off with her...

Took her?

I blink.

As it penetrates, my blood turns cold. Then it shifts and my blood pumps so hard and hot in my ears, my head might explode.

"Riley," Jase says from the front seat. "Hold it together, brother."

My throat is a desert. My chest burns.

Someone lays a hand on my forearm, and I hear, "Gonna be all right, bud."

I left her in a van at the four corners. Someone took her. Someone probably related to Grey's mate who was trying to kill Tyson, who poisoned several of our alphas. Because I left her in a fuckin' van in a dark parking lot. Because my head's been out of it.

He took my... my...

My vision blurs as rage seeps into my veins, shunting to my extremities. Soaking my skin from the inside out. This vehicle isn't moving fast enough.

My lungs are filling with water, like I'm drowning, like I'm back in the river searching for her, holding my breath until I can't hold it anymore, coming to the surface to gasp for air as my vision blackens around the edges. Swimming. The memory of my muscles aching floods, exerting until they burned trying to find her, desperate to get to her, unable to see her, unable to –

"Riley." Joel says. "We're almost there."

"Stop the car," I clip, expecting my voice to be garbled, expecting water to force itself out of my lungs.

I can't compute. I can't.

Lincoln pulls over and before his Bronco comes to a complete stop, I'm ripping my seatbelt off, shredding my clothes as I yank them off and shifting as soon as I've got the door open.

I'm wolf.

Nose to the ground.

Paws pounding the pavement.

Finding her.

I'll fuckin' find her. And I'll rip that wolf apart. That wolf that dared touch my mate.

I immediately sense her scent on the breeze, wafting through the air. Nothing else penetrates, not the car slowly following behind me, not the two wolves now flanking me as I run at full speed, knowing exactly where I'm going, what I'm doing, and why.

I smell her. I smell *him*. And she's in distress.

"THAT DIDN'T TAKE LONG. Give me the female your pack took, and I'll give you yours," one of the assholes I smelled the night before sneers, a gun pointed at me. "Take one step closer, and you're done."

I shift to human form.

I don't know how much time it took to find her, but it didn't feel like long. I had a single-minded focus, details of how I got here already hazy, but I know I found her within minutes of getting out of the Bronco by running through the thick brush not far from Mase's place.

My eyes dart around the dark space and I see her behind him, bound and gagged, eyes filled with fear. Copper hair messy. Blood? A small cut on her toe.

I'm roaring as wolf before I've even finished shifting from man to beast again and see the panic in his eyes as he sizes me up. He squeezes the trigger and misses me, but I immediately smell blood mixed with the gunpowder and know it belongs to Jase.

I'm on him, my teeth gripping his throat as I hear the gurgle while I tear flesh away, snarling.

He flails as he shifts to a wolf that's much smaller than mine and I don't let up. I'm ripping skin, tasting blood, hearing bones crack. He yelps before going limp while I continue to rip through flesh, shaking it with my single-minded focus taking every bit of my headspace until I drop him and see the life drained from his eyes.

I roar again at the corpse and then turn my focus to her. Taking her in by sight and scent.

She should smell like me, but she doesn't. A wolf taking her would think she's free, available to mate. But she's not. She's not available because she's mine!

The rage in my head coupled with her fear scent that's surging into my lungs reverberates through my chest, filling that hollow space that I know would be hers if not for the seven years. She's frightened. She needs comfort. She needs my scent, my purr, my touch, my cock, my mark. She needs my knot.

My wolf's eyes meet her eyes.

15

ERICA

Riley and I are eye-locked for a solid five seconds when something springs forth in me. It's something I haven't felt since the day I ruined everything.

Hope.

And then his eyes flash with something strange before they bounce to hit Lincoln's. Something passes between him and Lincoln before Riley turns and runs, leaving me. Again.

And I'm immediately weeping. I'm sobbing into my knees, my body bucking until I'm aware of warm, strong hands freeing me from the ties around my wrists, then ankles.

I look into the eyes of Lincoln who looks sad as he assesses me.

"You hurt?"

I shake my head. That was the most horrific thing I've ever witnessed.

"Is Jason okay?" I manage.

"He's okay. Just grazed him," the one I know is Joel answers while examining the dead wolf in front of me. "Where's the other one?"

Jason sits on the ground, examining the wound on his leg. He becomes a wolf, sniffs the wound, then shifts back to his regular form.

"There were two," Lincoln says.

Lincoln is dressed, but the other two are naked as they'd been wolves as they approached behind Riley's wolf.

My feet are free. But they're kind of asleep, so when I get up, my legs turn rubbery and Lincoln catches me, scooping me up into his arms.

"Some other guy punched Cicely as the other guy dragged me off. Is Cicely all right?"

"She's all right. Just a little pissed off," Joel says. "What happened?"

"I... that guy," I point, "was a wolf first and just flew up on me, cornering me with his snapping and growling and then changed to human before he said, *you're comin' with me*. And then he dragged me off for a couple minutes until we were in this bush where he had a phone and his clothes and he... he tied me up then threw pants on and got on the phone and talked to someone called Wyatt and said he got *their* witch. Meaning you guys, I guess. Said it was a bonus."

I try to will my heartrate to normalize, but it's not cooperating. I'm kind of dizzy. The guy was rough. Wrenched my shoulder. I'll definitely have bruises. I lost a sandal. I stare at the wolf's dead body, his clothing and phone in a heap beside him.

"Oh shit. I don't know if I'm about to barf or pass out," I mutter.

"Which feels stronger?" Lincoln asks.

"P-pass out."

"Got you," he assures, carrying me to his truck.

The wind picks up and I think it's the cool breeze that keeps me lucid and talking. After choking on a sob, I ask, "Who was he?"

I look toward where Riley went, more emotion clogging all my chakras.

"We'll figure it out." Lincoln sets me into the front passenger seat as Jason and Joel put the dead wolf into the back. And then they're slamming the hatch before getting in.

We're on the move. Without Riley. Going in the opposite direction to where Riley ran.

"I lost a shoe," I mutter, staring at my feet as I try to take deep breaths.

"I'll find it," Lincoln tells me. "Drop you off and then I'll look."

"It's okay, you don't have-"

"I'll find it," he insists, voice angry.

"Thank you," I whisper.

And nobody speaks for the rest of the drive as the two get dressed in the back seat. And then we're back at the corner where my van sits.

But we don't stop there. We pass it and keep going until turning left at the corner where Roxy's is. We go down a long road paved with homes until we stop we pull up the driveway of a large character home with a wide porch at the end of a dead-end street.

"Where are we?" I ask, breaking the incredibly loaded silence. It's like I can feel fury coming from all three of them.

"My and Jase's place," Lincoln answers as he puts it in park.

"Why?" I ask.

"You're not staying in that van after that shit tonight," Jase answers for him. "Give Linc your shoe, babe."

16

RILEY

I'm staring at Linc and Jase's house, teeth bared as I stride toward it. When I fluidly become my human form, my teeth are still bared. I stalk up the driveway toward the front steps, nostrils flaring, fists clenched.

The door opens before I'm there. Linc holds it open and tips his head, gesturing for me to enter.

"Why the fuck is she here?" I demand.

I know I left her in his care, but sure as fuck didn't expect him to bring her to his house.

"Because she's not safe in a goddamn parking lot by herself," he snaps back. "Fuckin' obviously," he adds, giving me a judgmental glare that makes me want to rip his goddamn head off.

Before I fully form my next thought, I hear a car at the same time as sense movement behind me.

Tyson shifts from wolf to human form, coming up beside me. Mason's truck pulls in, Greyson is with him.

I straighten up. My nose is *that* weak that I didn't smell them before I heard them. All I smell is her. In there. Still afraid. And behind Linc's and Jase's scents, which makes me near rabid.

"Grey's been briefed," Mase advises, coming toward me. "Let's get inside and talk."

"We can talk here," I fire back.

"Riley, this is bullshit," Tyson puts in.

"Talk to me," Grey requests, hand landing on my shoulder.

I thaw just slightly, taking in the sight of Greyson. "I haven't seen you in days. I should be congratulating you on your mating," I say, voice a little gruff, "but clearly I'm not in my right fuckin' head because of shit with her.

How 'bout you talk to me? What's the deal with your new mate? Should I say congrats or condolences?"

"Congrats for sure." Grey smiles.

"Congrats, brother," I say with sincerity.

His smile widens and he gives my shoulder a squeeze before his hand drops. "Thanks, man."

"Talk to me," I request.

"I'll do that. Let's go inside. Get this over with so I can get back."

"Back to your mate?" I ask.

"Yeah," he says.

And by his face I know he's looking forward to getting back to her and I can't help but feel stung.

"You left her alone? With all this happening?"

That's fuckin' rich coming from me after I left mine alone.

"She's safe. Got two alphas there." His eyes are lit with something. They're silver. Glowing briefly. "But it's makin' my skin crawl to leave her in someone else's care."

"But is she trustworthy or..."

"Come inside; I'll explain." He jerks his head toward the house. Where *she* is.

My insides twist with ugliness.

"I'm not going in there," I state.

Though I state it, looking rooted to the spot, the truth is that every fiber of my being is fighting to stay, fighting to not rip in there and tear her out of here, away from them. Because I smell her from here. I smell all of her. And I've got the worst case of blue balls in the history of the world blending with jealousy and shame. My mate is being protected by them because *I* left her unprotected. The epitome of a wolf shifter's relationship with his mate is that he protects her at all costs. Though this sure isn't the epitome of a shifter relationship.

I'm so bloody incensed right now I could easily lose it and do shit I know I'll regret. And I'm not sure if the crux of my anger comes from what she's done to me, how her feelings keep penetrating my anger, or my opinion of myself.

My behavior is what got her abducted tonight. I didn't do my job as her mate. I'm fucked in the head, losing my basic senses, and I nearly lost it all, all my control, when I felt her emotions coming at me after she watched me rip that fucker apart.

"What's goin' on?" Grey asks.

I have no words.

He jerks his chin up. "Okay, how's this? You're pissed off. You're pissed at her for what she did, rightly so, and you're pissed off because you want her."

My lip curls.

Mase speaks up. "You're also probably holding back for fear you'll hurt her or scare her. Because the image in your mind for seven years has been her frightened face as you lost her."

I flinch.

Grey leans a hip against the banister of the porch and continues, "I had a chat with her oldest sister Vivica on the phone an hour ago. Just gonna say, that girl in there grieved even harder than you did." He points to me. "Believe that or not."

I scoff.

"I'm serious, Rye. Think about it. You're out here thinkin' it's over, thinkin' there's no hope, but you've got the hope she's at peace at least. It takes you time, but you find a way to move on, focus on your pack. While-" He points at the house "*she's* out here hurtin', torturing herself for the hurting you're doing, while unable to do a fucking thing about it but wait."

I take a step back. More like stumble.

"Her hands were tied, Rye. Completely. Though it *was* her doing, she was practically a kid. What? Twenty-one years old? Barely a fucking adult. She fucked up. And she suffered. She was forced to hide, man. She didn't want to."

"Grey. I can't." I lift my hands.

"How many times over the years did you wish for a do-over? How often have you sworn you'd do anything to get her back?"

Grey knows he scores with that as I flinch harder.

"Well, you didn't lose her, Rye. Some shit just got in the way. And now the way is clear, brother."

He stares, waiting for me to speak. I don't, so he keeps going. "She's yours, bro. The one meant to sire pups with. Meant to keep you warm at night and light up your mornings. Fuck, Savage. Get your goddamn head out of your ass and claim your mate."

I turn, ready to walk away, but crash into Tyson, who's looking down at me from the two or three inches of height he has on me, which feels right now like two or three feet.

"How many times in your life did you fuck up badly? Ever?" Tyson asks. "Saint Riley?"

I let out an impatient huff as I step back. I do not need this right now. I don't have the goddamn capacity for it.

"We all fuck up. You've never made a mistake you wish you could take back? Your mate doesn't deserve to be heard? Did I not deserve to be heard when I fucked up with my Ivy?"

"Ty –"

"I fucked up so bad with my mate I never should've gotten another chance. But I did."

"This is different," I grind out.

"How?" he demands. "Your mate is here to face what she did and fix it. Should I have not been heard? Do people not deserve a chance? Should Ivy have forgotten I existed because my instincts took over?"

I grind my teeth.

"You think a witch's instinct isn't to use magic?" He waits for a beat, then says, "You know what you need, cousin? You need to be locked in a room with her until this gets worked out."

"Not a bad idea," I hear Lincoln say from behind me.

"Agreed," Grey chimes in.

I slowly turn away from Ty and face the rest of them, seeing hardness in each of their expressions.

I grind out, "The pack isn't supposed to get in the middle of a mating, so how about you all mind your own business?"

"The mating hasn't happened, though, has it?" Jase weighs in. "And because you're fighting fate, you're not you. You know you're not. You need to sort this shit before you lose more of yourself. Before we lose you because it feels like we're losing you, man. You know how bad this can go and you know you'd step in to help if it was one of us."

My eyes skate across them. They're all looking at me like they don't get me. Though fuck, *I* don't get me.

"You need this," Ty says from behind me. "How do we make this happen? Can we vote?"

"Bring forth the motion, Ty, and we'll all vote," Grey invites.

"No," I deny, laughing it off.

Ty steps into my periphery and crosses his arms over his chest. "I want Riley and his mate to go stay at my cabin. For a week. They should be able to work things out within that time if they're left alone together."

I scoff. "This is some horseshit."

"I vote yes," says Linc.

Joel states, "Same."

"Aye." Grey nods and looks to Mase.

Wait a fuckin' minute. I shake my head. "Guys. I am not doing this. I'll decide if and when I-"

"Yeah. I vote *yes*. It's a good idea." Mase cuts me off, looking me in the eyes. "It probably won't take a week. It'll probably take an hour."

"Nice of you to think this is no big deal, Mase. But it is a big fuckin' deal."

"It's the biggest deal, Riley," Mase states. "It's just that you've been refusing to deal with it. The Riley Savage I know doesn't run from anything."

"Fuck this."

"I also vote yes," Jase says. "Six yesses. It's gotta happen, Rye."

I'm thrown and feeling even more disconnected from them because all six of these assholes are unanimously voting to lock me up for a week with the one person I can't bear to be alone with. Because if I'm alone with her again, I don't know how the hell it'll go.

"Oh, it's like this?" I scoff.

"Stacy's brother's gonna be a problem," Grey states.

"Stacy?" I ask.

"Lily wasn't her real name. You ripped apart her cousin Jimmy. She's gonna be torn up about that because he's blood, he's pack to her. But you were within your rights to do that, Rye. He's her brother's henchman and he was gonna go down regardless. I feel it – we're gonna have a battle on our hands with this clown, so go Rye, fix shit with your woman while we work on shit here. We'll cover it all until you're ready to pitch in. I'd love to have the luxury of a week locked up with my new mate, but as it's her family problems cropping up here, that's not an option I can take time to indulge in. So, you go fix shit with Erica."

"If it's not fixable?" I ask.

He gives me a pointed look. "Then it can be severed. You can cut her out of your system like my father did with the woman who gave birth to me. You've got a case to argue that the differences are irreconcilable like with my old man. I already asked Vivica about it, and she assures me it'll be your choice. But take the week. That's what I'm adding to this vote. Not only that I vote with Tyson to have you two in the same space to work things out, but also that you give it a week before you make your decision."

"I'll be the first to agree with that motion," Mase says.

My eyes cut to him. I feel betrayal course through my insides at this shit. And that's not right either. Nothing's right. Nothing. Not how I'm acting, certainly not how I'm feeling. I'm not myself, I know it. I also don't know how to articulate it so these guys will leave me alone, which is what I want most right now.

"We know there's been magic involved," Mase tells me. "I know what that does to your head. I lived it, Riley. I lived in hell while shit got sorted out. That's gotta be what's happening here with you. You're pissed off. You're hurt. You're thrown for a loop since everything you thought you knew for years is wrong. You're denying what's yours and that's fuckin' with your senses. Not just your senses, it's fucking with our connection, too. And then tonight she got taken."

A growl involuntarily rumbles out of me. From somewhere dark inside me. The place that meant I ripped a shifter's throat out tonight. I killed somebody. Because he took her. Put his hands on her.

But then I left her on the ground with tears in her eyes, her heart hammering in her chest so hard that it felt like it was in my chest. There was blood on her body, and fear in her soul. I can *feel* her soul. And every bit of me doesn't want to feel it. But I do. And her soul has been shredded. It's in tatters. I push the thoughts away, slamming the proverbial wall down again to try and block that connection that's been forming since I pinned her to her back in her van the other night in the village.

Yeah, it's trying to form, and as I've been struggling to block it, it's taking everything I've got. Maybe that's why I feel so screwed up. Why my senses are off. My connection with my pack. Fuck, the connection with myself, even.

Bile rises in my throat, hitting my back teeth.

"You're angry. I understand angry, Riley Savage," Ty says, squeezing the back of my neck. "I understand it better than most."

"This is why you're getting tough love from us right now, Rye." Linc leans forward, adding his hand on my free shoulder. "'Cuz we know you. And you need it. I know nothing about the mating bond, but Tyson and Mase do and I'm with them. This is what you need. Time alone with your mate. It makes sense to me. Enough time to figure out what's next. You're not functioning. You're not you right now. Leave the rest to us. We've got the business. We'll handle shit with Grey's mate's brother. We've got shit here. Get things sorted, bro."

"You've been carrying a heavy load," Grey adds. "For a long time. Because you didn't know how to go on otherwise after her. But now's your chance to figure it out. We're here to share the load. You've got a second chance here. You're getting what you wanted most for seven years. You're getting what you lay awake nights aching for. Most don't get that, Riley."

I shake my head. "I hear you guys. I do. I *am* fucked right now. Absolutely fubared, and I don't know what the hell to do. You're all pissing me off, but I'm not so far gone that I don't get it. I know I'm not myself. I know you all give a shit."

"This isn't going away unless you deal with it," Grey says. "If you don't, you know what'll happen. You know that's why we're sometimes called in to help with other packs and mating issues. When an alpha denies his mating bond and rejects it, things go very wrong in his head; it fucks with his wolf, and it often affects his entire pack."

I know this. I just don't know what to do about it.

"Trust the process," Mase advises and gives me a look filled with wisdom from first-hand knowledge.

"Yeah," Grey agrees. "If you decide you wanna move on, cut it off at the neck, we'll make it happen. I'm getting to know the Young sisters and they're open to me being an extended member of their coven. They could use me. I've got a lot to learn, and it feels right that I explore that, but I know in my gut that despite my father telling the truth when he says severing the connection with my biological mother was necessary, that doesn't mean I think it's automatically the answer here. We're mated to who we identify for a reason. There's a reason Stacy showed up in the diner and seemed like an enemy, but is now mine."

"You happy?" I ask.

He smiles. "It's right. It's early but I already know it is. Even if it's complicated. But it's right; I know it in here." He thumps his chest. "You will too if you let instinct lead instead of letting emotions screw with you."

I sigh.

He keeps talking. "There's a reason the birth order between the Brennan sisters got sorted out with magic so they'd wind up with who they belonged to. There's reasons for what happened to you and my cousin Erica seven years ago. I don't know her. Not at all. Nor her sisters, but through my conversations with them so far I feel a connection with them. And based on my conversation with Vivica, Erica needs your time after spending seven years working hard to be the kind of woman who could earn your forgiveness for her fuck up."

"What's that mean?" I ask.

"All I know is she was forced to hide from you and it's not what she wanted. The rest? That's for you to find out. But bottom line: she fucked with magic before she knew what she was doing and got into a tight spot. She wasn't allowed to fix it and Vivica says she's suffered for it every day since. Seven years of suffering. I'm telling you more than I'm supposed to tell you, but I'm giving you all the information I have because this is you and me here. Family comes first. They're blood, but you're family. Maybe they'll feel like family soon, but you? You're part of me. You're part of all of us. And you need to give this a shot so you'll know why it happened this way and so you can decide what to do about it. You can't just keep struggling like this. We'll lose you. You'll lose yourself. And you're too important to us, so we're trying to help here."

"He's right, Riley," Ty says. "How about if I come with you to pack a bag? Then I'll drive you to the cabin. Someone can drive her to you. I'll ask my Ivy and the other women to make food in the morning and we'll drop it off to last you the week."

"Ty," I mutter, backing away, feeling the urge to shift, to flee. "I'm not-"

"You'll have time to work on it. It's happening, Riley," he says, leaning forward.

I look to the sky for deliverance.

The earth shifts beneath me, nearly knocking me off my bare feet. My eyes snap to meet Tyson's. His eyes go reflective and he partly shifts. It snaps back inside him before fully emerging. There's a staticky energy coming at me from all six of them. Something in our bond. They're exerting this over me. And it makes part of me angry. The human part of me. But something in the animal part of me retreats and tilts his head to bare his throat enough to show I respect our pack bond. Our pack bond snaps my resolve.

Our bond has been stronger than ever since Tyson joined us. This is who we are. This is my pack, my team.

I *do* need to do this. Not because I want to. Because of them. Because they believe in this so strongly, that I'm compelled to do this if I'm part of this pack. Our bond is that strong, has that much influence over each of us. This strong connection to one another is how we mentally stopped Tyson from killing Mase in the town hall dance that night. And it's how they're compelling me to do what they believe I should do right now.

It goes without saying that as a pack, we'd only do this if absolutely necessary, and I know I'm sunk.

I've only got the time it takes to round up some shit at my house to come to terms with the fact that I'm about to be locked in a small cabin for seven days with Erica Young.

17

ERICA

I'm sitting on the couch between Cicely and Bailey when Lincoln and Jason come back inside. Bailey's eyes hit Jason, whose leg has already healed after he shifted. It's obvious she's worried about him. I was, too, but they said the bullet just nicked him and shifting healed him up a hundred per cent.

Bailey was shaking with panic when I recounted what had happened to me tonight. They'd arrived just minutes after we did, Cicely bringing a bottle of booze, saying she was fine, that it was just a bit worse than a bitch slap and had healed after just one shift. She was more pissed off about what happened than anything, that someone dared put their hands on her that way. She showed genuine concern for my wellbeing. In all this, I guess I'd sort of forgotten Cicely is a wolf shifter, too.

Bailey arrived carrying two tote bags filled with snacks. I had a shot of rum, but didn't touch the snacks.

Bailey says, "So, Riley didn't stay? Not even after all that, huh?" She's asking me, but her eyes are bouncing between Jason and Lincoln.

"Nope," I reply. "Just ripped apart the guy, then looked at me for five seconds and left." I pour a second shot of rum and down it.

THE ROOM GOES QUIET, and energy zings around me in a way that makes me feel like they're all communicating without words.

"Saddle up, we're headin' out," Jason tells me, coming back in from outside.

I get to my feet after setting my glass on the table and look at the girls. "You guys wanna hang out with me on my bus?"

"Sure," Bailey chirps happily.

"She's not sleeping in her van after all this, Jase. She can stay with me," Cicely offers.

"She's goin' to Tyson's old cabin," Lincoln pipes up from behind Jason.

I shake my head. "I'd rather stay where I am in the parking lot. Until he's ready to talk."

"Riley's meeting you there. You two are bein' locked in for a week," Jason advises.

"What?" I whisper.

"We took a vote," Lincoln explains. "Can't resolve your issues if you're not in the same space. You're gonna spend a week there and see what conclusion he comes to."

I blink rapidly as I process this. A week alone in a cabin with Riley?

My heart sinks. Because a week with Riley that isn't what he wants hurts. It's happening because his pack voted for it to be so.

"Um…" is all I manage to verbalize.

"Right," Jason claps, "C'mon, Erica. Bay…can you talk to Ivy? Help her organize provisions for a week for them and have it dropped off to Ty? He'll deliver it all in the morning."

"Why don't the men ever organize food provisions?" Cicely mumbles as Bailey happily chirps, "Absolutely."

"We could," Lincoln offers, "but the result'd be beef jerky, Fritos, and beer for a week."

"True," Bailey says with a giggle.

Cicely rolls her eyes.

Bailey then jumps up and hands me the tote bags. "Take these bags of snacks. There's chips, crackers, chocolate, a cheese ball, some nuts." She passes Jason the tote bags when I don't take them.

"But…" I try.

"No, Erica," Lincoln denies. "Riley needs this. I don't know that it'll be easy, but it'll be progress. You said you're here to sort shit with him, right?"

"I'd rather he come to talk to me of his own free will. How are you getting him there with me? Isn't he going to be… uh… hostile or-"

A new voice enters the space by saying my name.

I turn to see the man I instantly know is Greyson Blackwood. My cousin. We haven't met yet.

"It's been a couple days and that hasn't happened, he's gotten worse. So this is what needs to happen. It's been decided. He's on board. Albeit reluctantly."

I hold out my hand. "Greyson. I'm so glad to meet you."

He stares at my hand a second and I drop it, crestfallen, thinking he's another wolf shifter who's afraid of physical contact with me. But he surprises me by instead pulling me into a hug.

"Me, too. We'll catch up another time though, yeah? Let's get you there and get this show on the road."

I almost burst into tears at the affection he's just given me. I put my arms around his middle and sink into his strong warmth. After a minute of silence, I look at his face. He's very handsome. And I know those kind, silver eyes. My sisters Jessie and Vivi have those same eyes. So does Danica in color, though hers are more almond-shaped. Mine aren't far off either, though mine are flecked with a lighter brown. Some of his facial features are reminiscent of my father, actually. And now I'm feeling emotional; I'm barely holding onto the tears.

"You look a little like my dad," I manage.

"Where is he? Will I get to meet him?" he asks, eyes soft.

I shake my head. "He died when I was twelve."

He squeezes my shoulders. "Sorry to hear that. Hey... this? It's gonna work out however it's supposed to. Can't say it won't get ugly first, but Riley Savage is a good man. The best. You both need this."

I force myself to swallow and then nod. Greyson leads me outside, Bailey and Cicely following.

"Good luck," Cicely says, then holds out the bottle of booze. "You might need this."

Greyson takes it for me.

"Your brother seems pretty awesome," I whisper to Bailey.

He lets out a low laugh in response and messes up his sister's hair. She looks at him with affection.

She squeezes my hand. "He is *very* awesome. Now, go. He'll get you there. Go get your man. Maybe the sooner you get yours, I'll get mine." She looks at Jason wistfully.

He sees and hears this and doesn't react. In fact, he seems oblivious.

And then her eyes search mine. "Do you know what's gonna happen with the rest of the council members? I mean… who they'll mate with and when?"

"Bailey…" Greyson reprimands.

I shake my head. "Please don't ask me that. I can't answer any of those questions."

She scrunches up her nose. "Any hints?"

"I have some vague bullet points, but nothing solid about the rest but even if I did, I can't say anything. I'm sorry."

"Drats. Anyway, go get your man. When it's all sealed, we'll have a girls' night and celebrate."

I give her a sad smile.

"Positive thinking, Erica," she urges, then repeats, "Positive thinking."

Yeah. Right. Sure.

"See you there. I need to take this opportunity to get a run in." Greyson passes the bottle to Jason and then pulls his shirt over his head and tosses it while kicking off his boots as his jeans drop and quickly, before I can even shield my eyes from his nudity, he's already shifted into a large, silvery gray wolf. He immediately breaks into a full run.

"Erica," Jason says, opening the passenger door of Lincoln's SUV and gesturing for me to get inside. As I do, he squats to gather Greyson's clothes and gets in the back with Joel.

I blow out a long breath as I buckle the seatbelt.

WE'RE PULLING UP TO a small one-story cabin. I know of this place. It's where Tyson was raised. Where Tyson and Ivy mated and spent their first few weeks together.

There's a classic old pickup truck already here and I see forms on the open porch that takes up the front face of the cabin.

Lincoln turns his SUV off.

A light goes on in the cabin and now I can make out Tyson stepping back outside to stand with Mason and Riley. There are two gym bags at Riley's feet. Headlights shine a light on him, my van pulling in behind us. Riley's body language can only be interpreted as... hostile.

Lincoln says, "Your ride's here because your belongings are in it, but we're gonna ask you to let us take it and park it back at our place."

Joel had me hand over my keys when we got to the gas station, and he got out and drove it here.

"Why?" I ask.

Greyson is here. Naked. He's opening the passenger door and helping me out, saying, "We're asking the same of you that we asked of him. Give it seven days."

"I thought you left," I say, averting my eyes from his nudity.

"Needed a run before I go home. I'm heading there in a minute. You'll give it seven days?"

"What if he leaves?" I whisper.

"He won't leave. But we're asking you not to leave, either." He reaches into the back seat and grabs his jeans and pulls them on. I keep my eyes averted until I hear the zipper go up. "Sorry," Greyson says, "I'm semi-decent now."

"He won't leave?" I ask.

"Pack bond," is his answer.

I hear Riley grumble something from the porch, but Greyson is talking again. "Seven days, you two stay here and figure things out. After those seven days, we move forward. Either you two move forward together, or you don't."

I swallow.

"If he wants out, will you cooperate?" Joel asks.

"I will," I answer, voice betraying my emotion.

"You've said you aren't using any magic in Arcana Falls, but this isn't inside the village limits," Mason inquires. "Do we need to worry about you pulling magic on Rye to get what you want?"

I shake my head. "Nope. Breaking rules got us here." I stare at my feet.

"Right. We should get your clothes and whatever you need from the van so we can head out," Greyson says loudly, obviously for everyone's benefit.

I rush into my bus and grab my toiletries bag, my belt bag and phone charger. Greyson grabs my suitcase and gathers the half a dozen dresses from the rack of clothes I've hung in the tiny cupboard.

"Two things. Something I gotta say and then a question, Erica," Greyson whispers just as I'm about to leave the bus.

I wait expectantly.

"If you want this," he says carefully, "if you really, *really* do, you gotta be patient with him."

I barely nod, but I know Greyson reads the emotion in my eyes. He gives me a soft look.

Most of my family is female. I have a feeling I'll like having Greyson Blackwood as a member of my family.

Though then again, Riley will cut me out of his life in seven days, so Greyson won't likely bother with me after that.

I nod some more to show him I'm in this.

"Good." He rubs my back. "Also... is she dead or alive?" he asks earnestly.

I blink in surprise.

"Soleil Young," He says. "I don't know if I need to know her, but I wanna know if she's alive at least. For starters, anyway."

"We think she is," I say softly. "But I really don't know much about that entire situation. I've never met her."

He lets out a breath and I watch his eyes change shades from a dark brown to a silver color.

"Me either," he says.

"If you ever need to reach out, we might be able to help, Greyson. Me, Vivi, and Ronnie cook up a pretty useful locator spell together. Though I'm under sanctions right now, they could work it without me. Or I could help if it's after all this. And Aunt Mimi said she's happy to answer your questions. I'm sure she knows way more than we do."

A swallow works down his throat. "Not sure about that, but I appreciate having the door open. Thanks, Erica." He gestures for me to head out the door. I step out and head in Riley's direction.

"Hey? Program my number in your phone," Greyson says from behind me, then his voice drops, "If you need anything, call me."

"Oh," I feel discombobulated. "It's in the bus," I say, darting a glance over my shoulder at Riley who is on the porch, looking tense, looking at the trees off in the distance. "The cupholder in the front, I think. And maybe could you grab my cooler? I have some food in there."

"I'll grab it, sure," Greyson agrees.

"We brought some supplies from Riley's kitchen," Tyson says as I walk toward the cabin, getting closer, feeling like I might be heading for my doom.

He continues, "I took them inside and left them on the table. Some need the fridge or freezer right away. And I'll be by in the morning with more food," Tyson tacks on.

"And to make sure he hasn't murdered me?" I joke.

Nobody laughs.

I can see from my periphery that Riley's eyes are on me now, but I can't bring myself to meet them.

There's an awkward moment until Greyson is back. "I added my number and called my phone from yours, so I have your digits too. Here."

I slip it into my dress pocket. "Thanks," I whisper, then I'm again hugging myself.

"It'll be okay," Greyson tells me, putting his hands on my shoulders and squeezing reassuringly.

I hear growling. And it moves through me with a strange sensation.

Riley's doing that. And his eyes are on Greyson.

And suddenly there's heat in my underwear. I'm mortified because I could swear I see both Lincoln's and Joel's nostrils flare. The sound of Riley growling is arousing. Against my will. Oddly. Because I have no idea how I could even feel that right now with all that's happened and happening.

And I think they can all smell it on me. God, the indignity I feel has my cheeks hot now, too.

"She's a relative, man. Chill out," Grey jokes, eyes on Riley, but he also lets go of me.

"Biology," Mason explains, not meeting my eyes. "Don't be embarrassed, Erica. Just biology. Let's go, boys."

Great. Confirmation that they smell it. *Just great.*

My clothes, Riley's bags, and some other bags are on the porch by the door. I bite my bottom lip and shiver as things seem frozen in time for a beat.

"Now, brothers," Mason repeats.

They pile into cars and my van. I watch them pull down the long, winding driveway, past the two hundred-odd-year-old weeping willow. I bet it's full of magic. I'd love to tap into it. I have a feeling it'd share a whole lot of magic with me willingly. Maybe I can test that out in a week. When all this is done with. Sadness swamps me.

Right now, I'm standing on the grass in front of the porch for a moment, unsure of what to do with myself.

We're here. This is it. This is *it*. The moment I've been waiting for. For seven years.

God, I don't know if I can do this. I'm terrified. Terrified to speak the words. Terrified of what he'll think, *how* he'll react, how much it'll hurt when he tells me he wants me out of his system and then walks away with zero emotion on his face.

Though zero emotion is probably better than anger or worse – pain. But, this is really happening, and I don't know how I'm going to hold myself together. I don't have a good explanation for all this. I was young, careless, broken-hearted, and selfish. He's not going to forgive and forget. How could he after all it's cost him?

Riley turns and goes to the door, so I stare at his back as he opens it.

Instead of going through, he holds it wide and gestures.

"Go in. I'll get this stuff in."

"I'll help," I offer.

He shakes his head. "I've got it. Go in."

I move past him, catching his scent, feeling emotion well up so fast and full that I don't know if my body will buckle, if I'll burst into tears, or burst into flames. But I walk inside and take in the small, shabby but tidy, rustic space through unshed tears that I blink back.

18

ERICA

Seven Years Ago

I drove to Drowsy Hollow with mascara tracks down my cheeks and my grip on the wheel so tight my hands were aching like I had arthritis.

My twenty-first birthday was in a few days, and I wasn't just getting presents. I'd also been planning to give away one. A big one in my eyes. I was going to give Devon my virginity.

Today, plans changed. Because I found out he's been cheating on me.

Six months, I wasted with him. Six months of my life. Not only did he cheat, he cheated with Tawny, who is supposed to be my friend. He's been sleeping with her for over a month. Over a month while lying to my face with his forked tongue – *that snake*.

And looking back, I figured it probably wasn't the first time. Because not only did he cheat, but he was overheard telling his friend he was only hanging in there to get my cherry and then he'd be done with me and my "quirky ass".

And it turned out I was the laughingstock of my friend group. Because I'm ridiculous. Ridiculous, quirky Rikki Young, holding onto her virginity for the perfect man.

I'm now convinced that the perfect man doesn't exist.

I drove here to escape the nonsense of my regular life. The nonsensical "regular" life I constructed for myself.

Along with spending a lot of time on my craft the past three years, I'd been trying to live a double life, the second one being more of a "regular" life.

I moved out and got a roommate. I also got a regular job about eight months ago, wanting to make sure I lived as an adult in the regular world, thinking it'd make me better at the craft because I wasn't only living in the world of the Young coven. Being in the community instead of spending all my time with witches would make me a better person, a better witch, wouldn't it?

Turned out, it just made me miserable. The competition out there was stiff. For jobs. For genuine friendships. In dating. I surrounded myself with people my age and that was a mistake. Because almost all of them turned out to be back-biting, plastic, two-faced jerks. There was only competition, no camaraderie. Except for my roommate Priya, who told me the truth about Devon.

I confided in her this morning that I was going to give it up for my birthday and she cracked, sitting me down and showing me evidence of everything that's been going on. The texts where I'm the butt of jokes. Video of Devon with Tawny at the nightclub with their drunk, glassy eyes and their hands on one another in a way you knew they were getting up to no good behind my back. A text from Tawny to Priya admitting she'd gotten drunk and slept with him once and initially felt bad, but couldn't seem to stop since then and wanted advice on what to do about it.

As kind as Priya was to tell me the truth, Priya held onto the information for a while, too, worried about sharing it. Maybe even taking Tawny's side. And she'd shown me signs of the same personality defects as what was in the rest of our friend group, probably because she spent so much time trying to fit in.

I knew I was done. It was time to move on. I'd go back home to Aunt Mimi's. Back to work at the shop. I'd give up my job at the call center and go back to basics. Back to people who gave a damn about me. Back to dancing to the beat of my own quirky drum. I was done trying to fit where I didn't belong.

I'd spend a couple days here with Aunt Lyrica, reconnecting with who I am, do a cleansing ritual to rid myself of any lingering bad vibes, spend some time in the forest, give Aunt Lyrica's apartment a deep cleaning for her, then reboot my life back to the previous settings, back to a life that felt genuine.

Shuck the shoes, the business suits, and the fake life. Get back in touch with and in synch with my environment, my family, myself.

I dashed tears off my face as I pulled down the main strip of Drowsy Hollow, approaching the little diner down the street from the dry cleaners. It was a sweltering hot summer day and as much as I loved my van, I thought it might be nice to have something with air conditioning.

As the thought occurred to me that it might be nice to go pick up some pies and have them for dinner (something me and Aunt Lyrica often did – skip dinner and go straight for dessert, especially at this diner, which was known for their pies), the door to the diner opened and a beaming, sparkled beam of light shone down, spotlighting the delicious man coming out of the diner with a smile on his face.

Riley the wolf shifter.

My heart tripped over itself as he held the door for an elderly lady following him out, pushing a wheeled walker slowly. Very slowly. She got caught up in the doorway and he helped her out. And his smile, aimed at her sank a sharp arrow into my chest.

No such thing as the perfect man? Maybe not perfect, but I'd bet this van I'm in that I love so much that Riley the wolf shifter was pretty damn close.

No, the saving of the virginity I've been doing, because I wanted giving it to someone to mean something, shouldn't have gone to Devon. Fate intervened. It also shouldn't have gone to the four boyfriends I had before Devon, three of which got tired of waiting, one of which moved away before he lost his patience.

But a man like Riley might deserve it.

A man who would choose a lifelong mate and be faithful to her for life. All hers. Never cheat. Never intentionally hurt her. Not make fun of her behind her back with the intention of taking something from her that she's been saving for someone who would appreciate it. Someone kind. Patient. Genuine. So handsome he takes my breath away.

Before I found out about my family's secrets, about the coven, about everything supernatural that my mother tried to protect me from, I'd been planning to save my virginity for marriage – because I was a romantic.

For all my parents' flaws, they were madly in love with one another and showed it every single day. I wanted *that*.

And then despite being eighteen, nineteen, and twenty years old and being the only virgin I knew, I've held onto it. And thinking back to that while looking at the beauty of the dark-haired, green-eyed, muscled Riley Savage with the beautiful smile... I knew I was right to save it. I was also pretty sure that what I'd learned about wolf shifters only added to my resolve to save it for someone who'd care that I saved it for them.

Because what I saw that day three years back along with what Aunt Lyrica told me about their nature, their pack structure – it made me even more of a romantic.

She said most shifters, particularly alpha-male wolf shifters, mate for life. That the alphas give a claiming mark to their love that deepens their connection. She told me their mating relations were special, that while he might play the field until he finds his fated mate, he saves certain things for her only. He'd only lock together with his true mate through an expanding knot on his penis. He'd give her pleasure like she'd never get anywhere else. The knot also worked to prevent pregnancy on others, locking his seed up inside him, until he was with her, his one. It would release and expand for his mate, giving her his children.

And I thought it was romantic. Sexy. I swooned, especially at the idea of that gorgeous specimen of a man giving me something special just like I'd give him something special of mine.

I thought that since he'd save that for his one and only, it'd be romantic if whoever she was... she saved that all for him, too.

Devon charmed me, acted like it meant something to him that I was *that* kind of girl. And as hurt as I was, looking at Riley the wolf shifter and remembering that about him, I was so very glad I didn't give it up to Devon.

A horn was leaned on behind me, so I realized I was still idling by the diner even though Riley was walking in the opposite direction. In my mirror, I saw him glance over his shoulder at the blare of the horn. Panicking, I surged forward.

And that's when I bumped into a fire hydrant. Hard enough that water began spurting out.

OF COURSE HE CAME TO my rescue. He's just *that* perfect.

One second, I was taking in the reality of the geyser in front of me, and the next, he opened the door and gently led me out, holding my hand.

Holding my hand!

And the electrical jolt I felt? Like real electricity, more energy than I've ever felt when practicing magic – which meant we both should've been zapped on the spot as water dripped from his face and shirt.

"You okay, darlin'?" he asked, looking straight into my soul with those vivid green eyes.

And I couldn't even form a sentence.

"Here." He tugged my hand and pulled me further away from the water fountain, then released me. He got in my bus and expertly backed it up into a parking space as a dog and two kids ran through the water happily down where the spray tapered a bit.

Concerned faces around us turned to smiling faces as an old man caught up with the kids and pulled his t-shirt off, then boogeyed through the water.

"Just a little scratch," Riley said as he examined the front bumper. He looked underneath and frowned. "Nothin' major. You lucked out there."

My cheeks burned.

Now there were more people playing in the water on the sidewalk.

A firefighter came with a toolbox, and I stood dumbfounded, dripping wet, and feeling like something in my life had strangely, inexplicably, but also fundamentally shifted.

Riley turned to face me and smiled.

Ding. Warmth and magic zinged around my chest, wanting to explode like fireworks.

Yeah. I could save myself for a guy like this. I could sacrifice even more than a van for him.

A guy who holds the door for a little old lady who is moving slowly? He didn't show an ounce of impatience.

A guy who helped me when I did something stupid. Who was then smiling at me.

A guy who called me *darlin'* in a way I *felt*. I felt it like warmth spreading through my veins.

A guy who lives in a community of people that help one another, that are there for each other, unlike the community I was trying to make myself part of where they were all competitive, backstabbing, and opportunistic – itching for the next bit of gossip to spread and only looking for their next dopamine rush and nothing of any true substance whatsoever.

Not like this guy. This guy? A guy who lives in a world of magic.

A world where I could probably be myself instead of hiding who I am and what I come from.

If only.

"You need help getting somewhere?" he asked. "You all right?"

I shook my head. "I'm okay. Just a bruised ego. Thank you for your help."

"You sure?" He eyed me from head to toe and then back to head again. "You want a towel?"

I took stock of myself. Dripping wet, my dress pale pink and pretty dang see-through.

I covered my chest and watched his eyes sparkle with mischief as he scratched his jaw.

"You carry towels in your back pocket?" I asked.

His shoulders shook with silent laughter. He patted his backside with both hands. "Not today. But I could nip into the diner and ask if they've got something." He jerked his thumb toward the restaurant.

"I'm not going far. I can leave my bus parked here in fact. Thanks for saving me the trouble of parallel parking on this street. Wasn't looking forward to that."

He laughed. "Innovative way to get yourself a valet."

The water was shut off and people were grumbling.

"It's hot. C'mon, sir! Turn it back on!" a kid called out.

"Yeah!" the old man that had run through the water chimed in.

"Sorry folks," the firefighter apologized and looked at me and Riley. "You okay, little lady? That you that hit it?"

"Guilty. It was an accident. I'm so sorry about that," I called over. "Do you need my insurance information?"

How much was this little blunder gonna cost me?

"No harm, no foul. All hydrants on this block were slated for flushing on Monday, anyway. You just let us check this one off our list first. Don't concern yourself. You cooled these folks off, too." He shrugged and then waved before heading down the street.

Weird. That was it? No fines? I guessed I lucked out.

A familiar song played, increasing in volume. The ice cream truck. It pulled up beside us. The wet elderly man, the wet kids, and the wet dog trotted over as the window opened.

And until now, I associated the ice cream truck song with the death of my parents. Because I'd heard that song just moments before they died. But now I had a new memory to link to this song.

"You want one?" Riley asked, gesturing to the truck.

My eyes landed on the graphics on the side. On the banana split. I really, really did.

I felt like I was in the middle of a *meet cute* romance movie.

But suddenly something hollowed out in my chest, and I got a dark and foreboding sensation. And the sudden urge to get to Aunt Lyrica.

I don't have the vivid clairvoyance gift Vivi does, but what I *do* have is a finely honed sense about my family, about people I care about. Many times since my eighteenth birthday when I got this sensation, something was wrong with someone I cared about. Aunt Lyrica told me she and Aunt Mimi had often discussed my connection to all of them, similar to the gift Aunt Lyrica had with all her relatives. They said they believed I'd have similar gifts to her and had believed it for most of my life.

I knew something wasn't right and needed to get to Aunt Lyrica.

"I can't. But I really wish I could."

He looked disappointed. "Sure you don't want a banana split?" he tried, as if he knew what my eyes had landed on, though the whole side of the truck was filled with graphics. "Who can turn down a banana split?"

"Really, I've got to go. Sorry I got you all wet." I reached into the van to grab my purse and keys.

He smiled and shrugged. And there was something salacious in his expression as he eyed me from head to toe again. And based on my mood coming here today, you'd think I'd be disappointed and chant to myself that all men are dawgs.

But instead, there were butterflies divebombing in my belly and I was feeling incredibly shy despite that niggle in my gut that told me I had to get to Aunt Lyrica's STAT.

"Thanks for your help. Bye!" I waved and hurried down the street.

"Hope we meet again!" he called out.

I looked over my shoulder at him and tripped. I didn't fall, thankfully. Embarrassed, I faced forward and broke into a jog to get to my aunt, feeling like his eyes were on me until I turned the corner to take the shortcut through the alley that'd take me to the back of her building.

She was unconscious on her bathroom floor when I got into her apartment above the drycleaners.

I was still wet from the fire hydrant when I got to the hospital, but a nurse gave me a pair of scrubs and a towel while they looked her over. Thankfully, she'd gained consciousness as the paramedics got her onto a stretcher. They helped me convince her to get checked out despite her blowing it off like she was absolutely fine.

I called the house and Jessica answered, aghast at the news as I told her it was either pure luck (or pure fate) that I happened to be in town.

The hospital didn't like her blood sugar levels, nor some other numbers in her bloodwork, so they admitted her and would be keeping her overnight. Aunt Mimi and my sisters would arrive the next day, would shut down the store for a few days, then stay a couple days and we'd all celebrate my birthday in Drowsy Hollow.

I took that moment to tell Jess I wanted to move home and come back to work at the store.

She relayed that to Aunt Mimi who said, "Good."

And that one word gave me comfort.

AUNT LYRICA SENT ME back to her place for the night, telling me she was fine and that I could pick her up and bring her home the next day. She'd have the nurse call when it was time for me to come.

I got into a full but opened bottle of wine I found in Aunt Lyrica's fridge, feeling sorry for myself after my failed 'regular life' experiment and wondering if I'd ever meet the man who'd be worthy to have my virginity. A man hopefully at least a little like *Riley the wolf shifter*. I stared out the window and saw a shooting star. I wished on it for Aunt Lyrica. There was a second shooting star a half a minute later and I wished on that one, too. Wished I'd get to give my v-card to someone I'd never regret giving it to.

I sat down with plans to watch some sappy romantic comedies on TV to keep my mind off worrying about my ailing aunt. Me and my sisters weren't ready to lose her. Weren't done learning from her. Not remotely. I needed her to get well. And I wanted more time with her. We all did.

As I sipped the sweet wine, I had no idea how dangerous it was. I later found out it was spelled wine. It lowered inhibitions to help people go after what they wanted. A confidence-booster that Aunt Lyrica had prepped for one of her regulars.

I should've known better. She told me on my eighteenth birthday visit to never consume anything unsealed in her fridge without first asking about it.

But it didn't even occur to me until it was too late that the wine cork had been replaced with a stopper. Because I'd thought, *I could use some wine*. I also found out much later that one glass would've affected anyone, even someone with a strong alcohol constitution, and I had no such constitution. I was a lightweight, so drinking the whole bottle, I was pretty tipsy. Beyond tipsy, leaning toward drunk. Drunk and determined I already had my abilities, and after three years of constant study, and I should be able to write spells. I was convinced I could and should write a spell around what *I* wanted. The closest-to-perfect man I could think of.

Riley. To make him choose *me* as his soulmate. I felt like I could do it and furthermore that I *should* do it. I didn't want to play the field anymore. I was tired of waiting for my perfect man. I was tired of dating. The dating pool felt like a cesspool.

So, full of spelled wine and confidence, I dug through Aunt Lyrica's supplies to gather what I needed before heading out in the midnight moonlight barefoot. I stopped at my bus armed with a cornstalk from Aunt Lyrica's broom, which I rubbed all over my steering wheel before gathering some more of my own supplies. I locked up and wandered to the far end of the eerily quiet town, then down the dirt road behind the rusty, old water tower, singing to myself until I happened upon a beautiful tulip tree that was so big, it had to be the grandest tree I'd ever seen. It seemed to sparkle with magic to my drunken eyes. To beckon me toward it, offering to let me take what I needed from it. I often found myself compelled to hike deep into the woods, often finding a powerfully magic tree on my route. They called to me.

My magical abilities weren't bibbity, bobbity, boo – voila, magic. I was learning to work with energy. To seek and request it and then direct it along with my spells and sometimes potions to hope for the desired outcome. We used crystals, candles, herbs and spices. We practiced with intent. Good intentions. We tried to give more than we took. We didn't try to hurt people and we were told that though we could help dispense bad karma, so to speak, we had to be sure about it before doing it or it could come back on us. Magic didn't always happen straight away. And it didn't always go the way we wanted it to. Sometimes spells were perfect, and things didn't work out. Sometimes you got more than you bargained for. Sometimes I had to pay tolls for things I did. Sometimes people who benefited from my magic had to pay those tolls. I was warned that sometimes a screw-up happened and it could have a domino effect, so it was important to be cautious.

If you didn't have goodwill banked from your deeds you might not have success gathering energy. If you asked for energy, you could also be denied with or without reason. It would be a crap shoot. But between the wine giving me all the confidence in the world and the magnetic force of that magical tree, I was going to try.

I knew I was in the forbidden woods. These woods that were haunted by the energy of a man who'd never got to live out what fate had promised him via one of my ancestors.

Auntie told me how bad of an idea it was to work against fate, how hard fate would push back. For some reason, it didn't work for Holden Holloway, the angry being who haunted the woods. I felt very drawn to Holden's story, and I would later learn why.

Under that grand tree, I tipped out the contents of one of Aunt Lyrica's tote bags filled with the ingredients I'd brought.

I mixed up my chosen items in one of my small clay bowls.

Beet root powder, often used in love spells. I added clove powder as it's an aphrodisiac. I dumped in some mugwort, honeysuckle, and hibiscus which all attract love and lust before I sprinkled in some smoked paprika for maximum magic enhancement.

I lit a candle, dug my toes into the grass and arranged some specific crystals of mine while I meditated, using my wand and the corn straw from the broom I'd brought to mix the concoction. After mixing it counterclockwise three times, I carefully pulled one of my hairs and along with the stalk of straw, tied both into a knot around Lovers and Two of Cups cards. I didn't have anything else that represented him, but he'd touched my steering wheel. The cornstalk held Aunt Lyrica's juju, too, so I figured it wouldn't hurt.

I was wrong. I wouldn't find out until later that one should never, ever fuck with another witch's broom without extreme caution.

I meditated on the fact I wanted Riley to be my happily-ever-after. I wanted to be his mate. To be only his. For him to be just mine. I gave my wish to the tree, who sent it to the earth and the sky for me. And I touched the tree trunk, giving my thanks while hoping it would be so.

But what I didn't know was that Riley wouldn't choose his mate. Fate would. And it had already chosen me. I didn't know I'd get what I wanted if I'd exerted patience and waited for our turn.

Again, patience was never my strong suit. My lack thereof was going to be my downfall. And Riley's.

After casting the spell, I hung out and felt like I was sharing energy with the tree. It was immensely beautiful and intoxicating. Adding that to the wine I'd consumed, I was pretty dang drunk.

By the time the sun was coming up, I was still feeling the effects and decided to hide my implements in the bushes and keep walking. See if I could find my way to that magnolia tree where I'd first seen him. Maybe I'd see him on the way to or from a wolf run. Maybe he'd take one look at me, and it'd be the beginning of our happily-ever-after. But then I got sidetracked by the sunrise and the biggest, most beautiful field of wildflowers I'd ever seen.

19

RILEY

Seven Years Ago

My father asked me to quote a small job on the old water tower road leading to The Hollow. Somebody wanted a quote for a retaining wall and a fence on a wood lot. I got there and found it had nothing but a dilapidated shed on it with a couple hunter tree stands. They wanted us to put together the quote at a quarter to eight in the morning. On the dot. An oddly specific request especially considering there was nobody here to meet me while I did it.

I stepped onto the land, noting a faded homemade laminated sign that read 'no tresspassing' (yes, *with* the typo). Further in, there was a "smile, you're on candid camera' sign that looked like it'd been there at least a decade.

I measured the lot from the marked property line posts and jotted the numbers down so I could write up a quote when I got back, wondering if I was picked up on a trail cam or if it was just a sign to give would-be trespassers pause.

Did they want me here at a specific time for a reason? As a test to find out how punctual Savage Construction is? I figured *whatever*. Do my job and not worry about it. Then, something hit my nose.

Something... strange.

Something beguiling.

I shrugged that thought off because I didn't think I'd ever used the descriptor of *beguiling* in my life.

Instead of heading for the company truck, I kept going down the road, led by the scent, the scent that was gaining strength.

I couldn't place it. Not food. Not floral. Whatever it was, I had to know the source. Had to know with an overwhelming intensity that had me almost ready to shift so I could figure it out faster.

But I know better. The mystery call for a strangely requested quote could be a trap. No way would I shift and reveal my nature in an unknown situation like this in broad daylight without any of my pack at my back. Not that I can't handle myself in a tight spot, but *shit*... I couldn't ignore the niggle of anxiety. Like something wasn't kosher about this situation. Though everything in me told me to investigate further.

Guardedly, nose twitching, I moved down the dirt road deeper into the forest, noticing how the scent gained strength, thinking that the air felt strange, though I couldn't pinpoint why. I wondered if it had anything to do with the old stories we'd all heard about this section of woods being haunted. And then I heard singing.

And the scent got much stronger. And somehow even better. *The best*.

As I got closer I recognized the song.

There She Goes.

And my eyes widened at the vision as it sharpened into focus. Not only did my eyes widen, the crotch of my jeans tightened.

A vast field of flowers in purple, pink, and yellow. A redhead dancing. *That* little redhead with the freckles over her nose. The fire hydrant. Hippie van. Transparent pink dress covering a fuckin' exquisite rack. Banana split.

I stared, watching her twirling around with flowers in her hair, flower bunches in both fists as she sang.

The world stood still. No, she was the world. She was all that was in it. Until she collapsed. Panic struck hard, so I broke into a full run until I was standing over her.

She was smiling.

She wasn't unconscious. She lay in the grass, surrounded by flowers, a flower wreath tied in her wild, curly copper hair. Her eyes were closed, thick lashes lying against her cheeks. And she looked happy. Beautiful.

Greyish eyes opened and she startled, mouth dropping wide open before she cussed. "Holy horses." She started blinking rapidly.

"You okay, darlin'?" I squatted.

Her irises had flecks in them the same color as her hair.

"Am I... okay?" She frowned, little lines appearing over the bridge of her lightly freckled nose.

She was wearing a patchwork quilt-patterned long dress in earth tones, long tassels hanging down from the collar. She looked like some sort of earth goddess there in the flowers with all those blossoms in her hair.

"Are you? You were singing and then you collapsed."

She smiled wider at me. And then she broke into a fit of giggles.

I tilted my head curiously.

She's what I smelled. The scent was all around me. Not the flowers. Her. Soft, fragrant, beautiful, and...

Holy fuck.

Mine.

I think this girl is mine.

Mine?

I blinked in surprise.

Couldn't be. Could it?

Mase was born first, meaning it should be him that mates first. And not until we take on our roles in the council. Nobody was talking about that happening yet. Not even whispering about it.

But she was mine.

I knew it. My wolf knew it.

"I didn't collapse. I swooned."

"Swooned?"

"At the beauty of all this," she said, gesturing to the space around her. "The sky. The flowers. Did you see all the flowers? I twirled and sang until I was overcome with the beauty. And I swooned."

"Who are you?" I asked.

"I'm... Rikki."

"Rikki. I'm Riley." I held my hand out.

She smiled a gorgeous smile at me before she held her hand out.

It was filled with flowers.

I accepted the bouquet, changed hands and helped her to her feet. She'd tied it into a bundle with a long stem from one of the flowers.

She was tiny. I had at least a foot of height on her.

"Rikki, are you drunk?"

She laughed. "I was last night. I think it's mostly worn off though."

Though she was now on her feet, our hands were still joined. I looked at her small, dainty hands. They were warm, soft. I wanted to touch more of her. I wanted to sink my nose into that gorgeous hair. I wanted to count her freckles. I wanted to put babies in her. Immediately.

"Where are you from?"

"Here. I was born here but I don't live here anymore. I'm just visiting."

"Well, Rikki who's visiting… this is gonna sound crazy, but… I think we should spend the day together."

Her eyes widened in surprise. It was fucking adorable.

What I wasn't saying was, "And the rest of our lives, too."

She wasn't a shifter. She needed to be primed for all I had to say, all I planned to do.

"Do you have a boyfriend?" I asked.

She shook her head. "Not as of yesterday."

"A husband?" I pushed.

She shook her head again, smiling shyly. "Not as of ever."

"Nobody for me to compete with?" I tried, giving her a flirtatious smile.

"Nobody who could possibly be a contender, Riley," she replied and did it in a way that felt weighty. Like she already knew me, knew this about me.

Strange sensations bloomed in my chest.

"Wanna take a walk with me?" I asked, still holding her hand.

"I'd like that."

So we walked through the field of wildflowers, holding hands, each of us with a bouquet of the blooms she'd picked in our free hand.

Once we got to the dirt road on the other side, I noticed her feet were bare.

"Where are your shoes?" I asked.

She snickered. "I left them behind."

"Behind? In there?" I tipped my head toward the field.

She shook her head. "I took a walk last night and left them behind." She shrugged.

"Fueled by alcohol?"

"Actually," she said softly, pink tingeing her cheeks. "I'm not much of a shoe person."

I laughed, then I plucked a little green inchworm out of her hair and she watched me set it on a tree trunk.

"Bye," she whispered to it, "Thanks for keeping me company." And then she swung my hand as we continued walking.

My face split into a wide smile.

This girl was *different*.

"Tell me about yourself, Rikki."

"How about you go first, Riley?"

I laughed. "Weird but I can't think of a single thing to say."

"That *is* weird. How come?"

"Maybe because all I can think of is how much I wanna kiss you."

A swallow worked down her slender throat. And there was lust in her eyes. And… yes… arousal between her legs.

"Hold you. Take you home," I added huskily, "And keep you."

She didn't startle. Didn't look like she wanted to run. Her eyes didn't show as much as a hint of panic. Instead, she stared at me with wonder as that irresistible fragrance intensified. And it surprised me, but it felt very right.

She got up on her tiptoes, dropping her bouquet and reaching for my jaw. And I didn't hesitate to move in and touch my mouth to hers, not letting go of my bouquet until she let out a sweet little whimper that went straight to my cock.

When the second bouquet dropped, my fingers dove into her hair as our tongues touched.

Kissing this girl felt right. Righter than any kiss. Like she's mine.

"You're gonna think this is crazy, but… I meant every word I just said."

"It's not crazy," she said against my mouth. "It's… it's amazing. It's everything I've ever wanted."

I frowned.

"I mean… it *is* crazy. But… in the best way. It's… wow. I'm embarrassed now." Her cheeks tinted pink. "I'm feeling a little woozy. Do you mind if we sit down for a second?"

She advanced a few paces and plopped down on her bottom under a tree.

"You need water? I've got some in my truck. I'll be… I'll be right back. Stay here. Yeah?"

"I'll be okay."

"Stay here, okay? Don't go anywhere or I'll have to hunt you down."

She nodded, not looking remotely tweaked by my poor but accurate choice of words.

I ran.

I ran fast, feeling elation blended with concern. Elation at finding her but concern at her sitting alone under a tree feeling unwell. I grabbed my lunch pail, which I knew still had supplies leftover from yesterday's lunch on a job site and looked inside. Water. A couple protein bars, a packaged cupcake, and an apple.

I grabbed it and booked it back to her.

There she was, sitting where I'd left her in her pretty dress, with all those flowers in her hair, her little toes digging into the grass. Watching me. Smiling at me like I was a genie coming out of a bottle to grant her three wishes.

I sat down and opened the lunch pail.

"Always pack a big lunch. Waters aren't cold but better than nothing."

"Thank you," she whispered.

I uncapped one and passed it to her and then watched her drink a few mouthfuls.

"Better?" I asked a minute later.

She nodded slowly. "Yeah, I think so."

I passed her the apple.

"I'm okay."

"Eat the apple, Rikki."

She took it and examined it. "She's a beauty."

I smiled and our eyes met.

"What? It's the perfect apple. It should be in a food commercial."

I tilted my head. "Good thing you're here to eat it, then. It'd otherwise sit in my hot truck in my lunch pail today probably rotting."

"Good thing you met me then," she said, eyes twinkling.

"Yeah. Good thing. Eat the apple, Rikki," I repeated, "I need to know you're all right. An apple a day…"

"I just stayed up all night. Drank too much wine last night." She shrugged.

"Stayed up all night? Tell me about that."

She shyly dropped her eyes.

"Where were you that kept you up all night and brought you to a field of wildflowers this morning without your shoes?"

"A long story. I'll tell it to you some other time."

I smiled. "Okay. Mystery girl? I kinda like that. Gonna bite that apple or am I gonna have to get bossy?"

She gave me a sexually charged look as she took a bite. And I couldn't fuckin' wait to take a bite out of her. She closed her eyes as she chewed. As if she was savoring the best apple she'd ever eaten.

I watched her chew, then swallow, then take another bite. She moaned. And my cock was harder.

"So, we meet again," I said. "Under drier circumstances." Not counting her panties, which I knew were soaked for me.

She smiled. "We meet again. Just like you hoped for."

"Yeah. Lucky us," I repeated and leaned back on an elbow.

The sky looked extra blue. The grass looked extra lush. And that apple extra-red, extra juicy. And the girl? She looked and smelled amazing. Perfect.

I looked at our feet. At my big, scuffed work boots. At her dainty, dirty feet with the leather anklet on the left one. A little silver ring on her right second toe.

Fierce emotion rushed through me. Protectiveness. Like I needed to protect her from something. Someone. I didn't know what or who.

"Is everything okay?" I asked. "Do you need help with something? Someone?"

"Why do you ask?"

"You rushed off yesterday after driving into a fire hydrant and yet I find you early the next morning dancing by yourself with no shoes on in a field of flowers a couple miles from civilization. And you say you don't have a boyfriend as of yesterday, so…"

"Would you believe me if I said I've never been better?"

My eyes roved her pretty face as I took in details about her I knew I'd remember forever. Big eyes. Cute freckles. Spiky, thick eyelashes. A girl-next-door innocence to her that I liked. I licked my lips and said, "For some reason, yeah. Yeah, I do believe that."

She threw herself back on the grass and smiled at the sky, then at me.

"Want a bite?" she asked, holding up the apple.

I leaned over and bit from it while she held it out. Eyes locked. Heat simmering between us, about to hit a rolling boil.

"Best damn apple I've ever tasted in my life," I declared.

She nodded slowly, like she got me. Like she got the deeper meaning here.

She couldn't *get* it, not without my explanation.

She sat up and took another bite. Once she finished the bit in her mouth, she announced, "I was about to redesign my life."

"Oh yeah?"

"Yeah. It wasn't working. I was a square peg trying to fit into something round and prickly. So I figured I should go back to what I was doing before."

"Or you could move onto something new," I offered.

"Yeah," she whispered, as if she knew exactly what I was talking about.

"Feeling better?" I asked. "More water."

She nodded. "One more sip. And yeah. Much." She took a big mouthful.

"Wanna walk some more? Or are your feet sore?"

"Why would my feet be sore?"

"Walking all night with no shoes on," I said and then I lifted her small foot and inspected the bottom of it.

"I do that all the time," she waved. "I practically have shoe soles built into the soles of my feet."

"Nope. These aren't rough," I said, running my finger along the arch. Her foot was dusty, blackened from her walk, but soft.

She giggled and pulled her foot back.

"Ticklish?" I asked.

She nodded. "Very. I hate it."

"Oh yeah. So you wouldn't like it if I..." I walked my fingertips along her side and she pulled away, laughing, eyes lit up and so fuckin' pretty I felt it like a kick in the chest.

"No tickling!" She jumped up and took off.

And little did she know, as a predator, when someone or something runs from me, I've got no choice but to chase it.

I caught her in no time, lifting her up over my shoulder like a sack of flour.

"Got 'cha, now I get to keep ya," I declared triumphantly, giving her behind a playful whack.

She laughed as I swung her around, so she was in my arms bride-style.

"Tell me about yourself, Riley," she requested, taking another bite of apple. And then she held it up for me to take a bite, too. So, I did.

And then I did tell her about myself as we shared the rest of that perfect apple. I didn't get into the depth of my true self, but I told her about my family, about the work I did for my father's construction company, how I was taking over soon and had plans to expand from renovations into building new structures, how my buddy Mase was joining me to help me build it up into a bigger company. How we had a couple close friends who could help out with bigger jobs once we got them. About how I've lived in a little village near Drowsy Hollow my whole life and went to school for one year in a bigger city my first year of college, quit and then came back, knowing I never wanted to live anywhere else in my life. This was home. It's where I want to be. Where I want to raise a family.

I talked for a long while, her patiently listening. When I stopped, she started talking. She told me she liked the idea of planting roots. She had friends that loved to travel and jet-set but that wasn't her. She wanted a small-town life with a community that helped one another, that knew one another's names. She wanted stability and dependability. She wanted shared history. She wanted to nurture and grow rosebushes that would be in her family for generations to come.

This was right. She was definitely mine.

Still, I warned about the pitfalls of small-town life and having everyone know your business. She said she wasn't bothered by that and understood it as she always wanted to know everyone else's business. This got me laughing. She'd fit right in.

We kept walking, hand-in-hand, mostly me doing the talking. And before I knew it, it was nearly noon.

She glanced at my wristwatch with me and startled.

"I have to go somewhere," she whispered in a panic.

"Can you get someone else to handle it?" I asked.

She bit her lip. "Let me make a call and find out what's what." She reached into the pocket of her dress and pulled out a phone. "Shoot. Eight per cent. That won't last very long."

"You can use mine," I offered.

She shook her head. "It's okay. Give me one sec?"

She wandered away with her phone and I told myself I shouldn't listen, but couldn't help but try. But as I strained to hear, I couldn't hear her talking. And I found that strange because I can hear better than most shifters. But then my own phone rang and it was my father, wondering where I'd got to, asking if I'd gone to price out that job.

I whispered to him that I found *her*, my fated mate. And that I might not be back for a while. He asked if I wanted him to get Lincoln and Jase to vacate the house I shared with them. An alpha needed alone time with his mate, but I hadn't expected to mate so hadn't gotten my own place yet. Of all six of us, only Joel had his own pad. Mase lived in an apartment above his parents' boathouse.

I decided I'd rent a cabin at Sleepy Cove, a small resort across the lake from our village with a handful of cabins for rent that we'd done some renovations at. I'd been there the day before to pick up a check and they had plenty of vacancies.

When I got off that call, I went looking for her. Sniffed her out and found her in a clearing near the ridge overlooking the river that fed into Chariot Lake. And I wanted to show her the Arcana Falls. I wanted to show her where I live. Introduce her to my family. But first... I wanted to make her mine. I wanted it with an ache I've never felt.

She ended her call and something about her posture bothered me.

But I was feeling a lot of things right then.

I'd heard that the claiming urge can come on suddenly, fiercely. And while I still had command of myself, my control was beginning to fray. I needed to get some facts out, so she knew what was about to happen.

I had to fully disclose who I was and what it'd mean after I took her and made her mine. I was more than anxious to make her mine.

"I have to tell you some things," I admitted.

She had her back to me; she was staring ahead.

"You're gonna think it's crazy," I added.

I felt anxiety at the fact that she still had her back to me. Something about her posture didn't feel right. But then she turned to look at me and the emotion in her eyes hit me in the chest.

I knew she was mine without a doubt, knew I wanted to look into those eyes every day for the rest of my life.

There was something strange working in them, something I didn't understand. But I knew I wanted to learn everything about this quirky mystery girl and that's exactly what I'd do.

"I know this is highly irregular to someone like you, but it's not for someone like me. I... know, this fast, that you and I were supposed to meet."

She looked around us, looking panicked.

"Rikki, I need to talk to you about who I am. About what I am," I admitted. "You're gonna think it's a little crazy, that I'm off meds, but I promise you I'm not."

She didn't say a thing.

I held my hand out. She didn't make a move, so I tagged her hand and tugged, bringing her to a nearby boulder large enough to sit on.

Once she was on my lap sideways, I toyed with one of her long curls.

"I'm a shifter. I can be in this form, and I can be in another form. The other form of mine is a wolf."

She chewed her lip and stared at her fingers, which twined with one another nervously in her lap.

I covered her hands with one of mine and squeezed reassuringly. "I spend most of my time in this form, though I need to regularly let the other side of me out."

I stopped talking. I searched her face for a reaction. Panic was rising in her expression.

"Rikki, we identify our fated mates by scent, then set eyes on them and know down to our bones they're meant to be ours."

She shook her head.

I ran my hand up and down her back. She was shaking. I didn't want to frighten her. I didn't know how else to do this other than to try to explain. The urge to nurture was now stronger than the urge to claim, down to her reaction I guessed.

"There's a reason we met yesterday. A reason why I was drawn to your scent today. It's you. You're the one."

Her lips parted. She was about to speak.

"I promise you it's true. I'll show you. I'll show you my wolf and you'll know I'm not lying. I wanna take you home, Rikki. Take you home and make you mine in every way."

I ran my nose along her throat. She shivered.

I dropped my voice to a low whisper against the ridge of her ear. "It's a biological urge that's hard to shake. But I promise, I'll take good care of you. I'll undress you. Make love to you. Make you feel good, baby. And I'll give you my mark and my knot. My mark will be a bitemark right here." I caressed her throat.

She sank into me instead of retreating, but a tear trickled down her cheek.

"And then," I whispered against the ridge of her ear, "it'll be the beginning of our forever."

"Riley," she whispered, brokenly.

Our eyes met.

And then I noted her expression wasn't of lust, or of fear. It was something else. Something stark. Bleak. Grief? I didn't know.

Did that phone call contain bad news?

She pressed her lips sweetly against mine. And it felt so right. Except that she was crying. She pulled back, swallowed hard and looked directly into my eyes for a beat before abruptly scrambling off my lap. She promptly tripped and fell.

"Whoa. You okay?" I helped her to her feet.

She looked around with a strange, confusing expression.

"Rikki?" I repeated.

"It's not me."

"What do you mean?"

"It's not me, Riley."

"It is. I know it is."

"It's not me. It's a mistake. I have to go. Oh God; I'm so sorry. I have to... I have to go."

She broke into a run, running along the trail that butted the ridge, leading down to the river that fed into Chariot Lake.

"I'm sorry if I scared you. Let me explain. I promise I'm telling you the truth. I..."

She looked over her shoulder with panic in her eyes and kept running. "I'm sorry! I can't! This was... I made a mistake."

"I really am a wolf shifter. I'll show you." I pulled my button-down shirt off and threw it. "Don't be afraid. I promise when I'm wolf, you won't get hurt. I'll show you and then I'll look like this again and take you to a place where we can talk. Where I can make you mine. It'll be okay, Rikki. I promise. I'll be a good mate."

"I'm sorry. So sorry. I..." She shook her head, backing away while looking in multiple directions. Then she stumbled and tumbled backwards.

I blinked with confusion and felt frozen, rooted in place for a split second before I could move my limbs.

Horror washed over me as she disappeared from my view.

Finally, I got unstuck and moved as quickly as I could. My vision blurred as I stared over a cliff that overlooked the river. The river was moving fast, like a waterspout and it rippled as I saw a shadow move across the wake.

And I couldn't comprehend it because I didn't think we were this close to the edge. But we must have been. I dove straight in, determined to save her.

20

ERICA
Now

I set my quilt on the back of the couch, fingering the flannel square of Riley's shirt before I turn my attention to putting the perishable food into the nearly empty refrigerator.

All that's in the fridge are some bottles of water, a few jars of condiments, along with three large cans of peaches. There's a box of food on the counter, so I add in the milk, cream, a half-full carton of eggs, some deli meat, and a wrapped brick of cheese along with a box of half-melted popsicles to the freezer. The box of groceries also has half a loaf of bread as well as a jar of peanut butter. I put in the fruit, yogurt, and milk from my cooler.

This is an old but tidy little cabin with a compact kitchen, a round kitchen table and chair set, and a small living area that's dominated by a wood stove. In front of the stove are a ratty old Archie Bunker type armchair, and twenty-odd year old large and comfortable-looking three-seater couch and scratched circa 1970s wood coffee table. I see a small alcove with three doorways leading to other rooms behind the couch, which faces a big picture window, the wood stove kitty-cornered beside it.

He comes in with my suitcase and stack of dresses and walks by, not looking at me, taking them in one of the rooms.

When he passes me on his way out, I'm leaned against the wall, hands behind my back, gripping my left wrist with my right hand while I watch him go and come back with his bags, which he takes into a different room, again with zero eye contact.

He goes out one more time and comes back with the bottle of booze and bags of snacks, which he sets on the table in front of the wood stove.

He turns to me, looks me over and says, "I'm not gonna murder you."

I swallow.

He's staring at my feet.

"No shoes."

My belly dips. "I lost one when that... guy took me. Lincoln has the other. He said he'll find it for me."

He growls.

I startle. And my underpants go damp. Or I should say *damper*. Strange to have such contradictory responses at the exact same time.

He shakes his head and runs one of his hands through his hair.

He's angry. Looks almost wild. He hasn't shaved in a while and his hair is a mess of dark curls. He looks almost unhinged. I mean, clearly it's been quite a night. His green eyes are hard on me. Digging deep into me.

His nostrils flare and I'm sure it's because he can smell what his growl did to my underpants.

His jaw clenches.

Is he ready to hear what I need to say?

"Riley, I..."

He lifts a hand to halt me.

I clamp my mouth shut.

"Not tonight, witch."

My eyes close and it takes work to swallow.

He goes into what I can see is a bathroom, between the two bedrooms. I stay rooted as I hear the shower turn on.

I let out a sigh and my eyes land on the booze bottle Cicely contributed.

I find a clean glass in the dish drainer on the countertop and pour myself a shot. Okay, a double. I drink it back and once I recover from the burn, I sit down on the couch, empty my lungs, and plead with my heart to *please* slow down.

I wait, taking deep breath after deep breath. Then, hearing noise outside, I peer out the window and my heart kicks back up again because I see a giant wolf with something in his mouth approaching the cabin.

He drops something on the wooden steps and meets my eyes, jerks his chin up in greeting, then turns and runs away.

I squint and realize it's my shoes he's dropped for me.

Thanks, Lincoln.

I open the door and go outside to get the sandals.

When I'm back in, I see Riley, in just a towel, looking tweaked.

I hold my shoes up in explanation. His expression relaxes just slightly. I open my mouth to speak, but he turns and goes into the room he dropped his bags in and slams the door.

Was he tweaked because he thought I was leaving?

I'm still a lightweight with alcohol and I'd had a double before we got here, so I feel a little wobbly when I go into the bedroom carrying a bottle of cold water I'd grabbed from the fridge. After setting it on the little table beside the bed, I open the doors to a large wall cupboard. As I'd hoped, it's filled with linens, so I make the bed up, then think about the little kitty-cornered fireplace and how nice it would be to sleep by a fire. With Riley beside me. Spooning me. Pressing his lips to my bare shoulder. Rubbing my stomach. A big, round stomach. Wedding rings on our fingers.

Sadness swamps my body again as I take two clean towels from the cabinet and head to the bathroom so I can shower the dirt from my body, especially my feet, wishing some special soap existed to wash the dirt from my soul.

21

RILEY

I'm growling at the ceiling while lying on the twin mattress in this tiny room. Because first I was flooded with her sorrow and now her scent surrounds me. And it's intensifying by the steam of the hot shower she's in.

She's in there, a thin wall the only thing separating us. No clothes on, undoubtedly running soapy hands over her wet skin.

The visual hits me like a freight train and I'm suddenly sprinting from the bed, leaving the towel that had been wrapped around my waist behind.

Without premeditation, I'm ripping the bathroom door off the hinges to get to her. It crashes to the floor, then I'm hauling the shower curtain aside and taking in her form amid the steam. She's shocked. Dripping wet. Naked.

Mine.

I growl in her face as I grab her and haul her up into my arms.

My gums ache as my canines elongate, a pinching sensation coursing through them with the urge to bite.

Intense urges control me now. More than I've ever felt, not *that* day I identified her, not yesterday or the day before. My control has snapped and left the fuckin' building. It's on me so strongly I no longer have free will.

I guess it's my primal instincts that are now in control. Tired of waiting, tired of battling with me. Mase wagered it'd take an hour, but it's only been twenty minutes.

She's now on the double bed in the other room and I'm on top of her, one hand full of her hair, holding it tight as I stare at her creamy throat while my chest rises and falls with deep breaths.

"Riley," she whispers brokenly, tears filling her eyes. "I'm so, so fucking sorry, Riley."

I snarl and slam my hips forward, impaling her with my rock-hard, aching cock, feeling like her body splits apart at the seams with my forced entry.

She grabs my shoulders and screams at the intrusion as our eyes are locked.

And I have zero control. I'm in the rut. My cock is in charge. The witch and I are just dragged along for the ride.

Hot slickness wraps around me, and I smell the faint tang of her blood on me, too. I drag two fingers through the space where we're joined, lift my hand and inspect the tinge of pink. Yes. *Mine.* I taste it and groan, supremely pleased she saved this for me.

She's jolting at my touch and though her face is pained as she holds on, she doesn't ask me to stop. She swallows hard, staring deep, telling me with her soulful eyes that this is mine to take. And take it, I will. I have no choice.

I'm not gentle; I can't be. I'm slamming my hips forward over and over, muscles straining in my neck as primal instincts buzz in my blood.

She still has those freckles on her nose, like so long ago, and I resist the urge to count them. Seeing the tightness in her expression, I somehow find the sense to not continue to be a completely savage neanderthal and find her clit with my thumb as I continue to rut. I rub circles over it and feel her body relax marginally as she lets out a little grunt of more pain. She's so tight and hot around me, it feels fuckin' perfect. I rub faster circles and feel another gush of wet. I watch her pretty pink nipples harden, then focus on her pulse throbbing in her beautiful, creamy neck for a minute before I brace one elbow into the pillow and move wet strands of copper hair away from the curve of her throat where her neck meets her shoulder. I'm salivating as my teeth extend further while a growl rolls up from the depths of me. Another hot gush of her essence helps ease my way in and out of her tight, fluttering heat as I clamp down on her throat.

Her body jolts as she cries out. I rub faster, her slickness coating my fingers as my cock continues to slam inside over and over. As I taste my mate's blood in my mouth, emotions surge through me. Hers. Mine. And it's so much. So much emotion, I can't untangle it all.

I'm marking her, making her mine.

Mine!

Urgent, carnal need crests over me again and again while pain shoots through my cock and my balls. I piston harder and harder, unable to stop myself until my knot snaps out for the first time, revving up painfully. The pain and vibrations sending the rutting need into overdrive. And I can't move.

Fuck, it hurts.

Fuck, it's right. The most right I've ever felt inside a woman.

I'm coming inside her. Coming with soul-altering fierceness, pleasure spiraling out of control in me as she whimpers loud. Her head is thrown back and she's climaxing, mouth open, eyes filled with wetness. Her blood trickles down her throat and I lap it up while continuing to grunt like the animal I am. My seed spills into her, my knot vibrating so hard it's audible. The painting on the wall rattles, the vibrations are *that* hard. I can't tear my gaze from her convulsing body as I pull whimper after whimper from her parted lips.

Her fingers grip my biceps as she continues to cry out and then one hand slides to catch my hand and her fingers twine with mine.

"Riley," she whimpers.

Remorse shunts through me at what I've done, what I'm doing, what I can't stop myself from continuing.

She saved it for me and I'm fucking taking it without being gentle. Because I just can't be.

Her legs are trembling. Her back is arched. And she now wears my mark. I lick it again and she shudders. The bleeding has stopped.

And not only do I feel the greatest pleasure in my life at mating her, at knotting her, at tasting her, I can feel intense emotions pulsing inside my chest in a place I know once and for all is hers. A tangled ball of love, remorse, pain, and pleasure. I've hurt her. Immensely. And yet she doesn't want it to stop, loves every second of it. Because I'm here and finally touching her. She knows she's mine. It's crystal clear in my head that it's all she's wanted for years.

My knot continues to pulse, the slickness of our combined juices pooled between us. She's jolting, whimpering, and clinging to me while I rut like a monster, grunting and groaning as I take.

I collapse on her when it finally stops.

I twist so she doesn't have to take all my weight and am on my side. But I'm still inside. My knot hasn't deflated yet.

I blow out breath after breath, trying to slow my heartrate, listening to the internal snarling of my furious wolf who wants out. He wants out now. He's angry. He feels separate from me instead of a part of me, and it's an odd sensation that I can't wrap my mind around. And I've got the odd sensation I'm about to shift against my will, but before that can happen, my knot deflates halfway, my cum spills out of her, but then my knot tightens and starts revving again.

My body bucks as I painfully come some more while she whimpers and trembles, clawing the sheets at her sides, legs pulsing out of control while spilling wet slickness into the puddle we've made.

She grabs my face and our eyes lock for a beat before she rams her tongue between my lips. I give in after a split-second of stone-cold stillness before I groan and take a deep drink of her, tasting her sweet lips again, finally, after so many years. Another thread of control snaps as I bite her lip and take her mouth like it's my God-given right. Our tongues twist up together and I run my thumb along the mark I've put on her, making her jolt even harder as she seizes in pleasure under me. I flip to my back and still attached, she rides me, holding my shoulders while still kissing me.

Her sweet mouth moves down my more-than-stubbled jaw and she nips at my throat too, wanton, throwing her wet hair back as she rides my knot like a woman possessed and determined to take everything I have to give. I run my hands up her torso and tweak her nipples as I growl, then sit up enough to take one into my mouth. I bite down.

She cries out in pain, but continues orgasming at the same time. Our pain and pleasure weave together in my chest as her nails dig into my biceps. I feed on her tits like a starved man who's finally getting nourishment.

I feed while growling. Can't stop.

Releasing the bruised nipple, I move her onto her back, slamming my hips forward without being able to pull back out because my cock knot continues pulsing, deflating half way so I spill seed over the sheets as she's too full of it before going full again and vibrating harder. My vision blurs as I process how she saved herself for me for all this time. All this time.

And after leaving her in a fuckin' parking lot for days instead of protecting her, she gets taken. She gets taken and has to watch me savagely murder the man who took her. So I can continue being an asshole to her before taking what she saved for me – no sweet words, no romance, no prep whatsoever while refusing to hear her out. No, I just rip a door off, rip into her and take her like a goddamn monster.

Some other paper-thin thread in me snaps and leaves me feeling like it might be the final thread. Like I'm completely, utterly broken inside as I smash my fist into the wall above us.

22

ERICA

Riley stills on top of me. He's still inside me. He's fisting the sheets with his now scraped knuckles, and I see anguish slashed across his features. He looks into my eyes for a long, exposed beat before he looks away.

"Fuck," he says gruffly and then he rolls to his back, taking me with him. He's still inside me.

As much as I know the biology, the meaning behind what we just did… the knot, the bite…nothing could have prepared me for the reality.

I prop myself up with my elbows so I can look at his face. His bleeding hand shields his eyes as he blows out a long breath.

His body language right now? He's unhappy. Supremely.

"Um…" I start.

He grinds his teeth and still doesn't take his hand away from his eyes.

"Riley?" I inquire, barely whispering. He's bleeding. He might want ice for his hand.

"We have to wait a minute for it to go down."

"It?"

"My knot."

"Oh."

And I know now that he'd be pulling away if he could. But he can't. And now pain slashes through *me*.

My vagina feels like it's on fire. That was rough. Painful. But I wouldn't change it. Because it was Riley. Riley and me and it probably won't happen again. I saved it and gave it to him. It was his, nobody else's. And despite everything, I'm glad it went to him.

Yeah, it hurt. A lot. But then it felt good. And rough. But more good than anything. I felt sensations I didn't know my body had the capacity to feel. And feeling him? Touching him? Being touched by him? What a trip.

I'm very aware of our bodies touching. Skin-to-skin. But instead of basking in the afterglow of giving my virginity to the man I've loved for ten years, the man I was destined to be with, the man I've hurt beyond repair... I get to feel raw and on the verge of empty, knowing I'm about to be empty because he can't wait to pull out of me, away from me. He's so angry he just put his fist through the wall while still inside me.

This hurts.

He lifts his hand and looks into my eyes. I don't know how to read what I'm seeing. Regret. He regrets this.

Mason's words of earlier ring in my ear. "Biology."

That's what this was. He was driven by biology and now that it's over, he wants to push me away. But we have to wait for his knot to go down first.

Well, this is awkward. And immensely fucking sad. My chin wobbles and I do my best to stop the tears from flowing.

There's a long beat of silence before I jerk in surprise because it's vibrating again. Riley's back arches and I can't take my eyes off the smokin' hot look of pleasure on his face while feeling it myself. That knot is buzzing against a sensitive bundle of nerves inside me again and my muscles are contracting around it. We let out twin moans as I bury my face into his shoulder and he grips a handful of my hair, moaning out loudly, masculinely. Holding me tight.

This is what I've been holding out for. It really fucking hurt at first, but then it transcended into something ethereal. Something otherworldly. Something magical.

I'll never be the same. *Never.*

I also know that although he's feeling physical sensations, I can tell he's not remotely near the same metaphysical space as me. I can only imagine he wants to fly through another window; he'd just burst through the roof if he could fly – anything he could do to flee the witch that betrayed him. Because despite the biological response that made him *mate* with me, Riley Savage hates me.

IT GOES ON SO LONG and so intensely that when the vibrating finally stops, I'm utterly exhausted. He tries to position me on my side, but it isn't comfortable for me since he's much larger than me, so sensing this in an eye lock where I know he reads my discomfort, he rolls to his back, and I flop listlessly on top of him, tucking my head under his chin.

"How long until it lets go?" I finally ask.

He's so warm. So comfy to lie on. I feel like I could lie here forever.

His answer is just an exasperated breath.

"It's not supposed to do this, is it?" I ask a few minutes later, daring to look up at his face.

"No," he says, not looking at mine, looking off to the side. He can't even bear to look at me.

And lying here like this, there's nothing I can do but rest my head on his shoulder and fall asleep.

I jolt awake what feels like just seconds after my eyes have closed because he's vibrating inside me again.

My vagina is protesting. Sore. Totally new to all of this, but Riley's knot doesn't seem to care.

Abruptly, I'm flipped to my back and he's groaning into my ear, his hot breath dancing across my skin.

I grab the back of his head and hang on tight as another body-spasming orgasm rips through me, making every nerve ending in my body jolt. Orgasms with Riley Savage inside me make me feel like magic makes me feel. But times a hundred.

I'm limp, aching, and utterly exhausted at least thirty minutes later when it still hasn't let up. I'm a ragdoll, a slave to sensation as I can do nothing but ride it out.

He passes out after it finally stops, on top of me. Dead weight. I'm too sleepy to try to convince him to flip us back over. I fall asleep, too.

TWICE MORE BEFORE THE sun rises, it happens again, the fullness and vibrations pulling me out of sleep.

The first time, I actively participate, digging my nails into his back, which I think he likes, because he lets out a deep, vibrating growl and kisses me like he actually wants me. It goes on for ages and his eyes glow bright green. I dare to stare straight into them while I come undone. After it finally stops, he lifts me up as he gets to his feet and as I'm about to ask where we we're going, he hits the light switch, then lays back down.

Then sometime later it happens again, though this time I barely move, just cried out until hoarse, limply lying there while I felt the muscles in his shoulders and biceps ripple, watching him fist the sheets in the moonlight as his masculine groan undoes me. The second time it's mercifully only a few minutes long.

I WAKE UP ON TOP OF him, the sun shining through the open gingham drapes. Nothing is vibrating. But he's still inside me. His knot hasn't let go.

We're at the wrong end of the bed, so he must have moved us away due to the mess we made. I'm relieved there was a mattress cover with vinyl backing on this mattress when I put the sheets and covers on last night. Clearly, these shifters have experience with this kind of... mess.

His arms are around me. And my heart spasms because I know it's not because he wants to hold me. One of his hands are tangled in the length of my hair. The other is on my behind.

I wince, my muscles aching. I feel like I've been through a long battle. My vagina, particularly. My mouth is a desert. I see the water bottle I brought in last night on the bedside table, so I stretch sideways to reach for it and it's too far.

I feel him go tense underneath me and then both of his hands are gone, not touching me. My heart shatters a little bit.

"Water," I rasp. "Can you move just a little to the right?"

He moves us over and I snatch it, uncap it, and take a long, needed swig. After I swallow, our eyes meet.

And I don't know how to read his expression. It's hard. A direct stare. And I feel so exposed.

"Want some?" I croak out.

"Bend your legs?" he requests gruffly, and I tuck in.

He sits up, me straddling him as he takes the bottle from me, finishing it off.

We're face-to-face, chest to chest, out of necessity. My hair is everywhere. I try to tame it, self-consciously.

"Kind of a predicament," I say softly.

He scoffs and crushes the emptied water bottle, seeming like he's doing everything he can to avoid my eyes. He tosses it to the table beside the bed.

"Is there a trick to get it to ... uh ... let go?"

"No clue," he mutters. "Never knotted before this."

My heart divebombs. I gave him something of mine and got something of his. Even if he didn't want to give it to me.

"Need my phone," he tacks on.

He scoots a little until his legs are dangling, then he wraps both arms under my butt as he rises. I loop my arms around his neck and wrap my legs around his waist, holding on. I wince as he stands, feeling my very sore private parts stretching some more.

The revving abruptly starts up again.

"Uh oh," I squeak, head rolling back because it's awake and at what feels like full volume. And I have no choice but to react. These sensations are otherworldly.

He sits back down, sensations taking over by the look on his face, too. I bury my face into his throat and wrap my arms around his back. I hang on, trying to just... ride it out.

It feels so fucking good. Good between my legs despite the soreness and it feels good to hold onto his strong, solid body. His skin is hot, his muscles bulging. As soon as one orgasm is over, another is hot on its heels. And his hot hands are on me, gripping me as he lets out a sound that's at least part animal. Liquid seeps out of me and it's hot and sticky and the air smells like a country store. Cinnamon and flowers and apples.

My sisters and girlfriends all talk about the elusive multiple orgasm that only seems to happen on a blue moon, but this is beyond multiples. Multiples and consecutives and I need it to stop. I'm like a ragdoll, just convulsing.

Mercifully, it's over in what feels like about five minutes.

Mercilessly, his knot still won't release me.

"Fuck," he groans.

"Are you sore, too?" I ask.

Our eyes meet and he frowns. "Fuck," he barks then rubs his forehead.

Okay, so if I'm reading him right, he's not sore. But now he knows I am. And he's feeling bad about it? Maybe?

"Hang on," he says and wraps his arm under my butt to carry me to the other room.

We walk over the bathroom door, which is laying in between the other rooms and move into the other room, a small bedroom with a twin mattress on the floor, a bookshelf with some children's books, a stack of a couple boxes, and a little kid's desk and chair. He squats to fetch his gym bag from the floor. He sets it on the desk and unzips it with one hand, the other arm still wrapped under my booty.

He takes out his phone and dials.

"Aunt Cat? Hey."

"Riley!" she replies cheerily.

I can hear her loud and clear what with our proximity to one another.

"Got a problem," he states.

"Oh?"

"My knot won't release."

"Your..." She lets that hang.

"Nope." He looks mortified as his eyes flit over my face and then look away from me, off to the side.

"How long has it been?" I hear her ask.

"Since somewhere around midnight last night."

"That's about when your mating scent released. We can smell it all the way here. Didn't expect that since Greyson's scent is still lingering."

He's staring over my shoulder, studiously avoiding my eyes. I bite my lip. My left hand is over his shoulder, my right hand is dangling. It's pretty dang awkward to be attached to someone in this... manner... when they don't even want to look at you.

"It hasn't let go."

"In ten hours? Not even for a little?"

"Not at all."

"Oh."

"You've never heard of this?" he asks.

He carries me back to the other bedroom and sits on the bed. I tuck my knees in and examine my fingernails as he wraps an arm around my back. Not affectionately, either. Perfunctorily.

"Not in our pack, so I have no idea how it's resolved. Um... why don't you try getting into a warm bath? And then call me if it doesn't work. Meanwhile, I'll get on the phone and see what I can find out."

"Fuck," he mutters.

"Don't worry, sweetie. I won't use your name. And congratulations," she says earnestly.

He doesn't respond.

"Love you, Riley," she adds.

"Love ya," he says and then he ends the call.

Yeah, I'm sure he wouldn't want it getting around that his parts are malfunctioning. That's something other men might rib you about. And congratulations aren't in order when you've accidentally mated with someone you hate. Though his aunt probably doesn't know it was just a biological reaction to being in the same small space.

Something dawns. I haven't gone pee in about ten hours. Thankfully, I don't feel the urge to go. Probably because... I can only guess... all the sex has used up whatever moisture is in my body? Who knows? I'm not a doctor. Though, I did just drink almost half a bottle of water.

I'll try to put it out of my mind, so I don't inadvertently trigger my bladder, which has always been prone to the power of suggestion.

We're on the move again and in the bathroom. I'm relieved it's a giant lion-footed soaker tub much like the one in Cicely's apartment. Hopefully it'll be big enough. Riley is not a small guy. He blows out a long breath and then climbs in and squats with me wrapped around his middle as he pops the plug in, turns the water on, adjusts it, then sits down and scoots backwards. My back is to the taps.

It's wide enough, but barely. My knees are pressed into the sides of the tub, and I try to shift myself so it's not as uncomfortable on my knees and my ankles, which are wedged in tight.

Our eyes meet. His dart away.

I chew my cheek.

"Too hot?" he asks, still looking anywhere but at me.

"No."

My vagina hurts, and my knees and ankles aren't feeling so hot either. My whole body aches, in fact. Though not nearly as much as my heart.

A sob chokes out against my will, and I cover my face with both hands, totally losing it.

"God damn it," he cusses.

He gently pulls my hands away from my face. I can't stop crying. I'm sure I look like an ugly mess right now. Naked. Stuck.

He's got a less hard look in his eyes.

He's about to say something and then his expression changes.

"Shit, try to relax your muscles, okay? You're clamping down on me and..."

The vibrations start up again.

"Oh God, not again," I whine as he grabs the sides of the tub with both hands and throws his head back with pleasure.

I blow out a deep breath, feeling not only that his knot is vibrating, but also that his legs are trembling. I look at his face. He's feeling good. I'm just the sore one at this stage.

Wait... no...sensations are rising in me now, too. I grip the sides of the tub as well and while the sound of running water roars in my ears, I quickly lose myself in sensation and ride the wave. God, that's intense. But just as soon as it slows, the revving of his knot intensifies, and my orgasm is piggy-backed by an even bigger one. He stares at me, watching me unravel.

There's an intensity in his eyes that I don't have the capacity to decipher. I feel naked. Not just clothing-wise. Like he's seeing something I don't want him to see. We're not in the dark. The bathroom is bright. And I'm so... exposed.

While we climax together in an eye-lock, longing overtakes me. Longing for him to want this; want me. For him to love me instead of loathe me. I cry out his name and he grabs the back of my neck and pulls me in so our lips fuse together. He groans into my mouth, the sound branding me his. I'll be forever his, even if he's never, ever mine.

He's still gripping the back of my neck as the vibrations slow, and eventually stop.

The tub is very, very full, but I wait, holding my breath, wondering if the hot water will relax him enough that his knot lets me go.

He releases my neck and scoots forward abruptly, so he can reach around me to twist the taps off before he leans back, slicking his hair back with wet hands. He stares at the ceiling with an exasperated expression. Even though he just kissed me, which is an intimate thing to do. I'm a little confused and a lot hurt.

"Since we're here, can I wash my hair, please?" I ask. "It's kind of... everywhere."

He tries to hand me a bottle without looking at me, but I say, "I'll use this one, thanks." Then I stretch to reach to the opposite corner and grab a salon quality bottle of shampoo instead of the bargain brand he has in his hand.

He sets the bottle down.

"Can you, uh... lean forward so I can wet my hair?" I ask, not wanting to break his dick, though maybe it wouldn't. Maybe it's made of supernaturally indestructible titanium-like material.

He leans forward so I can more easily lean back. I close my eyes and enjoy the heat of the water as I lay for a luxurious second without any outside stimuli. Of course not counting the inside stimuli of a large penis with a supernatural bulging knot lodged in me and the knowledge that he's leaned forward, likely trying to look anywhere but at me.

I sit up and take a few minutes to lather up. And then I lean back a little and he gets the message as I lean back and submerge my hair again, scrubbing at it to get the foam out.

He's not looking anywhere else. He's watching me do this with what looks like a carnal expression. And then he flexes his pelvic muscles and I frown.

I'm feeling even more full.

Is it about to start again?

"Oh shit." I sit up. "I think it's about to happen again."

He nods, face scrunching.

I brace.

He groans with pleasure.

I grab onto him and press my forehead in his throat. He grabs the length of my hair and holds on.

It's a fast one, thankfully. But it's another big one and I'm limp when he rises with me in his arms. My two unused towels from last night are here along with both piles of our clothes from yesterday, but before I reach for a towel, he's got it and wrapping it around me. He grabs the second towel and moves us back to the bedroom.

I do my best to dry my upper body with the towel he gave me while my wet legs hold onto his wet skin. He sits on the bed, me straddling him and he gives up his efforts to dry himself out of frustration, I think, since he can't easily reach his lower extremities, so before I tackle my hair, which I realize belatedly did not get a dose of conditioner, I shimmy the towel around his back.

Our eyes meet. But nothing is said. And his expression still holds so much hostility, so after drying him for a minute, I realize he doesn't want this but isn't saying anything, so I tug the towel up around my hair and squeeze the length within it.

He lifts his phone and makes a call.

"Riley?" the female voice answers.

"Didn't work," he mutters.

"Okay, um, I could drop off something to help you sleep. It-"

"Won't work. Slept a little last night. Still knotted."

"I'm still waiting for a callback from a second contact. The first one, Dr. Blakely, he had no advice except to just enjoy it."

He growls.

And it releases a gush of wetness from me.

"No, no, no, fuck! Oh shit!" I say, as the vibrating revs up like a racing bike about to pop a wheelie.

"Gotta go," he grunts.

"Fucking SOS. Someone save us; I'm not sure how much more I can take," I weep as it's throbbing inside me, buzzing, pulsing, and whatever else it's doing.

He stands up and puts me against the wall and braces with both hands, my legs wrapped around him. And he bounces me a little as he vibrates inside me, groaning with pleasure. Is he doing this because he has the urge to move? Because this isn't the typical thrusting-type sex I'd expected, though I guess you can't thrust when you're locked in.

It doesn't last long on the wall before his knees buckle a little, so he's sitting on the bed again, holding onto my ass as his mouth latches onto my neck where he bit me last night.

I let out an animalistic-sounding cry at the entirely new sensations now pouring through me. More wetness between my legs. Stronger throbbing vibrations. His hands travel up and down my back, then squeeze my shoulders before one hand goes back to my ass and the other tangles into my wet hair. He's still sucking the spot on my throat and my eyes are rolling back in my head.

"Omigosh, why are you doing that?"

"Hoping it doesn't hurt so much if I...do... more for you."

I frown.

He's trying to help? With more? I don't need more. More might kill me.

"God, that feels so..." I start, and then he sucks harder. "Ah!" I dig my nails into his back and whimper.

Man, that feels good. The combination of his mouth on that spot, the claiming spot, along with his hands on my skin *is* helping. A tear trickles down my cheek at the reminder of what the claiming spot means.

More of his semen is leaking from me. This bed needs to be changed. I need water. I need... "Ah! Riley!" I call out loudly. I need a minute. A minute, please, God...

He halts what he's doing and as my eyelashes continue fluttering I notice the fact that his nostrils are flaring.

He jumps up, still grasping my butt, thankfully... because I'd probably break his dick and / or it'd rip me apart if he didn't support me like this. The vibrations halt as he looks out the window and then shoves it up with one hand. I look over my shoulder and see the surprise on Tyson's face. He's on the porch with boxes. I see a blonde head in the car outside. Ivy. They're both here.

"Fuck. Tyson, what are you doing here?" Riley demands.

"I'm sorry, Riley. Brought food. Back to whatever you were doing." He snickers.

I flush scarlet. The window isn't a full-length one, thankfully, so he can only see my bare back, not any of my nudity. But it's obvious that Riley's carrying my nude body.

"Man, my fuckin' knot won't release."

Tyson startles and frowns. I bury my face in Riley's neck. Mortified.

"We've been attached since last night," Riley grunts.

"Fuck, really?" Tyson sounds shocked.

"Your mother's tryin' to help me figure out how to get out of it."

Tyson laughs.

It. I feel like I'm *it*. An inconvenience. An embarrassment.

"Not fuckin' funny, man. It keeps goin' nuts on me. Like it's got a mind of its own."

Or, I guess he's thinking of his knot as *it*. That still doesn't make me feel better.

"Is your witch controlling your knot for her benefit?" Tyson asks.

I gasp at the audacity of the accusation.

"I'll have you know that *no*. Absolutely not!" I snap, looking over my shoulder at Tyson, who has his eyes averted.

God, I have to make sure I don't flash him my boobs.

Tyson laughs again. "It's very fuckin' funny, cousin. Maybe it's your wolf, your instincts telling your body to hold onto her because this is where you belong. Inside your female."

Riley growls.

I wince because my traitorous body also reacts to the growl.

"Get the fuck gone, Ty," Riley says gruffly.

"Listen to your knot. Your wolf. This is where you're supposed to be. Stop fighting fate and maybe it'll let your knot let go for a few minutes and give your mate's princess parts a reprieve."

Gah!

Riley storms to the bed with me and trips. We land hard.

Tyson calls in loudly. "My Ivy's pregnant. I'm gonna be a father!"

"Congrats," Riley grinds out, sounding angry.

"I'll put all the food inside for you since you're…" He lets that hang.

"Yeah. Okay," Riley practically grunts as I start crying out again as his knot buzzes inside me.

He covers my mouth, trying to stifle the sounds and I accidentally bite him, my body so out of control with sensation.

This does something to him, obviously, because his eyes flash like liquid emeralds shining with light and he growls again and attacks my mouth, grabbing my face and thrusting his tongue into my mouth.

Whimpering around his tongue, I pull back and grab his face with both hands and stare deep into his eyes.

"Riley, please, try to-"

He roars out the rest of this orgasm, then punches the wall directly over the headboard.

I was going to ask him to try to relax.

23

RILEY

"Try to-" she starts to say, but halts when my fist crunches into drywall above her head.

And now she's trembling.

I feel like an asshole.

I hear hammering outside the room. What the fuck is Ty doing out there?

I squeeze my eyes tight and blow out long breaths as regret swims through me.

"Maybe... he... um..."

I try to let go of the tension in my body and meet her gaze under me.

Her hair is all over the pillows. She looks so fuckin' pretty it hurts. And when this little witch comes, fuck me, she's the most gorgeous thing I've laid eyes on.

Fierce possessiveness floods my system as my eyes lock on my mark on her throat.

My knot flexes and loosens. I pull my hips back. No. Not enough.

"Fuck," I grumble.

Her chin trembles and it feels like a kick in the gut.

"Leavin' now. Call if you need anything," Ty calls out.

"Thanks," I call back.

And then we lie there for a long time.

She clears her throat.

"Say what you gotta say," I mutter, staring at the holes in the wall.

"Maybe he has a point. Maybe because you're fighting biology because of how much you hate me, you... your..."

I sigh.

Hate myself more like.

She clears her throat again. "If you try to blank your mind, meditate maybe, maybe it'll help. I could talk you through some meditation."

"The sound of your voice sure as shit isn't gonna calm me down," I mumble. "I need food." I sit up, lean over toward a t-shirt on top of her bag and snatch it up.

"Put this on at least," I grumble.

Her expression? Hurt. She's hurt because she thinks I don't want to look at her nude body, but it's more like I'm hoping if I can't see these beautiful tits for five seconds maybe my knot will let go. I can't articulate it. Can't form much more than basic grunts at this point. It's like I've devolved or some shit, so after she's got it on, I carry her out to the kitchen to see what sort of food Ty dropped off.

Not only are the looks on her face doing me in, the emotions flooding my chest mean I'm getting it on the inside, too. It's too much. Too much emotion from her on top of the shit I'm feeling.

No, I don't think this is my wolf. I've got a weird sensation that I'm alone in this. Like my wolf has vacated the premises of my fucked-up brain. It's like I'm more than half empty. Never fuckin' felt this way. It's different from the grief when I thought I lost her. It's different from the anger when I found out she deceived me. There's definitely guilt over what I did to her last night. What she's been through because of my inability to function. I don't know how the fuck to describe these emotions other than to say I don't know myself right now.

Tyson fixed the bathroom door and put shit away, thankfully, as navigating putting groceries into the fridge with a woman attached to my pelvis wouldn't be easy. A quick glance shows me several meals already made that'll just need warming up or throwing into an oven. I see sticky notes on some of the casserole dishes with instructions or names of what's inside.

I catch a faint aroma and it takes too long to realize is Lincoln's scent in the air and a beat later, there's banging on the door. My nose isn't working properly, just like my dick.

"Stay there, Linc!" I demand, pushing back the urge to growl so it doesn't set her, then me off again.

"Hey Rye!" he calls out. "Sorry, bro... just brought you a microwave. Ty phoned and told me about your..."

Fuck.

"Don't finish that sentence!" I order.

Linc clears his throat. "Anyway… brought you the nuker from the office so you can warm up food."

"Count to ten slow, then bring it in. I'm stepping into another room first."

I take her into the closest room, the bedroom.

Our eyes meet as I hear Linc's footsteps coming in. Putting the microwave down, then retreating. "Call me if you need anything, brother. Congratulations, by the way. Another down, three to go."

I flinch.

"I'm movin' out. Figure we should have our own pads as it might not be long for Jase since all four of you were pretty close together. Anyway, call me if you need anything."

"Thank you, Lincoln," she calls out. "For the microwave and for finding my shoes last night."

"You're welcome, Erica. Welcome to the pack. Later."

I bare my teeth, then hear more footsteps. The door shutting. I move us back out.

"Coffee cake." I spy the container on the counter. I open the fridge. "Fruit salad. Yeah?" I look at her face. "Nothing to heat up to get us some fuel for starters."

She doesn't try to hide her sadness and it feels like a kick in the nuts. She swallows, then nods. "Could I make coffee or tea?"

I move to the counter and lean her against it while opening the door to the cupboard (I know from visiting Ty and Ivy here) has the filters and coffee.

Not easy filling the pot and making the coffee with a woman attached to my cock, so she pitches in, swiveling sideways as best as she can, taking the pot and filling it with water, scooping the coffee into the filter I've pulled out, and pressing buttons after I've slid the filter basket into place. After she presses the button, I pull out two forks from the drawer and she lifts the cinnamon streusel coffee cake my aunt makes and holds it while I get the tub of fruit from the fridge. I move the chair sideways and sit at an angle letting us both access the table.

After she pulls the lids off both containers, I grab a hunk of cake and offer her the first bite.

She startles with surprise and then leans forward and nibbles a little dainty bite off the end, eyes on mine.

"Fuck manners. I'm fucking starving." I shove the rest of what's in my hand into my mouth.

Yeah. I'm fucked in the head right now, but something made me feed her first at least.

She smiles a gorgeous, beaming smile, but then it disappears just as fast as it appeared and that's probably because of the grouchy look I feel on my mug. Watching that pretty smile die makes my gut churn.

Taking it in stride, she takes my cue and grabs a hunk of cake with her fingers and attacks it like she's half-starved. I follow suit and grab another big chunk. My aunt sure makes a great fuckin' coffee cake. Every couple that mates in this pack gets one of these sent over.

Our fingers clash a couple times as we both go for the fruit salad, not bothering with the forks that are right beside us.

The coffee maker beeps, and she perks up with excitement, head turning to look at it. I lift her and move us to the counter. She twists the tap on and rinses her hand before she reaches into the still open cupboard and pulls down two cups and sets them on the counter. I pour into both mugs as she reaches up for the sugar bowl.

"Cream, sugar?" she asks.

I move us to the fridge and grab the cream.

"Lots of cream, no sugar," I say.

She adds sugar to one, and cream to both cups and stirs and lifts them both. I carry her back to the chair and she sets them on the table.

She snorts.

Our eyes meet.

"Guess it's like being in a get-along shirt."

I frown.

She explains, "Our neighbor when we were kids living in Drowsy Hollow before we moved away... they had two really rowdy boys that used to fight all the time. I was just a little kid, but I vividly remember them being put in this giant dad-sized button-down shirt on their front lawn and on their back was a sign taped saying *the get-along shirt*. Their parents would get so fed up with them fighting and when they hit their limit, they'd have to wear this shirt together, only having use of one arm each as the other arm would be stuck inside the shirt so they'd have to work together to make sure they managed to... you know... accomplish things. They'd have to wear it a whole day and by the end of the day, they wouldn't be fighting, they'd be working together. That's kind of how we have to be right now."

I reach for another handful of cake and eat it.

She deflates before reaching for her coffee and blowing on it.

The shape of her mouth fascinates me as I watch her blow into the cup and then lick her lips.

"Shit," I grunt, going hard inside her. She sets the coffee down, knowing what's coming.

The minute my knot revs up, her pussy clamps down hard, pulling a groan from me.

She winces and then buries her face in my shoulder.

"Oh no," she cries out.

I hate that she's sore. I hate that I can't find words to communicate that to her. Because I'm so majorly fucked up. My senses are wrong. My body is traitorously holding onto my mate because it doesn't want me taking off on her again and I know, bone deep, that if it let me go I'd instantly shift with the need to run for the forest, looking to devour everything I can sink my teeth into. To blank out my rage. At this situation. At her. At mostly myself for the way I'm acting and how I'm failing at everything.

I can't believe how good she feels. How while this is happening I know I could stay inside her like this forever. When my body finally lets go, I know I'll miss the feel of this and want it again. And again and again. Knot her again and again until the end of time.

I ripped this girl out of the shower and fucked her raw, taking the virginity she saved for me. I took her virginity viciously. And I did this just an hour after she watched me murder someone who took her, who had that opportunity to take her because *I* left her unprotected. In a fuckin' parking lot. I can't believe how my body continuously ruts her against my will. Against *her* will.

I'm pissed at my pack brothers for locking me in here with her.

I'm furious with myself for murdering that shifter before asking questions, without finding out what the fuck he was doing with my woman, in my village. I'm so pissed at how frightened she was as she watched me do this as wolf, pissed that she could've been hurt, that the fucker even set eyes on her never mind forcefully took her, tied her up, frightened her. Touched her.

I can't settle down and evidently, my reactions are controlling my knot. Every time I have either a negative or a lustful thought specifically about my mate, my knot starts up again. It takes us both to orgasm regardless of whether I'm thinking negatively or noticing how beautiful, how desirable she is, how right she feels. How addicted I am to the sound of her voice.

How many times did I ache, wanting this over these past years, thinking I'd never get to experience a knot? Even thinking about the color of her hair sets it off. I dreamt about this color so many nights, but my dreams didn't do justice to how beautiful it is, how much I love sinking my fingers into it, how it looks in my fist and spread across my chest.

Finally, my knot stills and we're still for a minute, recovering. Her soft still-damp curls are all over my arm as she catches her breath with her face buried in my throat. I catch myself stroking her hair and examining it between my fingertips before our eyes meet and I pull my gaze and my hand away.

She shakily lifts the cup of coffee and takes a sip. And then another.

And then she sets it down. "I better not drink anymore."

Our eyes meet again.

"In case biological stuff happens," she elaborates. "I can't exactly...go to the bathroom by myself right now."

She's probably emptied her bladder and not realized it during any one of the many times my knot has gone off. We've both spilled a lot of liquid on that bed in there. I don't bother enlightening her. Potentially embarrassing her. Though maybe our bodies are in a state of pause with this unconventional mating.

"You're probably fine to drink. Don't get dehydrated. Finished?" I manage, gesturing to the food.

She tears off one more hunk of cake. I take a sip of my coffee and then snap the lids on the cake and the fruit salad.

As I get to my feet, supporting her behind with one arm, she grabs the fruit container and I move to the fridge and open it. She sets it inside.

"What now?" she asks when I close the door.

My eyes flit over her face.

"Can we talk, Riley? Could I... explain my side of things?"

I feel my lip curl.

"I guess you're not ready," she says sadly.

I sigh and go to the couch, sitting. She tucks her legs on either side of me.

"This uncomfortable?" I ask.

"Not now. But it might become that in a few minutes."

"Tell me when and I'll move to my back."

"Okay," she says, eyes searching my face.

"Talk," I mutter. "If you're sure you want all this on the table when neither of us can go into separate rooms to process afterwards."

Not that I wanna hear this. Just... what else do we do? Can't put this talk off forever, can I? I don't know if whatever she has to say will make it better or worse. Not sure how things could get much worse, so might as well...

"Yeah," she mutters. "But... it is what it is. And I know what I say won't make things suddenly okay. But... it's been almost seven years and... seven years in a few days." She gets a faraway expression for a second, then shakes it off, as if reliving it, as if it hurts to do that. "It all happened a couple days before my twenty first birthday, and that's irrelevant I guess, but you were a big factor in my life since a few days after my eighteenth birthday, when I found out I'm a witch, and... though you didn't know it, I saw you a couple times between then and when we finally met. And... wouldn't you like to know? I mean... haven't you wondered since you found out I'm alive if there might be a reason? More than that I'm just this horrible person who tricked you?"

I push my anger away. Or I try. Because if I get angrier, this knot is liable to start up again and I know she already aches from the way my body has been punishing hers.

"Clearly you haven't rehearsed this speech," I mutter.

"No. No, I haven't," she admits softly. "Because what happened haunts me. Haunts me, Riley. And whenever I think on it I can't function that well and I... need to function. And I know you'll never forgive me. I know this... all this with us right now is just biology. I know when we get through this week that you agreed to-"

"That they pushed on me," I correct.

Her eyes drop and she pouts while shrugging. "I'll give it back to you. Your life. I'll cut myself out of your life for you. So that you can finally find happiness. You just have to request it."

Her eyes move back up to meet mine. I stare deep, despite that it hurts to look into her eyes. I know I need to look. To listen.

"I'm listening," I say, and it comes out soft.

"I can't take back all the pain I caused you. I really wish I could. Believe me, please, when I tell you I never wanted this. I wanted *you*."

I grind my teeth.

She twists her fingers between our chests nervously. I stare at her hands while she resumes talking.

"I just went about things the wrong way. I fucked up. It's on me. If I'd waited for nature to take its course, I would've had what I wanted, and this was a hard lesson for me. A lesson you never should've had to be the scapegoat for. But I didn't know that. And it's still no excuse, so I don't even know why I'm saying it. I pleaded my case for you to be free of this... this pain because of my actions when I stood trial. They wouldn't." She shakes her head. "They wouldn't let me free you of this pain and God, I pleaded on my hands and knees, Riley." She chokes up and covers her face with her hands. "I tried so hard. They wouldn't let me. They made me punish you as a punishment to myself."

"Who?" I demand, moving her hands away from her face.

"The supernatural council collective. They found out what I did, found out fast, and they arrested me for it, made me stand trial. I... I wanted you. I wanted you and I did a spell not knowing I just had to wait. I'm so impatient so some who know me might not believe I'd wait, but I would. I would've waited if I'd known the alternative was hurting you. I drank some spelled wine that I should've known better than to drink, not that I knew what it was, but I knew better than to consume anything opened in Aunt

Lyrica's fridge without asking what it was first. But that day... my heart was broken because my boyfriend cheated on me, and Aunt Lyrica was in the hospital so I was sad and broken-hearted, and I didn't think. I just drank the wine. And the wine... yeah... it did what it was spelled to do."

She startles, eyes widening, and I realize it's because I've bared my teeth. I try to clear my expression, feeling the anger rise at what she's just said. Because she mentioned a boyfriend? The flash of anger I feel at anyone else touching her has me ready to shift and rip shit up.

She resumes talking. "And I saw you that day, so I went into a trance and hit that fire hydrant and left and then between finding my great aunt unconscious on the floor, then the ambulance and the hospital..." She takes a breath.

My fuckin' head is spinning.

"I drank wine spelled that makes you lose your inhibitions and go for what you want. And I did. I got drunk and wrote a spell and went into the woods and you found me the next morning in the wildflowers. I just went for what I wanted. And I wanted you. I..." She wipes her eyes with her shaking fingers and takes another deep breath. "Okay, I'll back up a bit. I saw you right after I found out I was a witch when I turned eighteen, three years earlier. That's a whole other long story but I didn't find out I'm a witch until my eighteenth birthday. And that's the day it felt like my life started. My aunt was training me and took me to a tree near your village. You couldn't see us because we were cloaked, but you were talking about building a tree house with your friends and you were just so..." She shakes her head. "I was smitten. She told me about how wolf shifters live, and it sounded amazing. The way you mate for life, how you care for your mates."

I scoff.

She gives me a sad smile. "Yeah. I know how weird that sounds now. But then I saw you again. Because I broke the rules and spotted you for just a minute after I drafted a potion that let me be invisible to you. Then the next time I saw you, I was in the supermarket in Drowsy Hollow. And you were so gorgeous and smiling and there was banter with some of your relatives and you were just so... everything. Fast forward a year to a couple days before my twenty-first and I came here upset because that guy cheated on me and I was angry and crying and driving to see Aunt Lyrica and get away for a couple days, but then got to that main strip of town and there you were. I saw you in the street holding the door open for an old lady with a walker. I drove into that fire hydrant and... and we met."

She swallows and takes a lungful of air before resuming. "Then I had this sense something was wrong, so I left instead of getting a banana split and something *was* very wrong. Aunt Lyrica was unconscious. So I got my aunt to the hospital, and I was upset at that and at Devon and Tawny, a former friend and... anyway, I drank the wine in Aunt Lyrica's fridge not knowing it was spelled. Then I went for what I wanted. Because the wine gave me the nerve. And seemed to turn off my common sense, I guess. I went for what I wanted. A man who'd be sweet and kind to his family and to old ladies. Who'd never cheat on the woman he loved. I thought wolf shifters chose a mate for life, I didn't know they were mates that fate chose. I tried to insert myself as yours, which was really, really wrong."

"But it was the truth," I manage.

"But I didn't know that at the time, or I could've waited. I would've even if it was hard. But there we were, and you were telling me stuff about you, and I was sobering up realizing what I'd done and feeling bad about the spell I cast because I wasn't fully trained yet and wasn't supposed to cast spells. Not to mention I was fucking with fate and when I made that call because I was supposed to pick my aunt up from the hospital, I got told off, told I was mucking around with fate – that what if you had a real mate out there somewhere and what if I just robbed her of her fate and created a ripple effect? And that's not who I am. I might've wanted you for myself, but I wouldn't have taken you from someone else if it was supposed to be that way. You know?"

She waits.

And then she shakes her head. "I guess you don't know. Then really realizing what a mess I'd made because they knew what I'd done – because Vivi got a vision and a witch from the council did, too, and Vivi's freaking out because I broke a bunch of rules and ripping me a new one, telling me they're about to combine their powers and spell me out of there because I'm in huge shit and absolutely can't let you mate me. I have to, no matter what, find a way to get out of your sight before you go all feral alpha and mate with me anyway. I was told I had to prevent you from seeing them spell me out somehow, so I panicked and when I felt the energy buzzing around me and knew I was about to be spelled out of there. I didn't know what to do, so I stepped off that cliff."

There's silence for a minute and I'm sure we're both remembering that moment.

"But Riley, I never landed in that water. Because they pulled me into Aunt Lyrica's covenstead. We were told to wait there. A council member who helps oversee the covens and is all-knowing, all-seeing and frankly a tyrant lent some of her and another witch's power to pull me out. We had to sit there until they got there, and I was arrested. Actually arrested, made to wear this necklace that stops me from using my powers, and put on a plane and sent to Eastern Europe. They put me in a cell for a week. They put me on trial and then I found out the truth. That I *was* your fated mate, which was why I was drawn to you so much. But it wasn't our turn."

A tear flows down her cheek. "We'd get our turn. Or we would've if I hadn't fucked up everything." She wipes her eyes again.

I grind my teeth and press my fingers to my temples.

"Riley, I was young and stupid and fucked everything up and then I couldn't fix it. I had to wait. They said I had to wait until I was instructed to go to you and admit everything. Until then, I had to hide my existence from you at all costs. I had to live my life knowing you were hurting, thinking you'd never find love, thinking I drowned. I was forbidden to contact you, told that if I broke more rules I'd feel the consequences, that my whole coven would be stripped of our magic. And while I'd give up magic for you, I swear I would've to spare you this, there would be fall-out. More than a ripple effect, because our coven manages a lot of things for a lot of supernaturals and it would fall apart like a house of cards and then blow up like a mushroom cloud. Many lives would be affected, not just ours. So, my hands were tied."

She shifts uncomfortably on my lap, so I take the hint and move us so that I'm on my back, her on top of me, able to stretch her legs. She props herself up on my chest to keep looking at me while she resumes talking, lips trembling, face soaking wet with her tears, eyes bloodshot.

She pulls a quilt off the back of the couch and fingers it.

"I'm so sorry, Riley. I would've fallen on my sword to save you from this, but I wasn't allowed. The wrath that'd rain down if I didn't abide would be disastrous. For so many people. So many supernaturals. I take full responsibility for my actions. I hoped you'd move on. That you'd forget about me. That time would dull things until it was time for me to face you and apologize to you."

I scoff.

She sniffles. "They had my bus towed so you couldn't figure out who I was. My aunt and my sister went back to find my wand and my other implements, and they brought me your shirt. I put it here."

She shows me the patch of flannel on the quilt she's holding.

"This quilt has things that are important to me. Some baby clothes. Things I wore on momentous occasions. One of Dad's shirts. A piece of Mom's Christmas tree skirt. Your shirt." She fingers the flannel and her chin wobbles. "I tried my best to do the best I could to help people who needed my coven. I kept… I kept track so that I could show you how hard I tried. I wrote a bit down, what I could because I have to keep some things secret, but I wrote down hints and saved them all in a jar. I brought the jar. It's in my bag. And I know it probably won't matter now, so I feel stupid even telling you, even thinking that keeping track of my deeds would mean anything to you."

She waits for a second and when I don't speak because I really fuckin' can't, she continues.

"So… when your knot lets go of me you can just… stay in the one room and I'll stay in the little room until the week is up and I'll… I'll get my sisters here and notify the supernatural council you want a severing."

I don't say anything, so she rests her cheek on my chest and wipes at her eyes some more. Shuddering from crying so hard.

"Then it'll be over, Riley. I'm sorry that I have to be so close to you while you process this. I'm sorry about all of it. So sorry I can't adequately explain…"

My eyes slam shut, and I work down a bitter swallow.

We're quiet for a long time. There are birds off in the distance making noise, but it's otherwise eerily quiet.

She nuzzles into my chest; I don't know if she realizes this. She's drawing figure-eights on my shoulder with her fingertip for a long time while sensations of love flood me through our connection. I don't know if she knows I feel it. I only know I'm feeling too much right now. More her than me. And it hurts. She hurts so much that if I were standing, this girl's sorrow would bring me to my knees.

I listen to her breathing as it slows back to normal. She sniffles occasionally. Wipes her eyes. My chest is damp from her tears. It feels like they've seeped straight into me.

I'm grinding my teeth so hard, it's a wonder they haven't been reduced to dust.

She's asleep.

I examine the copper curls fanned out on my chest. How right they feel. How wrong *I* feel. How fuckin' angry I am that all this happened.

I need my phone. But it's in the bedroom, so the calls I need to make will have to wait.

24

ERICA

I'm jolted awake by the pulsing inside me. I don't know how long we've slept but I'm certainly awake now, on top of him, that knot making me grind into him like my life depends on it.

I don't know how it still feels good after it's tortured me for the last however many hours, but it does. His hands clasp my butt as he lets out a throaty, "Mm. Ah!"

I whimper and bite down on his shoulder while gripping his hair, which I can tell drives him wild because one of his hands tightens on my ass while the other slides up to grip the back of my neck as he makes the sexiest throaty sounds.

Now we're probably soaking the blanket on this poor couch. Shit. Should've ... oh God, ogodogod!

I let out a shuddering breath as I'm overcome with sensation before it slows and finally stops.

And as I float back down to earth, I have a thought. An idea. I reach under him and slide my fingertips between his butt cheeks until I find the tightened creased skin back there and I push my fingertip in.

"What the fuck!" he shouts and then we're upright, him standing, and me quickly wrapping my legs around him and hanging on despite that he's holding me with an arm under my butt because he's looking at me with an infuriated accusation.

A small laugh escapes. "I thought it was worth a try."

He gives his head a hard shake. "Don't ever fuckin' do that again, woman!"

Another laugh escapes. I can't help it.

He growls at me and then winces and waits, expectantly before breathing out relief, I guess, that his growl didn't wake up his knot again.

"The fuck, Erica?"

I purse my lips, trying to stop the smiling, but I fail.

"My sister told me she did that to her boyfriend to see if he was into it and he jumped off her like his balls were on fire. I wondered if it might shock your body into letting me go."

"Never again," he repeats, looking furious. "Never, you hear me?"

"Okay," I squeak. But he looks insanely annoyed with me still and probably partly because I can't wipe the smirk off my face.

He squats and lifts my quilt from the floor and sets it on the couch with what looks like care, which throws me, before he walks us into the bedroom and aggressively grabs his phone from the bed.

And heat rises in my face as I get a little pissed too.

"Chill out," I mutter. "Not like you didn't invade me and *my* body without warning."

He stops mid-step and looks at me. And the change in his expression looks a teensy bit contrite.

"We need to clean stuff," I snap, looking back at the bed, thinking of the couch now, too.

"I'll have it all cleaned for them when this shit is all over with," he mumbles, then takes us back to the kitchen and pulls out two bottles of water, then takes us back to the chair beside the couch and sits down. I tuck my knees in by his hips and accept a bottle from him while he's texting on his phone. Acting almost like it's totally normal for me to be attached to his dick like this.

And I'm fighting the urge to cry, a giant, burning lump in my chest. Because yeah… this *shit* will all be over, eventually. For him.

Did I feel better after unloading my story on him? I wasn't exactly articulate in my explanation. I wasn't even all that easy to understand, I'm sure. I should've rehearsed it. But at least now he knows. And I don't feel better. I don't know what I feel, other than sore between my legs, my entire legs in fact. I feel bruised from the waist down.

He said nothing. He didn't shout. Didn't say anything. I don't know what he thinks. Or, I guess I do. He wants this *shit* over with.

While he taps away on his phone, I take small sips of my water until I've had enough. I cap the bottle and put it on the couch beside us. And then

I work my messy hair into a long braid to keep it back off my face. I have nothing to tie the end with, but it should hold for the time being. I look around, waiting for him to finish doing what he's doing.

Eventually, I hear the swish of a text and watch his eyes scan the screen. He's texting, fast, mouth looking hard, eyes the same. I blow out a sigh and shift uncomfortably. He takes a hint and rises, throws the soiled blanket from the couch off and lays down on his back. I stretch my legs out and put my head on his shoulder, resisting the urge to look sideways at the screen that's hovering above us as he continues tapping away.

Finally, he puts the phone down and it immediately rings.

He sits us back up and lifts it.

"Riley," I hear.

"Yeah Linc?"

"Just talked to Jared. His old man told him about a case around fifteen years back where a male got stuck in a female. Three days they were stuck."

"Yeah?"

Riley's eyes meet mine.

Three days? God, no.

"He shifted and his wolf let go," Lincoln says.

"What was the situation?" Riley asks. "Fated mates?"

"No. That's the difference. They were missing. Jared's dad was on the case to locate these two. Turned out they'd eaten some weird mushrooms together as wolves. Woke up locked together and lost. Couldn't break apart and the effects lasted a while so they think that's what fucked his knot up and made the shifter disoriented. Or because they weren't fated, so he malfunctioned somehow. Weird situation, bro. She belonged to someone else. Got ugly. Anyway, that's irrelevant here, what's important is that when he shifted, his knot released her. You tried that yet?"

"Nope. Thanks, Linc."

"You gonna do it?"

Riley's gaze is still holding mine. And I know he's read the sheer terror on my face at the idea of this.

"Don't think that's a good idea."

"What about a half-shift?" Lincoln suggests.

"Haven't done one yet. Haven't practiced enough to figure out how."

"Shit. Well, think about it. It could solve the problem. A full shift, I mean."

"Later," Riley says and ends his phone call. He looks at me.

And I feel panicked.

And like I can't possibly handle him changing into a wolf while he's inside me.

Because he'd be inside me! And because what if his wolf decides to rip me to shreds? I saw that angry wolf. It was terrifying the way it drove those huge teeth into that guy and gave him the death shake, blood flying everywhere. The sounds the wolf made. He wasn't a nice guy, had been rough with me, but he died a brutal, painful death.

Riley searches my face and I know my eyes are betraying my emotions right now.

"Don't worry; I won't shift while I'm... while we're..." He looks away. But then he hardens inside me, and the vibrations begin.

My head lolls back at the sensations and I let out a shuddering breath. He moves quickly, taking me to my back and then he's groaning into my neck, onto the claiming mark. It's making my body sing. It's singing a soulful, loud lament. I'm whimpering out loudly, unsure if I'm feeling more pleasure or more pain. Because my vagina feels like roadkill that's been run over thrice.

"The couch," I mutter because I don't want us to make a mess on it.

He lifts me and we don't make it to the bedroom. We finish on the floor.

25

ERICA

I wake up on top of him. We went to bed early after we worked together to heat up and then wordlessly ate some lasagna someone had sent. It was delicious. When I remarked on that, he grunted in reply without looking at me.

The only other conversation was when he said he was tired, and I suggested we try to at least change the sheet before getting into bed. We quickly gave up on the disaster of trying to get a fitted sheet on all four corners. Instead, throwing a couple clean towels down and then an extra comforter on top.

We can't easily do the dishes, but luckily found a package of paper plates on top of the refrigerator.

It was barely dark when we got into the bed, me lying on top of him.

I know we both lay there for hours awake without talking. I was trying to meditate, as difficult as it was given my predicament. Working at reflecting. Trying to calm my mind. Trying to relax, so I could sleep and get through the next day.

His phone made noise a few times, so he quickly grabbed it texting with somebody. I tried to ignore it, but couldn't stop myself from concocting imaginary conversations where he was complaining to someone about how awful it was to be stuck with me while I had no choice but to lay on top of him.

Yelling at me would've hurt. Calling me selfish. Calling me a fucking idiot. I knew forgiving me and throwing his arms around me to declare his undying devotion and relief that he finally had me in his arms wasn't going to happen, but the silence really, really hurts.

And worst of all, I can't even be mad about it or say anything. Because he owes me nothing.

My limbs are stiff and sore. I'd do questionable things for a lonely hot bath where I could stretch out. I'd really love to feel the earth beneath my feet. Feel the energy. I'm itching to be outside but know it's not practical.

He stirs and opens his eyes. And he startles at seeing me and it's like he doesn't know me for a second. Or like he can hear my thoughts, maybe, and knows I'm full of negativity right now.

"Another day in the honeymooner's paradise," I grumble.

I still don't need to go to the bathroom. Small blessings. But I *am* thirsty, I do want coffee, and I'm pondering asking him if we can sit out on the porch to drink it.

He sits up and swings his legs over the side of the bed while I wrap my ankles around his back.

"I'd like a clean shirt," I say.

He reaches for the floor and pulls one of my bags closer, then grabs fabric and drops it.

"Oh. Yeah, a dress would be good. It'd at least cover my behind, too."

He's still. Grinding his teeth. And a long moment passes.

Finally, I ask, "Can you pass me that? And a bra would be good."

He grinds his teeth some more before he lifts my bag and slaps it on the bed, gesturing like, *you do it.*

Great. He's in a fine mood this morning.

I pull out an orange bra and then stretch to reach the dress he dropped on the floor. It's a brown, rust, and sage patchwork pattern. I've had it for years.

Oh.

Shit.

Images race through my mind.

This is the dress I wore *that* day. That's what this attitude is about. I don't even remember packing this when I left to come here. But I must have.

I stretch and he gets the drift, moving so I can reach for the pile of dresses on hangers thrown across my other bag. I haul a different dress from its hanger. A navy-blue ankle-length jersey t-shirt dress with long slits and pockets on both sides.

I casually stuff the other dress into the bag, knowing my cheeks must be the color of my hair.

I whip my t-shirt off, then clip the bra on and quickly pull the dress over my head, not looking directly at his face the entire time, but catching that he's doing his best to not look at me. Still, I feel my cheeks flame all the same.

My eyes hit his face as he rises and carries me to the kitchen with a miserable expression on his handsome face. I'm mourning the expressions I used to see on his face whenever I'd see him. Before all this. Before I fucked everything up. He smiled all the time. He looked happy. I ruined that.

He haphazardly starts working on the coffee. I reach to take the pot from him so I can wash it, but he swats my hand away and grouchily does it himself, one handed, the other arm propped under my butt.

"I can help," I offer.

"No," he clips. "I'll do it."

I hold my tongue and let him do his thing. Have his temper tantrum. And it's ridiculous. Because he has to dump the old coffee grinds and rinse the basket out, change the filter and scoop in more coffee and it takes forever because he's stubbornly doing it all one-handed.

Once he flips it to 'on', he's reaching for the fridge door and one-handedly moving casserole dishes around until he finds what he's obviously looking for. A batter of some sort, filled with vegetables. It's uncooked and shredded cheese floats in the concoction.

He elbows the fridge shut, peels a Post-It note off the lid, then turns the oven on.

"This all right?" he asks.

"What is it? A breakfast casserole?"

"My mother's. Takes about half an hour to bake."

"Oh. Okay."

Riley's mom.

My belly dips. Riley's family? I want to ask about them. His parents. His siblings. I remember every word he shared about them with me that day before it all went wrong. I also know of them from ledgers and some interference done a while back, but I'm suddenly aching at the idea of extended family. In-laws. He's the oldest of three. A brother named Brody who's a year younger. Traveling. He'd been traveling for two years when Riley and I met. He's actually destined to rule his own pack as an alpha. Vivi told me and I wonder if that's happened yet. Riley also has a sister named Trina who's probably college-aged by now.

I have married coworkers and acquaintances who bitch about their mother-in-law. About deadbeat brothers-in-law or catty sisters-in-law. I've always wanted a mother-in-law. Not having a mom anymore, it's the closest thing I'd get to a mother. I have Aunt Mimi, but a grandmother to my future babies? And a father-in-law. And…

Loss sweeps through me.

I won't get to meet his mom. If I did, she'd probably want to publicly stone me in the town square. His dad probably wouldn't think much of me either. I know how I'd feel if I met significant others of my loved ones who treated them terribly. My heart sinks.

RILEY'S MOM'S BREAKFAST casserole was good, though I didn't have much of an appetite, so far in my head about how much his family must loathe me. The coffee he made was a little on the strong side and I wasn't a fan but drank it anyway. The weather is stormy today. Like Riley's mood.

After we ate, I told him I really needed to wash my face and brush my teeth. With all the drama yesterday and not getting a minute to ourselves, neither of us had seen a toothbrush. This was another too-intimate moment of navigating me doing that and washing and moisturizing my face and then waiting patiently while he did a quick wash up with some bar soap and brushed his teeth.

By the late afternoon, though, I'm concerned. There's been no more oscillating of his knot and we're just joined. Laying around. He's exuding this absolutely miserable vibe and I really, really want a minute alone. To cry, or scream, or something. Walk on two feet. Not be attached by the vagina to a man who hates my guts. To make a cup of herbal tea and go sit in the rain, asking it to wash my soul clean. It's felt tarnished for so long.

We've spent all our time today on the couch, each with our eyes on our phones, not talking about anything, just listening to the rain pound down for hours upon hours when finally, I put my phone down and speak up.

"Riley?"

His eyes bounce from his screen to my face looking just as miserable as this morning.

"If you think it might work…you can try to… shift."

He looks surprised.

"I'm a little scared, but… you're obviously miserable like this and –"

"And, what? You're not?" he snaps, making me rear back. "Your feet haven't touched the floor in nearly forty-eight hours. You can't tell me you're happy to lie on top of me or have me lie on you for the rest of our lives."

I promptly burst into tears. Big, ugly, noisy ones.

"Fuck," he clips.

And then his knot starts up again.

IT STOPPED ABOUT AN hour ago, after going for what felt like an hour, but neither of us has spoken since.

I *am* tired of not being able to put my feet on the floor. I've spent the better part of all this time lying on top of him. I'm worried about my lack of bodily functions, thinking that clearly there's magic at play here, though I'm not the orchestrator.

I don't care that it's raining out. I'm a dance barefoot in the rain sort of girl – or I used to be, back when I was happy, back before I fucked up our lives. But I'd settle for a walk in the rain, digging my toes into the grass.

I used to be the barefoot bohemian dancing and singing witch in her long dresses with flowers in her hair and hearts in her eyes. I doubt I'll ever be her again. She jumped off a cliff into a mountain of pain and loss.

I catch him staring. Not looking away. Actually staring.

I look away, self-conscious suddenly.

"Okay," he mutters.

My eyes bounce back to his face.

"Okay?" I query.

"We could try it," he says. "Me shifting. If you're willing."

My jaw drops and then I swallow hard, processing the fact he's giving me a choice here.

"Do you think your wolf will attack me?"

He frowns and shakes his head sharply. "No. Fuck no."

I bite my lip.

"You don't believe me?" He raises his eyebrows.

"I have no reason not to believe you. But, just sayin'... he was really vicious and scary and I'm..." I'm shaking as I leave that hanging, visions swimming in my mind of blood and teeth.

"If you don't trust me..." he starts.

"I trust you," I blurt, grabbing his shoulders and squeezing. "I do, Riley."

And I still do.

He flinches and if I'm not mistaken, his eyes soften just marginally before he lifts us up and carries me to the bedroom. He puts me on my back.

"If he stays inside... um ... me, will you be able to switch back to yourself fast?" I ask, heat creeping over my face.

"Yeah," he says. "If it doesn't work right away, I'll switch back. I'll switch back anyway since you're so afraid of me when I'm wolf."

My heart trips over itself as he hovers over me, hands braced on either side of my face, looking supremely pissed off.

He closes his eyes and bites his lip, looking nervous for a second.

My heart is pounding so hard I'm afraid it's going to explode.

And then it happens. Fur bursts forth as his facial shape changes and his limbs stretch out into the much larger animal form.

I'm free. Not attached.

I gasp as I'm underneath the giant, brown wolf.

My vagina is on fire. On. Fire. But empty. Blissfully empty.

And my heart hammers hard in my chest. I'm terrified.

Switch back, switch back, switch back!

He doesn't switch back. The giant, chocolate brown wolf with bright green eyes looks down at me. Sniffing.

Sniff. Sniff. Sniff.

Omygodomygodomygod. My heart is about to split out of my chest and run for its life.

His giant paws are on either side of my face, the rest of him directly on top of me. And he's absolutely massive, so he takes up the whole bed. He's not crushing me, though, so that's a relief since I'm sure he has to weigh close to three hundred pounds. He's huge, fluffy, but also looks muscular. And he's warm. Very warm.

He drops his giant head enough to sniff the top of my head.

"Riley?" I whisper. "Shift back now, please. This is a little... uh..."

Now his wet nose is touching my nose. He sniffs again.

"Scary," I whisper.

He looks into my eyes, and I shut mine because I'm thinking... *don't make direct eye contact!*

A loud, deep bark shakes me to my core.

I jolt in absolute fear and my deepest instinct is to call upon magic to save me. But I can't, can I?

Will this be how it ends? All this time, all of this, and Riley's wolf just gets rid of me? Rips my throat apart like that other guy?

I whimper. "I'm sorry. I'm sorrysorrysorry. Please don't kill me."

He barks again.

I open my eyes and he's still almost nose to nose with me.

God, he's huge.

He leans back slowly, not far, but a few inches from my face, and then a giant pink tongue swipes up my cheek. I freeze.

He licked me!

He drops on top of me, and I hear a strange thumping sound. His tail? His tail is wagging!

He's like a giant, gorgeous, chocolate brown wolf puppy that's full of happiness.

Nothing like what I saw the other night.

"Holy smokes," I whisper.

He barks again, doing a little pouncing action with his paws on either side of me. Kind of a... *let's play* motion.

I choke on laughter.

"Hi," I say.

He barks again and pounces again a little, making the bed shake.

"Oh my God. You're not gonna kill me. Are you?" He very slowly tilts his head to the side as if to say I'm completely off-side, and then barks again, which is scary as shit, but he's not aggressive. Not at all.

He's so big, and soft-looking and... happy-looking that I give into the urge to pet him. I tentatively reach up and he sniffs my hand, then licks it, so I touch his mane and give him a little scratch.

"You're so soft."

He doggy-smiles at me and then pants.

Wow.

I have both hands up now, scratching him under his ears. He flops off me, to the side, and shows me his belly.

I laugh and reach over and start to scratch. He jiggles around on his back, loving the scratching. His right leg then starts to jerk, like I've found a ticklish spot.

"You're absolutely fucking adorable, you know that?" I say, scratching harder. "And I thought I was strictly a cat person."

He barks loud, startling me so badly, I fall off the bed and land hard on my ass.

"Ouch."

His head pops over and his eyes are on me, looking excited.

"You understand me, don't you?" I ask as I rise to my feet.

I'm standing! On my own feet.

Phew. Weird.

He gives a soft little ruff.

"I thought wolf shifter people and their animal counterparts weren't two separate personalities," I say thoughtfully. "That doesn't seem to be the case here, does it?"

He puts his chin down and sighs.

The playful pup look is gone and replaced by a different expression.

"Because Riley's not right, right now, is he?"

The wolf stays still but his eyes look up at me and he sighs again.

"Yeah. I'm so sorry about that," I say, tears springing up in my eyes. "It's my fault."

He stretches and licks my hand.

My chin trembles.

I lean forward and wrap my arms around his neck and cry for a minute, sitting down beside him. It feels good not to be attached to Riley. My body feels really strange, though. My vagina feels utterly foreign to me.

The wolf stays put while I cry, hugging him, then finally he licks my jaw.

"I have to tinkle now. Finally," I say, wiping my eyes.

He follows me to the bathroom.

"Wow, my legs are like jelly," I mutter. They're sore and numb and just feel... strange after not being used for almost forty-eight hours. "Wait here, okay?"

He sits just outside the door.

While closing the bathroom door softly, I say, "I'll just be a minute."

I catch my reflection in the mirror. I look pale. Shocked. I *am* shocked.

"You're a good boy, aren't you?" I call out and hear his tail thumping in response.

I lift the length of my dress and sit down on the toilet. After peeing for what feels like an eternity, I finish up, get up and look in the mirror again. I've often had trouble looking at my reflection for the past seven years. Will I ever feel better about looking into my own eyes again?

I blow out a breath as I wash my hands and then wash my face.

When I open the door, the wolf stands by the front door.

"Do you need to go out?" I ask.

He lets out a soft *ruff*.

I open the front door and follow him out.

Fresh, rainy air. Oh yes... it feels good. The world feels vibrant even though it's gray right now with the rain. I taste raindrops on my tongue and there's something new to it. Something... odd.

Something tingles in me, maybe just a reaction to finally being able to stand, but I feel very, very alive. Very aware.

He runs off the porch steps and I follow, filling my lungs with the humid air and feeling like every blade of grass, every leaf or willow branch is speaking to me all at once. I walk toward the weeping willow tree and relishing the feel of the wet blades of grass under my feet, press my hands against the trunk.

Energy pulses in the air, wanting me to play.

The wind picks up and he barks at me. Once. Sharply.

"What's wrong?" I ask.

He barks again and headbutts me.

"What is it, Scooby?"

He barks and I back up. He headbutts me again in the lower belly and then bites the hem of my skirt and tugs gently.

"What?" I ask.

He backs up slowly and I follow, hoping my dress doesn't rip.

He does this until I'm back on the porch steps.

He then walks away from me, sniffing the ground as he goes, then he lifts his leg and pees. There are tooth punctures in the hem of my dress. I sigh and turn my gaze skyward. The sky is gray, dark, wet, and the air feels so good. I lift my arms out wide and tilt my head back and just soak in the feeling. Everything is fresh, crisp, almost feels... new.

The wolf sniffs the ground and then pees again a little. A strange, spiced, almost floral fragrance fills the air.

I watch as the wolf takes a few steps, then lifts his leg again. And then he repeats it. A few steps. A tinkle. A few more steps. Another sprinkle.

He's clearly marking some territory or something, which is strange as this is Tyson's place. Though Riley and Tyson are close and from what I know of this pack, their wolves should be close, too.

Yet Riley's wolf is marking as he moves around the cabin's perimeter. He keeps going, getting to a garage not far from the cabin and goes behind it. I wait a few minutes until he appears again, coming from the other side, trotting happily back up to the porch and then looking over his shoulder at me as if to ask, *are you coming*?

I get the door opened and follow him back inside.

IT'S DARK NOW AND RILEY'S wolf is on the couch beside me, his head in my lap as I stare at the fire I made in the wood stove. It's still raining and there's a slight chill in the air. I put a bowl of water down for him and he drank some and has seemed content.

I don't know when Riley is planning on showing his face again here and it's getting late, so I'm hungry.

"Do you want some food?" I ask.

The wolf lifts his head, so I get up. He puts his chin down on the couch and just his eyes follow me as I move to the kitchen, looking back at him.

"I was thinking of more lasagna, but that's probably not your thing, is it?" I look into the fridge. "They brought us a cooked rotisserie chicken. How about some of that?" I take it out and take the lid off.

He doesn't seem interested.

"Then maybe some more of that gooey, cinnamon cake. God, that's good. I could have that for my birthday cake every year from now on and be so stinkin' happy..." I sigh.

I warm up some lasagna and pour myself a glass of wine from a bottle of unopened wine I find in the fridge. It's golden, crisp, sweet, and delicious. I examine the label. *Quinn-tessential Honeymoon Reserve.*

"Ooh, this is good." Then it dawns that whoever sent it probably figured me and Riley would drink it together. As part of a romantic dinner.

"Guess I can have a romantic dinner with Riley's wolf if nothing else," I say, "So far, you're better company anyway."

His tail thumps in response.

"He's kinda grumpy. And not much of a conversationalist. Though I guess that's down to the company he's forced to keep for the week."

The microwave beeps and I set my plate on the table.

"Yeah, I know – self-deprecation isn't endearing. But you try living in this head of mine for seven years. Do you want some chicken?" I ask, plucking some off the bone and putting it in a bowl on the floor beside his water dish.

He watches me do this but doesn't come over.

"No? Okay," I say. "It's there if you change your mind."

He jumps down off the couch and goes to the door and paws it.

I open it up and let him out. He runs off, fast.

"Oh," I mutter to myself.

And then I go to the table and eat, not remotely enjoying the solitude, though I do enjoy the wine and pour myself a second glass.

The rain picks up and hits hard. After I finish eating, I wash my dish, clean up the mugs and cutlery in the sink, and then take the opportunity to change the sheets properly and put a clean blanket from the armoire over the couch.

I take a quick shower and put on a nightgown. With underwear. When I look out the window, Riley's wolf is on the porch, lying down.

I open the door.

He comes in.

"Still you, huh? Is Riley coming back?"

He jumps up on the couch and lies down.

I stick another log into the wood stove from the basket, sit beside him, and open up the e-reader app on my phone.

He puts his head on my lap.

I try to read, but I can't focus.

I turn my attention to the wolf instead, running my fingers through his soft fur.

"You know, it really sucks," I mutter.

His eyebrows jut up enough to let me know he's paying attention.

"Wolf shifters identify their mate, right? They look at her and know. I looked at Riley when I was eighteen years old, and I knew. *I knew* that was the man who would be *the man*. The man who'd be everything to me. And I was so sure that if he was mine, I'd be everything to him. I took every opportunity to come back to Drowsy Hollow to see if I could catch a glimpse of him for three years until I finally fucked up and drank that wine. And it made me go after what I wanted most in the world. I wonder if all witches fated to mate with wolf shifters identify their mates first. I'll have to inquire and see if there are other witch/wolf shifter pairings. Maybe I'm the only witch who's dumb enough to do something about it."

The fire crackles and the rain picks up again. I wrap my quilt around myself and rub the flannel from Riley's old shirt on my face. "I used to sleep with this and swore I could smell him sometimes. He smelled so good that day when I ruined everything. I knew I loved him. I knew it was more than infatuation. Those few hours we spent together, the way he looked at me, his presence, everything about him. And I wish I could go back and change everything. Save him all the grief I caused." I wipe my eyes. "I'd wait the seven years. I'd wait twenty, thirty, forever if it meant I wouldn't hurt him."

Riley's phone rings from the coffee table.

Grey calling.

I answer.

"Hi Greyson, it's Erica."

"Erica, hey. How's everything?"

"Um... well..."

"I heard you two were-"

"Stuck? Yup. Copulatory tie to be technical. Yes, I Googled it."

He laughs. "Sorry, it's not funny. Though it probably will be when you all look back on this later. Since you answered, I take it that's over?"

"He shifted and it let me go. But now it's the wolf that's here and he's been here for... like... four hours or something."

"And... how's his wolf's demeanor?"

"He's totally different from Riley. He's very sweet."

Greyson laughs.

I hold the phone.

The laughter dies down, and Greyson starts talking again. "So, seems like there's a bit of a separation happening. We've seen it before when the man and his wolf aren't simpatico."

"So they're not usually a separate personality? Because from all I thought I knew, they aren't supposed to be."

"No, they're not supposed to be."

"So, where's Riley then?"

"In there. Like his wolf was. Watching."

"So... not like... dormant, sleeping or something like that?"

"No. He's watching, listening, and probably pissed that he hasn't gotten back in."

"Not just enjoying not being here stuck here with me?"

"He's there. He's just in wolf form, though sounds like if the wolf's sweet and Rye wasn't, he's split. But he's still in there. And knowing him, pissed off at being locked out."

"Shit, so stuff I've said about him to his wolf, he'd have heard?"

"Yeah."

"Shit," I say, stroking the wolf's head.

Greyson laughs.

The wolf looks up at me and his eyes glow green just briefly.

I jolt in shock.

Was that a message?

The wolf puts his head back on my lap.

Greyson keeps talking, "I'll call in the morning and see if anything has changed. Think his wolf was tired of him being a dick so now he's holding out."

"Oh... like... refusing to let Riley back in?"

"Probably."

"Yikes. Could that go on for a long time?"

"It's been known to happen."

"Yikes," I say. "What does it mean when his eyes glow?"

"Riley's? Riley's wolf? Any of us on the council - our eyes can glow when we've got heightened emotions."

"Like anger?"

"Yeah. Among other emotions. The wolf is calm, sweet as you said, so don't worry. You need anything?"

"I'm good," I tell him. "Though if Riley isn't back by the morning I might need someone to drop off some doggie kibble if it's not too much trouble."

He laughs heartily. "He doesn't need dog food, Erica. If he's hungry, he'll let you know to let him out so he can go hunt."

"Oh. Maybe he did that. I put some roasted chicken on the floor in a bowl and he doesn't seem to want it."

"He won't eat that. He'll bug to be let out and when he's hungry."

"I think he did that. Right after he peed all around the place."

"Makin' sure everyone and everything knows you're his," he says.

My eyes boing. "Oh."

"Later, cuz," he says, laughing.

"Later, cuz," I parrot.

And then I set the phone down and lean over to look the wolf in the eyes.

"So, if you're in there, Riley, I'm not sure if... Scooby Dooby here is holding you back from getting back in or not, but... I like him. I hope you two work it out if you're in some sort of argument right now."

The wolf pants while seeming to listen to every word I say.

I lean back, put my feet up on the coffee table, and get back into my e-book.

26

RILEY

I've always had dominion over my wolf. We've always been *one*. In synch. Until the past couple weeks where I now realize I've been systematically splitting in two. Until now, specifically, because my wolf is showing himself to be too smart, too even-tempered to go along with the asshole behavior I've been pulling.

Clearly, he's distanced himself from me and barely made himself known the past two days. Not since I made the snap decision to take what was mine. It's only in hindsight I realize this. He was part of me when I ripped Greyson's mate's cousin's throat apart. But departed after I mated her.

Now I know there was a separation happening. We've heard of it plenty of times working with other packs who needed help. He was biding his time. Waiting for me to let him in. So he could fuckin' take over, and lock me down. The fact he's been able to do this shows how fucked up I am.

He's put me in time-out. And being in time-out, I'm getting an opportunity to see her through new eyes. His eyes. I'm also seeing how much more relaxed she is when I'm not there, which says a lot. She's still sad. Incredibly sad. But she prefers his company to mine. And him? He loves her. Deeply. And he's pissed at me for being such a dick.

When I couldn't get back in, felt him push against my own will and win, at first I was livid. Because I'm in control, because I'm me. But also because I want answers about the supernatural council that sentenced her, *no, sentenced us*, to that extreme punishment. If she's meant to be mine, if I'm meant to be hers, then what the fuck was the difference *when* it happened?

Why was such a harsh punishment delivered when she felt so drawn to me that she used the tools she had to get what she wanted? I'd have done the same. Alpha male shifters do it. They identify what they know is theirs and they take it.

The Young witch saw me, wanted me, and broke some rules to have me. Which didn't cheat a true mate out of her fate because she *is* my true mate.

I need to know the deal. Yeah, punish a witch for breaking a fundamental rule, sure, but a punishment this harsh? With both of us suffering for seven years when we're meant to be together? A punishment like this putting a wedge between what should be our bond?

I'm infuriated at what it's done to her. At how different she is since the day we met. At what it's done to me. So infuriated it's made me a hard ass dick who couldn't pull his shit together. Couldn't function. I'm broken. I was pissed off, angry, but then seeing her after all this time and the warring feelings, then feeling her pain? Having her emotions chase me? What came at me through our connection that day in the restaurant made me splinter apart inside. I'm her mate and I can barely talk to her. I'm her mate and there's nothing I could've done to protect her through this. I'm her mate and I'm the one breaking her even worse than she's been broken. All this time she's waited to be able to come to me and this is what she gets?

I haven't even purred to comfort her. All I've done is rut her, scowl at her, let her down, and shut her out.

I'd been messaging Joel, Grey, and Jared to ask them to help me get answers about her punishment, about the supernatural council. In my time on the Arcana Falls pack council we haven't dealt with any non-shifters on the supernatural council. We've dealt with two wolf shifters. That's it.

But I'm not getting my answers as I can't control my wolf to use my phone and can't get my wolf to let me in or get his furry ass to Joel's place so Joel can tell me what he knows, obviously, since I agreed to stay here a week. So for now... I wait.

I wait. And I watch. Watch her talk to him, feel her stroke his fur and tell him he's better company than me. Feel her emotions as she tells him she loves me. Feeling strangled that I can't speak, can't touch, can't run away from her emotions.

Then I watch him mark the perimeter of Ty's place, take down a buck then hunt for and eat two fish, drink a half a pond's worth of water, piss on four more trees, take a giant shit, then he swims in the river and takes a long run back to the cabin's porch, napping while he waits for her to open the door.

And seeing but not feeling her stroke his fur in front of the fire while she drinks tea and eats pistachios and yogurt-coated raisins, maybe I'm a little jealous of my wolf. Wanting to feel those fingers in my hair. Missing the heat of her pussy clamping around me over and over. Am I beginning to thaw? To see reason? Beginning to hit the capacity where I'm finally processing and gaining perspective? All I know right now is the more I think about it, the angrier I am that some assholes decided to punish us both this way. And angry at the way I've behaved, how it's put me right where I am now – trapped.

No, I'm not right yet, but maybe this *time out* isn't such a bad thing.

27

ERICA

I wake to sunshine spilling in through the window, Riley's wolf, who I'm now affectionately thinking of as Scooby snoring softly beside me, his paw on my palm. I look at him and get a burst of affection.

The part of Riley that doesn't despise me.

Now my chin trembles. I hold myself together and rise, stretching while my legs dangle.

Immediately, he's pouncing off the bed and dancing in front of me with excitement.

"Good morning, Scooby Dooby!"

He pounces back up, knocking me back on the bed and licking my face, making me giggle.

My giggle halts because his eyes suddenly glow.

And then they stop. Was that Riley?

"I need to pee. Do you need to pee?" I ask.

He hops off the bed and trots out.

I let him out and then go to the bathroom.

Waiting for the coffee to finish brewing, I look around from the porch and there's no Scooby. After making my coffee, I unplug my phone from where it's being charged and take it with me to sit on the porch with my morning cuppa. Instead of sitting on a chair, I sit on the ledge and wiggle my toes in the grass. There's so much energy out here right now. I'm practically tingling with it. It's as if I'm being invited to play with it, which is such a new, odd sensation.

I see a missed text message on my phone.

Vivi: How are you?

I reply with a flower emoji.

A flower lets her know I'm okay. The more flowers, the more okay. One will do today.

She responds promptly with two eyeball emojis. One eyeball means she's okay. She's a bit better than okay.

I'm not big on texting and generally keep it short and sweet with my sisters, particularly with the secretive nature of some of our conversations. We've adopted emoji use for our conversations and identifiers. I use a flower. Ronnie uses hands. Jess uses lightning bolts. Dani just uses thumbs up or thumbs down, won't subscribe to our coded system. She's our most serious sister. I'm the most whimsical, likely followed by Jessie, the other redhead in the family. Or, I guess I used to be…

I wish they were nearby. That I could talk stuff out with them. And that's not really me. I'm not much of a talk-out-her-problems kind of girl. I love having people around me and will always lend an ear though it's rarely my style to bend someone else's ear. But I'm craving that right now. Vivi would put my head in her lap and give me a scalp massage. Ronnie would paint my fingers and toes. Jess would try to make me laugh, try to cheer me up. Dani would give it to me straight and tell me how to fix all my problems.

And I know that now that I've sent Vivi two text replies since I got here with the one flower both times, if there's one more single flower text, she'll call me to try to get me to talk.

I can't. I can't articulate the pain of this situation to anybody. I told Riley and that was harder than anything I've had to do. I'm tapped out and don't want to explain my feelings about Riley's reaction and our time together so far to anybody. It hurts too much.

The wolf trots happily in my direction.

"My life is shit," I tell him. "At least I've got you, huh, Scoob?"

The wolf's tail thumps on the porch where he's now lying down.

He looks content.

"For now at least," I add softly, thinking that life will soon need to change for me. But to what, though? What will life be like after Riley?

LATE EVENING

Not sure how Riley and I can work out our issues since he's not here, but given that I know he's just going to tell me he wants a severing at the end of this week, I guess he found a loophole. Now he doesn't have to put up with being in the same space as me. Maybe he doesn't even want Scooby to let him in.

I've put some of the food Riley's people sent over into the freezer so it wouldn't spoil and stuck to mostly stuff we'd already gotten into.

I'm on the couch with my drawing app open on my phone, my S-Pen in hand as I draw a picture of half Riley's face, half his wolf's. No fire tonight as it's balmy and hot outside, so instead I've got all the windows open and a table fan I found in the smaller bedroom blowing from the front windowsill aimed at us.

I STARTLE AWAKE ON the couch when all the hair on my body feels like its standing on end. Scooby is growling, showing his teeth.

He's staring at the door.

I get to my feet and his eyes cut to me and he barks. I immediately sit, feeling like he's given me an order.

"What's wrong?" I whisper.

He keeps snarling and snapping at the door. Something flies through the open window where the fan is propped. It lands with a hiss and fog fills the cabin before I get the chance to make out what the projectile looks like.

28

RILEY

I'm pushing, hard, trying to get my fuckin' place back because the scent in my wolf's nose isn't just danger, it's related to the fucker whose throat I ripped apart. Family to him. Relative, not immediate, but still related and I know that's him. He's alpha and he's got two men with him. Also shifters. Beta.

Three men are outside the door of this cabin where she sits, needing protecting. I smelled them ten minutes ago and I've been trying to get in since then, pushing hard.

And my wolf is pushing back against me, not letting me in. I'm enraged, locked in my own wolf's mind. He wants at these guys. Wants to rip them apart. Wants to protect her and doesn't trust me to do it. With all my might, I've sent alarms off hoping it alerts my pack through our connection. That dusty corner inside my mind blares like an alarm and all I can do is hope that it got to them, that I haven't fucked myself beyond all recognition with my malfunction, cutting me off from them completely.

The door flies open, and I see two men flanking a bigger one, the alpha. The alpha is masked and wearing a face shield and armor. Riot gear. The other two guys have gas masks over their faces. The alpha has a weapon pointed at my wolf. A dart gun of some sort. The other two guys have regular guns. They're all wearing gas masks and they immediately grow hazy through my wolf's eyes.

"What the hell?" Erica shouts over the sound of my wolf growling. As he lunges for the door, the alpha pulls the trigger and a dart lodges in my wolf's forehead. He still lands on top of the alpha who falls, landing hard on his back.

My view is fucked as my wolf's vision immediately blurs. This fucker jabs him with something sharp in the side. I feel the pain of it as well as hear the yelp of my wolf while my mate screams, enraged, shouting, "You motherfucker!"

I push hard, push with all my might, because I need to protect her. With everything I am, I know it.

I NEED TO PROTECT MY MATE!

Finally, strength rushes through my senses and I feel myself fusing with him again. I'm shifting, melting into my own form slowly, too slowly.

The dart falls out of my skin and hits the floor as I'm on the alpha fucker, grappling for his throat while I'm still shifting. Too slowly. I'm only half-shifted. I push, pull, push, push, pull, PUSH and I'm through.

"Grab her!" the alpha fucker belts out to the guy to his side as I lift him clean off his feet by his throat. He shoots me a second time. This time in the throat.

"I'd say nothin' personal, buddy," he grinds out as I drop him, "Just need to confiscate your witch. But it *is* personal. You killed Jimmy and when I know that potion has worked its way through your system, I'm gonna kill you. Kill you *and* take your witch. She's gonna be *my* witch."

As I go down to my knees, there's mayhem.

Mase's and Linc's scents hit me. And I feel elation for a beat that they'll stop him, that they'll protect her for me. Through the haze I see them rush in as barking, growling, teeth-bared wolves, but they get shot with darts. First Linc drops, then Mase.

I'm on my belly, cheek smushed to the floor, swimming toward unconsciousness.

My nose is filled with my mate's scent. She smells good. She smells better than anything I've smelled in my life. She smells even better than she smelled before. Why does she smell so... no... I can't close my eyes; I need to stop them. They've got her. *No!*

"Rikki," I groan and see them dragging her kicking and screaming past me through the cloud of smoke. The space darkens and she blinks out.

29

ERICA

"Rikki," Riley groans before he passes out, and although I can just barely make him out with the smoke filling this place, I see his hand on the floor, reaching for something.

Hearing him call me that... *God...*

Two men in masks drag me out the door. One has me under my arms, and another has my ankles. I'm fighting despite the fact that my eyes and lungs are burning, but they're much stronger than me.

I nail one in the nuts with my foot, and he grunts, then slaps me across the face. Hard. The tallest of the three guys, dressed like he's part of a swat team shouts, "Forget her feet, cover her eyes! Gag her. Quick! Don't let her see you or use her mouth. Fucking told you guys to be careful with your shit or she'll cast a spell."

"It's hard Wyatt, workin' against the alpha's claiming scent," one says, and now a hand covers my mouth. Another covers my eyes. Something gets tied too tight around my head and is pushed over my eyes.

"Let me go!" I try to shout anyway, but it comes out garbled.

I'm dropped roughly on my belly, and someone pushes my head down so my face is smushed into the wood as I try to drag in clean air.

Well, that's some bullshit. I can cast a spell blindfolded and gagged. I don't need to say a spell aloud or see these assclowns to do it.

"Push through," the guy that's still inside calls out. "He's incapacitated and she's ours for the taking. Don't let her talk. But don't fuckin' smother her to death, I need the witch. Get her into the van and I'll deal with them. Three fewer Arcana Falls super-alphas to worry about in one maneuver? It's our lucky day, soldiers! Super-alphas? Such a bullshit abomination."

The guy is venomous.

"If this is a witch with decent skills, I can get me the strength these seven have, no problem."

How dare he threaten to deal with Riley after already hurting him! I'll show him a spell...

Though... oh... oh shit; I can't use magic. I can't use it here.

Fuck. Fuck, fuck – wait... *Not* fuck.

I'm not actually in the village of Arcana Falls. I'm in between Drowsy Hollow town and the Arcana Falls hamlet.

A technicality. I'll take it and hope I'm allowed. Though even still, he's talking about hurting Riley! So screw the rules. Screw everything if it means Riley gets hurt.

And I can't let them take me somewhere. Can't let them 'confiscate' me. Can't let that guy hurt my Riley or the other two wolf shifters that ran in to help. If I'm punished again, so be it.

I don't let myself linger on rules or *what ifs*. I fight. I fight because the life of the man I love might depend on it. I can try to chant a spell in my head, but I don't know how much goodwill I've got, not after all that's happened lately. I need to ground myself. Even one of my limbs. Some part of me needs to be touching the earth so I can connect with that weeping willow and ask for help. I don't know what kind of help it'll share, but I have to try. I have to try something.

But hands grasp my wrists as someone is trying to tie them together. My ankles, too. So I kick, I struggle as something is shoved in my mouth.

I fight my way partly off the porch, falling to the grass, biting, kicking, and flailing blindly as I dig my toes into the grass, sending a request quickly to the weeping willow tree at the road. A request for energy. For help. So I can stop these guys. So I can save Riley and his friends. But it hits me that it's not even necessary because vibrations are already zinging through me.

The zing didn't start at my toes where I'm grounded. It's coming from inside me, gushing through every part of me as power spurts from my pores. I'm easily able to shimmy the wrist binding off, then I haul the bandanas off my face as the men who had ahold of me have been blasted several feet away, as if by a massive whoosh of air. Lightning bug-like blue sparks flit around me. They're crackling with energy. Energy of mine! I haul the bandana off my mouth before pointing at the one to my right.

A bolt of heat leaves my hand, cutting through the rope binding my hands and a visible bolt of energy zaps him in the chest, knocking him to the ground. He jerks and jolts repeatedly like he's being electrocuted. My eyes dart to the other one who's pointing his gun at me with fear in his eyes and I envision the negative life force that makes up who this guy is being pulled from his body. His skin starts smoking. He drops his weapon, twists to run, but falls flat on his face.

Smoke rises from his skin and the weeping willow is swinging in a windstorm, sending energy to me as my hair whips everywhere. A large limb flies our way, landing across the two of them. The tree limb catches on fire. The two men are on fire now with it.

I didn't need to connect with the tree that way. Something's different. It's like there's an abundance of energy available to me. Inside me. More than I can comprehend. I can channel it, I can bend it, I can feel it like it's part of me. I can access as much of it as I want. I release it back into the sky and earth, gently, like setting down a delicate and priceless heirloom because I don't know where it needs to go and don't want to cause harm to anything other than the bad guys. I don't know what that was or where it came from, but it was frighteningly effective. I don't have time to ruminate, to dissect it because of what's happening around me. I send my gratitude to the willow and rush back up the porch steps. I need to get back inside and stop that asshole from hurting Riley. I silently plead for more of whatever I need to make sure he hasn't hurt Riley or his friends inside.

I hear the sound of a gunshot. And another. And yet another.

No!

Though it's hazy with the smoke, I make out through the back kitchen window that at a distance, Joel and Jason are rising from the ground back there. They'll help! One goes left, one goes right, and I know they're racing around either side of the cabin as I turn my attention to the floor where that guy in full riot gear looms over Riley's bleeding body, a gun in one hand, a knife in the other.

"No!" I scream and point at him.

He startles and looks at me with fear.

"No!" I scream again, an electrical charge building up inside me and I suddenly know I could set him on fire with rage at the notion of him hurting Riley. I can't do it fast, can't risk an out-of-control fire in here with Riley and his friends, so I slow it down. I slow it down and amid the smoke already hanging in the air, I'm fairly certain new smoke starts to rise from his riot gear as more sparks flit in the air around me. The bad guy lifts the knife again, and I know he intends this to be the end of the man I love.

I want to hurt him. I want to finish setting him on fucking fire, but Riley needs help.

I need him gone!

The universe answers my need with energy that whooshes out of the space, straight out the door. I feel the remnants of his energy, the most foul energy I've encountered and I don't normally feel bad energy like Ronnie does. I needed it out of here, away from me as if it's an infectious disease.

I plead with the universe, "Please let Riley be okay!"

I fall to my knees at Riley's side. He's bleeding from the right side of his chest, his shoulder, his side, and his leg.

Joel is suddenly beside me. "Erica?"

"Riley's hurt! And two of the guys," I cry out, eyes burning from the fog that's still hanging in the air.

"I'm all right," I hear Lincoln say. "Mase? You okay?"

"I'm okay," Mason chokes out and I can see him in his human form on his hands and knees. He's bleeding. There's less smoke in here, but one of them is coughing. Now both are coughing.

"I'll open all the windows; air this place out," Joel says.

"The bullet was sucked right out of me." Lincoln says. His shoulder is bloody.

"Out of me, too," Mason says. "She sucked the bullets out when the asshole with the gun got sucked out."

Did I?

I cough out some excess smoke and get a better visual of Riley on the floor. I drop to touch him, summoning clean energy, clean air; I don't even know how I do it, but I do. The bad air is sucked out, quickly, like it's being vacuumed out of here and everyone's hair is blowing, it's that strong.

It's so strong, it pulls me a few feet away from Riley, so I set it down. Riley's friends are staring at me with shock.

The smoke is gone, Riley is breathing clean air. So are the rest of us. Lincoln and Mason are close, looking at Riley with me. He's bleeding in multiple places and bruises are forming on his torso. But he has a pulse. I somehow cleared out the bad air so he can breathe and at least he still has a pulse!

I channel everything good I have inside me into his skin.

"Be okay, be okay, Riley. I love you so much. Please be okay."

I feel hands on my shoulders.

"Hey, Erica?" Greyson is here.

I whimper. "Please be okay, Riley. He stabbed him and shot him with two darts, Greyson. Threw a smoke bomb in here and shot Lincoln and Mason with darts and then I heard three gunshots."

"We're okay," Lincoln says, pressing a hand against the wound in his shoulder. "He shot each of us with darts and then again with a regular gun, but then he got sucked out and the bullets went with him."

"We're all here now, all seven of us. Everyone else is okay, Erica," Greyson says. "Ty's gone after the fucker. We'll catch him. Find out what he did. Hey. It's okay."

I'm sobbing. "It's not okay if Riley isn't okay," I whimper, wrapping my arms around the limp, unconscious and bleeding man that I love. "There's too much blood. He's been stabbed and I think he got shot."

"Riley, man, wake up and shift," Greyson calls out, jiggling Riley's shoulder. "Shift and heal, brother."

"What are you doing?" Greyson then asks.

"I'm sending every bit of good energy I have inside me into him." I press my hands to his chest and touch his mouth with my lips. "Please Riley, be okay. I don't know why or how but it's like I have new magic, Greyson. I got the bad air out of here and I got the bad guys away and, and… I don't know how I did it." I'm shaking.

"Take a deep breath," Greyson orders, looking into my eyes. "Keep sending good energy at Rye. I wanted to make sure you guys are okay, now I wanna help Ty chase that fucker down. It's my mate's brother."

I try to send more good energy. "Riley's hurt really bad, Greyson."

"Keep at it, cuz. Tell me everything, somebody," Greyson orders, squeezing my shoulders. "What's with the two-man bonfire outside?"

Jase speaks up. "She blasted those betas with magic. They dead?"

"They're on fire so I'd say."

"They tried to take me," I whisper.

Lincoln continues. "This alpha was stabbing and kicking Rye while I was coming to. And then he shot all three of us. Got my shoulder, Riley's gut, Mase, where'd he get you?"

"Back of the leg. Guy's a bad shot. I'd have gone for the head."

The idea of that has me ready to barf.

"I almost set him on fire, too," I say. "But I didn't want to burn everything in here up, so I whooshed him out."

I hear a car and then running across the wood porch.

I look over my shoulder.

A dark-haired lady with green eyes and a medicine bag.

I cry out with relief.

"I'm gonna catch up with Ty. Help track that fucker down. Be back. Good job, Erica." Greyson drops a kiss on top of my head and then he's rushing out.

30

RILEY

I come to... enraged, fighting something. My vision is blurry, my skin is slick with sweat. My head pounds. I feel like I got into a fight with a knife and a pair of steel toed boots and lost. Strong hands are on me, holding me down as I flail.

I need to shift and heal, to fight, but I can't. I'm stuck. Where's my mate? Where is she? I have to save her. Everything is so fuckin' blurry.

She was snatched not just once; my bullshit meant it happened to her a second goddamn time. Right under my fuckin' nose.

"Where is she?" I holler, vision clouded. I think I smell her, but my nose has been fubar'd lately, so I don't know.

Hands tighten on me. Smells are familiar.

"Riley, it's okay. Don't shift just yet, please. I'm drawing some blood. Hang tight."

Aunt Cat. The adrenaline in my system subsides a touch.

That's Joel and Jase in my nose; they're holding me down.

"There. Got it, Riley," Aunt Cat says.

Where's she? They got her!

I'm trying to get up. Hands guide me to sitting but stay on my shoulders.

"It's okay, bro," Jase says. "Take a couple breaths."

"Why's it so fuckin' blurry?" I fist my eyes, trying to shake this – whatever it is – off. "Where's Rikki?" I demand.

Aunt Cat pats my shoulders. "Lie down, Riley. She's okay. She's here, she's fine."

"Where?"

"Erica, come over here, honey," Aunt Cat says, "Show him you're here."

I feel warm hands on my chest. Hot, smooth hands. Hers. Warmth envelopes me. Comfort blankets me. I grab her wrists. I smell her.

"You're not hurt?" I manage to get out.

"Ease up there, bud," Jase says, and I growl in response and grab his throat with my right hand, hanging onto her with my left.

"Rye," Joel clips in a harsher tone. "You're hurting her. Ease up! That's Jase you're choking, brother!"

I let go of Jase but keep my grip on her.

My eyes still swim with floaters, but I can make the color of her hair out in the blurry haze. I let go of her wrist and reach for her hair. She catches my hand with hers before I get to it.

"Riley," she says, sounding choked up. "Let your Aunt Cat look after you, please?" She sniffles.

I blink a couple times to try and clear my vision. I'm sifting through all the scents in my nose. Jase. Joel. Grey further away. My Aunt Cat. My mate.

"Everybody out," I demand.

"Riley?" Aunt Cat calls. "I've got some medicine here for you and I drew blood because-"

"I need a minute, Aunt Cat. A minute guys."

My mate's trying to pull away. I tighten my grip on her.

She makes a pained sound. Too tight.

"Sorry," I breathe through the intense throbbing. So much fuckin' head-throbbing. "Not you out. Them out," I manage.

"Rye, maybe you should-"

"Out Jase," I snap. "So fuckin' help me..."

"It's okay," I hear Rikki say. "I'll be fine."

I hear the door shut.

"Where are we?" I demand, sniffing the air. "Can't see very well."

"The bigger bedroom at the cabin," she says.

I tug and she comes closer. Not close enough.

"Closer," I demand.

She gets up on the bed beside me.

I pull her until her face is almost close enough to kiss.

"Ouch."

I release her wrist and catch her by the waist, pulling her on top of me. "Sorry," I say.

She doesn't resist. I smell salty tears. Her salty tears. She's crying.

"They hurt you?"

"I think I did more damage than they did. To me at least. Are you okay?"

"All three of them? Badly? Incapacitated them?"

"Kind of worse than that with two, but don't worry about that right now; your friends are dealing with it."

"No," I growl. "Explain. I don't want shit being kept from me. I don't want my pack getting between me and you. Or anybody else. Enough of this shit!"

"You got stabbed a couple times and shot and the smoke bomb went off in your face and damaged your eyes. Your aunt gave you medicine.

"Where am I shot?" I need to shift to heal but I don't want to shift in case I can't get back in again. I need to figure shit out like this, as man.

"The bullet got pulled. It's... it got pulled from you, Mason, and Lincoln. Two of the bad guys are dead. Tyson is looking for the one who was shooting everyone. Let's worry about letting your aunt get you well, okay? That's all I'm trying to say."

"What did they give me? My head is fuckin' pounding and it's so goddamn blurry in here."

"The tear gas bomb or whatever that was went off right in Scooby's face."

Scooby. I could almost laugh.

She keeps talking, "Then it was so close to your face when it went off. And they don't know what the darts had in them, but your aunt is gonna do lab work on all three of you that got hit. She doesn't want you shifting yet. The other guy was kicking you and stabbing you, too. That's why you've got bandages. You lost a lot of blood."

"Who?" I grasp my head and moan with the pain.

"Greyson said it was his mate's brother. Try to rest, Riley." She's pulling away.

No. No!

"Stay. Lay down with me," I demand, grabbing her.

There are several bandages on my body. They feel tight, foreign.

She lays down at my side.

I pull her closer and twist, putting my head on her chest. I've been rough. I've hurt her.

"Sorry I'm being rough. I... need you here."

She stills.

The pounding of her heart, though it sounds a little fast, is comforting. She wraps both arms around me.

"I'll stay. Close your eyes and rest, please, okay?" she chokes out. "Your aunt thinks you'll recover fine, but you need to rest your eyes. She took blood to make sure, to find out what they gave you, and she injected you with some pain meds for your headache and bandaged the wounds."

"Don't leave," I demand.

"Okay," she says softly.

Stop crying, baby. I'm gonna fix it. Gonna fix all of it.

I think the words, but realize I can't manage to verbalize, because I'm sinking. I'm sinking into her scent, fingers on one of my hands threading into her soft hair as my body grows heavier. She's filled with troubles. Pain. Worry. But I'm gonna fix it all.

31

ERICA

A vibrating noise startles me and it drags my mind back to being stuck together for two days. But it's not happening inside me; the sound is coming from his chest. And it's not feeling like that same sensation; I'm not stuck. There's nothing sexual happening here. Though, maybe I *am* kind of stuck. Because this sensation sliding through me feels soft, sweet. It's kind of lulling. Like I *want* to be stuck. Glued to Riley Savage for the rest of my life. My eyes drift closed, and my body fully relaxes. So strange, feeling relaxed for the first time in... weeks, I think.

No, no *kind of* stuck about it. It's absolutely lulling me into what feels like a happy, cuddly dream-like state. Like... I've never been this relaxed in my life. Like... I'm in a field of soft, warm flowers. I smell floral scents in the air, and the crisp smell of a fall morning. My favorite scents.

I don't know if this reaction... this affection from him is about to wear off or not. It hurts to feel this, because I know it's not mine to keep. Though it should've been. And loss tries to sweep through me, but it can't. Because this sensation I've got now is stronger.

He needs me here to comfort him for some biological reason, so I'm here. I'll just take a little rest maybe. I won't hope for anything.

Riley's Aunt Cat slips back in and smiles, mouthing *sorry* as she reaches toward the table beside the bed. I'm fighting to keep my eyes open.

"What's happening?" I mouth, pointing at him.

She tilts her head curiously.

I whisper, "He's vibrating, but not like before. Like ... from his chest."

A bright smile spreads across her face. "Alpha's purr. That's not the first time he's done that for you, is it?"

"Alpha's purr," I whisper.

She frowns.

He's out. Complete dead weight on me, making that sound while he holds me.

"They do that to comfort their mates," Cat advises. "They use it in both good ways and in evil ways at times. Your first time hearing it? For real?"

I nod a little, feeling choked up. I could die happy just like this.

"Evil?" I query.

"Never mind that." She shakes her head. "He's giving you something you need. Comfort. Enjoy it. It's a good sign." She tucks the blood sample she already took from Riley into her medical bag. "I'll message in a couple hours and see how he's doing. Here's your phone." She sets it down. "I sent myself a text, so we'd have one another's details. If you need me, reach out and I'll come back. I think it might just be time he needs. He took two of those darts and the others took one each and they're already beginning to feel better. Like I told you, Riley is strong. Those other shifters don't know who they're up against. Their potions and noxious substances keep failing because of how much strength our council alphas have. They've got no idea." She winks.

I nod, feeling like I'm putty, glued to the bed.

"There's eyedrops here if he needs them. If he can't shift to heal within the next twelve hours, we'll wanna change out those bandages and give his wounds another cleaning. The darts affected the others' ability to shift for just a bit so not sure if it'll do the same with him."

"Okay," I say, and I'm listening but I'm also fixated on what she said.

The alpha's purr. She said he's doing it for me. For me? He's so disoriented, it's probably just instinct. Though I don't believe he's doing it for me, whoa, do I like it.

I take my fill of it as I sink into bliss.

I want to bathe in it. Smell this scent forever. Keep these sensations like they're still mine to have. If only I could bottle this scent, this sound, so that whenever I want, I can just have a whiff and a listen. That would help when he moved on and left me behind. *Yeah. Me with my nose forever in a jar.*

The cabin is likely empty now, but I've been told two alpha shifters named Cade and Gus will guard the perimeter of the place. Greyson was going to brief them on everything. Cat showed me pictures of them on her phone after saying they'd stay out of the way unless absolutely necessary. I recognized Cade from Roxy's.

Greyson's new mate's brother is evil. I hope they catch him before he does any further damage.

I'm guessing right about now his mate and I are sharing top spot for the most hated women destined for shifters from this pack. Though she's got the benefit of having a man who doesn't appear to be angry or hating on her, despite what she did. Greyson seemed pretty happy the other night.

Riley's purr lulls me to sleep. His scent in my nose, that sensation in my body? His head on my chest and my fingers in his hair? I'm floating, feeling like I'm wrapped in warm rose petals.

32

RILEY

Someone has her. They're pulling her away but I can't see them. She's crying out in agony and although I'm reaching for her, I can't catch her hand as she claws for me.

"Riley, please! Save me, Riley!"

I stretch and stretch and can't reach her. She's floating away from me, being pulled into a dark hole. And the fear on her face feels like a thousand knives sinking into my flesh everywhere.

I jackknife upright in bed, sweat dripping from my hairline.

It's dark. I don't know if it's dusk or pre-dawn. But my vision feels sharp again. I've always seen well in the dark but it's as if I can see even better. Her scent is in my nostrils. She's next to me. Safe. Here. Mine.

Her eyes are on me, and I plainly read concern in them, though she likely can't see more than my outline.

Before I can calculate it, I'm on her. I'm on her, dragging the long dress up and getting it off her hot, arching body. Her underwear go first, then her bra.

It's gone now and my palms are filled with her breasts, her nipples pebbling against my life line, my love line. She arches higher for me as I take one tip into my mouth, tasting her skin, listening to her sweet sounds as little whimpers rush from her lips. My palm slides down between her thighs and I find her dripping wet for me, skin out in goosebumps. For me.

Mine.

I dot kisses up to her throat until I feel the raised skin of the mark I put on her. I draw that warm skin into my mouth and suck, feeling my pulse quicken as she cries out. She rides my hand while whimpering some more, eyes filled with lust, with longing.

I could stare at her in the dark forever. Because she's looking at the outline of me with unbridled want, not realizing how well I see her, I don't think. Not realizing how well I read her and how right now without the pain she's been carrying, reading her makes my very essence sing. Because she isn't hurting right now. Right now, she wants me. She loves me. She aches for me.

I pin her with my hips, driving forward again and again, sinking into blissfully hot, tight, beauty. She's perfection around me. Her legs wrap around my waist as she digs her fingernails into my back.

My knot snaps out like a switch has been slapped and right now I don't give a fuck if it stays there forever. I want this. I want to know she's safe, that she's here, that she'll never be out of my reach again. Nobody dragging her from me. No disappearing off the side of a cliff. No clawing at nothing trying to get back to me, back where she belongs. Nobody dragging her away from me. Fuckin' no!

I roar out as my knot spins and my hot cum fills her. My mouth finds hers and she tastes like everything I've been wanting for seven long years.

We're a tangle of bodies as I turn around to my back and she digs her knees in by my hips.

My little witch's head is thrown back and as her hair spills around her shoulders, down her back, I take a handful of it and use it to hold on. My knot deflates and now she can move. I help with that by holding her hip with my free hand and bouncing her.

The sounds she makes. The way she feels. The sensations inside me? Profound. Right. It's all for me. She saved herself for me. She didn't let any man touch her, not for all that time while she waited until she could finally be mine.

Thank fuck her sister stopped me in the bar that night. Because since setting eyes on her, I've never laid a hand on a woman with lust in my mind. I've never imagined fucking anybody but this girl. My girl.

My Erica. My Rikki.

I tried to imagine it with that bartender, *tried*, but it wouldn't materialize because it wasn't meant to happen.

I suck on her full bottom lip as I flip her to her back again and rearrange her legs up over my shoulders, kissing her calf and rubbing her clit as her legs tremble. I keep at that swollen, wet clit while sinking inside her tightness over and over. After she comes again, I flip her to her belly and fuck her from behind, biting her mark again, wanting to mark her all over again all over her body so she knows she's mine, so she knows I'm here, on her, in her. Never again letting her doubt that this is where we both belong, hanging onto one another.

My hands grip my mate with purpose, ownership, because she's all mine.

I growl the word *mine* and come again before collapsing on top of her.

I fall asleep with her under me like that.

Exhausted.

The remnants of the headache nags at me, but I fill my lungs with her scent. And her scent is blanketed by mine, as it should be. I feel tired and drift toward sleep again, my chest rising and falling with vibrating purrs.

I hear a sweet little sigh under me.

I press my lips to her throat where I've marked her and my eyes close as I sink back into a dreamless sleep, feeling troubled because though she feels good and right, I know there are claw marks scored across her heart from my actions since she showed up here to try to make things right.

But now it's on *me* to make things right.

33

ERICA

I wake up to sunshine streaming in the window, across the fluffy brown form that has his furry chin on my belly, bright green eyes looking into mine.

I'm feeling both happy and sad at seeing Riley's wolf.

"Hiya Scoob," I whisper, scratching behind one of his ears.

He stretches and licks my chin, his tail thumps against the bed, then his fur melts away and he's Riley again. And he's on me. He's on me and he's naked. We both are.

"Hey," Riley replies gruffly as if it was him and not his wolf I'd been greeting.

I drop my hand. My mouth also drops open.

His eyes coast over my face, then his knee nudges between mine and he guides the tip of himself to my entrance. Immediately, I feel my body react and ready itself for him as he slides an inch into me, pulling a gasp from my lips.

He slowly moves inch by delicious inch until he's fully inside, then his eyes drift half shut, and his mouth is on mine, those pillowy soft lips touching mine, then the tip of his tongue licking my bottom lip before dipping in just enough to touch the tip of my tongue.

I whimper and my legs wind around his butt as he deepens the kiss. My fingers dive into his soft, messy, curly hair. He pulls three quarters of the way out of me and then slams hard. I cry out. Loud. Oh my goodness that feels fucking amazing. He does it again, our eyes locked. His eyes sparkle with what looks like mischief.

What?

His hands cradle my face, and his mouth is a hairsbreadth from mine as his eyes rove my face.

I feel... seen. And scared. Scared out of my mind.

Sheesh, he smells good, feels good.

He pulls out and then slowly drives back in, to the root.

It's slow and deliberate. He's awake, looking in my eyes, and holding me, staring at me while he makes love to me. That's what this feels like.

Making love. Not just biology. Not just an urge that comes from innate behavior.

But... it can't be.

Can it?

Don't hope, Erica. *Don't.*

Something shifts and he goes from gentle to wild. Like something inside – self-control – has shattered. He pins me, wrists cuffed over my head by his hand and he's glaring into my eyes like he's furious. It's gone from making love to fucking. Hard fucking. And it's incredible. Riley Savage fucks into me over and over and over. His pace is punishing, his grip likely bruising. And I'm along for the ride, staring directly into his gorgeous green eyes, not protesting, because he can fuck me as hard and as long as he wants. I'm his. I'm his for as long as I live, even if he has me sever our connection, even if he wants to forget I exist and find someone else. Someone else to love. To have a family with. To wake up beside each and every day.

A tear drifts down my cheek, landing on my shoulder and I choke on a sob.

"Fuck!" he snarls and then he lets out a roar as the vibrations rev up and take me over the edge, hurling me into an eruption of sensation punctuated by light and noise. Noise that comes from the depths of me.

His eyes flash a glowing green before his mouth clamps onto the bitemark on my neck and this sensation sends things into overdrive. He sinks his teeth into it, not enough to break my skin but enough that I feel it. And it feels like a light show crackles and sparks from between my legs. I'm not sure where I begin and end. I close my eyes to hide from the intensity. I feel like I'm folding in on myself, falling apart. This could be the end. This could be the last time.

I convulse around him, holding onto his knot as tight as I can with my inner walls, wishing I could keep it forever. Keep *him* forever.

"Yeah," he groans softly, sexily, licking, then pressing his lips against that mark on me and then he stills as I take his full weight.

I luxuriate in it, until he slides out of me, and I'm left feeling empty.

He sits up and throws his legs over the side of the bed, giving me his back.

I stare at the muscles of his shoulders, back, and arms for a minute before I swallow down a giant lump of harsh emotion.

He stays like that, hunched, forearms resting on his thighs. It's a position of defeat, I think.

"Are you okay?" I ask in a whisper. The bandages from those stab wounds are on the table. He must have taken them off before he shifted. His skin looks healed. He looked pretty rough yesterday with at least five different wounds, one of them round, from the bullet.

"Head's still a little sore," he says. "Can see at least. And I just ran a shift test as you saw and it's all good. Healed up and he let me back in."

He looks over his shoulder. "Scooby did." He shrugs with half a smirk.

A joke?

"I didn't realize it until I was too far gone to stop it," he says. "Man and beast splitting in two. He took over because I malfunctioned." He winces and puts his hand to his forehead.

"So you became separate personalities?"

"Basically." He rubs his forehead.

His head still hurts.

"There's ibuprofen." I gesture to the table where my phone lies between the bottles of medicine and two bottles of water. "And eyedrops if you need them."

He gets to his feet and looks at me, looking like he's weighing what he's about to say next. His expression drops.

I quickly twist to reach the bottle, then shake two pills out into my hand. In the handoff, I drop them on the bed.

I'm shaky. Unnerved. He ravished me last night. And just now. And it was incredible. He didn't get stuck. And he purred on top of me afterwards last night. And right now he's standing here naked, glistening still from the wetness between us, looking at me like he's about to tell me it all meant nothing. That it was only biology.

He lifts the pills and pops them into his mouth as I uncap the bottle of water for him and offer it.

He takes it. Our fingers brush and I chomp down on my lip, willing my body to stop shaking. I'm not sure what to say or do.

His eyes are on me as he sips.

"You used magic," he says after he drinks half and passes it back to me.

Grateful, I take a few mouthfuls and put the bottle down.

"When they tried to take you," he adds and then his expression hardens.

"Hopefully I won't get in trouble, but uh huh. We're not technically in your village, which was where I was told not to use it, and the situation was extreme, so… fingers crossed."

That's an understatement and I haven't even begun to come to terms yet with how different my magic felt. Like it was on a hair trigger. Like I had an endless well of energy and good will to draw from. Like the tree couldn't wait to share it with me. And I conjured wind. And lightning burst from my hands and… I can't even wrap my mind around the two shifters that died. Bad guys. But they died.

I'd do it again, too, if it meant saving you.

"They tried to take you," he says, leaning toward me aggressively.

"Yeah."

And he tried to kill you. I don't say it. And Mason and Lincoln.

His eyes glow briefly while his jaw muscles bulge. And it makes my heartrate kick up.

"Do we know any more?" he asks, and steam might as well be coming out of his nostrils with how angry he looks.

"Something to do with Greyson's mate and that whole plot to poison and shoot Tyson and … stuff."

"Where's my goddamn phone?" he clips, eyes slicing across the perimeter of the room.

"I don't know."

He walks out. I can't help but admire his naked form while also shrinking a little with the amped energy coming from him.

And now I'm going into ponder-mode.

Before I get very deep into the maze that's my brain, he's back with his phone and I avert my gaze, because… it'd be rude to gawk at his beautiful, long, thick penis.

His body is insanely fit. Muscles. Flat, defined belly. Tanned skin. That delicious facial hair which can safely be called a beard at this point because it went beyond stubble days ago.

He quickly skims his phone, grinding his teeth, which makes his jaw muscles bulge. He tosses the phone to the table beside mine before climbing back into the bed.

"I'll let you get some more sleep," I say, scooting down toward the bottom of the bed so I can get out. It's early but I'm awake so I'd might as well get up.

He grabs my wrist.

I wince and our gazes lock. "Oh no you won't."

I won't?

"How'd this happen?" he asks softly.

Softly? Yeah. So softly, it feels the opposite of how it's supposed to feel. Instead, it's like an ice pick is jammed into my heart.

I frown. That's a soft look in his eyes, too.

I stare and my mouth drops open. He's rubbing his thumb along a bruise ringing my wrist while examining it.

"Those assholes?"

"You did it when you grabbed me last night."

His eyes hit mine with shock and then pain slashes through his features and he looks away.

"I did that?"

He clenches his jaw so hard I hear his teeth grind.

"It was when you were first regaining consciousness. I'm not holding it against you. I… understand, Riley."

"I'm sorry," he says softly, looking into my soul. "Beyond this, how are you?" His thumb caresses my bruise slowly, sweetly.

"Do you really wanna know?" I rasp, my throat feeling like it's got a cactus lodged inside it.

"Yeah," he says. "Are you okay?"

My eyes fill up. "No."

"No?"

"Not at all."

He reaches out and hooks a hand around my neck and crushes me to him. I gasp in surprise as his mouth crashes into mine and he groans.

"Everything's fucked up," he says against my mouth. "I'm fucked up."

I choke on a sob, nodding. He kisses me again, hungrily and almost... desperately, holding my face now with both hands as we fall onto our sides on the pillows.

Why is he kissing me? Why is he holding me?

"So fucked up," he adds and then he's purring.

I nod some more.

The purring halts.

"I'm so fuckin' angry. I've been steaming mad for days. Angrier than I've ever been."

"I'm so sorry, Riley," I whisper. "I..."

"Shut up."

I flinch.

"Shut up and let me talk."

I wince.

He's holding my face tenderly in both hands. His gorgeous eyes are liquid green pools. "I'm fucked up beyond all recognition, witch. Because of what *you* did."

"I know... I fucked myself up, too."

"Shh."

I clamp my mouth shut.

"But, Rikki, even more than what you did, what *they* did. The assholes who punished you. Who punished *us*."

My back straightens as he stares into my eyes. "What would you have done if they hadn't taken you that day, if they hadn't magicked you out of there? When you let me think you'd fallen into the river?"

God, his eyes hold so much emotion. Then again, that's one of the things that first drew me to him. Because every time I've looked at this man, those eyes hold so much.

Laughter. Camaraderie. Lust. Anger. Hate. I don't know what I'm looking at right now but they're soft, hurt, and so, *so* beautiful.

My answer tumbles out quickly. "I'd have gone wherever you wanted to go and done whatever you wanted to do, Riley." I swallow and then add, "I wanted to be yours the first minute I saw you. I would've clawed my way back over that cliff to you through anything and everything in the way if they'd allowed it without those severe consequences. I swear it on everything I am. I didn't want to stay away; I had no choice. No choice."

His eyes close and his mouth contorts painfully as he swallows. "So then you don't need to be sorry. You didn't set out to hurt me. You wanted me. And you're supposed to have me. *They* need to be sorry because they got in the way. They chose to be so goddamn cruel to not just you, but to both of us. Don't ya think?"

I swallow with difficulty and then my mouth drops open. Words don't come out. I must look like a gasping fish because after a minute, he continues talking.

"Did the punishment we got fit the crime when we're supposed to be together anyway? I wanna know who made that decision. Who did this to us?"

Me. I did this to us. That's what I've always felt.

"No," he says, caressing my face. He must be reading my expression because I haven't said anything in response. "It's not your fault. Who sentenced us to this punishment?"

"Members of the council did."

"Who?"

"It... it was a committee of four of them."

"Who, baby? Who?" he demands.

Baby?

"Um, Lucinda Alexander, and-"

"Who's that?"

"A witch. A very powerful one."

"Who else?"

"Uh, Sergei Voitenko, vampire. Looks young but he's one of the oldest in the world. Also a wolf shifter named Mitchell Blakely, and another witch: Aviva-"

"Mitchell Blakely?" Riley cuts me off.

I nod. "Yes."

"He was just *fuckin'* here. He was here and…" He jumps out of bed and starts pressing his phone screen with aggression.

He paces the room a minute while I stare at him, feeling something dangerous crackling in the air. He's absolutely livid.

"Mitch? Riley Savage here. You need to fuckin' call me. Or show up. You have some goddamn explaining to do and I think you know why." He tosses the phone, and it hits the wall.

I jump.

"He was just fuckin' here." He rakes his hands through his hair, staring at me, looking infuriated.

I swallow hard.

"Tell me what happened."

"We got the impression there was a deadlock type vote, that the vampire and the shifter held out on agreeing with the punishment the witches chose. We waited days for them to come to an agreement. Finally, my sentence was delivered, and my sister Ronnie saw Sergei leave immediately after that, looking pissed off. He and Mitchell obviously agreed before he left, even if he was mad about it. We figure he held out the longest."

"Be back," he mutters and walks out, making another call.

A minute later, I see him outside, pacing while barefoot, wearing a pair of grey lounge pants low on his hips while talking on the phone.

I get out of bed and clip on a clean bra and then struggle to put a pair of panties on, stumbling around the room like a deer with new legs. I throw on a brown and cream floral halter top maxi dress that comes to my ankles. I twist my hair into a bun, grab an elastic to hold it in place, and go to the bathroom. I use the bathroom and then wash my face and brush my teeth all while thinking that I don't know what the heck is happening here. I'm skittish, shaky, and just… thrown.

After the coffee maker is going, I turn the fan on. It's a scorcher today. I look around and the floor didn't stain from all the blood. The guys cleaned it up, not letting me lift a finger, just telling me to stay by Riley's side while Cat bandaged him up.

And he's okay. He looks totally healthy today. I'm so grateful. Grateful but not hopeful.

Because I can't let my heart go where it's trying to go after our conversation. Yes, he wants someone to pay for what was done to him. To ... us. Which throws me because I've never looked at things from that perspective. I've always looked at it like I'm the one that did it and I'm the one that needs to pay for it, hating the fact that Riley got punished, too.

I give myself a shake. Though he's placing blame on them right now, that doesn't mean he's going to forgive me. It doesn't mean things are going to be okay with us, that I'm off the hook and that we can build a relationship from here. How could we? A relationship on top of the charred remains of our hearts because of what I put him through? I can't let myself hope for anything.

Two more days and then he'll have fulfilled the one-week agreement and we'll go our separate ways. Right now he's mad at them, but he's still likely got all sorts of rage simmering beneath the surface for me.

He's been through trauma after trauma. I'm the reason he and his wolf split and his wolf locked him out after he was forced to spend all that time attached to me. I'm the reason he spent seven years in mourning. He got hit with drug darts, shot, stabbed, and almost blinded by a gas bomb. Beaten while he was unconscious, too. Of course he's pissed off.

Maybe he'll go on to fight with the ones who sentenced us, but hopefully he keeps his head clear and doesn't do anything reckless. I know from personal experience how harsh they can be.

I look at my phone and see a text from my sisters' group chat.

Vivi: Checking in, Erica.

I tap the flower twice. And then decide to add a third. And it's not exactly true, but another single flower reply could mean involvement from them. It's also not entirely a lie. I'm counting my blessings, so I'm a little better than I was. Because he's healed physically. So have Mason and Lincoln. He's speaking to me. And not that it should count, but I've had several orgasms in the past twelve hours not counting the many other ones over the past five days.

More than that, I got to feel what it feels like to lay underneath him, feeling his warmth, listening to him purr and feeling like he needed something I was able to give him. My presence. The soft looks, too. The soft voice and the soft looks and…

I shake it off again, my face hot as I root through the fridge and pull out a package of bacon and the half-full carton of eggs and shakily set about finding the rest of the implements needed to cook some food.

My phone rings. Vivica.

Shit.

"Hello?"

"You're lying about the third flower, aren't you?"

"Sometimes it's not good to have such perceptive relatives," I mutter.

34

RILEY

I'm about to step into the cabin, but I hear her talking on the phone. I also hear the person talking to her. My hearing is back at what it was. Maybe even sharper.

Though I'm raging with anger, still, and I've just been on the phone with Mase and Joel getting updated about all that's going on, I've now got a new focus. My mate. My mate who saved my life yesterday. And Mason's and Linc's. My mate who killed two assholes. My beautiful little witch who has been hurting for seven years waiting, wanting to be mine.

Ty didn't find that alpha asshole Wyatt Meadows. But Grey and Joel have been working on learning as much as they can about him and his pack.

My council co-alphas are capable, have shit under control, and will keep me in the loop where necessary, so I'm determined to focus on her, feeling like doing that will get me back to myself so I can do the right things, so I can move shit forward and deal with the garbage that got piled on her.

I wait and listen.

"You're lying about the third flower, aren't you?" the female voice on the phone accuses.

I can usually hear this well, but I haven't been at this level for the past week. My sense of smell has sprinted past full capacity, too. And I'm feeling closer to myself.

"Sometimes it's not good to have such perceptive relatives," my mate grumbles.

"What's happening?" the female on the phone asks.

"The pack bond means he had to be alone with me for a week to work things out after he wasn't able to stand being around me, so they sent us to Tyson Savage's cabin. Under duress."

"I know that much. Greyson told me."

"He's pretty cool, isn't he? He looks a little like Dad, Vivi."

"Does he?"

"Yeah." My mate sniffles. "A little."

"But we can talk about him later," the sister asserts, "Now explain things with you and Riley to me. Pretty please."

"It's too much to get into. I just need the rest of the week and then we'll be able to move forward with the rest of the plan."

I bristle. *Plan?*

"Is that gonna be how it goes?" Vivi asks. "The plan?"

"I ... expect so, even though he's acting weird." Rikki sounds distraught.

What plan? My mind races to the warning that Graydon Blackwood gave me about witches doing shit behind your back. What's this about? Was everything I was beginning to feel while my wolf locked me in wrong? Is this witch out to fuck me over? Again?

Alarm bells are ringing in my head.

I flex my jaw muscles, ready to push in and demand answers. But the pain of the notion keeps me rooted and listening instead. *No.* She saved my life. Everything she did boils down to how she feels about me.

"Does he want to end things?" the sister asks.

"I don't even know. He's acting weird."

"Elaborate, Erica."

My mate huffs. "It's not gonna make much sense unless I explain the whole thing. He's just outside talking on the phone."

"Just give me the gist, then. Maybe I can help you figure it out."

"He was furious. He hated me. We got stuck together because his knot was in me and wouldn't go down. We're also talking kidnappings, shootings, murders, getting stuck, and so much more. I can't get into it. He could come back in any second and there's a lot that's happened."

"Has he heard your side of things?"

"It... yeah... But it took a lot to even get him to listen. And then he... it was like he wanted to crawl out of his skin. And Scoob... his wolf locked him out after that, which isn't supposed to happen, but it did because he was so screwed up because of me, fighting the mating instincts because he hates me so much. Things were bad. Like, really bad. The shit I did to him split him into pieces of his old self. It was horrible to watch. But then other things happened and he's back in his own skin properly I guess and now he's *not* acting like he hates me and I... I won't get hopeful, you know? Hope is dangerous."

"Hope's not dangerous, sis. Aunt Mimi wants me to ask if you've mated with him, but you just said his knot was stuck, so that answers that."

"Yeah, but it was just biology. His urges. Instinct. I don't want to read it wrong. I'm sure in a couple days when the week is up he's gonna want the severing. And maybe he'll have forgiven me enough to buy me some good juju for that other situation coming up this fall. At least I hope he will."

"He might not want a severing."

"I mean, how could he not, though? That's been my plan all along. Explain. Apologize. And then let him finally move on with his life. "

Pain slashes through me as I hear her sniffle before continuing, the pain in her heart worming its way through mine.

"But then he purred for me and made love to me and now he's mad at other people, not me, and..." Her voice is wistful. Dreamy.

"Other people?"

"The people who chose this punishment. I'm... gotta admit, I'm confused, Vivi."

"Of course he's mad at the people who doled out that punishment. It was a bullshit punishment, Erica. We've all said that for years. Except you. We wanted to help you find a way out because it was so harsh and there you were... so broken up about it. You just took it and frankly, you shouldn't have. It broke you. You might have broken some rules, but you didn't deserve that."

Her emotions are pulsing toward me in a way that has me wanting to rip the door down and purr for her. But I need to hear the rest of this. Gain some more insight. Her plan is to let me go. But she doesn't want it. She's sure *I'll* want it.

"I had no choice, and you know it."

"I do know it, baby sister. You sacrificed everything for the greater good. And you'd keep doing it, too, because that's who you are. I also know you've beat yourself up too hard instead of realizing how harsh and unnecessary it was. Drinking that wine was an easy mistake any of us could've made. Any of us! The wine plus your heartbreak was the cause, but what happened after... it didn't need to go that way. They didn't need to punish you so severely. Didn't need to punish him that harshly either. I'm not surprised he's pissed at them. In fact, I'd be surprised if he wasn't. Of course he was angry that you were alive and hiding for all that time. Now he knows why and now you two can move forward. Forget the severing plan, I'd lay money down it won't happen. Your biggest ambition with that spelled wine wasn't to get rich, take over the world, or anything other than to have true love, Erica. God, think about it and realize you're not the bad guy here."

"Stop. I can't get my hopes up. He's mad at *them* now, but that might not erase all his anger at me. It's probably just temporary. He's been dealing with a lot and once he sifts through it all he's probably gonna realize he needs to start over. Start fresh with zero baggage."

"Making love to you, purring for you? That sounds pretty damn real to me."

"Biology. I think he's just having a biological stress reaction and... fighting his instincts messed with him. Maybe it's still messing with him. I need to hold fast and let the rest of the week ride out without hoping. I'll guard my heart."

I bare my teeth.

"Guard your heart, Erica? When have you ever been able to do that?" the sister asks.

"Stop knowing me so well, Vivi," she mutters.

I press my forehead against the door and sigh.

Vivi asks, "Does he even know that if the mate bond is severed, it'll only be severed for him? Not for you? That you'll live in pain for the rest of your life?"

Now I'm grinding my teeth.

"I'm not about to saddle him with that guilt."

"Erica..."

"No, I could probably use a fresh start, too."

Bullshit.

"Bull pucky," Vivi hisses, echoing my sentiment. "Of course you'd leave out the part about how bad it'd be for you. You've become addicted to wallowing in guilt. Enough."

"Stop," Rikki hisses. "I better go. He could be back in here any second and I'm making him breakfast."

"You don't eat breakfast, so that tells me you're looking after him. You're making him breakfast while simultaneously guarding your heart against heartbreak that you've been feeling non-stop for a decade since you laid eyes on him?"

"Shut up."

"While you prepare to let him live on happily without you and you won't even bother to tell him you're gonna give away the chance for you to also get closure and healing too because you bank up good stuff to give to other people. Because that's you, baby sis. Good stuff for everyone else, not you."

I frown.

"Not always," she fires back, "You know how impatient I am. How it often screws things up."

"Cut yourself some slack, Erica. For fuck's sake. Grab onto some happy and don't let go. You deserve it because you're you, but you especially deserve it after all you've been through."

"Goodbye, Vivi! Hanging up now."

"Good, Erica, because this was cliché as fuck."

I stand there a second, fists clenched, jaw clenched, and hear nothing else. Then there's the sizzle and scent of bacon and I hear an egg being cracked.

I open the door.

Her posture changes and though her back is still to me, it looks like she's bracing. And brace, she should.

I erase the space between us, turn the stove off, catch the back of her neck and spin her around to face me. She drops the whisk; it clatters to the floor as the bowl of eggs she was mixing falls into the sink.

Her eyes are wide with fear.

"You're my mate," I tell her, mouth an inch from hers.

Her eyes widen even further.

"I've been shitty since you got here. And you know why."

She frowns.

I grab her hips, hoist her up, and set her on the counter before moving in closer, palming both sides of her face.

"I'm done being shitty. I'm done, Rikki."

"Riley, I..." She looks so torn. She swallows. "I understand why you malfunctioned, and I take full responsibi-"

"I heard you on the phone just now. Heard every word you said and every word your sister Vivica said. My ears are working again. So's my fuckin' brain, I think." I tap my temple. "Finally."

She jerks back.

I run my finger across the bruise on her left wrist. "I'm done being a shitty mate. Leaving you unprotected to fend for yourself. I need to make it up to you. And I'm gonna do that, little witch. I'm gonna fuckin' do that." I kiss the bruise on her wrist.

She shakes her head and opens her mouth.

I cut her off before she can speak with a kiss and then I'm carrying her to the bedroom.

As soon as her back touches the mattress, I shimmy her dress up. She's wearing strappy black panties. They're gone in a flash and then my mouth is between her legs, tasting her.

"I've wanted to taste you for so long. I thought fate ripped away that chance."

She blows out a breath and then her mouth forms into a little O as my tongue swipes across her clit.

"And now you're here. In the flesh. Mine." I tighten my grip on her. "Never letting anyone or anything come between us again, mate."

She's wet for me, now whimpering for me. Squeezing my neck with her thighs, arching into my mouth as she fists my hair.

Swiping my tongue through her pretty, tight, pink folds, I latch onto her clit and suck hard. She cries out and it's a near feral sound. I slip two fingers into her slick heat and nudge her back door with my pinky. Swirling my tongue around her and gliding my free hand up her torso, under her dress, until I yank the cup of her bra down and get her silky nipple between my thumb and index knuckle, I apply pressure. Pressure with not only that hand, but also my mouth and my other hand.

A steady pumping of my fingers for a few minutes is followed by my pinky nudging in just a little. She comes so hard, she screams. And I'm ravenous for her, loving watching how she reacts, falling apart in my grasp. Riding my mouth and fingers, gasping for air. The hottest look on her face.

I can't wait to get inside her. I move up her body and lift her, spin her around, and then I'm on my back, guiding my cock into her dripping wet pussy. My beautiful mate's eyes are lustful and she's looking at me like I'm a god.

I like that look a lot.

I sit up and pull her tighter into me, bending my knees. "Ride me, little witch." I grab the bun in her hair and pull the rubber band out, so her curls fall in a gorgeous copper cascade. And then I whip the dress up and off before I latch onto a perfect pink nipple and take a pull.

She isn't moving enough. She's lost in sensation. Sexy as fuck with all those curls and those fuckin' freckles. So I help, grasping her hips, thrusting mine as I move her the way I want her.

"Mm, you feel so good, baby," I grind out as my eyes drink in her naked body.

She whimpers and grabs my face, crying out a melody on a perfect pitch as she holds on. And then I've got to hold on tighter as I knot her. Because I'm overcome with how good it feels. Not good; amazing. Amazing to know she's here, mine, taking my cock, tightening around that knot. She fits like she was made for me. She *was* made for me. She's mine. She's been through hell and back for wanting me, and she's still willing to crawl through fire for me. Saving lives. Trying to take on my pain. But she won't. I won't fuckin' allow it. Nobody's gonna get in the way of us again and it's my job to make her happy.

"Beautiful," I say against her mouth and use my thumbs to wipe the tears off her cheeks. "My mate. You're here. Do you know how badly I ached for you?"

She sobs. There's guilt pulsing from her inside my chest.

"No, baby. Don't. Don't feel guilty. Don't be sad. You're here. You're alive. And you're mine. Nobody's ever gonna keep us apart again. Fuck them. They're gonna answer to me for what they did to you. What they did to *us*." I wipe more tears away as my knot continues pulsing.

"Oh Riley," she sobs.

"I feel your pain, baby. I also feel how you feel about me. I'm gonna get this pain outta the way so we can be happy. Okay?"

She sobs harder and holds me tight, her hot pussy milking me in a way that has to be magic.

Then I'm coming again, hard. I roar as sensation takes over and I'm unable to speak anymore. Instead, I suckle my mark on her while we ride out the sensations until I fall to my back, and she goes limp on top of me. My knot releases, but I feel her walls squeeze like she wants to keep me inside. What my mate wants, she gets. From now on.

My cock responds by going hard again and my knot returns as she sighs into my throat, nuzzling, practically purring herself.

I'd feel completely at peace right now except for the fact that I feel what's happening inside her. And it's a war. She's at war with herself, her conscience I guess. She's spent the better part of a decade feeling immense guilt. And I'll bust my back figuring out how to fix it.

There's also the not-small fact that there are people who will answer for this shit. I can't wrap my head around why the supernatural council collective would be so fucking harsh against a twenty-one-year-old witch who'd only been practicing for three years.

Shifters take their mate without regard for rules. Steal them from fake mates. Take them from their packs, their families, without a second thought. Why is my little witch being punished so harshly for going after what's rightfully hers? She identified me before I identified her for a switch. *That's* what happened here.

And my head is finally straightening out. I see clearly. I feel her. I feel myself. My shit is fusing tighter together by the minute.

I've got the faint scents of Cade and Gus in my nose as I know they're watching the perimeter of the property from a distance, but close enough to intervene if any shit goes wrong.

I'm also feeling slightly better after my calls. Joel, Jase, and Linc are taking turns manning the surveillance cams and my father and Mase's father are taking turns with four of our men at the town hall while several continually scope the area outside our village on four paws at night, on two legs during the day.

We're in code orange right now, the dial veering toward red. Sussing out and figuring out a plan to deal with the situation with Greyson's mate's brother and the rest of that pack.

What we know at this stage is that it's a pack in Silver Hills, about six hours northwest and Stacy's brother Wyatt Meadows is the alpha. They wanted Ty dead because he allegedly killed their father several years ago after a dogfight match and an argument with Uncle Cornelius. They're a pack that keeps to themselves and Stacy says they think our pack is an abomination. They want to take the rest of our super-alphas out and absorb our pack into their own, taking over this territory as they're power-hungry and want dominion over the magic in the region. They lost their witch, a witch who was a hostage and forced to make potions for them. Losing their witch explains why they want mine.

I don't know what men, potions, and firepower they have still at their backs, but we do know they're only too happy to enlist the help of chemical warfare against us. They masked their scents to sneak up on this cabin the other night. But not well enough because my wolf caught their scent. And that might be down to the fact that I was locked out. My senses were fucked but that doesn't mean my wolf's were.

I've insisted I'm brought into things if I'm needed and that I want to know everything. I've assured my co-alphas I'm on the way back to being myself.

They're insistent that I focus on my relationship. And I plan to do that, too. I feel capable of doing it all.

I hold her for a while, a long while enjoying how right she feels. Languishing in her scent, the sound of her breathing, knowing she's awake but feeling mostly content being still. Purring for her. But when hunger niggles at me, I slide out from under her so I can go finish cooking up the breakfast she started.

I turn the bacon back on, crack a few new eggs and drop some bread into the toaster.

I wander back in a while later with two cups of coffee and she's resting her head on her elbow lying at the bottom of the bed, staring out the window. I set the plates down on the edge of the bed, kiss her softly and feel that she watches me leave the room. I come back with breakfast, set the plates on the bed, and sit.

She gnaws on her lower lip while looking at me with an unreadable expression. I'd ruminate on the fact it's a good thing I can read her emotions, but I can't, really, as they're a tangled mess right now and I don't know her well enough yet to untangle them. I do know she feels at war with herself.

I take a piece of bacon from one of the plates and hold it out in front of her. She sits up and reaches for it. I shake my head and touch her lips with the tip of it. She opens her mouth and takes a little bite.

I see the outline of the glass jar I've spotted a number of times the last few days. It's inside one of her bags, so I set the meat on the plate before stretching to grab it.

"Riley," she whispers, looking panicked.

"Said you put notes in here over the past seven years to show me about things you did while we were apart?"

"Every piece is a fact or an outcome of someone I was able to help."

"Yeah?"

"Most are people you've never met, but also a couple you have met. But I'm not sure about this now. Maybe you shouldn't read them."

"You wrote them for me to read, right?" I ask.

She twists her lips adorably, looking conflicted.

"I didn't want to sacrifice your happiness for all this," she says. "I didn't want to pick magic over you, but I was stuck. So stuck. And hurting. And aching for you. Just aching to tell you the truth so that you could move on with your life once you realized how badly I fucked things up. I wasn't allowed. But now, here... I can give you the choice. You can choose to sever our connection and then you can move on. Maybe find someone worthy of you." She swallows. "But asking you to read those? Now it sounds kind of dumb and self-serving."

"Doesn't seem dumb to me. Of course I wanna know what you were doing while we were apart."

I grab a fork, saw off a piece of fried egg and fork it up, bringing it to her mouth. She hesitantly opens her mouth and accepts it. I set the fork down and unscrew the lid.

She fidgets, so my eyes bounce to her; she looks worried.

"Just so you know, I didn't know what you were doing, Riley. I wasn't allowed to look into you or ask anyone any questions. I could only guess."

"I went off for a few months. Hunted a lot. Howled in grief a lot."

Her lip trembles.

"But then I came back and tried to focus on my pack. I got appointed to the council and it probably saved me. I threw myself into it. Found out Tyson's alive and that helped, too. Gave me hope."

She smiles. "I..." she swallows. "I might have helped with that part a little bit."

"Yeah?" I ask.

"It's not in there but..." she gestures to the jar. "we turned the volume up on all your scents to make him want to come to the village that day. So he'd show himself."

I caress her face and she leans into it. We hold one another's gaze for a long moment before I turn my attention to the jar.

Inside are many folded pieces of paper. Mostly white, but some pink, yellow, and one blue. Some are Post-it notes. Some are lined or unlined sheets of paper. I dump them onto the bed between our plates, unfold a white one and read aloud.

"Helped Ronnie with locator spell to find an abducted child. Ransom was due two hours from the time we found him."

My eyes meet hers. She looks down at the plate.

I lift a slice of toast and hold it out. She reaches to take it, but I pull back and instead touch the corner to her mouth.

"I'm feeding you breakfast," I say. "I'm taking care of my mate right now. You got a problem with that?"

She shakes her head, looking bewildered.

I hold it out again and she takes a bite.

I set it down, wipe the crumbs from my fingers on my pantleg before folding the piece of paper up again and dropping it into the empty jar. I reach for another piece of paper.

"Kept bad guys away from girl in danger. Chicago."

She moistens her lips and elaborates, "She's going to do great things in her life. Vivi saw it, saw she was in danger, and we were really close by, had gone on a girls' shopping and theater trip. We intervened to keep them from getting her. They were human traffickers. We also kinda helped them get caught on another occasion."

"Good," I remark and pass her a cup of coffee, then put the paper into the jar and pick up a yellow Post-It. I unfold it.

"Redirected love letter from wrong house. They will have two babies. One baby will grow up to be a veterinarian and save many pet lives."

I smile, put the paper in the jar, then lift a pink piece of paper.

"Saved lives by containing entity in Drowsy Hollow woods. Helped facilitate journey to fated forever love."

I give her a pointed look. "Same woods where you and me met?"

She nods. "Aunt Lyrica died that day. It was a race against the clock to get here on time. I was gonna fail so we did a different remote spell and... it worked out. Mostly."

"I know who this is. We stay out of those woods after dark in the fall. My grandfather was chased as a young wolf by that... thing... and was lucky to make it out of there."

"Aunt Lyrica helped him get out of there," she says. "I saw it in one of her ledgers. He needed to get out of there otherwise there wouldn't be you, wouldn't be Tyson, you get the idea. This is why it's so important my coven keeps their magic. The effects are far-reaching."

"I can see that," I say.

She pulls her lips tight and eyeballs the plate. I lift up some bacon and she takes a bigger bite than last time and chews it while watching me lift another piece of paper.

"I give thanks to your Aunt Lyrica for it."

"I miss her. It was a blow, losing her. It was also quite a hairy experience trying to get things under control with those woods."

"So you'll do it again this year?"

"Not exactly. Things have changed. I can't get into it, I don't think. I may need guidance from Aunt Mimi on what I can and can't tell you. Sometimes when someone finds out about our magic or when they learn they benefit from it, they have to pay a toll for the knowledge."

"Your Aunt Mimi might have a problem with me," I warn. "I wasn't exactly... polite when I met her. Or when I knocked on the door to her house.

She didn't look pleased, either, when she saw me tracking her around her town."

She nods. "I know. She raised me since I was twelve and is the closest thing I have to a mother. She's the elder and leader of our coven, mostly retired now, but she still dabbles a little."

"I'll win her over," I say and give her a smile.

She smiles back, but it's hesitant.

I turn my attention back to the jar and grab another folded paper. "Matched up kidney donor and recipient? AJS. Nice one. What's AJS?"

"Just the initials of the recipient so I'd remember. We've been involved in a few similar situations. Some other things were going to get in the way of that one because of some magic performed by an irresponsible coven. One of their elders came to us to ask for help. We occasionally work with some of them. It was destined to happen, so we had to help get the interfering thing out of the way."

I drop the paper in the jar.

Another: "Helped woman find out her husband was cheating in time for her to meet the love of her life. Now happily married and spend thanksgivings feeding homeless."

Next: "Reunited a man with his adult child that didn't know he existed in time to give him a bone marrow transplant."

"More eggs?" she asks.

I lift the fork and she gets another bite.

"Your sister said you don't eat breakfast," I say.

"I do when I've been extraordinarily active multiple times leading up to breakfast time."

"Guess you're now a breakfast person," I tell her, lifting a slice of bacon from the other plate and popping it in my mouth.

Her eyes light with humor, but I'm not sure she believes that this is real. I'll prove it.

After washing it down with some coffee, I lift another piece of paper from the bed. There are dozens more of these.

"Delayed a flight with Vivi and Jessica's help. Might have saved 327 lives."

"Vivi got a vision."

I give her a pointed look and sip my coffee again before reading the next one.

"Worked with Jessica to redirect stoned airline mechanic away from their job so they would not make a critical error."

"Vivi called from the dentist's chair all frozen mid-filling because she got a vision of someone slipping a drug into a woman's macchiato in a coffee shop." She sips her coffee. "It might not have hit the airline mechanic until she was at work. We think Vivi got the image for good reason. Could've caused a problem with that flight."

I read another. "Helped a student find their acceptance letter into a prestigious program. It went to the wrong house. That student will meet the love of their life in that prestigious program."

My mate softly responds, locking my gaze with hers. She has such beautiful eyes. "They've probably met by now, in fact. Sometimes it's lives at stake," she says, "And sometimes it's love at stake. And love is worthwhile. Sometimes we're called to intervene and maybe that intervention is only a small piece of a bigger puzzle. Butterfly effect kind of thing. You know what I mean?"

"I do," I say without breaking eye contact until I have another folded piece of paper opened. The only blue one in the batch.

She bites her lip and looks nervous. Red creeps over her cheeks.

"Helped your mom narrowly miss a head-on collision with a truck during an ice storm."

I do a double-take and read the paper a second time, but in my head.

"Helped your mom?" I ask.

"Yours. Yeah. Whoops. Kind of selfish of me to list the extra detail. I'm not a complete martyr, I guess. It was her and your sister in the car."

She lifts a piece of bacon from her plate and feeds it to me.

"I'll read the rest of these later," I say after swallowing and scoop up the remaining folded pieces of paper, setting them all on the chair. I move the plates and the jar to the floor, feeling her eyes on me.

I roll into her and cup her jaw. "I was hungry for food. Now I'm hungry for you."

"I was enjoying my breakfast," she teases, looking embarrassed.

"I failed you, Rikki."

Her expression drops. "Huh. What? How did *you* fail *me*?"

"I'm your mate. It's my job to protect you. I didn't."

She jolts in surprise. "You didn't know."

"Doesn't matter. It's my job."

"But it wasn't yet. You couldn't know."

"Doesn't matter. Still my job."

"We...you..." She looks adorably confused. "That doesn't make sense. It was an impossible situation."

"Right. Like the one you're in right now, little witch?"

She opens and closes her mouth, looking speechless.

I scoff. "Because to me it seems like that harsh punishment is to blame more than you here. You beat yourself up, but you were in an impossible situation, too."

"How could I not? It's my fault. I drank the wine that was already opened. I cast the spell."

"Did you know the wine was open?"

"It didn't really dawn on me until later. I was being careless. I can't be careless. I know better."

"We're all guilty of that sometimes aren't we?"

She doesn't answer.

"Right," I continue, "And did you then do something awful, or did you do what the universe intended anyway?"

"I forced it to happen early, Riley. It wasn't time."

"But did they have to make us wait seven years? Did they need to deliver that harsh of a punishment? Could they have found some other way to get their point across without putting you through torture? Without me being left to mourn you when you weren't dead? Leaving me to blame myself thinking I'd scared you off that cliff?"

She blows out a long breath.

"Woman, I couldn't do anything about it then. But I can do something now. So I'm gonna do what I can do to fix this for us. Because it's my job. My job and my honor, mate, because I'm supposed to keep you safe. In here, too." I lay a palm on her chest. "You suffered for seven fuckin' years and I could've been there to fix it, but I wasn't."

"That doesn't make sense, Riley."

"Nope," I reply.

"You couldn't have stopped it." She pleads with me to believe her.

So I do the same. "I don't see how you could've stopped it either if it was meant to go this way or if powers higher up than you deemed it be this way. So how about we do what we *can* do? Take care of one another going from here. Yeah? You were made for me. I was made for you. We fit. We just haven't gotten the chance to let it be how it's meant to be."

"But... you were so mad at me."

"I was. I was furious. But I didn't have all the facts. And I'm still angry. At a lot of things. The last few days I've been most angry at myself."

She looks confused.

"Time to fix that. Time to work on us."

"Us?"

"Us," I confirm.

She shivers. "You have to request a severing."

"What?"

"I've been so sad for so long Riley. I don't know how to not be sad. I'm probably too broken at this point, so it might be best that you request a severing and then move on."

"Me move on and leave you wallowing in pain when I could fix it?" I volley.

"I don't know if you could fix it." She tries to move away.

I stop her, holding her face with both hands. "When I not only get to fix it, when I get to have you? Don't think I can fix it? Watch me."

"I don't know how you could forgive me. I also don't think *I* can forgive me."

"Think you could have it in you to forgive me for completely malfunctioning when you came here to make it right?"

"That wasn't your fault."

"See? You've already done it. Now I'll help you forgive yourself. But gotta say, I'm gutted over what I did, how I acted. After all you went through you then have to deal with that shit?"

"It was normal. You were shocked. Then you thought I betrayed you on purpose." She shrugs.

"And then your pain leaked all over me, little witch, and fuck did it hurt."

She looks about to crumble. I pull her close. She presses her forehead into my chest.

I purr for a minute for her and she sniffles, sinking deeper into me.

"I feel your feelings. When you're sad. When you're excited. When you're torn about something. You got here with a fuck-ton of emotions and they came at me like a hurricane. I soaked it in, Rik. Yeah, it fucked with me. Badly. Feeling all you were feeling is what's fucked with me the most out of all of this."

"I'm sorry, Riley."

"Stop apologizing. I'm done hearing it. I don't need it. Okay?"

She nods and looks into my eyes.

"Then that fucker takes you and you have to watch me end him… making you fear me, fear my wolf?" I grind my teeth. "Never killed another shifter, a human either. But something snapped when he took you, when I saw you bound and afraid. Then to make it worse, I take you and mate you that way? Rough like that? After I took you and mated you that way, my psyche splitting in two… my knot holdin' on because my body knew even if I couldn't get my head together that we belong together? Then jumpin' ahead to being in time out for that time and seeing you through my wolf's eyes, seeing you a little more relaxed, having time to think things through and un-fuck my head? But then you were again in danger due to my fuckin' negligence, I finally snapped out of it because above everything, you're here. You're alive. That's what matters. You're here, you're mine, and you want me. And I don't wanna lose you again. Correction: I won't lose you. There's nothing in the way anymore if I can get my head outta my ass. I get to have what I've been fuckin' aching to have for seven years. My head's out and it's staying out. I'm sorry, baby. So fuckin' sorry for leavin' you in a parking lot vulnerable. And… I'm sorry about something else, too."

"What's that?"

"That I took your virginity that way."

She jolts with surprise.

"Yeah, your sister, Jessica? She showed up at a bar where I'd planned to hook up with a random stranger to work you out of my system. She showed and told me you saved it for me. Saved it after everything."

"I didn't know if you'd want it."

"Of course I'd want it. I'm wrecked over how I took it. It's been fucking with me since right after it happened. Fucked me sideways that I did that to you, lost it like that."

"It was always yours to have, no matter which way you took it. I'm just glad it went to you."

"You're a fucking miracle, Erica Savage."

She jerks in surprise and stares at me a second.

"Yeah, Erica Savage. You want a wedding? You don't need it, whatever. You're my wife in my eyes and my pack's eyes now. No severing, little witch. Not now, not ever."

She begins to weep. Hard.

I lay down with her and purr.

"I..." she sniffles, "I don't want anybody to pinch me right now because if this isn't real, I don't wanna know."

I pinch her ass and she giggles, tears in her eyes. Love in her eyes. I kiss her and purr some more.

"I don't want you to fall into things and then realize you made a mistake not getting a fresh start when it's what's best for you, Riley."

"Baby, I swear I'm never gonna feel that way. Not ever. I'm really glad you saved that for me. I'm also really glad your sister stopped me that night because it's only been you for me. Since the day you bumped into the fire hydrant."

35

ERICA

I want more than anything to believe him.

I *do* feel too broken to be fixed. I didn't think it was possible. Him. Us. A future.

He purrs for at least an hour with me lying close, my head on his chest, and it feels so good to be held, feels so right to hear that noise, smell his scent. I don't ever want it to stop, but nature calls, so I finally get up and go to the bathroom, feeling his eyes on me as I leave the room.

I refuse to look at myself in the bathroom mirror, fearing facing the idiot in the reflection. The self-loathing slithering through me is intense right now, though not enough for me to pull away when he touches me. Not enough for me to resist letting the warmth seep in when he holds me, when he purrs for me.

When I come out, he's dumping the contents of our breakfast plates into a trash bin by the fridge.

"It went cold. Didn't get enough to eat. Want something else?"

"Yeah," I say and approach. When I get to him, he's setting the plates into the sink. I get up on my tippytoes and wrap my arms around his neck.

His eyes sparkle and he gives me a wide smile.

I thread my fingers into his hair and stare into his eyes.

God, I could look deep like this forever if he looked at me like this all the time.

"What do you want, little witch?" he asks, voice gravelly.

And my belly dips. I want to make him happy. That's what I want. I want him to always look at me like this.

"I want you," I say.

And then I drop to my knees, taking his lounge pants with me.

His cock bobs up and I watch him grip the counter on either side of himself as my mouth wraps around him.

The look on his face is hot. Sizzling hot.

I pop him out and say, "I've never done this before, so feel free to make suggestions." Our eyes are locked as I wrap my lips around him and take him in deeper.

And the look on his face is all the encouragement I need to do my best to make it good for him.

"Fuck, that's some magic right there, little witch," he groans.

And then it seems like he loses his ability for speech as he grips the counter harder, throat bobbing.

"Oh, well since I'm not supposed to use magic," I say, planting a kiss on his hipbone. "But when it comes to you? Fuck the rules."

"Get that back in your mouth," he orders, eyes looking dangerous. His fingers thread into my hair.

So I get back to it, feeling heat and moisture between my legs at the command.

"I'm gonna come down your throat if you don't stop that," he warns, not long later.

My reply must be clear as I gaze up at him communicating with my eyes and more suction that it's exactly what I want. It must be clear because he wobbles and then it happens. He comes in my mouth.

And it's an awesome thing to watch. Muscles straining in his neck. Fingers flexing. Lips parting, eyes flashing with satisfaction.

"You looked fuckin' breathtaking on your knees looking up at me, while taking my cock, looking at me like you want to give me everything."

I sit back on my heels.

"I do," I admit, licking my lips.

He lifts me up and carries me to bed.

"You're still hard?" I asks as he throws my legs up and lines up, rubbing the hard crown of himself through my wetness.

"That answer your question?"

"I figured you'd need a breather. Mortal men would."

"Nuh uh. It's good to be a wolf shifter sometimes," he flashes a grin.

"Except when your parts work when you don't want them to?"

"Was it so bad?" he asks, mouth touching mine.

I smirk.

"I agree," he replies softly, and then slides inside.

36

RILEY

It's the following day, early afternoon and we've been alternating between fucking and sleeping while getting acquainted.

I've told her about work, updated her about my family, about the pack as well as given her the gist of both Ty and Mase's matings, which she enjoyed hearing about considering her family's involvement.

She told me about her sisters, her aunts, about losing her parents and went into more detail about how her nature was revealed to her. She also shared that she loved everything about being a witch, feeling in tune with nature especially.

"We need food," I tell her.

"Yeah," she whispers, then swings a leg over my torso to climb on top of me. "But first this."

I guide my cock to her entrance but hold it there.

"We need sustenance after this time, little witch. Or you're gonna be the cause of my death by starvation."

We skipped dinner last night and haven't eaten yet today.

"Okay," she whispers against my mouth and then greedily pulls my hand away so she can sink down onto me, letting out a sweet little moan.

"Seven years to make up for," I say against her claiming mark.

"I'm down for that," she replies. "Think we're doing okay so far."

"We sure are," I say. "Love that nobody's touched you. You saved it all for me. Baby, that makes me very fuckin' happy. Thank you, for saving it for me."

"Nothing past second base and that's before my twenty-first birthday when I cast the spell. I turn twenty-eight soon."

"I haven't touched anybody either. Not on purpose."

Her eyes bore into mine and I like that look.

"Had a few make passes. A few sneak attack kisses or gropes but I was the recipient and never reciprocated. Never wanted anyone after I thought I lost you."

"I hoped you'd find someone," she says, swaying softly on me, leaning back, her gorgeous curls touching my thighs.

"I hope you're lying to me right now. Then let that be the last lie you tell your mate, darlin'," I run my hand up her stomach and caress her breast.

"I didn't want you to be lonely because of what I did, Riley."

"I found ways to busy myself."

"I wouldn't let anyone call me Rikki after that day. Dad used to call me that. I'd lost the two most important men in my life, and I didn't feel like Rikki anymore."

"You want me to stop?" I ask.

She shakes her head. "I like hearing it from you."

I squeeze her thigh with affection. "It's mine then. To everyone else around here, you're Erica."

"Works for me."

"Thank you for writing me all those notes. I'll read the rest later. I understand what you went through. I fuckin' hate that you went through it. Thank you for saving my life yesterday and Mase and Linc's, too. I'm gonna make up for lost time. I'm gonna make you happy, little witch."

"You've already done that, Scooby Dooby."

I smile.

"So... seven years with nothing. A virile man like you? Did you ever touch yourself and think of me?" she asks, a naughty grin on her face.

I like the look of it, too.

"Almost every night," I tell her with my own grin. "Some mornings, too."

"I touched myself while thinking of you," she tells me, voice husky.

"Did you?"

"Yes. A lot. Sometimes used toys. Imagining being with you. It was nowhere close to how good the reality is."

"Show me," I request.

She looks shy all of a sudden, so I take her by the hips and bounce her on me, rocking my hips. "Touch yourself," I whisper.

Her cheeks go pink and she chews on her lip.

"Never be embarrassed with me. Not ever. It'll rock my world to watch you touch yourself while you ride my cock. I mean it. Do that for me?"

"Okay," she whispers, eyes bright with emotion.

And I know this girl would do anything for me. This is what I've been waiting for. Her. My mate.

I pull her latest cute little dress (that she's only had on for five minutes) up over her head and toss it, then watch as she presses her fingers against her clit. She rubs in little circles and it's hot as sin to watch her doing that with me inside her.

"Show me better," I say. "I wanna see more."

She leans back and spreads her lips wider.

My knot snaps out and begins vibrating inside her. This makes her whine, arching, grabbing my hair with both hands. She stares into my eyes as she loses it. And I fuckin' love it.

"Don't stop. Keep going," I demand, pulling her right hand down and pushing it back between her legs. I watch her fingers, eyes darting up to take in the look on her gorgeous face as she whimpers, then she's crying out louder. Music to my ears. My mate has a beautiful voice.

My phone rings. I can see the screen from here.

Mitchell Blakely calling.

Fury takes over and without calculation, I grab it.

"Mitch," I clip.

Her face changes and she looks horrified, covering her mouth. My knot is still going so although her hand covers her mouth it doesn't do much to tamp down her reaction.

"So, you've mated, I take it," Mitch says in his thick Scottish brogue.

My knot halts. "I'm inside her right now," I snap. "And you've got some goddamn explaining to do."

She jerks in shock, looking angry with me. She's about to get off me, but I stop her by grabbing an ass cheek.

She leans over and bites my neck. And it's hot as fuck, rather than punishing.

"Sorry, baby," I whisper, squeezing her ass.

"We'll need to meet then," Mitch replies, sounding business-like. "Prepare for me and some other guests. I'll be in touch with details on our arrival. The next few days, I'd imagine."

"Are you fuckin' kidding me?" I snap.

"No, Riley. I'm not."

"Unbelievable. You sound mighty blasé for the shit you've put us through. Get your ass here, then," I say.

"Keep a tight leash on her until then, Riley," Mitch advises.

"Excuse me? You wanna lose your fuckin' teeth?"

"After mating you, we ascertained her powers would be amplified. Significantly. Be careful, Riley. If the other witches are correct, she could be dangerous."

"Dangerous?" My eyes search her face.

My mate can obviously hear him because she looks baffled.

"Dangerous, Riley. Lots to update you about. I'll be in touch. Just ask her to be careful. Safe. Not to wield any powers without some guidance from the SCC. Please? Tell her it's an order."

"I'll make that request," I say.

"No, Riley. Give that as an order to your mate. From us and from you. Exert the mate bond if you must. I'm not jokin', lad. It's important. Please tell her so."

"I'm not about to blindly agree to anything without a meeting and an explanation about why things have gone down the way they have. I'm not very fuckin' happy. In fact, call me the polar opposite of happy right now because you and whoever else made this decision caused a shitload of unnecessary pain to my woman, not to mention me."

"The SCC witches deemed it necessary, my friend."

"I'd take your word for it, but I happen to have zero trust and a whole lot of animosity right now so get your ass here as soon as possible so we can hash this out."

"Do not forget who you're talking to, Savage. I realize who you are and how powerful your pack is, but do not forget that the council that oversees all supernaturals is involved here and it's advisable for you to hold your temper in check. I'm on your side. I'm one of you and believe me, if anyone fucked with my mate the way we fucked with yours, I'd be just as livid."

"Yet you were part of it."

"There are reasons, Riley. I didn't agree with their approach until they took the time to explain why they had to be so harsh."

"Not sure any of your reasons can possibly justify what was done, but I'll listen to what you have to say. I'm making no promises of future cooperation after this. The SCC crossed the goddamn line."

"Need I remind you I sided with you guys after that cock up that just happened with Mason Quinn and his mate's ex-fiancé?"

"Seven years I thought she was fuckin' dead!" I shout.

"I know," he says softly.

"Seven years she felt so guilty she's practically unrecognizable."

She jolts, looking devastated.

I keep going. "I'm freshly mated after seven years of fuckin' grieving my mate who wasn't actually dead, so maybe you all oughta tread carefully with me right now. I know who I'm talking to. I know who I am and what I stand for, and this was cruel. You're a bunch of cruel and heartless bastards and as her mate, it's on me to straighten shit out."

"I can see this conversation isn't going to go anyplace productive until you get all the details, so let me get off the phone here so I can make some calls and gather resources. We'll come see you. I'm not holding anything you say against you, Riley, but please be reasonable with the other council members. They're not all as understanding as I am."

Incensed, all I manage is, "Bye." I end the call and toss the phone.

She's got pain in her eyes. And awe, if I'm not mistaken.

She opens her mouth.

"No point," I cut her off. "We'll see what they say."

"My magic felt crazy-strong when those guys grabbed me. Like I didn't even have to work for it. Like... I did stuff I didn't know I could do."

"No magic until we know more, maybe."

She nods. "Yeah. I killed two men. It just came out of me, and I didn't know they'd die."

I hook a hand around her neck and bring her mouth to mine.

"I killed two people, Riley. I've never killed before. Maybe I'm gonna get in trouble for that."

"They deserved it. Just like the fucker I took out. And I did that on purpose. How about a bath together? Relax us both."

She nods again, looking in thought.

"What's on your mind? Something besides guilt you don't need to feel?"

"I think I want Aunt Mimi here for whatever this meeting they're talking about is. And my sisters."

"When I hear back from Mitch, you tell 'em."

She nods.

"Bath?" I ask.

"Okay."

"Then we'll eat something. For real this time. I'm dyin' for a big, juicy steak and all the fixins. I'm gonna ask one of the guys to drop off food from Roxy's. Got any cravings?"

"A banana split," she tells me.

"Ice cream? We need food, woman."

She elaborates, running her fingers through my hair. "You offered to buy me a banana split the day I hit the fire hydrant. I really wanted it."

"Oh yeah?" I ask, anger already coming down a notch.

"I hadn't wanted to eat ice cream since the day I dropped my ice cream cone watching my parents burst into flames. But I wanted ice cream that day by the fire hydrant. I didn't have any. Haven't had any since I was a kid. But I really, really wanna share some ice cream with you."

I smile and caress her face. "You hungry for something with nutrients first?"

She sighs. "Bananas are very nutritious; I'll have you know."

I smile.

"Need to take care of my mate."

"Just so you know, I often eat dessert for dinner."

"Eat some food like a good little witch and then you can have dessert."

She pouts.

I hold my ground.

She sighs. "Okay, how about some garlic bread with cheese and a bowl of creamy soup of some sort?"

"I'll make it happen," I vow, kissing her.

"SO... BABIES," I SAY, soaping up her shoulders.

She stiffens.

"Mase and Ty's mates are pregnant already. Best keep at makin' up for lost time so we have a chance of our firstborn being born in the same year for the next council." I kiss her earlobe.

"Um..."

I twist, turning her so I can see her face because her emotions are going a little berserk right now. It's a strange sensation.

I jerk my chin up in question. "You don't want kids?"

"It's not that. I do want kids. As many of them as I can have."

"Can't have them? Mase's mate thought she couldn't have kids. Turned out she just couldn't have 'em without Mase."

"I want kids, Riley. Your kids."

"Good. I sense a *but* coming."

"I can't tell you when I might be able to give you kids because of something I did." She looks panicked. Stricken even.

I wait. But she says nothing, so I say, "You wanna explain?"

"I um... see... this is another reason I wanted to give you the option of a severing. Because-"

"Don't," I clip. "Not happening. Not ever. You hear me? Stop sayin' that fuckin' word."

She winces.

"Tell me," I demand.

"Well, now you're pissed with me, and I understand why, but can we get out of here and dry off so I can explain?"

I summon some patience. "Yeah. If you promise to stop saying severing. If we have issues to figure out, we'll figure them out."

"Okay. Stop being mad at me. Please?"

"Wolf shifters mate for life, little witch. Stop suggesting anything otherwise and I'll stop being testy."

"Okay."

She looks contrite as she stands. I get out quickly so I can wrap her in a towel, which I can tell she likes by the soft expression on her face. The face she made for my wolf while I was locked in. I wrap another around my waist and lead her to the bedroom and say, "Sit down."

She sits on the end of the bed, wrapped in the towel, so I grab another towel from the cabinet and begin drying her hair, then I dry her little feet.

She's ticklish, so she squirms. "Nooo tickling!"

"Not tickling on purpose," I tell her, then I pin her to the bed and then drop a kiss on the pad of her left big toe.

"You're so sweet, Riley."

I toss the towel on the back of the chair. "Okay, tell me. No wait…" I sniff the air. "Sean's here and he has food."

"Sean?"

"Beta in our pack. Meet me in the kitchen."

37

ERICA

He's halfway into his steak dinner when he gives me a pointed look. "Kids?"

I wince.

"Tell me," he orders.

He looks so sexy sitting across from me eating his big meal with his wet hair and his bare chest. He's in just a pair of lounge pants and although I'm enjoying watching him enjoy his food, I just want to crawl into his lap and make out with him. And more. I want his mouth between my legs again, with as much vigor as he devours that meal.

I shove away my extreme horniness and take a big breath, setting down my spoon. "I made a promise that helped me save someone's unborn child. It was really messy. They made mistakes and had to atone and... it's a long story and I don't think I can give out too much detail, but we performed a spell that puts that child in a safe place until his mother can safely carry him."

"All right," he says. I know he doesn't *get* it.

I continue, "It's to do with the woods where we... where I... you know."

His eyes flash. He knows I'm talking about the entity that haunted those woods.

I continue. "I promised his fated mate that I would carry their baby if I couldn't get him back to her. They made some mistakes and had to pay a toll. It's a pretty harsh one too. Sometimes that's how magic works."

"I get that you're drawing parallels here between them and us. But not sure I get it completely, babe. Surrogacy?"

"A supernatural surrogacy. I made it so I can accept the pregnancy if something stops her from being able to carry, such as her death. I can't become pregnant any time soon just in case I have to do that."

"So, if we hadn't gotten together and that happened there'd be a birth, an immaculate conception sort of thing?"

"I'd just be a host. He's already been conceived; I moved him from her womb and he's in a state of pause in a safe place in the fae realm. They allowed me to use it twice. I won't be able to use it a third time. He's safe until he either gets put back into his mother's body, or he'll go into mine."

"I see," Riley says carefully, looking like he's considering this for a moment, then asks, "Why's it your responsibility to carry their baby?"

"It's not. Or... it wasn't. But I offered. So, now it is."

He regards me without saying anything, so I continue.

"I won't break that promise."

"Pretty big sacrifice, promising someone that."

"I never make promises lightly. That couple has been through a lot. Like... *a lot a lot*. And I don't know if she'll survive where they are now. It's a long story, Riley, but they're locked somewhere now and when it's time for them to come out, I'll find out if I need to carry their baby."

"What if you go into heat? Because now that we're mated, it could happen. In fact, it *will* happen. It's just a matter of when."

"I know that there are heat cycles that go with the moon when mated to a shifter. Or that just go because of biology. I didn't expect this."

"This?"

"Us. I didn't know when I'd have to come face you, although when I did that, I did suspect it'd be soon. And I really didn't expect you to want anything other than to sev – *end* our bond. I guess I would ask you to try really hard to not impregnate me."

He snickers. "Not sure it works that way."

"We could use birth control."

He shakes his head. "Won't react well with heat mixed with my chemistry. It put Ivy's life in danger. Nobody knew she was on the birth control pill until it was almost too late. She got real sick. So sick, Ty thought he was gonna lose her."

I'm about to tell him I'm talking about condoms, but he speaks again.

"Is there some way to keep this unborn child safe if you get pregnant until after you've given birth to our baby?"

"If Isabella is dead when we bring her back to this realm, their child will immediately be in my uterus. I've already cast the spell. When I write spells, I have to have all contingencies figured out, but... I didn't think of *this* contingency."

"Why not?" he asks.

"I thought there was no hope for you and me," I admit. "I thought you'd just see me as an enemy. I knew there was a possibility you might even have found someone else to spend your life with." I swallow hard.

He bares his teeth.

I shrug.

He sighs. "What if you're already pregnant when this happens? If she dies..."

"I... don't know. I have to research that."

"I'm not saying I don't respect the promise you made, but when an alpha goes into the rut, baby..." He gives me a pointed look. "I don't need to tell you this. You've been here the past six days with me."

I twist my fingers in my lap. "See, I made this promise knowing there was a good chance I'd have to face you before things got resolved with that other situation, but I've always been so sure you'd sever our bond. I only hoped you and I would part on cordial terms so that it'd build me some good will and I could use that good will to help that couple even further."

His expression goes dark, so I stop talking.

"Sorry for saying the swearword, there, Scooby Docby."

He snickers at the endearment, but then sobers. "Talk to your coven. Your aunt. Find out what can be done."

I wince. "I don't think anything can be done. I just need to wait."

He drops his napkin aggressively.

"So you're expecting me to do what? Stay away from you so I don't impregnate you? What if you're pregnant with my baby and this other pregnancy jumps the queue and hurts our child?"

"Birth control would-"

"You can't drug yourself to fight off having my baby, putting yourself in danger, because you want to have someone else's."

"I'm talking condoms, Riley."

He gives me a look like I'm suggesting he dip his dick in boiling oil.

"What they went through, Riley…"

He thrusts a hand through his hair, pissed off. "And we haven't been through a lot?"

"But we're arguing over a baby that doesn't exist versus one that does."

"Our baby. Mine and yours," he says like that has a whole lot of weight.

Frustrated, I sift my hands through my own hair. "He or she doesn't exist yet. This other baby *does. Or will as soon as his mother is ready to carry him.*"

"If she's not dead," he says.

"Yeah," I whisper, hoping that she won't die.

"If you're not pregnant and giving birth in the same calendar year as the rest of the council's mates, there's a good chance our son won't be on that council."

"If the offspring born in that calendar year even *are* the next council," I volley.

He looks at me like I'm crazy.

"You don't know, Riley, if they will be or not. You don't know if your firstborn will be a council super-alpha. Your first child could be unable to even shift because I'm his or her mother."

He ponders that a second.

"It could be your child born in another year or it could even be other children from other pack members that make up the next council. You and the other six have only held the seats for what… just over six years? It could be thirty years or more before it's time for a new council. It could happen in a week. It won't… I know it won't because the next council hasn't been identified yet, but theoretically, it could happen any time. The coven will decide when that happens based on my sister's clairvoyance."

"The coven decides?"

I nod.

He frowns. "What do you mean?"

"Did you think your council just decided to retire and appoint you guys?"

"Pretty much."

"Ask, if you don't believe me. Aunt Lyrica used to advise on it. Now it'd be Vivica because she's got precognition and she's clairvoyant and will know when it's time."

"I didn't say I didn't believe you, witch. I just never heard of this shit."

I stand up and lean forward aggressively. "Don't call me witch like it's an insult one minute and an endearment the next, Riley Savage." And then I storm to the counter and start washing the few dishes in the sink.

I glare over my shoulder at him. His eyes blaze and he looks at me like he wants to punish me.

"So, I see you're a sassy little witch, sometimes." He moves to me and sinks his teeth into that mark, and it hurts a little. But more than hurt, it feels good.

I still scoff. "I'm a lot of things."

He spins me around so I face him.

"I can tell," he says with a dangerous look in his eye.

Pissed off, I say nothing. Even though I'm pissed off, I'm also wet, responding to the dominance emanating from him.

"When do you find out what the situation is with this other couple?" he asks.

"Halloween. Or very soon thereafter."

He sighs and thrusts his hand through his hair in frustration. "Well this is just fuckin' great."

Slouching, I feel crushed. Because I'm speaking the truth. I can't jeopardize their unborn child. We put them somewhere to contain possible damage, but we won't know if any damage to Isabella is contained to that place or if it'll seep out when the spell unlocks. If all is lost on November first, that child will be my responsibility to not only bring into the world, but likely to raise, too.

And here's Riley, wanting me. Miraculously. Wanting a family with me. After everything. And here I am hurting him. Again.

He takes a step back, anger in his eyes. "Fuck this." He throws his pants down to his ankles and steps out of them.

I straighten up and watch him go.

He's gone... just like that. I see his wolf through the window, take off into a full throttle run.

I frown.

I can't eat any more of my cheesy cauliflower soup or of my garlic bread. My appetite has vanished. So I put them in the fridge.

Roxy's didn't sell banana splits, had bananas and whipped cream, but Sean went to the supermarket in Drowsy Hollow and brought back the other ingredients to make our own. I have a feeling there won't be any dessert tonight.

I drop my head and study my dress pattern as I ponder what to do about all this.

38

RILEY

"What are you doing here?" Greyson's father Graydon asks after cutting the engine on his lawnmower. "You're supposed to be locked down with your witch for a couple more days, aren't you?"

"The Young coven is responsible for deciding when a new council takes over?"

He looks taken aback at my question and then answers hesitantly with, "Yes. Are they appointing a new council? You haven't identified the next generation yet."

"Why have we, the current council, not got a relationship with the coven?"

"I guess *you* do now," he says sourly.

"I need answers, Graydon."

He looks around and sighs, then takes a bandana out of his back pocket and mops his brow.

I lean against his car in the driveway. "I'm now waiting on a meeting with Mitch Blakely and a couple SCC members who are coming here to talk to me about my mating. About shit that's obviously been kept from me. Did you know they sentenced my mate to staying away from me, to letting me believe she's dead for seven years?"

"What? Why?"

"They did that to punish her for using her magic on a love spell to make me hers."

"No," he states looking genuinely surprised, "I didn't know that. Absolutely not. I'd never keep something like that from you. None of us knew."

"I need information here."

"I don't have any, son. We knew nothing about your mating other than what your father told us. He said you found her but lost her. A couple months after you left town we got notice to hand over the reins by a certain date and so we prepared for it and that's what we did. But you were all named for the next council when you were teenagers."

The council meets every year to study the pack's youth in competitive situations. Some years there are a few stand outs. We've done it the past five years, me and the other five before Ty came back, but nothing has stood out with seven young pack members at once. We've all been expecting it'd happen after we mated, as their future kids got to their teens. After losing her seven years back, I didn't think I'd have kids. Before that, we'd all been sure it'd be our kids together. Grey said he felt it and we know Grey's got half witch blood, so it seemed like his hope was more of a premonition.

"You told us you were turning things over because the six of us were ready."

"We turned things over because we were *told* you were ready."

"Why didn't you introduce us to the coven when we took over?"

"I pulled back on the relationship when my first mating was severed. They backed off as well. I wanted that family to have nothing to do with my son. They didn't push. I've dealt with Lyrica a few times over the years when I've had to, and it was never pleasant. Luckily, I haven't had much reason to deal with her. Nobody's bothered us from that coven much between Greyson's biological mother's leaving and now."

"Clearly the relationship is entwined."

"Clearly," he parrots. "This pack exists the way it does because of that coven, you know that."

Jase pulls over on the road, gets out of his car, and jogs in my direction.

"Everything all right, Rye?" he asks, tossing me a pair of shorts. "Code orange, buddy."

"I'm not stayin'," I advise.

He says, "You don't seem all right. Tomorrow the week is up. Things not smoothing out?"

"I'm not all right, Jase, but things are smoothing out with my mate. But I need to get back to her right now. Can you call a meeting for me? Seven of us go for a run in the morning and we'll talk in the cave after?"

"Yeah, sure," Jase replies. "I'll get word to the others."

"Thanks," I mutter.

"Mated life okay?" he asks, looking a little green. "I mean... beyond everything. All the shit you've had to deal with."

I drop a hand on his shoulder and squeeze. "It's everything, man. When you know it, you know it. Don't matter what tries to get in the way. You'll figure it out. Got a lot to talk about. Tomorrow though. Yeah? Gotta get back to her."

He doesn't lose the green look to him when he nods. I clap him on the back. "Nothing I can say will convince you. You'll look at her and you'll know, brother. You'll just know."

"You're not supposed to be here!" I hear.

Bailey is yelling out the upstairs window.

"It's all good, Bail," I tell her. "Bringing her home tomorrow."

Bailey smiles. "Good. Glad to hear it. Hi Jase."

"Hey squirt," Jase answers without looking up because he's watching Linc approach.

"Hey boys!" Linc greets. "How's things, Rye? Are you supposed to be here?"

"I'm on my way back now. We'll stay at Ty's one more night and I'll bring her home in the morning."

"You sure? Delay reality for as long as possible if you can, bro. Take an extra few days if you need."

"I'm sure. We can still be alone in my house with all the comforts."

"Aw, nice, man. Happy for ya, bro." He slaps my back and then hugs me.

"Wanna go finish your circle jerk somewhere else so I can finish cuttin' my lawn?" Graydon ribs us.

I don't know what I expected out of Graydon. He's a solid guy. A good mentor. I'm not surprised he knows nothing about all this shit with me, but I also don't get why the pack worked closely with the coven in the past and he didn't bother to tell us that when we took over. Not just him, the others as well.

I'll talk with my council co-alphas in the morning and then decide if we want to have a joint meeting with the retired council to get more information. I know things must have been strained when Graydon had his mating bond severed, but I think he should've handed off managing the coven relationship to someone else on the council, not to mention brief us on it when we took over. And it isn't like Greyson knows anything about this either unless he hasn't leveled with me about it. And that's not Grey. Grey would keep me in the loop.

I stay in human form and jog the few blocks over to my place, survey the place, and call my mother from the Savage Construction line to ask if she minds sprucing the place up for me and getting it ready for me to bring my mate home in the morning.

Mom is a little short with me and I know it's for two reasons.

1. I've been distant since all this shit came to light. She's hurt that I've shut her out.
2. She's worried about me being mated to a witch. She was friends with Soleil Young when Soleil and Graydon got together. When things went south with them, her friend moved away, and nobody would tell her what happened. I know she's likely worried. I'll introduce her to my mate in a few days and I'm sure that'll alleviate her concerns.

I'M PULLING UP TO THE cabin after talking to Cade and Gus, which I also did when I left, asking them to stay close to her as well as just now to let them know I'm taking her home in the morning.

I find her on the grass beside the porch, drinking what smells like tea, eyes on me as I approach. Emotion pulses in my direction, not just from her eyes; I feel turmoil from her place in my chest.

"Why did you drive here?" she asks. "Why are you looking at me like that? Did something happen?"

I approach and she sets her cup on the porch, and looks up at me.

I jerk my thumb up, motioning for her to stand.

She does.

Then she gasps when I lift her up and throw her over my shoulder, carrying her inside.

I close the door, lock it, and carry her to bed.

As soon as she's on the bed, I'm on her, lifting her dress up over her waist and lining up at her entrance.

I cradle her jaw with my free hand and touch my lips briefly to hers.

"We'll figure the baby stuff out. Sorry I was a dick about it."

She looks surprised. She looks ready to burst into tears.

"You said *fuck this*."

Pain pulses at me through our connection.

I shake my head. "Shit, baby. I didn't mean it like that."

Her chin wobbles and I feel like a bag of shit.

"I didn't mean it like that, Erica."

"No?"

"No, baby. Till death. Till. Death."

She lets out a long exhale.

"But I'm not staying away from you if you go into heat."

"Riley..."

I practically spit out with disgust, "I'll buy some condoms tomorrow. Let me have you as much as I want between now and then without 'em and I'll deal for a while if I have to."

She wraps her arms around me and squeezes.

"Thank you for being awesome." She pulls back and looks at me. Now she's got a huge smile on her face.

"I was a dick. I'm sorry, little witch."

"Yeah, but then you went back to being awesome. And you don't need to use condoms."

"No?"

"I talked to my sisters on the phone. They're all coming. They want to be here for this meeting with the SCC. Aunt Mimi didn't say much, but echoed what Mitchell Blakely said. That I should probably refrain from using magic until after the sit down. I could tell Aunt Mimi knows things, but I don't know what or how much. I told them I felt like I had new powers, that they were a little scary. They promised to help me figure that out. As for the baby stuff, Ronnie has some of Isabella's things and my things. They did a little investigative ceremony after you left and called me five minutes ago to tell me they think it'll be okay. Either we won't get pregnant until it's okay to do so, or we will and it'll still be okay because Isabella will be able to carry her baby." She smiles brightly at me. "They found a way to delay for a short time if she's not ready. I don't know details, but it seems like it'll work out. Ronnie sees kids for both of us. Both couples. No loss of children. None. Which means it'll work out somehow."

"Thank you for digging into that straight away, baby."

"I could tell it was important to you. Even if you said 'fuck this' and that might've meant you were done with me."

"It is important to me. Because I don't want anyone or anything stopping us from living our life together. We've had enough get in the way. And that made me selfish for a minute and I'm sorry about that. But what I was done with was fighting. I needed to run off some steam. I'm never gonna be done with you. Never."

"I'm relieved," she whispers.

I kiss her. She pulls back.

"I'm relieved because not only is it going to be okay, also… you acted like a dick which means you're not perfect. And that's kinda good because it might be really hard to spend the rest of my life with someone who is perfect and never ever screws up. Because I'm a big screwup. Big one."

I laugh. "If you haven't figured out after the last few days with me here that I'm far from perfect, you've got rose-colored glasses on, little witch."

She smiles and kisses my jaw. "I'm glad you're not mad at me."

"We've got a lot of things to wade through, darlin'. Can't promise I won't lose my cool once in a while, got a whole lotta testosterone in me. But if I do lose it, please gimme time to sort my head out and chances are I'll come back soon after with a calmer head about things."

"Okay, Riley," she says.

"You wanna whip us up some banana splits?" I ask.

"I want you."

"Yeah?" I ask.

"Yeah. And *then* I want *you* to make the banana splits. I mean, it's the least you can do after you threw that tantrum and left me here."

I throw my head back and laugh.

And then I sober. "I asked the guys to watch over you. Cade 'n Gus. I didn't just leave you here. I'll always have a mind to your safety, your wellbeing. Especially after fucking up but not just that, because it's my job. My job and my honor to look after you. Okay?"

She nods slowly, face brimming with sweetness. "Just tell me next time that you're going. Maybe kiss me goodbye before you go and tell me you'll be back soon?"

"I can do that."

"Thanks, fuzzy wuzzy."

I snicker. "Fuzzy wuzzy?"

She shrugs. "Doesn't feel right calling you Scooby Dooby. That's your wolf."

"I am my wolf."

"Even still... I'll keep tryin' pet names on for size until I find one that feels right."

"We're goin' home in the morning, little witch."

"Home?"

"Our place. We were here to sort ourselves. Feels sorted, doesn't it? Day seven tomorrow."

She smiles.

"Besides, our place has a lot more comforts. You are down to move in with me, right, mate? Be part of my pack? Make the village of Arcana Falls your home? Fair warning, if you say no, I'm gonna have to go the route Ty and Mase went and kidnap you."

"Of course I am," she whispers, looking emotional. "Since the minute I saw you, it's what I've wanted most."

I kiss her.

She breaks away. "But can you pretend to kidnap me? That sounds kinda hot."

I stare for a second.

"Because it's you, I mean," she says quickly. "*Only* because it's you."

I laugh, lean in and press my mouth to hers. "I bought my house from my folks a couple years ago. You can redecorate if you want. Haven't done much since I bought it. It's big. Got four bedrooms. Lots of space. The shop for Savage Construction is out front in the garage and we've got a building out back with all our tools and equipment. It's not far from Roxy's. Stumbling distance, in fact."

"That sounds perfect," she says. "And I do come with some stuff…"

My phone sounds off. "Got lots of room. I'm gonna go see what that's about," I say.

"Okay, I'll call my sisters and ask them to bring my stuff when they come, okay?"

"Good." I drop a kiss on her mouth and then go find my phone on the kitchen counter.

> **Mitch Blakely: We are coming to meet with you and your mate. We'll be there in your village Thursday. Early afternoon. Can you accommodate us overnight? 3 of us."**

I reply.

> **Come to the town hall. I'll work out accommodations.**

I message the council group chat.

> **Heads up. We need to accommodate 3 SCC guests Thursday. Want you all there for this meeting with me at noon.**

Joel responds.

> **Jase called and told us about the SCC. We'll all see you for a run in the morning. Congrats on your mating.**

> **Me: Thanks brother.**

Linc inserts a thumbs up in the conversation.

I smile, thinking about the fact the other three haven't answered because they're likely busy with their mates. Two of the three of them have already started building their family. And I don't know if it's fated for me and my mate to have a child soon, but love that her sister saw kids for us. I don't know if our kids will or won't be in the next council. If they will or won't be able to shift. But what I do know is I feel lucky.

A few weeks back I thought I'd have no chance at having kids, no chance of a kid being in the next council since I was considered a widower. I didn't think I'd ever want to hold and kiss a woman let alone fuck her, give her my mark, knot her, and purr for her. And now the idea that I've got my woman and that we can look forward to a future together… if none of our children are part of the council, I'm okay with that.

39

RILEY

Screaming jerks me out of a dead sleep and I half-shift before I realize it's my mate that's screaming and writhing in bed beside me.

I pull back. "Babe," I shake her.

She whimpers and thrashes.

"Rikki?"

"Riley!" she cries and writhes some more. Panic and adrenaline dominate my blood. Because she's screaming like she needs saving from someone or something and my instinct is to immediately spring into action.

"Erica!" I shout, pulling her into my embrace, holding her tight.

"Riley," she whimpers, voice sounding garbled. She's gasping for air. Gasping hard. Her heart is racing. Adrenaline surging.

I purr. I purr while holding her tight, rocking her, and she goes limp in my arms and then is weeping against my chest. That was my second time half-shifting. The first time when I was locked out and those fuckers threw the gas bomb through the window.

"What was the dream about?" I ask, stroking her hair.

"More... more purr," she mumbles.

I purr harder and lay back down with her, holding her close. She clings to me, body trembling. Her teeth chatter so I will my body temperature to rise while I continue purring.

She falls asleep.

I don't.

THE SUN HAS RISEN, and I know I'm late for the run. Her nightmare happened a few hours ago; I just wasn't about to leave her afterwards.

Couldn't. And I couldn't sleep afterwards, either. Because I'm angry. Stewing. Wanting answers from the assholes who put her through this, and even more – wanting a way to take away the fears that plague her sleep.

She stirs in my arms and looks up at me. Fuck, she's pretty.

"Good morning."

"Good?"

"Yeah. Waking up with you always is." She snuggles in and kisses my throat.

"You gonna be okay if I go meet the council for a meeting? I'll be quick." I stroke her cheek.

"Go ahead. I'm gonna sleep a little more, I think. Weren't you supposed to go when it was still dark?"

"Wasn't gonna leave you alone after that nightmare. What was it about?"

"Drowning." She nuzzles my throat with her forehead. "I often dream about the river swallowing me. Angry at me for my lies. Sorry you missed your run, snuggle bug. Sorry I woke you up."

"Forget the meeting. I'll see them tomorrow." I hold her tighter.

"No, it's okay. I dream it often, honeybear. I'll be okay."

"Honeybear?" I ask.

She scrunches up her nose. "Maybe not honeybear."

"How'd the snuggle bug one feel?"

"Meh. Not it."

I chuckle and drop a kiss on her forehead. "You sure you don't need me to stay?"

"I'm sure." She kisses my jaw. "This one had a better ending than any of the other ones."

"Didn't sound like a good ending from here," I mutter.

"Waking up to you holding me, purring for me? That's never happened before and that made it way better."

I brush her hair out of her eyes with my fingertips. "Be back in an hour or two. Go back to sleep, little witch," I kiss her shoulder and roll out of bed.

THEY'RE ALL IN THE cave when I get there.

"Didn't think you were gonna show," Grey greets.

"Sorry, guys. She had a nightmare."

Tyson looks me over. "Day seven. And you stayed to console her during a nightmare?"

"We're good. We're goin' home as soon as I get back. Owe you a new couch, Tyson," I add.

"Why?" he asks. "That thing is older than me. Can't imagine you damaged it any worse than…" He stops and I know realization dawns as to why I'm saying that. He waves a hand. "Don't worry about it. I'm the one that insisted you stay there. My Ivy's already picked out all new furniture for it anyway. We just need to arrange delivery."

"Right," I say, smiling.

He flashes me a grin. "So, you're good?" Ty checks.

"No. Not good. But not good not because of her, because of what was done *to* her."

I proceed to fill them in on all the shit she's been put through unnecessarily. How Mitch Blakely was part of the jury she had to stand trial in front of, telling them why there are supernatural council members coming the day after tomorrow. I also say their support in making sure the pack members treat her well is important to me. I don't want them treating her like an outsider who wronged me. I don't want her to feel anything but at home. They've already started spreading the word that she not only saved my life but also Mason's and Lincoln's. They assure me the pack is ready to embrace her.

"Yeah, Jase? Keep your fuckin' sister away from my mate. If she gets anywhere near her and pulls any of her typical bullshit, I will call a pack-wide vote, nominate to have her booted."

Jase raises his hand in a non-verbal gesture that lets me know he gets it. Sherry Creed hasn't shown her face much since Bailey punched her in the face for blowing shit up with Mase and Amie at Tyson and Ivy's wedding reception.

Mase's jaw flexes. I know he's still not past his animosity with Sherry Creed. Jase's eyes bounce to Mase's with apology.

"Jase isn't responsible for his sister's bullshit, boys," Joel advises.

"No, but I will have a word with her," Jase replies.

After I finish bringing them up to speed, Ty makes sure to crow about his brilliant idea to lock us up.

I roll my eyes at his ribbing and when I've had enough, give him a playful shove, which lands him in the water.

He comes up laughing, then hugs me, pounding my back and congratulating me.

That all done, Grey gives me his update, filling me in on what I've missed from his camp. He's enjoying time with his mate who was only doing her asshole alpha brother's bidding. Ty holds no ill feelings toward her, but wants to talk to her when Grey's ready to bring her out in the open so he can get more info about her father, the man she says he supposedly killed, which is what fueled her alpha brother's plans.

He needs to be stopped. He's gonna come at us again, we're sure of it. Joel and Grey are still doing some fact-finding and will keep me in the loop about the next steps, which I absolutely want to be part of.

He tried to steal my mate twice. He shot, stabbed, and drugged me. Shot Mase and Linc, too. Grey does know from his mate that her brother wants our territory. He wants to rule our pack since he considers it a status symbol. We've got the largest pack known in North America and he thinks it's ridiculous that it's looked after by seven alphas. Figures he could handle it all by himself. He wants the council alphas dead as a show of his dominance and superiority, and he plans to accomplish it by having a witch at his command to do his bidding.

We'll be tackling that issue after this SCC meeting coming up. All seven of us will be there and then when that's behind us, we'll work to disable that shithead in Silver Hills. And maybe Rikki's coven can help. Grey's already talked to the older sister Vivica about all this and they've agreed to be on-call for us.

I fill him in on my conversation with his father and he is not pleased, tells us his father has made the topic of the Youngs a no-go in his household. We agree Greyson and I will share managing the coven relationship going forward.

"Where are we gonna put 'em?" Joel asks. "The three from the council."

Ty speaks. "If it were normal guests, I'd have them at my house since we have so much room. But can we keep these people outside the village somewhere? Drowsy Hollow? I don't trust them here."

"Good point," I reply. "I'll call the couple who owns the resort across the lake with those cabins for rent. See if they have a vacancy. Maybe Mase can ferry them back and forth on his boat."

"Good idea. Not sure I want them here either. I'm happy to run 'em back and forth," Mase replies.

40

ERICA

Being driven into the village of Arcana Falls feels strange. So much has happened since I first drove here. No way would the *me* of a week and a half ago believe that in such a short time I could get to where I am now.

Getting held and purred for by Riley.

Eating banana splits in bed last night with Riley. The best banana split I've had in my life.

Having sex dozens and dozens of times with Riley.

Mm, Riley...

And is he *ever* good at sex! He knows how to kiss. He's a god with his tongue. And that swirling, buzzing, steel-hard instrument of his? I'm its slave. Honestly. I can't get enough of it.

And he is over the moon at the fact that I saved my virginity for him. Over. The. Moon. It feels pretty awesome to have validation that saving it was the right choice. That I will never, ever regret who I gave it to.

I certainly never expected at the end of the seven days together in Tyson Savage's cabin that I'd be ending it in Riley's truck, Riley's hand on my thigh as he drives me to his house, which he's calling *our* house.

We pass the intersection with big barn that is their town hall and gas station where my van had been parked, though I know it's still at Lincoln and Jase's place. We keep going past a dozen or so homes before we're pulling into a driveway on the left just before the next corner that I know has Roxy's Bar. In fact, I can see the roof of the building, which means it's easy walking distance, or... *stumbling distance* as Riley said.

Riley's place has neighbors on either side but not close. It's a double or maybe even a triple lot with a big garage out front, a big square building behind it that has three garage doors, and then there's the house beside the smaller garage. It's a big house. And it's cute as a button. It's Victorian style, not too dissimilar from Aunt Mimi's house on the coast. This one is white with black shutters and black trim. Two stories with a tall, peaked roof. The front of the house is dominated by a white porch that goes left and wraps around one side. Two dark wood rocking chairs with a little table between them grace the porch and the table has a little wooden lighthouse with 'welcome' on it. There are colorful flowers in the flowerbeds, rosebushes climbing a trellis along the side going up to a second floor which has a little peak over the half-hexagon bump-out window that I really hope is the master bedroom, because that could be a little reading nook right there, which would be amazing. And there's a waist-high white picket fence all the way around it. My dream happily-ever-after had a white picket fence in a small town where everyone is close. And my dream is coming true.

There's also a little red hatchback car in the driveway. Before I get a chance to ask about the car, as it doesn't seem Riley's style, he pipes up.

"What do you think at first glance?"

"It's amazing," I say with a big smile. "Can we paint the house black and the front door and the shutters orange?"

He parks beside the red car and laughs as if I'm joking.

"Grew up here. Big yard in the back. Little potting shed. Garden. Mom used to grow vegetables every year. Couple fruit trees back there, too. Fire pit. Barbecue."

"Can I have a sunroom greenhouse built?" I ask. "If there's room? Like the one Bailey's parents have? And maybe a second-story balcony off the master?"

"Helped Dad build that for the Blackwoods back in the day. I'll build you a greenhouse, little witch. No problem on the balcony. Can build a greenhouse directly off the kitchen. There's a door already there with two steps down into the back yard." He gestures toward the side where the porch wraps around. "Can put it right there so you can walk straight out into it from the house."

I smile wide, clapping my hands. "That'd be amazing."

He drops a kiss on my shoulder. "Look around and anything else you want done, I'll hook you up."

"I have everything I want," I say, leaning close so I can plant a big, wet kiss on him. He deepens it and I'm the one to break it, asking, "Any objection if I paint rooms black or red or cover every surface with glitter?"

"Not as long as you're in my bed every night," he says. "Paint the whole thing tie-dye if you want."

His eyes bounce over my shoulder.

I hear a beep-beep and see the red car's hatch rise.

A blonde ponytailed lady with an uncertain expression approaches the red car's open hatch and I know she saw us making out. She's dressed in yoga clothes and carrying a basket of cleaning supplies and a vacuum cleaner.

She also has green eyes. Riley's mom. She's fit and attractive and does not look remotely happy.

"Mom, hey." Riley greets, letting go of me and getting out of the truck. He rounds it and pulls her into a hug.

I should've known this was a possibility.

Riley then opens the door and tugs my hand so that I get out.

I'm super-self-conscious. I can't read her mind, but I'm imagining what she's thinking. I hurt her son and she's devastated that I'm here. My heart is lodged in my throat.

I'm incredibly self-conscious, too. I'd put my unruly hair up in a bun this morning, but Riley promptly pulled the hair band out so it's everywhere. I'm not even wearing shoes. And I'm wearing my patchwork earth-tones dress. Riley wanted it on me to carry me over the threshold, as it should've been done seven years ago. It's a little snug now and low-cut V-neck. When I used to wear it, I wore it with a tank top underneath. I'm not right now, so my cleavage is kind of spilling out of it a little bit. We didn't even shower this morning. Just had sex, coffee, packed up and drove here. I'm sure I look like a homeless harlot.

"Mom, this is my mate, Erica. Baby, Lucy Savage."

"It's very nice to meet you, Mrs. Savage," I extend my hand.

She shakily takes mine and swallows hard before pulling it away quickly. "Hello," she rasps and then turns to her son. "I cleaned up and stocked you up." She points at the house. Her hand is trembling.

"That's great, Mom. Appreciated."

"Trina and Brody want to come and meet ... her. Let me know when we can do that. I'll do a dinner," she says nervously, staring at the asphalt instead of her son.

"All right," he says, looking at her strangely.

"I'd better go." She hooks her thumb backwards.

Riley lifts her vacuum cleaner and puts it in her trunk. "Come here a sec." He tugs his mother's hand. "Baby, have a look around the back if you want. Don't go into the house without me. I'll be right back."

"Okay," I say. "Really nice to meet you, Mrs. Savage."

She gives me a shaky smile. "I...hope I got food you like."

"I loved your breakfast casserole," I say. "Riley said you sent that. It was very good."

She smiles but it doesn't reach her eyes.

"Mom's lasagna, too," Riley adds.

"Oh, that was yours? It was delicious. I ate three quarters of it all by myself." I rub my stomach.

She nods but says nothing.

"I'll just go check out the yard," I say.

"You want your shoes first, little witch?" he asks, eyes twinkling with amusement.

"Naw, I'm good," I say. "Sorry for my appearance, Mrs. Savage. I'm kind of a barefoot bohemian flower child." I shrug and smile.

She looks me over and says nothing.

"Not to worry though. I'll wash my feet before I go inside. Since it looks like you just probably did the floors. Is there a hose out here, fuzzy wuzzy?"

Riley's eyes sharpen. Not on me. On her.

"Riley," I say.

His eyes bounce to me. I give him a shake of my head, hoping he's not going to give her a hard time for the way she's being. I mean... I understand. I'm the girl who hurt him. She's just having a natural reaction.

I only hope people give me a chance to prove myself. I want so much to fit in here. This is what I've wanted for a long time. A small, close-knit community.

We don't have that in Marblehead. We keep to ourselves.

We had that in Drowsy Hollow when I was a kid and I want it again. And I know I'd have even more of it here because I don't need to hide my true nature. I'll get it here; I know I will. I'll work for it; I'll win all these people over. I'll become more like my old self now that I've got Riley. I can *feel* it rising to the surface in me.

"Don't worry about your feet, Erica," Riley says angrily and then looks about to blow up with his eyes on his mom, so I speak quickly.

"Mrs. Savage? About what happened with me and Riley all those years ago…I promise you, I'm not the wicked witch of the west, I try to be more like Glinda the *good* witch, but things got-"

"No, babe. Let me," Riley cuts me off, pulling his mom toward the garage.

"Okay. Bye. Thanks again," I say.

I meander to the back yard, through a gate beside the side of the house.

Bordered by the pretty, waist-high picket fence, I'm instantly in love with this yard. The grass needs cutting, and the flowerbeds need weeding but clearly, Riley's had other things on his mind. It doesn't matter though; I'm in love with it and can hardly wait to play in the dirt and get acquainted with everything growing here.

I can see myself out here sketching and painting. I can see me stringing fairy lights everywhere. Parties with Cicely and Bailey. With Ivy and Amelia. Maybe I'll throw a baby shower for them here! I calculate quickly – no, they'll be heavily pregnant in the colder months so maybe not an outdoor baby shower. Maybe by then I will have shown Riley's mother I'm not a wicked witch.

And Riley…

I can see sitting on that porch out front with him. Taking walks to the bar to catch up with friends or grab a meal. Eventually putting a swing set out here for children. I'm looking forward to that. All of that. There's plenty of room for a greenhouse without losing too much yard. I squat and stick my fingers in the soil of the back flowerbed and close my eyes.

Energy zings through my fingers. Not just a little either. This place is filled with magic. I can see it and smell it and I can definitely feel it. And it wants me to play.

"Not yet," I whisper. "I need to know more about my changing skills first."

"What 'cha doin' little witch?"

I turn and face him.

"Talking to the dirt."

He laughs.

"No really. But mostly envisioning all the ways I'm gonna enjoy this yard. Not to mention the area. It's very magical."

He smiles and then goes serious. "Sorry about my mother. I set her straight."

"No, please don't be sorry. I'd be skeptical if our son got together with someone who'd been supposedly dead for seven years, too. I hope you weren't harsh with her."

"Not harsh at all. Just set her straight is all. She knows now what's what. Word's gettin' around that you saved my life and Mase and Linc's lives. That we'd all have bled out and died if you hadn't stopped that shithead. That you didn't stay away because you wanted to. That I'm a hundred per cent *with* you. That you and me are forever and gonna be very happy. But she's been ignoring the phone, not answering the door and keeping to herself the past few days."

"Worrying about you," I whisper.

"And to say she's feeling guilty for how she was just now is an understatement."

I shake my head. "She saw you in pain. She was bound to be worried about who I am and what I might be capable of."

"She knows the truth now. And I probably should've called her earlier and put her mind at ease. That's on me. Anyway, it's sorted. Prepare yourself for some grand gestures. Stopped her from coming back here and throwing her arms around you."

"Aw, you should've let her. Been a long while since I got a good Mom hug."

"You want I can call her back?" He jerks his thumb toward the driveway, teasing.

"That's not necessary. Neither are grand gestures."

"To Lucy Savage it is. I told her your family is heading this way for the meeting. She's gonna take in your Aunt Mimi and give her the star treatment. She's gonna call Ivy and Amie and ask if they can take your sisters between 'em. They've got lots of room there. I mean, so do we, really, but I'm not ready for company."

I shake my head. "They'll stay upstairs above the drycleaners. Kathleen moved here to Lorenzo's, so it's vacant again. Place holds some nostalgia for us since Aunt Lyrica used to live there."

"Five people in an apartment?"

"Yes. We're close. We're always piling into a big bed or throwing sleeping bags on a floor and having sleepovers. Don't worry. They're fine in the apartment."

"If you say so. You call your family about bringing your stuff here?"

"They'll be here tomorrow. They're renting a cube van."

"You got furniture and dishes and shit like that?" he asks.

I shake my head. "Nope. I lived with them in Marblehead. I'll leave all my bedroom furniture there for when I visit. Then we'll have a nice place to stay by the ocean. Got a big bedroom there with a balcony that overlooks the water that I share with Dani whose room is beside mine. You'll love it."

"Sounds good, baby. It's a nice spot. I saw it when I went lookin' for you. But if you don't have furniture and dishes, why do they need a cube van? I somehow have a hard time believing you've got hundreds of pairs of shoes." He looks at my bare feet.

I snicker. "I have a few pairs. But no... I have a lot of art supplies, crystals, and plants. A teapot and teacup collection. And like... a lot of plants. Your little witch has a very green thumb and she's not afraid to use it." I hold my thumb out. "Did I mention I have a lot of plants?"

He plants a kiss on my thumb and pulls me close. "Guess I better get on that greenhouse, huh?"

I drape my arms over his shoulders. "Maybe next summer I'll set up a little fruit, vegetable, and flower stand at the end of the driveway."

"Not a bad idea. You wanna go see the inside of your home, Mrs. Savage?"

I bite my lip and nod eagerly.

Riley lifts me up and carries me.

I see two teenage girls riding bicycles past the house. They wave with big smiles.

I wave back and so does Riley. And then he takes me up the front steps and I pull in a big breath.

"You're acting nervous. Why?" he asks.

"I didn't think this was ever gonna happen. I'm just here hoping I'm not about to wake up from this dream. Though if it is a dream, it's way better than the kinds I usually have."

"Not a dream, Rikki. This is real. And it's very fuckin' overdue."

"Yay," I whisper, throat clogging.

He pushes the door open and carries me over the threshold. Me in that same dress, the same bare feet but a little older and a whole lot wiser.

And then he kicks the door shut and is kissing me before I can take much of anything in. Kissing me while climbing the long staircase with me.

I barely get to take in his bedroom because my dress is being pulled over my head and then I'm falling onto his bed.

His clothes are shucked off quickly and I'm eyeing his fantastic, muscled chest when he abruptly flips me to my belly, lifts me up by my hips, and then he's slamming inside me from behind.

I whimper but then manage a breathy, "Doggie style happens to be one of my favorite positions so far. Imagine that?"

He laughs and then groans as I reach under us and cup his balls.

My free hand clenches the high-quality bedding which smells like lavender as I whimper, seeing a vase of fresh white flowers on the nightstand. I turn my head and there's a bottle of wine in a bucket on the other nightstand with two long-stemmed glasses. Riley's mom may have been wary of me, holding a grudge, but she still spent effort on making this nice for us so that bodes well for the future as far as I'm concerned.

Riley sucks my throat at the claiming mark and then his fingers dive between my legs. He rubs my clit while plunging deliciously into me from behind.

I love the feel of the thrusts, the sounds he makes, the sounds our skin connecting makes, but then his knot comes out and I fall on my face, taking his weight on top of me as we groan out our orgasms together. This part

– the part where he falls apart and I feel it both inside and out – is my favorite part.

I'VE HAD A SHOWER IN the plain but spacious ensuite bathroom while Riley naps and now I'm wandering the house. The master suite is spacious and masculine with lots of dark wood. And though there's no reading nook in that bump-out, there's nothing in it so it's something I fully plan to utilize. It's tied for priority with the greenhouse. Riley's room is done with dark fabrics. Dark lamps. It needs a pop of color.

The bathroom is clean, white and spacious. The towels are black. It, too, needs color.

The other three bedrooms on this level are all ordinary and haven't been renovated, likely since before his parents left. One room is very girlie with floral wallpaper. Another room is painted blue, and I somehow know this was Riley's childhood room. The next room has been updated probably within the last ten years, but has more floral wallpaper that's a little more neutral than the girl's room. This is the only room with furniture, set up like a guest room, but it's underwhelming. There's a main bathroom, too, that's clean and spacious but probably hasn't been updated in about twenty years.

The winding oak staircase, which I'd love to stain darker, takes me down to the main floor where there's a big foyer punctuated by a giant glass chandelier. To the left is a big living room decorated with chocolate brown furniture and a grey rug. The walls are white. There's a lovely gray stone fireplace. I see a door to a bathroom and it's white. White walls, white floor, white fixtures.

To the right is a big entryway closet and French doors that lead to a dining room, but it's empty. It has great molding and a gorgeous ceiling but it's just plain white and empty. This is a room where family comes together so I would love to see it reflect that with warmth and personality. It leads to a kitchen, which also opens up to the living room, taking up the back of the house. It's updated, large, but also pretty plain.

White counters, cupboards, and backsplash. White floors. Black appliances, but it's ... sterile. There's a big island in the middle. The place has great bones and it's obvious that a bachelor lives here, started renovating but never put in any personal touches and didn't quite finish the whole place. Maybe didn't care all that much. There's a door here to the backyard and a short hallway with a powder room, an empty office-suitable room that has a wall of bookshelves, and a laundry room.

There isn't any art on the walls. The place has no plants. The furniture is comfortable but without much personality. Black, brown, white, grey.

Yeah… I'll enjoy injecting my personality into this space.

"What do you think?" he asks, standing behind me. I see he's in just a pair of dark drawstring lounge pants. And they're a little tented.

My eyes land right on the target.

"Is the tent for camping or are you happy to see me?" I ask. "Because you could fit a couple people under there, easily.

"Both. But only you're welcome in my tent. Come on over and get comfortable," he replies, deadpan.

I smirk.

He lifts me up into his arms and carries me to his couch.

"What's the verdict on the house?"

"Good bones," I say.

"Yeah?"

"But boring," I reply.

He looks surprised.

"I'm being honest."

"Good, be honest."

"It needs color. Life. Plants. Personality."

"Do what you want with it, baby. Make it home."

I clap my hands happily.

He thrusts his fingers into my hair and looks into my eyes.

"It's gonna be a fuckin' fantastic happily-ever-after, little witch."

I wrap my arms around him. "I love you so much."

And then I wince, because I just blurted it like that.

"Don't," he grinds out, emotion flaring in his eyes. "Don't regret sayin' that. Thank you for fuckin' sayin' it. I love you, too, Erica Savage."

"I really wanna give you a blowjob right now. Is that okay?"

He throws his head back and laughs. And then he quickly sobers and gives me a look I've already come to recognize. It means, "About now would be good."

"HEY RILEY?" I CALL out, walking my fingers up his chest.

It's nighttime and we're in bed, snuggled up. We just made love. For the fourth time today.

"Give me five minutes. I might not be a mere mortal but I'm also not a machine."

I laugh. "You're off the hook until tomorrow. I um… do you want to know how many kids my sister thinks we'll have?"

"How many?" he asks, voice very serious.

"Four," I whisper, feeling choked up. Happy. So, so happy.

He rolls over and attacks me, seeming very, very happy about that. Guess he didn't need a break after all.

41

RILEY

Coming back from an extra-long morning run with Joel and Jase, I catch a potpourri of Young scents before I even spot the big, white cube van that's backed in. Behind my truck is Rikki's hippie van and behind the cube van, a green Land Rover.

"They're here pretty fucking early," Joel notes. "A sign of coming days with the new in-laws?"

Jase shudders.

I chuckle, not minding in the least. I'm a morning person. So's my mate. She woke with me and the sun this morning after fucking half the night and was singing that song about sex and candy while making coffee in my kitchen when I headed out the door for my run.

I'm not surprised her family's here early, though figuring where they come from, they had to have gotten to The Hollow last night.

We get to my driveway and Jase's nose is twitching.

I give him a curious look.

He says, "Never smelled so many witches at once."

Joel's here after walking past the cut-off toward his own house since he had plans to go to Jase's up the street and around the bend. Jase recruited him to move some furniture over there today.

I resisted the urge to tease Jase that he's nesting like a she-wolf. I didn't tease because I know he's already all up in his head over it. He looks spooked, but he wants his place ready for when he brings in a female, so he's already cleared the nudie mags and car calendars out of the joint and he's having his mother and sister clean it later today after Joel helps him move some shit around.

Linc moved out yesterday; he's now setting up temporary digs in the one empty apartment out of the three above Roxy's bar and thinking about building his own house. Ty told him he's welcome to stay with his mate when it happens in the cabin since being above Roxy's when it happens might fuck with Linc. Wolf shifters typically den with their new mates out of the way. Old possessiveness instincts. And Cade has one apartment up there, Roxy the other, so that'd likely fuck with him.

He wants something deep in the patch of forest on Chariot Lake between Mason's place and Savage House where Tyson lives. He asked Mase to design a place for him and all of us to help build it.

I got a message to the surveillance room last night to give them the heads up that four Young sisters and their elderly aunt were coming today. I also told my mate to tell her family to check in at the gas bar so Cicely can converse with the control room, but I don't know if Cicely's open yet.

Since they're already here, it's a good thing we're all dressed due to the *code orange* around here. When life settles down, these Young witches will have to get used to shifter nudity when they visit.

"You guys are obviously coming to say hey, right?" I ask, because they're both following me up my driveway.

"Starved. Gonna be food?" Jase asks.

"We can whip up some grub. Might want your help unloading this truck, though."

"Works for me," Jase says.

"I'll help," Joel agrees. "Plannin' on spending the day helping him move shit around anyhow. And he probably doesn't have any food in his house."

"Probably not," Jase agrees. "But I'll buy at Roxy's after."

"Works for me. Breakfast here, dinner at Roxy's," Joel shrugs.

We follow the sound of laughter into the back yard where five beauties and their aunt are all hanging out. The patio table has an open box of donuts, a pot of coffee and a teapot I've never seen before – it's a big ceramic mouse wearing a skirt.

"That witch is so toxic, if she saged her house she'd wake up outside," the blonde witch I've already met says, and they all laugh together.

"Hey," I greet.

All gazes move my way.

I go straight to my mate who's the only one not at the table. She's sitting cross-legged on the grass beside the patio set, a fat black and white cow-patterned cat in her lap.

The cat takes one look at me and hisses.

"Hey, moondoggy!" she greets, excitedly reaching for me.

"Moondoggy?" I hear Jase ask behind me.

The other redhead who I already know is Jessica plucks the cat up and coos to him as I lean in and kiss my woman.

"Welcome to Arcana Falls, Young family," I greet.

I get smiles and hellos from all around the table, except from the old lady.

"Ms. Young. Nice to see you again."

She looks me over, her bright white hair in a tight bun. She's wearing a green and black gauzy dress that's buttoned up to her throat. A black pedicure peeks out from her Birkenstocks.

"My apologies for my behavior last time we met, ma'am," I tack on.

She extends her hand. I take it. She holds on and looks over at a curvy brunette dressed in denim coveralls beside her. That one reaches out her hand. "Nice to meet you, Moondoggy. I'm Veronica. People who love me call me Ronnie."

I let go of the aunt to take her hand and she smiles, staring at it.

"Fuck sakes," Rikki mutters and our eyes meet. She looks annoyed at the obviousness of what's just happened.

The brunette wants to get information from me by touch; the aunt's glance told her to do it.

"Hey Ronnie. You're the one who can read people when you touch them or their belongings, right?"

"And yet you didn't hesitate before accepting my hand. That's a good sign." She smiles at my mate who is beaming and then releases my hand.

"Riley, Ronnie's paying a compliment when she's touchy feely, even if it doesn't seem like it." My mate then gestures to the other brunette sitting beside her. "Vivica, our oldest sister."

"Shut your pie hole with that O-word," Vivica, who can't be much older than my mate grumbles.

She's the brunette I saw with the redhead at the bar that night. She and Veronica are so close in appearance, they could be twins. Vivica has longer hair and is slimmer than Veronica. Veronica wears glasses, too.

"And Jessie, who I think you met." Rikki gestures to the other redhead.

"Riley," she greets.

I kiss the cheek of Ronnie and then Vivica before I move to Jessie. I take her hand and kiss her cheek. "Thank you, Jessie," I squeeze her hand. "You know what for." I give her a look loaded with meaning.

She gives me a big smile and then gives Rikki an even bigger one.

"And that's Danica." Rikki gestures to a blonde who is looking me over with scrutiny.

"We've met," I say. "Like I said to your aunt, I apologize for how I behaved the day we met."

I reach for her hand, but Jase gets between us.

"I'm Jason Creed," Jase leans over and grabs Danica's hand before I get the chance. "Nice to meet you."

Fuckin' Jase.

"Nice to meet all of you. I'm Joel," Joel says. "Need us to unload that van?"

"Thank you, Joel, but it's done." My mate waves her hand. "Sisters are used to doin' it for themselves."

"Next time leave it for me, little witch," I say, approaching Danica and dropping a kiss on her cheek. I then move to Mimi and do the same. And if I'm not mistaken, Mimi thaws just slightly. "Nice to see all of you ladies. Welcome to mine and Erica's home. You're very welcome here. Any time."

My mate looks at me like she looked at my wolf after she realized he wasn't gonna eat her. Like she's melting.

The cat in Ronnie's lap hisses again.

"Who's cat is this?" I ask, reaching out, thinking it might need to sniff me.

The cat quickly darts a paw out and rips its claws across the top of my hand instead, drawing blood.

"Fuck," I mutter.

The cat hisses again.

I look toward the aunt. "Apologies, ma'am."

She shrugs. "No need to apologize for a word unless there are bad intentions behind it."

"This is Petunia. She's mine," Rikki says. "Very naughty, little Miss Toonie! Penny is my tabby and Oscar is my ginger. They're inside exploring."

"Penny and Oscar?" I parrot.

"My other two kitties," my mate says. "You want coffee, Hot Tamale?" She gets to her feet, "I'll brew another pot. Unless you want tea instead? How about you guys?" She looks to Jase and Joel.

"Coffee sounds good," Joel says.

"Yeah," Jase chimes in.

"Coffee, darlin'," I say. "Follow you in so I can talk to you for a sec." I reach for her hand, and she takes it and rises, then follows me inside.

"Nice dress," I say.

It's low cut, the back is mostly straps, and it's white with pink, red, green, and blue flowers all over it. Her feet are bare. I reach for her and tug the elastic out of her hair.

She rolls her eyes but doesn't say anything as I run my fingers through her curls and press her against the wall inside the door.

"Three cats?" I ask, tossing the elastic to the counter. I kiss her.

She smirks, then slips by me to go to the counter and starts working on another pot of coffee.

"You don't like cats?" she asks, looking concerned.

"Not particularly. And obviously the feeling is mutual," I say lifting my hand to show her the bloody scratch.

She grabs my bleeding hand and pushes it under the kitchen tap.

Three cats. *Fuck.* I scratch my jaw thoughtfully. "I'm a wolf shifter, mate."

She smiles, looking me up and down before patting my hand dry with a paper towel and looking it over. The bleeding has stopped.

"Yeah, Scoob. I think I noticed. And..." She lets that hang, smiling with her eyes and her mouth.

"Chances are, all three of them are gonna have the same reaction the one outside did."

Her expression drops. "Do you want me to ask my sisters to take them back with them?"

Shit.

I run a hand up and down her arm. "Nah, baby. They're your pets. I'll handle it. Any other pets I need to know about?"

"I have fish. And the three birds. They're kinda loud. A couple guinea pigs plus the two pet rats. Oh, and two bearded dragons and an iguana."

I choke on spit or something.

Her eyes light up. "Just kidding. I only brought the three kitties. Dani has all the reptiles. Ronnie's into rodents. Jessie has finches, but she frequently fosters pets from the animal shelter in the same strip mall as Mimi's shop, so we often have a menagerie of animals in Marblehead. Vivi has a rottweiler with three legs. Vivi's beau is looking after all their pets while they're here."

"You might need a spanking, little mate." I grab her ass with one hand.

Immediately, I smell arousal. Fuck, my girl wants a spanking.

I let out a little growl against her claiming mark. And she shivers. "Riley," she whines, gripping my biceps.

"Your family's here, baby. You're gonna have to wait until later for my cock."

She whimpers and kisses my neck. "Bummer."

"Bummer," I return, laughing.

"They're really happy for me, Riley. Like... really happy."

"That's good, darlin'. Love seeing all this light coming from you. Your smile. Your eyes. It's like joy is oozing outta your skin. And that scent coming from you?" I suck her claiming mark. "You smell both like you're dying for my cock *and* like it was inside you a few hours ago. Just as it should be."

She smiles even brighter, then her expression goes serious. "Aunt Mimi wants to be there for that meeting tomorrow for sure. So do my sisters."

Ah. Time to get serious.

I stroke her throat with my thumb. "They should be. And it's good they're all here. My recent understanding is that we should be working closer with the coven than we have been. Even if we don't need to interact day to day, we should have a relationship. Greyson's gonna oversee it since he's related to all of you, but I'm seein' myself just as involved since you're mine.

Since everyone's here, I should call Grey. Get him over here. Maybe the others, too. Have a pow wow before tomorrow's meeting."

"We should have them all over for dinner. Can we?"

"You cook?" I ask.

"Mm, not much. My repertoire is pretty limited. Ronnie's the chef in the family. She's more of a cottage witch where I'm more of a green witch, so I didn't get near the kitchen much other than when I was twenty and lived on my own for a few months."

"We'll barbeque. I'm good on the grill. Can you whip up a few salads?"

"Um... I can go shopping for meat for you to grill and then I can purchase ready-made salads. How's that?"

I chuckle. "Works for me."

"Excellent. I love parties." She smiles wide, radiating happiness that I feel in my chest as well as see plainly on her pretty face. "But, also, about you being involved with our coven for the pack? You should be. They're now your family, too," she says.

"You've got over six hundred new family members here in the pack, Rik. Hope you're ready for all that."

"I'm so ready," she whispers, leaning into me.

"You want a church wedding?" I ask. "I'm cordial with the preacher in town. Did some work restoring that pretty old church there."

She ponders this. "No. From the minute I saw you, I wanted you. And I knew you guys didn't do traditional church weddings, so I've never imagined one, not since then. I don't need anything more than what we have now. Except maybe some babies when the time comes. And it wouldn't hurt to have a pretty ring on my finger so people know I'm taken. Something really unique and audacious, though. Nothing traditional."

"I'm down for babies the minute we can have 'em, little witch. I'm sure you know that already. And when this SCC meeting is behind us, we've got some shit to deal with to figure out the rest of that nonsense with the Silver Hills pack. Everyone around here knows you're taken. You smell like me."

She sniffs her wrist and then wiggles her eyebrows.

I laugh. "But we'll go ring shopping. Maybe spend a weekend in your town so you can show me more of the area."

"I'd like that."

"It can't be estate jewelry, though. I don't want it to carry anyone else's juju like with Amelia."

She waves a hand. "We can zap the bad juju out if it's beautiful. And yay; it's settled. We should get back outside, Boo Boo Bear."

I smile, kiss her one more time, then swat her ass and lift the full coffee pot. We head for the kitchen door. But something dawns as I look around. The wide windowsill that overlooks the yard is filled with colorful plants. The kitchen island has a big bouquet of colorful flowers on it along with two stacks of fancy teacups and saucers and six teapots. Like the one I saw outside, they're all colorful, some of them quirky. I stretch my neck and see a jungle over in the otherwise empty dining room. There are at least twenty big plants in there in various pots.

"A lot of plants," I remark.

"Oh," she leans back and looks where my eyes are pointed. "That's less than half of them. The rest of them are upstairs. Gotta figure out the best homes for all of 'em."

I laugh. "Guess I'd better get that greenhouse built soon."

"Yeah, great. But those are all indoor plants. I like having greenery around me. When you build the greenhouse, I can grow *more* plants." She taps steepled fingers together while wiggling her eyebrows like a villain with the perfect plan to take over the world.

"Go enjoy some time with your family. I'll throw some pancakes and bacon on. Yeah?"

"Ooh. Sounds good, honeybee." She kisses me and skips back outside.

AFTER BREAKFAST AND time getting acquainted, Rikki's sisters and aunt are ready to head back to the Drowsy Hollow apartment. They got here last night and after the journey the aunt is still tired. The sisters offered to split up so some could help Rikki unpack, but she sent them off saying she was happy to do it alone, wants to do it by herself. One of her sisters muttered that some things never change, and they got into a little debate about it, but my mate won and convinced them all she can manage.

I like them all. The sisters are close and it's nice to see. I'm glad she had them all these years, though for the life of me can't imagine why they didn't set her straight on all that guilt.

In terms of their personalities from what I gather, Jessie and Ronnie are a little more on the whimsical side like my mate. Vivica and Danica are more serious. Vivica is warm. Danica is a little chilly, which I thought might be because of our previous meeting the day I caught my mate's scent, but quickly figured out she has a sharp, irreverent wit and put the tongue-lolling Jase in his place more than once as he shamelessly flirted with her. The aunt was quiet and observant. I tried to talk to her on the side about the meeting tomorrow, but she changed the subject.

When we see them to the driveway, I reach for the closest one to me, Danica. I hug her. I'm about to speak but she whispers, "Thank you for being the man she deserves."

I freeze.

She goes on, "She hasn't sang, hasn't laughed much, hasn't done much other than try to be worthy of you for seven years. But she's laughing and singing and smiling today. She worked her ass off to be good enough, Riley. I'm glad you're looking like you're worthy of her, too. I'm glad I made sure you caught her scent that day, though I'm sorry for the pain it caused you."

"Don't be sorry for that. It was about fuckin' time I found out the truth." I squeeze her affectionately and though my throat is feeling clogged, I hope my expression shows what I think.

Jessica is next in line for a hug. She, too, whispers to me.

"It's her birthday the day after tomorrow, Riley. Her twenty-eighth. We're gonna stay until the day after. You think we can cobble together a little party here for her?"

I whisper back, "How about a big party? Perfect time to introduce her to my pack. I'll introduce you to my mother and Bailey when you come back for dinner. Work with them? They'll make it happen and they'll make it special. We have plenty of room for everyone over at the town hall."

"Will do," Jessica says, giving me a wink and a beaming smile before reaching for her sister who's whispering with her aunt.

I get the aunt next.

"We'll speak later, Riley Savage."

"Yes ma'am," I say. "Again, I apologize for what happened when we met."

She taps my jaw with affection. "Help me up into this beastly vehicle, will you? It's not meant for shorter women and definitely not for women over the age of sixty."

"I'll give you a boost," I say and lift her carefully up into the seat.

Her eyes light up. "Erica, girl. You're lucky I'm not thirty years younger or I might spirit this one away from you."

Rikki laughs and then sobers and points with warning. "I don't care how much older you are than me, don't care that you raised me from the age of twelve, or that you're a more powerful witch than I am. I *will* fight you."

The aunt snickers and waves her hand dismissively.

"So nice to meet you," Ronnie says, hugging me. And then her body stills for a moment before she looks me in the eyes. "I'm sorry to say that though I know you two have had a bit of an uphill battle, you're gonna need to be careful. She needs you. Please take good care of her."

"I will. I promise," I say, feeling adrenalin spike in my bloodstream, like there's a threat looming. "Any idea what's ahead?"

She shakes her head. "It's Vivi that has that gift, but I get hunches more than concrete information. We'll keep you posted."

"I feel the same as these guys," Vivi chimes in, moving in for a hug. "You're a miracle worker. She's been smitten for a long time. And beating herself up almost as long. What a difference a little over a week makes."

"I've still got work to do," I admit.

"You've done wonders already. We couldn't stop her from beating herself up. Only you could. I'm glad you saw the truth of everything, saw her point-of-view."

I sigh. "Unfortunately, not quick enough."

She shakes her head. "Definitely right timing. Difficult things tend to happen with the right timing, even if the reasons aren't always evident. Call me if you need anything. Any help. Anything. My sister deserves her happy ending, and I won't hesitate to use magic to help her get it if anything gets in the way again. We're all of that mindset."

"Glad to hear that."

My mate is talking to Jase and Joel at this point, so I move her way after closing the Land Rover's door.

"Later," I dismiss the boys.

"See you at dinner. I'll bring some sausage," Joel says.

I hear cackling from the Land Rover.

My mate is laughing, too.

"We heard that," Jase calls over, teasing.

There's more laughter.

"I'll bring beer," Jase offers.

"Whatever you want, boys," I agree, bending at the knee and taking my woman up and over my shoulder, ready to take her upstairs and peel this dress off her body.

I hear honks from the van and the Land Rover as the Young family pulls out.

42

ERICA

Riley carries me upstairs and then he stops.

"What's wrong?" I ask.

"My bed is covered with dresses and cats."

"I have a lot of dresses."

"And cats evidently."

"The crazy cat lady starter kit includes three cats. That's just the starter kit though, so count yourself lucky I didn't bring six."

I hear hissing times two. I bite my lip.

He turns and takes me into the ensuite bathroom.

"Fuck," he mutters and adjusts me, so I'm cradle-carried instead of over his shoulder.

"Yep. Told you I have lotsa plants," I remind him, realizing he's cussing because he was about to take me into the shower, but the shower and tub are both filled with plants because they needed water. I threw the shower on for a while to mist some and filled the tub with a few inches of water for my orchids and bonsai trees to get their drink from the bottom.

He marches out of his room with me and halts in the doorway of the next room, which now contains about a dozen boxes of mine. The other empty room is full of my stuff, too, mostly grimoires and craft implements. The guest room that has another bed is now the cat room, though they'd made themselves at home in Riley's room. This room now holds three litter boxes, food dishes, one of three cat trees, plus the tote of cat toys.

"Three litter boxes?"

"Six. Three more are in your laundry room. They don't like to share toilets and it's good to have more than one per cat."

"Why the room with the bed and not one of the empty ones?"

"I thought they'd like this one more. They like people-beds."

"Clearly," he replies.

Oscar, my ginger male cat, sleeps on his back with all four paws up in the center of the bed.

Riley's gaze bounces to me.

I try to stifle a giggle and fail. "Set me down and I'll move Oscar."

He sets me on the end of the bed.

"Oscar," I jiggle my cat's chubby belly. He opens one eye and then closes it, pretending to sleep.

"Oscar…" I tickle his foot. He flicks it and rolls to his belly. "Off the bed for a little while, kitty cat. We need it." I lift him up and snuggle him for a second before stretching to plop him on the rug beside the bed.

Oscar looks over his shoulder at Riley and then walks to him and does figure eights around Riley's legs.

"This one doesn't seem to have a hate on for me," he says.

"He was a dog in his past life," I deadpan.

Riley looks at me like he's trying to figure out if I'm shitting him or not. I crack a smile and cackle, falling to my back.

Riley pounces, flipping me to my stomach, hauling my dress up, and then I hear the sharp intake of breath before he whacks my bare bottom. "Wicked witch," he breathes as I gasp at the sting and give him what I know must be a sexually charged look over my shoulder. I know it must be sexually charged because I've seen that kind of look in his eyes often the past couple days. The past couple of absolutely blissful days.

He hauls me over his lap. "Like this dress, baby," he says.

"Thanks," I whisper, feeling my face heat.

"How many dresses you got?"

"Probably seventy."

He laughs. "But no underwear?" He gives me a stern look.

"Got lots of undies. Just not wearing any right now," I reply.

"Two of my pack brothers were here. Don't do that if people are over."

"I didn't know you were bringing them home," I defend. "I wanted to give you easy access, Dream Boat."

He gives me a saucy smile. "You always wear dresses?"

"Always," I reply.

"I fuckin' like a lot that you're always in a dress. Love easy access. Don't mind workin' for access either."

I smile wide. "I have some very complicated bustier and garter belt sets."

His eyes flash. "Let's circle back to that later. Right now, I'm thinking back to you sitting cross-legged on the grass out back and knowing there was nothing between those guys and what's mine? Doesn't make me too happy, mate."

"My dress was covering the vicinity," I say with an eyeroll.

"And if I'd growled?" he asks.

I blink with fake innocence.

"In fact, I did growl in the kitchen and that means you went back outside wet for me. I think you need another spanking before you get your fucking."

"I think you might be right." I nod in agreement.

He bursts out laughing and then whacks my butt one more time before he turns me over to my back and disappears under the full skirt of the dress.

Riley takes his time kissing from my inner thigh upwards and then he runs a hot palm up my smarting behind before he grabs it in a way that can only be taken as containing a strong message. "Naughty little witch. Whenever I catch you without panties, you're gettin' a spanking." He sucks my clit and then growls directly against it.

And I don't know if I'm about to melt, detonate, or both.

"What else will earn me some domestic discipline, Wolfie?" I ask breathlessly.

He laughs low and it's sexy as fuck.

"Whenever I feel you're naughty or sassy. How do you feel about that?"

"I feel like I might start being extra naughty with a side of sassy."

He moves up my body and laughs against my throat, against the very sensitive bitemark he put there.

"Love my sassy little witch."

"Love you, Riley," I say back, looping my arms around his neck.

And then I grab a handful of his hair and try to steer his head back under my skirt.

He doesn't make me exert too much effort.

But then he exerts a whole lot of effort under my dress.

IT'S DINNER PARTY TIME and the gang is here. All seven council alphas. My family. Bailey and her parents. Her father didn't shake my hand and I felt tension when he and Aunt Mimi greeted one another, but her mother did shake hands with all my sisters, Aunt Mimi, and then gave me a hug. And though I saw him flex his jaw muscles, he also looked guilty at me catching him do it. I offered a smile. Greyson pulled him aside at that point and things looked a little tense for a minute before Carrie and Graydon sat down and joined the conversation.

Tyson's mom Cat is also here with her partner Stan and of course Ivy and Amie are here too with their men. I also invited Cicely.

We're in the back yard and though there's only one table, several people brought lawn chairs.

Riley is at the grill working on the burgers, chicken, and sausages. I texted the group chat earlier and my sisters shopped on their way back, bringing food for dinner, including six types of salad and a whack of dessert items as well as two pre-made charcuterie boards from the Drowsy Hollow supermarket. And people who came brought food, wine, booze, and other appetizers.

The gate opens and Riley's mother is coming into the yard wearing a pretty sundress and carrying a bouquet of flowers. She's on the arm of a good-looking man with long, dark hair and a salt and pepper beard that I'd know is Riley's father Atticus even if she weren't on his arm. He's carrying a bottle of booze as well as a tub of something. Though Riley has his mom's eyes, he looks a lot like his dad. You can see the strong resemblance between Lucy Savage and her sister Cat. You can also see that the males in the family take after one another. Riley and Tyson are standing together and it's clear that Atticus Savage is related to them both.

Riley's mom's eyes seek me out, so I rise.

"Thank you so much for getting the house ready for me. It was so thoughtful, Mrs. Savage, I-"

She throws her arms around me and squeezes me tight. "I'm so sorry I was rude. I just..."

"It's okay," I whisper into her fragrant blonde hair.

"What you've been through. You... you poor thing." She hugs me tighter. "Call me Mom if you want. When you're ready. Or... Lucy. Whatever you're comfortable with. No pressure. What can I do to help here? I brought potato salad." She pulls back and looks at me with affection shining in her eyes. And then she cups my face with further affection and my heart feels like it might burst.

I see my man over at the grill with his eyes on us, a big smile on his gorgeous face.

"Give her here. Share a little, woman!" Riley's father scoops me up into a hug. "Nice to meet you, Erica. I'm Dad. Pop. Or Atticus. Friends also call me Ace. Whatever you're comfortable with. Welcome to the family." He sets me on my feet and kisses my forehead.

"Hi," I rasp. "Good to meet you, too. I don't need any help, Mrs... Lucy-Mom." I giggle. So does she. "Just have a seat and let me get you both something to drink."

"Sit with Lucy, Erica, I'll go put those in water for you and grab drinks. Long island iced teas?" Cicely offers.

"Ooh. Sounds good." Lucy rubs her palms together.

"Whiskey and ginger if you've got ginger ale," Riley's dad requests, handing her the bottle of booze. "If not-"

"Brought a couple mixes from the store and ginger ale was one of 'em," Cicley says. "I knew you'd be here."

"Good girl," Riley's dad says, ruffling Cicely's hair.

"Thank you, Cicely. Beautiful flowers, Lucy-Mom. Thank you so much," I say.

"My son says you like flowers. I do, too."

"You've done a lovely job here with the flowerbeds. Riley told me they're leftover from when you had the house."

She nods. "I would've cleaned those up before you came, but heard you're a green thumb so thought you might like to do it instead."

"You thought right. I can hardly wait to dig in and play."

"I love gardening," Lucy goes on. "Got a smaller yard at our house, our new house, which is just at the start of Chariot Lake Drive. Come over whenever you want; I'll show you. Have you seen Carrie Blackwood's place? Me and Carrie are green thumb buddies, and we have similar landscapes."

"Oh yeah, her garden is gorgeous! I'd love to join that green thumb club."

"You're in!" she exclaims, clasping my hand. "Right Carrie?"

"Absolutely!" Bailey's mom replies from the other end of the table. "There was a lovely garden center just outside The Hollow, but the owner passed away and now it's empty. We have to go almost an hour to the next one."

"An empty garden center?" I ask. And then I bite my lip before adding, "Is it for sale or for lease?"

Lucy smiles wide. "I bet it is."

"It is," Atticus says. "There's a *for lease* sign with a phone number on it outside. Drove by it yesterday."

I get a shiver. "I could run a business like that."

"You sure could," Vivica puts in.

"Oh my God! I could help you! Or just invest and be a silent partner and help you part-time. I'm a teacher, so I have summers off. Or..." Her face drops, "I mean... I don't want to horn in on your idea. Sorry...I got excited."

"Horn in, Lucy-Mom! Let's do it!" I exclaim. "We could sell some of the wares from Aunt Mimi's boutique, too. I used to go to a garden center that had a housewares section, an indoor furniture section, and a clothing and jewelry boutique in it, too. It was amazing. I could even sell fruits and vegetables, too."

Her eyes are lit up. "This empty garden center is huge. It'd work. It's on around ten acres so you could grow loads there. We could use more shopping choices close to home."

"Hey Mom. Dad." Riley comes over and kisses his mom's head, then hugs his father.

"Me and Erica are going into business together. I'm gonna call that realtor about the Green Grove Garden Center."

Riley looks at me and I can tell he's checking to see if I'm on board with this. I hope my smile tells him that I am one hundred per cent down for this.

Cicely comes over with two big beverages with lemon wedges on the corner. Bailey hands Atticus his mixed drink.

"Cheers," I lift my glass.

Lucy lifts hers and taps mine, then speaks loudly. "Cheers to our new daughter, everyone's new friend, and new pack-member, Erica."

Everyone raises glasses. Bailey passes Riley a beer.

"And I wanna toast my mate's family, the Youngs," Riley says. "Welcome."

"Hear, hear," Amelia calls out. She and Ivy clink their glasses of boozeless fruit punch.

Everyone drinks to my family. Even Graydon Blackwood, who has a dark expression but raises his glass anyway.

And the rest of the evening is spent with a chunk of the Arcana Falls pack. And they know how to have fun. They eat heartily, laugh unreservedly, and show one another love and care while making me and my family feel welcome.

After we eat and have dessert and before we get back into the boozing, Riley calls everyone's attention.

"Okay, listen up. Tomorrow, we've got this meeting. They'll be here around noon. I want the council there. The Youngs. Graydon, if you could talk to the other retired council members and give them the option. It's not a necessity, but any of you that want to come, it'd be appreciated to have a strong showing of alpha pack members."

"I'll be there," Graydon says. "So will Lorenzo. I'll talk to the others."

"I'll talk to my pop," Jase puts in. "I'm sure he'll wanna be there."

"Appreciated. Let's not worry about this for the rest of the night. Let's enjoy our evening. Tomorrow, I'll say my piece and hear what they have to say for themselves. From there, if any decisions need to be made that affect our pack, the current council will meet before anything is decided. If whatever happens has to do with just me and my mate, me and Erica will deal."

"We're with you," Tyson agrees heartily. "Whatever you need, brother."

I watch as Tyson throws his arms around Riley, and they embrace.

Riley looks at me with fire in his gaze. "What they did to you, to us... it was cruel and reprehensible. I don't know what the fuck they'll say about it, but I'm not going to hold back."

"They've got far-reaching powers, baby, so please be careful," I implore. "We have to tread carefully."

"I still don't know what happened," Bailey says.

"Neither do we," Ivy speaks up, gesturing between herself and her sister."

"I'll fill you guys in," I say.

"I'd like to speak to you," Aunt Mimi says, rising, her eyes on Riley. "And you." She looks at Greyson.

Greyson's father looks annoyed as they walk by. I catch Grey give his dad an unhappy look before he follows.

Riley drops a kiss on my neck before he cocks an arm so Auntie can hold onto him while he escorts her into the house. Greyson follows. I watch Graydon stare at the house with concern in his eyes.

And then I give a succinct but brief explanation of what happened and why. Bailey, Cicely, Ivy, and Amie are all aghast with horror. Riley's pack brothers all look pissed off.

Lucy excuses herself, looking upset on my behalf. She says she's going inside to clean up and make more coffee. Two of my sisters slip in with her to help and ask Bailey to follow.

I try to get the mood to bounce back to something more jovial and feel like I'm falling flat until Mason's parents show up with a crate filled with bottles of wine and moonshine. This finally changes the mood. Mason's mom Skye is a hoot and promises to shop in my and Lucy's future garden center. She also asks to set up a wine and moonshine rack on consignment with us and we're even more excited about the possibilities. Cicely tells me she makes candles and handmade soap and wants to know if she can put some in our garden center on consignment, too.

"This is going to be amazing," I squeal and pour more of Skye Quinn's honey wine.

IT'S ALMOST TWO IN the morning by the time the last of everyone has left and I'm on top of the world. Because I have Riley. I have Riley, and I'm here, and he's not going to toss me to the curb.

My family gets along with everyone, and the way things are going, they'll be treated like extended pack members. I couldn't be happier. Amie, Ivy, Cicely, and Bailey are acting like they're my four new best friends and my heart is full.

My sisters took Aunt Mimi home so she could get some sleep and then came back. All were tipsy except for Dani, who chose to be the designated driver. Jase was flirting with her some more and I saw Bailey watching them, looking a little crushed. I'm glad my sister was sober and didn't pay Jase much mind.

I'm a little tipsy and wearing a perma-smile as I fall into bed.

Riley comes in a minute later, shucking his clothes off and dropping them into the hamper.

"Aw! You use a hamper!" I give him a melty look.

His eyes bounce between me and the wicker hamper and then his brows go up. He's confused.

"I don't have to pick your clothes up off the floor. God, you're perfect!" He laughs.

"I don't always use the hamper," I admit. "You might have to pick up my clothes occasionally."

"I'm happy to do that, mate."

"Aww. You're the best. What time is it, Mr. Wolf?"

"Dunno. Two, three? Why?"

"No. What *time* is it, Mr. Wolf?"

"Time to knot my mate?" he guesses.

"I guess you don't know that game," I say. "You're supposed to tell me how many o'clocks it is and then I take that many steps."

"Huh?"

"And then when I'm super close, or not, you decide as you're Mr. Wolf, and then I ask what time it is again, and you say *Dinnertime!* And then you chase me."

"Oh yeah?"

"Oh yeah," I nod.

"I could eat some dinner," he tells me, looking at me with carnal intention.

"Bon Appetit," I invite and throw my skirt up, giggling.

"What time is it, Mr. Wolf?" I ask.

He puts his knee to the bed, and I hear hissing.

"No room for me?" he asks, looking down at the bed.

There are two cats hissing again to give him his answer. Petunia is the ringleader, and she doesn't want him here.

"Little witch? Wanna get your pets outta here? Unless they wanna be catapulted outta the room?"

I laugh. "You wouldn't."

"No?" he asks, a wicked gleam in his eyes.

"Petunia and Penny, that's not very friendly," I tell them. "Penny just hisses when Toonie does. She's not cranky like Miss Cranky Pants."

"Don't care who, what, or why, just want them gone so I can fuck you, baby."

"How does the catapult work?" I ask.

He looks surprised.

"I'm joking. Don't throw my cats. I'll get testy."

He snickers as I get up and scoop one into each arm, then I carry them down the hall, put them in the guestroom bed with Oscar. I go back to Riley's room, shutting the door behind me.

"I had so much fun tonight," I say, putting a knee to the bottom of the bed.

"Good," he replies, leaning back and watching me crawl to him.

"Your pack is great."

"I know."

"Your dad is so nice. Your mom? She is awesome."

He laughs. "Evidently awesome enough to plan to go into business with forty-five seconds after she got here?"

I nod. "Yup. I would rock owning a nursery. A nursery and so much more."

"I bet you would, lookin' at all the plants here. You probably won't still need me to build you a greenhouse out back, then?" he asks.

"Duh. Of course I will," I reply.

He chuckles. "Get up here, woman." He opens his arms reaches for me, and I finish the climb up Mount Riley.

"I'm here," I announce. "But I wasn't gonna come all the way up here. Don't you want a blowjob?"

He gives me a sexually charged look. "The answer to that question will always be yes, mate. So no need to ask."

"Girls complain about doing that, but I think it's fun." I shrug.

"You're a little drunk there, mate. And fuckin' perfect for me."

"A little drunk, yes. I'd say Cicely makes a strong Long Island Iced Tea, but I'm also a lightweight."

"Apparently," he observes.

Then again, I drank three glasses of the wine Mason's mom brought, too.

"But it's good that I'm a lightweight and I'm a little drunk because it means I'll be able to sleep tonight instead of worrying about this meeting tomorrow. What did Aunt Mimi say to you?"

"Don't worry about all that, babe. I've got this thing. I'm gonna handle it. Don't sweat it, okay?"

"Riley," I get choked up. "I don't want them to do anything else to punish us. Please don't be all alpha badass with them. Please just... don't do anything that'll-"

"Darlin', they're not gonna fuck with us anymore. They're gonna answer for their sins and if I don't like their answers, we're done dealing with them. If I find avenues to complain about what they did to the other people on the council they gotta answer to, I'll do that. If we deem our pack just isn't gonna deal with them anymore, that might be what we do."

"But our coven's work..."

"Don't you worry about it. Let's see what they say, and we'll go from there. I'm not gonna have a kneejerk reaction, baby. I'm gonna hear them out and then we'll go from there. Okay?"

"Okay. I'm a little scared of my powers now, Riley."

"Why, baby?" He cradles my face. I snuggle in and lay on him.

"I always felt like I was working within the balance. Give and take. Give more than I take. Do everything with good intentions. Bank energy and goodwill so I have it when I need it. Share it where it's needed and warranted to help others. But when those guys tried to take me and I connected with the earth and sent my request to the roots of the weeping willow, it felt like I didn't have to ask. It felt like... like... there was no need for balance. Like all the energy was just mine for the taking. And then the anger I felt when that other guy was hurting you? It was a little scary. Felt so much energy when we got here yesterday, and I put my hands in the dirt. I can just use it up. As much as I want. But that's weird. It goes against everything I've been taught."

"We'll figure it out. Okay?"

I nod. I glazed over it with Aunt Mimi and my sisters. Maybe I should've been more direct about my fears. But the visit was all happy and fun and I didn't want to take the mood to someplace dark.

"I killed those two shifter bad guys, and I didn't even mean it."

"They deserved it."

"I don't want to fuck anything up. I don't want to risk hurting you, hurting my coven and our work, harming your pack that's being so, so fucking nice to me."

"You won't, baby. You won't."

I'm not feeling so sure.

Riley starts purring for me, knowing just what I need.

I feel myself sinking into his warm, comforting embrace and my eyes drift closed as it feels like I'm swimming through a warm, calm sea.

43

RILEY

I startle awake, shaking off a dream of the angry river. I dove in, certain she was in there, sure I could pull her out. But I just kept falling.

She's asleep beside me. I stare at her in the pre-dawn shadows, making out every feature. Listening to her breathe. Love floods me. My beautiful mate is here. Safe. Mine.

And my and Grey's conversation with Mimi Young comes back to me.

She told us as default coven lead after her older sister's death a few years ago, she was supposed to take on the responsibility of notifying the SCC before Erica finally revealed herself to me. They wanted to have a meeting first, before we mated. They wanted to control things, oversee my mate because of their visions of the sort of power she'd come into upon mating. Erica doesn't know her aunt broke the rules by not telling the SCC. Our eventual union has been a topic of interest for the SCC for years, apparently.

She told us it's likely they're going to put sanctions on her for not cooperating and furthermore, Mimi Young doesn't give a shit. She hasn't discussed her niece's new powers with her in any depth yet. She says that's Erica's business. She also told me she knows her niece has paid too much of a price for loving me already.

Mimi wanted to let it all play out without the council's interference. She felt since it was none of their business, she was leaving them out of it. The family decided to send Erica to me, tell her it was time, knowing it was the right time because of the birth order. Tyson and Mason had mated, so she said she'd argue that the council didn't need to know.

Mimi did not know Danica would reveal my mate's scent to me that day in the back of the drycleaners. But after that, the family had a meeting and decided it was time for Erica Young to move forward with her life without further SCC involvement. Mimi wants me and Grey to step up and support her nieces if something goes wrong in that meeting.

She then dismissed me and I left her and Grey alone for another conversation. Whatever that conversation was, I have no idea, but Grey left the party shortly after with a hard look in his eyes and a glare pointed at his old man as he said his farewells.

I'm skipping my run this morning. I decided that yesterday, wanting the whole morning with my mate, in case she's nervous. But I'm now wishing I'd taken the pack up on the late night run some of them went on last night as I've got pent-up energy.

I'm pondering going down to the Savage Construction office in my garage to run on my treadmill and get at least some of this energy spent.

But my mate stirs and looks at me with bright eyes and then a darker, sexually charged expression as her gaze travels over my chest. My favorite scent hits my nose. Her arousal.

I could run on the treadmill this morning. Or, I can exert my energy here since she fell asleep last night before I had a chance to fuck her.

"Ask me what time it is," I invite.

Her brows scrunch with confusion.

"What time it is…" I repeat, giving her a loaded look. I roll my hand.

Recognition hits her eyes, and she clears her throat. "What time is it, Mr. Wolf?" Though it's still dim in this room, I see amusement dancing in her eyes.

"Dinnertime," I announce and then disappear under the blankets.

"I'm supposed to run first," she breathes as my tongue spears her tight pussy.

"Next time," I say and then drive two fingers into her while I suck her clit. Hard.

WE WATCH MITCH'S RENTAL car pull into the parking lot of the town hall. It's Mitch with two women. This means the vampire who fought their decision didn't come. I plainly smell that they're both witches.

I feel my mate's nervous energy in the passenger seat beside me. I squeeze her hand. "It's gonna be okay, darlin.'"

She nods and squeezing my hand back, I know it's not just lip service. She believes me. She has faith in me. And it means a fuck of a lot. I drop a kiss on her hand and then let go so I can get out. "Stay here. I'll open your door."

Mitch, around my father's age, gets out looking like he typically looks, though he's dressed a little nicer in a solid black button down with new-looking jeans instead of his usual flannel over a t-shirt and worn denim.

The back passenger side door opens and a striking woman in, probably, her forties gets out and looks around. She has short, dark hair, dark eyes, expertly applied make-up, and is dressed in a designer black power suit and high heels with red soles.

The front passenger door opens and an older woman, maybe in her upper sixties gets out. She's plump, more bohemian than power suit, wearing a long skirt and a colorful blouse. She has her long, salt and pepper hair in a braided ponytail.

I open the door for my mate, take her hand and we approach, coming to a stop ten feet away.

"Lucinda Alexander, Riley Savage." Mitch gestures to the power suit wearing woman who gives me a once-over without expression. "And Aviva Starling," he gestures to the bohemian one who smiles warmly.

I fold my arms over my chest. "I'd say welcome to Arcana Falls, ladies, but not sure I'm feeling all that friendly given how you fucked our lives."

"Hello," my mate croaks.

"Erica," Aviva Starling greets and holds her hands out.

"Miss Young," the other woman returns formally.

"Mrs. Savage," I correct.

Lucinda Alexander doesn't react.

My mate steps up and accepts the outstretched hands.

I grind my teeth.

"Oh my," Aviva Starling says with wonder and her eyes cut to Lucinda who raises a perfectly arched eyebrow. "Oh my," she repeats.

She lets go of my mate and I grab Rikki's hand, not liking that this woman read her by touch.

Inside, there are chairs set up for the group that's here for support. As we cross the threshold into the addition that holds our meeting rooms and the library, which leads to the barn space where we usually have pack events, I see Jase moving ahead of us, likely to corral the group. By the time we're inside I see everyone is sitting down. My mother and Aunt Cat have left but they set the space up for us earlier. They put all the seating in a wide circle, which my father told me in a text message he and my mother decided on intentionally.

Nobody is sitting at the head or the foot of a table. Nobody will be up on a podium looking down at anyone else. To the side of the circle, which is full other than five empty chairs, two at one side, three to the other side of the circle, is a table with refreshments.

"A crowd?" Lucinda observes, looking annoyed.

"My mate's family and some of mine."

She says nothing.

"Hello all," Aviva greets.

"Everyone," Mitch greets.

"Feel free to help yourself to refreshments and then we can talk," I invite.

"I don't need refreshments ahead of this," Lucinda says.

Aviva moves to the table and selects a bottle of juice and a muffin before sitting down in an empty chair. "How is everyone!" she greets happily before taking a hearty bite of muffin.

Nobody answers.

Lucinda rolls her eyes and looks at the room with boredom.

Mitch takes a seat.

The room is silent, but you could cut the animosity with a knife.

"Mimi," Aviva greets. "How have you been?"

"Aviva." Mimi returns the greeting with an unreadable expression but doesn't answer the question.

Aviva opens her juice and takes a sip.

I look at Mitch. "Let's get this done then."

Mitch nods, then speaks, "Good morning. I was asked to sit on the committee for SCC treaty infractions by Erica Young against Riley Savage seven years back. I was one of the committee members chosen because I'm a wolf shifter. When a code of conduct infraction is up for debate by the Supernatural Council Collective, there are typically supernaturals from multiple groups. Two from the group of the accused, as well as two from other groups including wherever possible the group of the other party."

I pipe up. "Clearly not all parties involved, though, right? Because you're calling it an infraction by Erica Young against me, yet nobody called me to attend any trial or meeting."

"I realize this, Riley, but there's a reason for that and we will get into it. As I was saying, there was a committee to hear the issue as well as to discuss consequences. The other committee members were the two witches here today, along with Sergei Voitenko, a vampire elder. I invited Sergei to come today, but he couldn't fit this into his schedule. Lucinda happened to be here in the country, and Aviva got on the first available flight from Eastern Europe after my call. I was staying with Eddy, visiting with his pack in Washington, still, so didn't have a long journey to make back here."

I lean forward, giving him a look of impatience. I've always gotten along fine with Mitch. I know he's advised Aunt Cat on some medical issues several times and he's fishing buddies with my father and Andy Quinn, but he likes the sound of his own voice.

Mitch seems to pick up on my impatience, quickly adding, "Sergei advised he will gladly speak to Riley or Erica if they'd like. He left his phone number. I'll forward it to you, Riley."

"Uh huh," I say, impatiently.

"Should I continue or would one of you like to?" He looks to the witches.

"I'll speak," Aviva says. "Our aim with Erica's punishment seems harsh to you now, from what I understand."

"Understatement," I clip.

My mate squeezes my hand.

"Yes, but necessary. You see, most covens have a generation every two or three that is stronger than the previous few. We happen to know that the current Young coven generation is stronger than has been seen in many generations. Many. If not stronger than *any*."

The sisters all exchange looks that have me bracing.

Aviva keeps talking, "Knowing their potential for substantial powers and as we do on the supernatural council collective, we paid attention. While the first four born to the family are strong, formidable witches, we knew the youngest would be a force of nature. Quite literally. Lucinda saw it coming before you were born, Erica."

"What does that mean?" my mate asks.

Aviva looks at her with a kind look. "I think it might already be obvious to you. You are a force of nature. You no longer need to tap into nature in the way the rest of us do. We knew that your mating would unlock it. Level your abilities up, so to speak. Partly, we believe, because of where you were conceived, partly because of who your fated mate is. It's also this area. The magic in this region connects with the mating ritual, linking profound events in a supernatural being's life. Lucinda, as the senior seer of the council, was privy to some frightening statistics about not only your potential for power but also the fact that it would hit after you mated with Riley Savage. Another witch who has since died got a vision of you taking matters into your own hands after seeing that wolf shifter before the right timing. We had to intervene and guide events to mitigate risk."

How much intervention? The look on Lucinda Alexander's face is chilling. I don't trust her.

"You knew what I was going to do before I did it?" Rikki asks.

Lucinda replies. "What we knew specifically is irrelevant."

Aviva continues speaking, "But, we believed it necessary to delay you coming into excess power too early. Your efforts to hasten the mating would mean you'd come into power far too early, way before you were ready to handle being a force of nature rather than being part of the balance of nature. Erica, dear, you've got the potential for dark magic that even dark witches don't have."

"I don't get it," I say.

Lucinda speaks up again. "Witches operate within the confines of a code of conduct necessitated by the balance of energy. Give and take. Give more than you take. Erica has come into power that gives her access without cosmic repercussions hitting her. It's a big responsibility as well as a burden. And a delicate balancing act is required even if nature doesn't require it. Do you understand, Erica?"

My mate nods, looking a little pale.

Aviva adds, "You'll be asked at a certain point to take a position on this council. To help keep the balance in check for all supernaturals."

"What if I don't want that?" my mate asks.

"We already know you don't want it. But it's something you'll need to do. You are needed," Lucinda tells her.

"I don't understand," my mate says.

Mimi speaks up. "They wanted to humble you so that when you came into power you wouldn't abuse it. And from my perspective, so that you'd be submissive to their agenda."

All eyes are on her. The two visiting witches do not look pleased.

Mimi continues. "They therefore bestowed upon you the cruelest punishment they could give you so that you would be humbled. So that you would know what you could lose if not careful. So that when you got what was coming to you – your power along with your fated partner in life, you would be cautious."

"Wait a fuckin' second," I snap. "You all used our relationship as a tool to keep her humble? To make sure she was so fuckin' broken from having to live a lie for seven years so you could control her and her powers when she got them?"

Nobody says anything and that's my answer.

There's dangerous energy surging through the room. Rikki's sisters are all livid. Mimi still stands, glaring. My family, my pack members are all staring with awe in their expressions.

"Nobody seeks to control her," Aviva states, "And she's likely mated to you because of the strength of your pack. You're her protector. She was humbled, yes, taught the importance of balance, of following the rules. The news of her strength should not be widely shared as it would leave her vulnerable. And not only would your mate be too powerful for her maturity level if you'd mated right after she cast that spell, her location here and proximity to Greyson, also of the Young coven are factors."

Grey straightens up in his chair and looks confused.

Lucinda interjects, "Two Young coven members mating here, linking the coven and the pack further churns up a new, large hornet's nest of power here. You all have to be cognizant of that. Young coven: you need to direct Greyson Blackwood at the same time as guide your sister to keep both of them on the right path. If either of them veer into dark territory, it's on you all to report them to us."

"What the fuck?" Grey mutters.

"Greyson Blackwood has potential to be a powerful warlock," Aviva advises. "With training he can be. He should have been the oldest of a family of at least three, which was what was in the cards for Graydon Blackwood and Soleil Young if they'd remained mated. Greyson's mother's actions impacted that. When Greyson mated, he inherited the powers of what would've gone to his unconceived siblings as well as what was stripped from his mother. Wolf shifter matings are always monumental. They're that much more so with this pack due to the sorcery involved in forming this pack and linking its alpha males."

Greyson looks at his father. His father says nothing, but holds his son's stare and it's obvious that Graydon either has very strong opinions on all of this or maybe even has some knowledge of this part of things. Though I doubt he knew he should've had three kids with Greyson's mother. And I had no idea Greyson would come into his mother's power when he mated.

"Erica," Aviva calls out, "I would love to invite you to come to train with me at my sorceresses' retreat in Albania. We can help you learn to-"

"No," I reply.

All eyes cut to me.

"Absolutely not," I continue. "I don't trust you people as far as I can throw you. And believe me, I wanna fuckin' throw all of you."

"Riley," my mate whispers with panic in her voice at the same time as Mitch says my name in a warning tone.

"Mr. Savage?" Aviva's tone is placating. "Please understand, we only want to help. She needs help learning to not only wield but control the powers she has. And the SCC and all supernaturals could benefit greatly from her participation as well. Your soulmate is a loving and caring person, so she'll get a lot out of this as well. She-"

"No," I repeat. Everything in my gut tells me this.

My mate squeezes my hand.

"What sort of interference was there?" she asks Aviva and Lucinda, then turns her gaze to Mimi. "And how much of this did you know about?"

Aviva speaks. "Lyrica Young as head of your coven when you sat trial, knew everything. I don't know if she passed it all on to Mimi. But I'm sure Lyrica at least advised Mimi of certain requirements that were not met. We've also asked several times for confirmation about the mating, both from Lyrica and more recently, Mimi."

All eyes swing to Mimi as she speaks. "My sister and I raised and trained our nieces well. Erica advised that she hadn't mated when you made us work with you to yank her out of there the way we did and as you can see by my niece's husband's face, this caused deep damage. We objected to everything done. I did choose to let these two mend their relationship on their own. I did as you asked when he approached me in my covenstead and asked him if they'd mated although I already knew the answer."

"Yet you did not tell us when she decided to come here to enlighten him. She wasn't supposed to choose when to do that."

"Her coven chose the timing," Mimi advises. "It was within treaty guidelines."

"Not within sentencing guidelines, though," Lucinda states.

"And if that means repercussions, so be it. My sister and I have taught these five well. If you take my magic, I have no doubts they'll take care of me. But I've already implemented that my power will go straight to Greyson in the event of my magic being stripped. It will go to him and not to the SCC. My sister bequeathed hers to me upon her death, so if you think my niece and nephew are forces to be reckoned with now, you do not want to get on their bad side now, never mind if you take my magic and he winds up angry with you for it."

Rikki looks shocked.

Grey stares at Aviva and Lucinda with a glacial expression.

Clearly, Greyson and I need a catch-up.

"Your niece would've made a mess and if you were being impartial in this situation like you should be, you'd know it," Lucinda states.

Mimi's mouth opens but my mate speaks instead, and she does it sounding broken.

"I would've."

"Baby," I say, hating that tone in her voice.

My mate looks at me. "I would've made a mess, Riley. A royal one."

I shake my head. I hate seeing her vulnerable like this in front of her peers. I see them as predators and as a predator myself, I don't want her to show an ounce of weakness to these enemies. But here she is in all her beauty and vulnerability. I'm her protector and they're not going to get between us again.

"Riley, as a witch I've always been very aware of how much energy and goodwill I have stored. Until the other day at the cabin, I knew things changed with my abilities, but I didn't know why. I didn't notice until then that I've now got access to this vault filled with energy. It's endless, Riley. It's in me and it's around me. And that's a little terrifying."

"Which is why Mimi was to tell us when you were about to reveal yourself to him," Aviva says. "We interfered where we needed to, based on our gifts. We did what we needed to do just like your coven does what you're compelled to do, due to your visions and your desire to do good works. You have your work; we have ours. Your work is to do with people and other supernaturals. Ours is to do with supernaturals at your level. The only way to keep the balance was to make sure that this powerful young witch knew the price of her power. You now know it, don't you, Erica Young?"

"Savage," I correct.

My mate smiles shakily at me and then looks at Aviva. "I do. You're right."

"Bullshit," I clip.

"No Riley," my beautiful mate says with her heart on her sleeve. "I was always so impatient. I never looked before crossing the street. I just ran out going after whatever shiny thing I had my eye on. When I found out I was a witch, I broke the rules like crazy and dabbled with potions and spells before I was allowed to. I couldn't wait. I didn't... I wasn't mature enough. After what happened with us, after seeing what damage I could do with my bad habits of waving my wand before thinking things through, I took more time. More effort. I made sure to look both ways, to dot my i's and cross my t's. I became very careful and methodical so I wouldn't make mistakes. So I wouldn't cause any more unnecessary hurt. I'm so sorry that my personality flaws meant they had to-"

"No. Stop right there. Not true. You do not have personality flaws, baby. That's bullshit." I'm furious. I'm absolutely fuckin' furious. I'm ready to rip shit up.

"I had a lot of growing up to do. And I think I've done that, but I also think I *do* want some additional training," she says. "This new access I have? It's... it's big. I'm not entirely sure how to use it. And I don't want to hurt anyone or mess anything up."

Lucinda says, "She gets it."

Aviva nods. "She does."

"It was explained to me," Mitch speaks up, "And I'm bound by the guidelines of the supernatural council so I couldn't say anything. But I knew that of all shifters I knew that weren't of my own pack, there was no better pack for this witch to be fated to than this one, Savage. You're a strong, family-minded man who puts your pack above all. The only thing you'd put above your pack is your mate. And if you had to work for it, if you had to deal with some shit to make sure your pack and your mate were where they're meant to be, you'd do it. Even if it takes you a while to come around due to your anger at your loved one feeling pain."

I glare at him. Not sure how this fucker thinks he knows me this well. He's friends with my father, was good friends with Tiberius and a few of the other council alphas in that generation but he hasn't spent a shit-ton of time with me. Then again, he's not wrong. The only thing more important than my pack to me *is* my mate. *This* quickly. I know it with everything I am that she's my top priority.

Aviva speaks up again. "We asked to spend the night because it's a lunar eclipse event this evening and as you know, Erica, it's a big night for many covens. This would be a wonderful location to experience that. Together, we could have a really lovely experience, if we are permitted to perform some enrichment and good-will rituals with you. We can also help you flex your new muscles safely inside a circle, which I'm told you haven't really done yet." There's almost a question in Aviva's statement.

My mate has a guilty expression and I squeeze her hand. I don't know if these assholes know she took out two betas from Silver Hills with her powers but if they don't, they don't need to know.

"We've arranged accommodations outside the village," Greyson speaks up.

"Where?" Aviva asks.

"Across the lake," Grey replies. "We'll ferry you there when we're done here."

"If we could return tonight to the site where Lucinda and I pulled you out?" Aviva asks, eyes on my mate. "The area where you cast your love spell as well. Same area, I'm guessing. The area near the Holloway events of two hundred-odd years ago."

"Riley and I need to speak privately before we agree to anything," she replies and rises.

I rise as well.

My fury, my unease, it abates at her touch. Though I could've had this touch for seven years instead of just a few days, so it doesn't diminish my anger much.

"Can Riley and I go talk now?" she asks.

"You don't need to ask these people permission to leave, to talk to me, babe," I say, my emotions very evident in my voice. "These fuckin' assholes fucked our lives up, taking it upon themselves to make decisions for us, punishing us based on something you might or might not do."

"Riley..." she whispers.

"It needed to happen this way, Riley," Mitch states.

"Bullshit." My blood is pumping harder. I'm on a razor's edge here. "You people are fucked," I snap.

"Baby," she pleads, squeezing my hand.

"Things happened this way because they were meant to," Lucinda states. "Fate uses us to facilitate its needs and ensure balance, just like it does with your soulmate."

"Very much like the Young coven," Aviva adds.

I shake my head with exasperated disbelief. "Seven years you stole from us. Seven years you left her wallowing in pain based on a hunch?"

Lucinda says, "You two weren't supposed to mate until after Tyson and Mason. She jumped the gun. It had to be stopped."

I cut her off. "We mated after Greyson. I was supposed to mate before he did so that sounds like a load of bullshit."

"And has it caused problems? Have you had any mental difficulties? Because we requested the coven's ledgers before we got here and looked through them. It was noted that their interference with the birth order among sisters who are fated to alphas one and two affected alpha two's mental wellbeing."

Mason shifts in his chair uncomfortably. Rikki gives him a look of apology.

"Alpha one is Tyson and alpha two is Mason. We aren't numbers here. We're people who don't appreciate being fucked with."

"You're not privy to all the intricacies involved. Erica knows how these things sometimes unfold," Lucinda defends. "The next seven will be different from this seven. And these seven have been slightly varied from the previous seven due to events with alpha one. Things are fluid in magic. We react based on the information we're given, and on how the world changes, on how our visions direct us. There are many moving parts. We knew we had to stop the mating of the two of you seven years ago. We had to ensure that this one could mature to come into her power. Just like Erica and her sisters knew they had to facilitate keeping alpha two away from the second born Brennan sister until she mated with the first-born council alpha otherwise that would've gone very differently and your council of seven would be a council of six or even five."

"What?" Mason asks.

There's loaded silence for a beat before Vivica speaks, eyes bouncing between Ty and Mase.

"You two could've killed one another," she says, "You'd both have fought to the death. I saw it. I got alternating visions of either you dead, Mason, or both of you, Mason *and* Tyson. We had to find a way to stop it."

Mason rubs his forehead. Tyson's eyes narrow. They exchange glances then and I'm shook, imagining our pack without one or both of them.

Vivica continues, "The tethered bond your council had over you worked when it did because there were multiple generations and other strong alphas present, but if that confrontation had happened sooner than it did, there wouldn't have been enough of a tether and Tyson wouldn't have been as open to listening to the strength of that tethered bond coming from many people. We calculated how long it might be before Mason and

Tyson met and hoped it would be in a crowd. I saw the dance as the only location where it could feasibly work out. Thankfully, it did, although I know it was difficult."

Mason and Ty exchange looks and I'm sure one or both of them are thinking about how wrong that night went.

Tyson's lip curls and I give him a look loaded with meaning. Any anger he has about that needs to wait.

He seems to either get my meaning or decide himself as I watch his expression clear.

Aviva speaks up again. "We do what we can with the information given to us. That's what the Youngs did to help with the matings of the first two. You wolf shifters don't understand it because you haven't lived it yet, but Riley, you will see times when these witches have to spend hours, even days working through problem-solving tactics to do their work. It doesn't always just happen in a snap."

I see agreement in the eyes of the sisters as the woman continues to plead her case. "We had to do what we had to do to ensure Erica Young was ready for what was coming to her. We spent many hours weighing all the variables before a decision was made. I can see that Mimi Young did what she felt she needed to do by withholding information to give you two time to heal the breach, and-"

"The breach caused by your fuckin' asinine decisions," I snap.

Lucinda and Aviva exchange looks.

Lucinda speaks. "We won't deliver any punishments to you Mimi, for your part here. We know your time is limited and you'll want to spend what's left helping alpha four... Greyson... learn to wield his powers as well as hand the chain of command over for your coven."

"What?" Vivica asks.

"Time is short. Mine comes to an end soon," Mimi states. "Very soon. Within the next year I'll begin to decline. But I haven't announced who will take over for me as head of this coven."

My mate and her sisters all react. Vivica and Jessica both drop their heads. Danica and Veronica grasp one another's hands. I can feel my mate's sheer terror at the idea of losing the matriarch of their family. Her teacher. The mother-figure she's had since she was twelve.

I squeeze her hand.

"The ceremony tonight could bring you extra years with quality of life," Lucinda offers.

"But from that magic, you'd both take some of mine," Rikki speaks.

Aviva has the decency to look contrite. Lucinda says nothing.

"A coven trifecta in a place like this on a night like tonight could buy each of you more time," Rikki says. "Any witch over the age of fifty. And if I train with you, you'll have further access to my magic and that could mean more power for you. More goodwill banked on your end. A lot of it if my well is endless."

They say nothing for a long minute. Nobody does.

"It costs you nothing to share," Aviva finally answers. "You have an infinite amount of it at your disposal. Adding what you have to your sisters' individual gifts? Very powerful indeed. Couple it with Danica's healing strengths along with energy from the Starling and Alexander covens and it might buy Mimi five more good years, even. And will do good things for all three covens along with strengthening your bond with the supernatural council collective, which is never a bad idea. You may have an endless amount of energy at your disposal, but remember that there may come a time when you need advice, when you need goodwill that comes from relationships rather than magic. Having friends on the SCC is a good idea."

Rikki says nothing. I can feel emotions surging inside her and can tell she's processing information.

I pipe up. "My mate and I need time to talk. We rented a three-bedroom cottage for you across the lake. Mason can take you so you can rest in the meantime."

"Your father invited me to stay with him and your mother," Mitch advises.

"Our council here would prefer you host the witches, Mitch," I say to him carefully.

"And I have to say," my father speaks up, "Not feeling too hospitable, Mitch, finding out you knew all this for seven years and kept it from me."

Mitch looks unsurprised at my dad's reaction. Good, because he needs to take some responsibility here. Not hang out and golf, fish, or shoot the shit with his old buddies. He was just here and did plenty of that then.

"Wait," Rikki says. "What if I say no? What if I say no to tonight and no to the training? Are there repercussions?"

I growl and all eyes hit me. "You don't need to be afraid of these people, baby," I tell her. "I've got you. And furthermore, you're more powerful than they are."

I know by their expressions that I'm right. She is far more powerful than they are. I suspect she could crush them without flexing a muscle.

"Not quite, Riley Savage," Lucinda calls out, eyes sharp.

"Excuse me?"

"She'd have to flex a few muscles to take us out."

"Lucinda reads minds," Rikki whispers.

I hide nothing, I send all my animosity toward this bitch.

She smiles in response with a look that says she thinks I'm cute or some shit and lifts one shoulder in a shrug, then she examines her nails.

Aviva speaks up again. "We're going in circles here for the benefit of you, Riley, because we know the Young witches understand that we did not make these decisions lightly. We calculated all our options just the way they do when faced with important dilemmas. We knew that because of the nature of the shifter mate bond, that you'd heal your mate and that you'd come to a place eventually where you'd be able to move forward. All of this was for the greater good."

Lucinda adds, "You'll see that once your hotheaded alpha testosterone levels out."

I bare my teeth.

Aviva looks my girl in the eye. "You know this, too."

My mate squeezes my hand with reassurance. "Why don't we all take a break? Riley and I can go talk. Maybe my family can relax at..." Her eyes search the space. "Is Roxy's open?"

Mason answers. "They can hang at my house, Erica. Bunch of the women are over there waiting for this to be done. They've put out a spread."

"Thank you, Mason. So, everyone, we'll talk again in a few hours?" Rikki suggests.

Mitch gets to his feet. As do the two witches.

And then as the rest of the circle rises, I tug my mate's hand to get her the fuck out of here.

44

ERICA

The anger is practically seeping from Riley's pores as he drives us home. I know if I wasn't here, he'd have shifted and gone for a long run to try to burn it off. Instead, he drives a little too fast, but in less than a minute we're in the driveway.

I follow him inside. He slams the door.

"Unfuckingbelievable!" he shouts.

My cat Petunia hisses from her perch on the coffee table.

He points at my cat. "Fuck you, too."

She lifts a paw and licks it, not caring that he just swore at her.

"They're right. I would've messed up with all this power," I say softly.

"Baby," he reaches for my face with both hands, eyes softening.

I shake my head. "No, Riley. I would've. I wasn't ready seven years ago."

"I don't believe that for a second."

"I broke the rules constantly," I exclaim. "Made invisibility potions so I could spy on you when I was nineteen and got caught by Aunt Lyrica who warned me. But it bounced off me. I always read ahead in the grimoires. She'd tell me to only read twenty pages and I'd read forty. She'd tell me to do something level five and I'd try for seven or eight. I had no patience. I was supposed to wait five years to even practice and I was breaking the rules almost from day one."

"You're an overachiever."

"I broke the rules with blatant disregard and made that love potion!"

"Because of the magic wine," he adds.

"Even still. I was being careless."

"Wanting me wasn't careless," I tell her. "You identified your fated mate, just like wolf shifters do."

"If I approached without the spell, you wouldn't have wanted to immediately claim me."

"Did I not flirt with you that day when you hit the fire hydrant? I watched you run off hoping I'd see you again. We could've started dating. We could've built a relationship from there."

"You wouldn't have known yet that we're meant to be. It probably wouldn't have gone anywhere. I might've gone ahead and made a spell anyway because I'd want you a hundred per cent in and to be all about me and only me."

"We don't know that."

"Besides, if I was careful, I wouldn't have drunk the wine because I would've noticed it was open. Do you think if they hadn't stopped me that day and magicked me out of there, I wouldn't have let you claim me, mate with me?"

He sighs. "If only..."

"I would've, Riley. In a heartbeat. All my dreams would've been coming true. And then I'd have all that power and wouldn't be afraid to use it. I'd use it to solve all the problems I came across. For my coven. For your pack. For anybody I ran into. I'd be like a fairy godmother with her wand granting everyone's wishes without worry because I wouldn't have learned the importance of balance. I wouldn't have had important requests denied because I hadn't built up enough good will and energy yet. I'd have had you and I'd have had all that power and I would've felt invincible because all my dreams came true. I wouldn't have learned how to break it all down in flowcharts looking at all possibilities as well as probabilities."

"Baby..."

"No, Riley, I learned the hard way by losing you, by hurting you, that I have to calculate possibilities and probabilities and possible pitfalls. I learned to be cautious, careful, considerate of possibilities. I worked hard the past ten years to learn my craft. Even harder the last seven when I wasn't just trying to learn, but also trying to do good in the world. To do the right things, Riley, instead of the fun things or the easy things. To be someone you wouldn't think was just a selfish witch bitch. I didn't think I'd ever get the chance to wake up beside you. I didn't think you'd ever aim that beautiful smile at me again. I learned my lesson by what they put me through, and I won't take having a real chance with you for granted. Ever."

"Sweetheart..."

"Never. I'll never take what we have for granted. I'm so, so sorry you got hurt along the way, Riley. I am. I wish I could take that back. But I know I can't take it back without causing harm. Because you and me? We've learned how important it is to take care of one another, Riley. We both learned that, didn't we? You malfunctioned and got locked out of your own body and that taught you things, too. All this time you've been doing all these good things for your pack, taking care of people, being a good man, good friend, good son and brother. We've been on this journey that has been the hard apart, but we know what's important now. Imagine how much good we can do together? We've earned this. And we wouldn't know how easy it is to lose it, to lose everything you care about without going through what we've gone through. Especially me."

I let out a heavy sigh and watch him steeple his hands over the bridge of his nose.

After a long moment, he speaks, eyes fierce with emotion. "I don't give a fuck about me. I want someone to pay for putting you through that, Erica-baby. There had to be another way, a way that wasn't so fuckin' cruel. I can't stand what they did to you. After losing your parents violently like that. After all that pain and loss and then you learn you've got magic, which makes you feel happy and alive and then you get to dabble a little and then they pull that shit on you just in case you handle it wrong? Guilty before proven innocent? I hate that."

"I think it really was necessary, Riley."

He points at me. "I think they accomplished their mission of breaking you down so that you're so fuckin' humble that they can now use that to their advantage. Use you and your well of infinite energy. They wanna draw from your well of infinite guilt."

I flinch.

"But hear this: if all this shit was meant to be like they say it is, then one of the reasons you're fated to be mine is so that I..." He thumps his chest with his fist – "can make sure nobody fucks with you anymore. Nobody's gonna take advantage of that beautiful heart you've got, little witch. I won't allow them to mistake your goodness for weakness. I'll be your strength."

I face-plant into his chest and his arms immediately go around me. "We're so lucky to have a love like this. We've earned it, Riley. I really feel like we have. I'm never gonna take you for granted. Never ever."

"We *have* earned it," he says, taking hold of my face and tipping my chin up. "Nothing will ever get in our way again, Rikki. Never. I'll bust my ass to make sure it doesn't. And I'll damn well make sure people don't exploit the goodness inside you."

He marches me to the couch, sits and then pulls me down to snuggle.

And then he does exactly what I need without me having to ask for it.

He purrs for me for a solid half an hour.

I WANT AUNT MIMI TO have more good years. I want all of us to get more time with her. I want Greyson to have as much of her guidance as possible. I want to hear more about the potential for training, so I want to take Aviva up on her offer.

I talk Riley into arranging for them to be brought to the spot where I vanished off the side of the cliff so we can have our three-coven circle for tonight's eclipse. He doesn't like it, but to his credit he does what I ask. He sees how important it is to me.

Riley wants to go there first to scope things out and I decide to go with him, thinking maybe we can exorcise some demons for both of us.

We start off by walking down the long dirt road behind the Drowsy Hollow water tower, taking the same journey I took that night so long ago.

"The field of wildflowers isn't here," I say.

It's a forest that looks much older than seven years. And I'm confused.

"Was it magic?" I ask aloud.

"Maybe. Don't know. I haven't come back to this spot either. Not in almost seven years."

I've been here. But I never looked for the field of flowers like I'm doing now.

"Are we in the right place?" I check.

"Oh yeah," Riley says with certainty.

We keep walking, hand-in hand, Riley carrying my shoes, which I find so chivalrous and sweet it's made me melt. Even though I don't need to connect with the earth to find energy anymore, I don't think I'll ever stop. I love how it feels. I feel the energy. I feel things sprouting, blooming, growing.

I see a dying tree, and it's a fairly young one, so I pull away from Riley's grip and walk to it. I lay my hands on the trunk and then put my nose to it, inhaling with my nose directly on the bark. I don't know why it's dying, but suspect there's something missing in the soil here. That's not something I would've known before. Is this something new for me? If it is, it means my already green thumb might get even greener.

"You okay?" Riley asks.

"Give me a minute, please," I request.

And then I request enough of what the tree needs from nearby root systems. I can feel the difference, feel the willingness to give, the answering flood of energy ready to go where I want it, but I also do my best to communicate that I'd like permission. And I wait, listen, and focus on being open to the answer. I sense hesitation from one direction, acceptance from another.

I look at Riley, who is watching me with curiosity.

"This tree doesn't have enough nutrients in the soil. Somewhere near here, there was some pollution if my nose is identifying it properly. Don't know the details but I smell something's 'off'. My senses are more acute but I'm going to have to learn to translate them."

"Faint car fluid scents," Riley advises, nose twitching. "Someone might've driven in here and parked a bit. It's kind of rough terrain comin' in back on the road, so they might've sprung a leak somewhere and it leached into the ground."

"So," I explain, "If I weren't thinking about the balance, I'd have the other trees fix this tree without giving it much thought. And it might hurt other root systems, other ecosystems, an anthill, or some other seedling that's dormant and waiting for its turn to grow. But despite that I can do that, if I instead strive for balance, I'm asking for a little energy from a few places and listening for answers rather than just demanding it."

"Yeah, baby. That makes sense."

"If I were twenty-one and still super-green I could've seen this dying tree and if I had the powers I have now, I might've just directed energy here to fix it, not realizing what I could be breaking in the process."

"Makes sense," he says quietly. "But you talk a lot of fate, babe, and if fate made you identify me early, why would it want you to wait?"

"So I could learn patience, so I could get the thing *I* was missing inside of me to help *me* flourish without causing unnecessary harm to others."

His eyes flash with understanding and he drops a kiss on my forehead.

I rub the tree trunk and send my thanks through my toes into the earth because though the tree didn't get a giant surge of nutrients, it will get a trickle that I'm hopeful will help. And I'm going to help, too, by coming back here and checking on it, seeing if there's anything else I can do to help.

I catch his hand again and we walk some more, quietly, until I get a familiar sensation. And I think that sensation comes from Riley. I think the way he can sense things in me is reciprocal. I feel more and more in tune with him as the days go by.

We're here. Where it all went wrong.

I see him eying the rock he sat on with me on his lap. The air smells like apples and there's an apple tree behind that rock.

"Is that from our apple? The one we shared from your lunch?" I ask.

"Maybe," he says, staring at it.

I don't know where the apple core got dropped back then, but it's very possible it was dropped right here.

"The tree is young, the apples aren't ready, but I really, really want to come back here later for some. I want to plant a tree in your yard from fruit that comes from it."

"Our yard," he corrects.

"Let's go look," I say softly and tug his hand toward the banks of the river.

He hauls me behind himself protectively when we get to three feet from the edge, and I loop my arms around his waist and peer around his warm, strong body. I see the water below, down about a three or four story drop. The water is calm. The river doesn't look angry like it does in my dreams. Like it felt, for all those years in my mind.

"I wanna go in," I say. "I wanna jump in."

"Don't be crazy," he mutters staring down at the water while caressing my forearm that's draped over his belly.

"Look how calm it is," I say. "It's not angry with me."

He sighs. "I was pretty angry with it the last seven years."

"This river didn't deceive you," I say softly.

"I swam the other day in it, trying to make peace with it. Swam this river my whole life. The water here connects to where the Arcana Falls are. I should never have been angry with it. It's not what took you from me. You're also not the one that took you from me. They were."

"They did what they felt they had to do," I say.

His jaw muscles bulge and I know he's still frustrated.

"And some stuff we've done in our coven to help other people has undoubtedly frustrated or angered some of them. But here we are, Riley. We can move forward. We lost seven years we can't get back, but I gained a whole lot of wisdom in that time. And you were able to focus on your pack. You also got Tyson on board and reunited him with the family."

"Hm," is all I get from him as he stares down at the water.

"Can we jump in? Together?" I ask, moving around his body to stand at his side.

"You swim?" he checks.

"Like a fish. Lifeguard from age fourteen to seventeen at our community pool."

He shakes his head and gives me a squinty look. "See, if I knew that seven years ago, I might've thought you made it."

I give him a sad smile.

He kisses me. "Just teasin'. Someday we're gonna have to laugh about this."

"Someday. How long till we have to go pick those guys up?"

"We still have a couple hours," he says.

I reach for the hem of his t-shirt and pull it up, revealing his magnificent hot, tanned skin. I kiss his chest as I pull it over his head and toss it. It lands on the branch of a nearby tree and we both stare at it.

"Guess that's another one for the quilt, huh?" he asks.

I smile. "Yep. Monumental moments. This feels like one."

"It does," he agrees.

I undo his jeans.

"You're about to make this sexy, little witch," he warns, fire igniting in his eyes.

I shake my head. "Next time we come. This time, not so much."

His gaze softens. "I love you, Erica Savage. My little witch."

"I love you, too, my Mr. Wolf."

He smiles. I drop my panties and then look around to make sure we're alone before I turn around. "Unzip me?"

He pulls the zipper down on my dress and unfastens my bra. I drop them both and step out of the pool of clothing.

He's dropped his jeans and boxers. He steps out of his shoes and drops mine, then he takes my hand and squeezes. He's warm. Strong. He's even more than I hoped for when that little voice told me that it'd be really, really good to be Riley Savage's chosen mate.

"I want to go to Albania," I tell him. "Maybe go and come back before Halloween so I can do what I need to do for Isabella and Holden."

"Where you go, I go."

"It'd be okay for you to leave the pack with all this stuff going on here with Greyson?"

"If things get fucked sideways, we rush back. We can be back in a day, right?"

"I already checked flights. It's about ten and a half hours."

"We'll deal," he says. "I'm realizing how capable my team is. That I don't have to be at the center of everything all the time because my pack is all I've got. That's why we have seven alphas. To share the load. If they need me, they'll ask for me."

"Ready?" I ask. "To take this leap?"

"Absofuckinglutely."

I step a little closer to the edge. He steps with me. It's a long stretch of river with steep cliffs on either side for a little ways. Downstream, there's a little bank and a hill that looks climbable.

"On three?" I ask.

"Yeah."

"One, two…" I swallow. "Three." We step off the edge, holding hands.

It's not frightening. It's the opposite of that. It happens fast and when we land with a big splash in the cool water together, he's quickly wrapped me up in his arms, so we don't lose one another.

We're in the clean, clear, cool water together, and I open my eyes, seeing bubbles as Riley continues to hold me, kicking his feet to take us to the surface. I kick my feet too, to get us there faster.

We could be the only two in the universe right now; that's how it feels rising to the surface with Riley's arms around me. When we do break it, I'm smiling big. He kisses me. And I hold on tight, love flooding every nerve in my body for this man. My man.

"When I smelled you in the back of the drycleaners, I smelled you and I smelled this river, and the scent sickened me."

My expression drops.

"Now it's doing the opposite," he says.

"I don't think I'll have bad dreams about this river anymore," I tell him.

"Same," he agrees.

"I feel the energy in it. It's all good energy, Riley." I wrap my legs tight around his waist. "I want you," I say.

"I'm yours," he tells me. "Hold your breath." He goes under and lets go of all of me except my hand. We swim together like that for a while until we come up for air. "Keep goin'?" he asks. "Or are you tired?"

"Not tired," I tell him. In fact, I feel the opposite. I feel energized, elated, almost baptized in water - ready for my new life. With him. I feel ready to move on from the pain of the past seven years.

"Follow me, I'll show you the Arcana Falls."

"Okay."

We swim for a while.

"You are a strong swimmer," Riley says, once the falls are in view.

They're beautiful. Rugged. Not very big, but I feel so much energy here.

"Sure am," I say. "Swim team in high school, too."

He flashes a grin. "Under the falls. Meet you there?"

"Race you there," I amend and go under.

I come up first on the other side of the falls and the magic I feel here is incredible. And I can stand up; it's shallow.

He swims up behind me and loops his arms around my waist.

"Wow, Riley," I say, staring at the cave ahead. "This is amazing."

"Me and the guys often end our morning run here. Talk here about things."

"Kind of like your clubhouse," I observe. "You decided on here instead of building a tree house in that magnolia tree."

He smiles. "I remember that day. Weird that you were watching."

He catches my waist and boosts me up so I can climb up on the ledge.

"This is incredible." I squeeze water from my hair.

The wall of water ahead of us is mesmerizing. The stone cave walls around us look like they were molded from a whole lot of different rock types. There are a couple of long cushions over on one side with some small square pillows, too, that look like they come from a patio set. I go over and sit on one and then lay back and examine the ceiling of the cave. There's an opening up top revealing clear blue skies.

Riley lays down beside me.

"That felt good," I tell him.

His eyes travel my face.

"The jump, the water, the swimming. All of it. It felt great. Though it's really weird doing it naked."

He laughs, then his gaze goes serious. "Yeah," he says softly, caressing my jaw. "Except for the naked part." And then he moves in slowly and our eyes are locked.

His lips touch mine and then he's got my jaw as he deepens the kiss.

"Riley," I whisper.

"Erica," he returns.

"I love you," I tell him.

"I love you so much it hurts, baby. I'm so sorry I was such a dick when you got here."

"You said that already. Stop apologizing."

"Okay, mate. You gonna stop apologizing, too?"

"Touche, Mr. Wolf."

"What time is it, little witch?"

"Is it dinnertime?" I ask.

"Oh yeah," he says and then his mouth moves down my naked body. His mouth latches around one of my nipples and he bites gently, then sucks hard. This makes my body bow, makes my body sing.

His hand dives between my thighs and I'm slippery with arousal for him. I grab his biceps and turn him to his back. As I climb on, he guides his cock to me, getting just the tip inside. I'm ready to lower myself onto him slowly as he shifts to get more comfortable on his back. Just a little more in, he loses patience, grabs my hips and drives me down hard. It's so deep and I'm so full that I whimper, grab his face and cry into his mouth as he holds one hip and uses his thumb on his other hand to rub circles around my clit.

I bounce on him as he does, tightening around his steel-hard erection every time he's buried to the hilt.

He grabs my hair and then sucks on my claiming mark, and I crest over a peak, hitting a big, beautiful climax. Just as it's starting to ebb, he growls against my throat and the vibrations start. I collapse onto him, lost in sensation as he turns me to my back, and we ride out a big wave of sensation surrounded by beauty.

"UH OH," I WHISPER.

We've swum back to where we jumped in from and are holding one another, treading water just to the side of the banks we'll have to use to climb back up.

"What?" he asks.

"I wasn't real smart leaving my clothes up there. What if someone sees me? What if they come early?"

He laughs, looking up. "I'll shift, run up that hill and grab your dress and stuff. Drop it over to you."

"You're so smart," I say, smiling. "And good because I'm exhausted. Been a while since I've had a big swim like this."

"Stop treading, I've got us," Riley tells me. He's not panting. He's not remotely tired. He's got me. I stop treading water and it all hits me with a dazzling beauty that makes me want to cry. This feels so good. I feel so lucky to have this. To not be floundering by myself. Miss Independence has experienced some growth; I'm happy to have this man helping me. I don't have to prove I'm strong even when I don't feel like I am.

"What kind of magic you got, though, baby?" he asks. "Your aunt froze me in mid-air when I lunged for your sister back behind the drycleaners. Had me frozen in mid-air before I hit the wall. You can do that?"

"Dani told me. Nobody saw Auntie do that before. Could I do something like that? I think maybe, based on what happened with those guys that tried to take me from the cabin. They didn't freeze in mid-air; they were physically whooshed away."

"How'd you make that happen?"

"I asked for energy, I barely articulated what I needed. That's part of what made it so shocking to me. I wanted them to go and asked the willow tree for help. I wasn't sure what'd happen; I know that's an old tree in a magically rich area and thought it might give me something to fight them off. I've always been partial to weeping willows. I don't know how I knew what to do. I just... knew. And the tree threw a broken limb and it caught on fire."

"Pretty cool."

"Pretty scary. Also, I was really, really angry. The other guy wanted to hurt you. Hurt your friends. And I got mad. Then I used the energy inside them, and it seemed like it... fried them."

"Yeah, the guys told me."

"That was scary. I want more training, to learn what I can do, how to make sure it doesn't scare me, make sure I don't overdo it out of anger."

"You didn't know what you were dealing with. Now you've got some idea. You'll learn how to wield it, baby. You will."

I nod. "When Aunt Lyrica and I sat under a tree the day I first saw you and you were about to get close, she whooshed us back, but it was more controlled. This is why some more training would be good."

"Can you try and whoosh your clothes down here without gettin' them wet?"

"Let's find out," I say.

We swim to the bank where there's enough of a rock ledge to sit on and after ringing my hair out, I send my intention out into the universe, asking for our clothes. I hold my arms open and wait, envisioning them floating to me. Envisioning them staying dry.

We're both staring up. Nothing happens.

"Nope. Guess it's more complicated than envisioning them," I finally say. "They're not living so there's no energy. Maybe they need energy for me to move them. I don't have telekinesis."

Riley's nose twitches. "I know that scent."

"Hey!" We hear.

Riley pulls me closer to cover my nudity.

"Thought that was you two down there," Mason says, standing at the cliff's edge, also nude.

I shield my eyes. Holy horses, these Arcana Falls alphas are *built*.

"Sorry, Erica," he calls. "Junk's covered."

I give him a thumbs up.

"All these non-shifting women, hey Rye? Gotta change our habits. What are you guys doin' down there?"

"Makin' peace," Riley says.

"Ah," Mason replies after a few beats as if he does get it. "River and Rye's witch." Mason touches the side of his nose.

"Yep," Riley says.

He *does* seem to get it.

"Any chance you can walk about twenty paces and grab our clothes and shoes and drop 'em to us?" Riley asks.

"Sure thing," Mason agrees and disappears from view.

"Guess your powers worked mysteriously there," Riley says.

"You think? Might be just a coincidence."

"From what we've seen the last few months around here, I feel like there aren't too many genuine coincidences, little witch."

I laugh. "Fair point."

ONCE DRESSED, HE HELPS me up the hill; we're in a spot far less steep than where we jumped in with a gradually inclining hill and plenty of trees on it that I can use to pull myself back up.

It takes a couple minutes to do that, Riley protectively behind me, ensuring I don't fall. And then I hear what sounds like bickering when we get to the top. I see Mason and Amie there and she looks hostile.

"Hey," I greet her.

"Hey Erica," she says, and she's blushing. Not hostile?

"Did you catch an eyeful?" I ask.

"Of?" she asks, confused.

"Of us. Naked."

"Oh, no. Why?"

"You look embarrassed."

"She *is* embarrassed," Mason says, looking like he finds something very funny.

"They can skinny dip if they want to, Mase," she mutters.

He's still nude, cupping his junk. Amelia is fully dressed in jean shorts, a baseball hat, t-shirt, and running shoes.

He laughs. "That's not what she's embarrassed about."

"Zip it," she warns.

Yep, hostility. At Mason, not us.

"Runnin' with your mate?" Riley asks, looking at her attire likely.

"Running *from* her mate more like," Mason mutters, laughing.

"Shut. Up!" Amie snaps at him, face going redder.

"Just a little primal play." Mason shrugs.

"We are *so* in a fight right now, Doggo."

"Aw, c'mon, Wildberry," he says. "They get it. Don't you, guys?"

Primal play? That sounds fun. I don't get a chance to respond.

"No," she denies. "I'm going home. Bye, Erica. See you tomorrow maybe. Lunch at Roxy's? Twelve?"

"Um... not sure I can make it tomorrow."

"Me, Ives, and Bailey will be there so come if you can. If not, we'll do lunch in a couple days."

"Okay," I squeak. Tomorrow is my birthday. And my family is still here. I'm not sure what the plans are but now isn't the time to say that.

She walks off down the walking trail back toward town and Mason smiles at her back as she departs.

"Why here?" Riley asks Mason. "Got a big ole forest either side of your house."

"Filled her in on what I knew about you two. She was curious about the area, so we took a drive. The extracurriculars were unexpected."

"Ah," Riley says. "Though not really, right? Because the mood can strike anywhere."

"And it does," Mason says with a wink.

"You guys are worse than women," I tease.

This gets me sexy chuckles times two.

"Should you walk back up that trail naked, Mason?" I ask. "What if there are hikers?"

"I'll smell 'em before they see me," he says, touching his nose.

"Ah," I say.

Mason sobers. "Another reason I'm here… wanted to recon the area a little bit ahead of the magic witch circle."

"Good thinkin'." Riley nods. "Same."

"Lemme know when you're on your way back here. We'll meet by the water tower. See you guys later," Mason says and then he shifts into a giant pure white wolf and trots in the direction Amie went.

"I guess they're not entertaining my family at their house," I say.

Riley shakes his head. "Forgot to tell you he texted and said they'd gone back to the apartment in The Hollow for your aunt to rest and gather their stuff for this thing tonight. Not sure about this, babe. I'm gonna stick close."

"You can't be, Riley. Witches only."

"I'm your protector. How far away do I need to be? Because that's as far away as I will be."

"Okay," I say, leaning into him with a smile.

"Don't know what the fuck is funny." He frowns.

"It's not funny. Okay, it is a little. I like how protective you are." I wrap my arms around him.

"Good, cause this is who I am. Don't ask the SCC witches how far away I gotta be. Ask your aunt so the others don't know me and the boys are nearby."

"They might know anyway."

"Even still."

"Okay, pooky." I snuggle into his chest.

"Tell me that one won't stick."

"Pooky?" I ask.

His expression sours.

"I think it might stick actually. It feels right."

"The fuck it does," he denies.

"Aw, pooky… don't be surly."

"Pick another nickname. Or keep cyclin' through 'em. I don't wanna be pooky."

"I think you are definitely my pooky."

"I think you're bustin' my chops, little witch, and that'll earn you a spanking."

I clap my hands. "Yay!"

He shoots me a sexually charged look as he throws me over his shoulder and whacks my rump.

I giggle.

He carries me for about a mile like that before setting me on my feet by his truck.

Love is shining in his eyes as he opens the door for me.

"Love you, pooky," I say.

He shakes his head. "Get in the truck, wicked witch."

I laugh.

45

ERICA

"Just because you don't need to ask permission for energy, doesn't mean you shouldn't ask anyway. Just because you don't need to build goodwill to bank, doesn't mean it's a bad idea to do it anyway," Aunt Mimi says.

I'm taking her words to heart. Yes, I will learn and study some more. And I will continue to strive for balance. I can't imagine being careless with magic.

"Have you ever heard of powers like the ones they say I have?" I ask.

Aunt Mimi is a history buff and a well of knowledge on the history of witches. She could teach if she wanted to.

Auntie nods. "A couple times. One of Aviva's ancestors is one example. She went mad with it and self-destructed. It sounded like she didn't have a support system. That's not the case with you."

No, it's not. I have an incredible support system. Both with my family and now with Riley's pack. A smile spreads across my face.

Aunt Mimi says, "I think Aviva and Lucinda were coming from the right place even if we don't like the way it transpired. I might have chosen the same punishment for you back then if I were in their shoes. Lyrica agreed. Humble pie is an effective tool in many situations. But we hated this for you. We both did. Because we know your soul, girl. She would've loved to be here for today to see you have what you want, to see you responsibly coming into your full potential. She was very proud of you. As am I."

"Even though I was a brat who barely listened?"

"Even with that."

I choke up.

Aunt Mimi gives me her signature *don't you start* look.

Aunt Lyrica was angry when I got punished. She never seemed angry at me, though.

"Auntie... all these years, all you've done for us..."

"Don't start," she says and rolls her eyes.

I smile. "I love you, Aunt Mimi."

She swallows and looks away. "Love you, too. All five of you brats."

"Greyson's pretty great, isn't he?" I pivot quickly.

She smiles again and emotion lights in her eyes. "He is."

"You're gonna start!" I accuse.

"I'm not," she assures.

But I do think she's fighting it.

I laugh and drop a kiss on her cheek, then we get back to gathering what we need for tonight's circle. We leave the covenstead in the back of the drycleaners and pile into my bus with my sisters.

"Before we go," Aunt Mimi says as she lifts a tangle of necklaces from the pocket of her skirt and hands me a leather necklace with a pale green pearl charm. She hands Vivica a bluish one, Jessica gets an amber, Dani an ivory one, and Ronnie a pale pink.

"Pretty," Dani remarks. "Function?"

Aunt Mimi's jewelry sells out quickly at her boutique.

"Wear those, but don't draw attention to them." She eyes Ronnie. "You've got too much cleavage so stick yours in your pocket. Don't lose it. Make sure it stays on your body all night. Danica? Your ankle maybe. Someone choose their wrist."

"What are-" I begin to ask.

"I cultured the pearls myself with some protection elements as well as a blocking agent for mindreading. I got a vision a few months back, not very clear but to do with this moon tonight, so made and brought them with me to be sure. If they're not needed, no harm. If they are, we're covered."

"Do you have any concerns as of today?" Vivi asks. "Because I don't. I still don't like what they did to her back then, but everything today felt very genuine. My senses haven't been pinging."

"Mine have, but I can't describe what I'm getting," Jessie says. "Something stirring from beyond..." She shakes her head. "It's blurry, though. I'm not sure what it is that's reaching for us, but it's from another realm. I don't know if it's Aunt Lyrica. If it's our mom. I just don't know yet."

"Keep listening, Jessica," Aunt Mimi tells her, "And contingencies, girls. Always."

"I haven't planned for any," I say. "Shit."

And it's not like me.

"You've been kinda busy, cut yourself some slack," Vivi says as Aunt Mimi gives me a look that tells me she has.

And this is why she is the elder of our coven and why we need her. I can smell the rose, sage, and chamomile on the leather, all of which help block mind-reading. I put it on and tuck it into the tank top I'm wearing under my dress.

As I turn the ignition, Aunt Mimi clears her throat and says, "Girls, as Lyrica always said, *whether you're in your favorite dream or the middle of a nightmare, alone or in a crowd, always be mindful of potential pitfalls and exits. And... work out a plan for how to use that exit should you need it.* Remember this for when you don't have me to do it for you."

I PARK BY THE WATER tower beside what must be Greyson's car as he was going to drive Aviva and Lucinda here.

Riley is with most of the other alphas on the council nearby. All of them, as far as I know other than Jase, who is guarding Greyson's mate Stacy.

The moon is high and the ring around it is bright. Greyson scans the surroundings and I'm guessing he's taking in sights, sounds, and scents. I'm not picking up sounds as much as energy. It's quiet. No frogs or crickets. The energy here right now is abundant. His eyes bounce from mine to the back of Lucinda's head, then back to mine. If I'm reading his expression correctly, he doesn't trust her.

Hopefully he's just being protective. Nobody has spent enough time with him yet to know what his strengths are beyond the fact he can be persuasive. I wish he'd gotten time with Aunt Lyrica who would know.

"This walk becomes too much for you, Aunt Mimi, you tell me, and I'll carry you," he says.

She smiles at him. It's one of her rare wide smiles and I don't know if he knows how rare or what a gift it is, but his gaze softens, and he holds out his arm for her to hang onto. I see her hand him something. He eyes what's in his palm and sticks it into his pocket. A protection pearl charm for him, too, maybe? I'm not sure.

Aunt Mimi is small and of course she's getting on in years now, but she's never seemed frail to me. Maybe it's how slow she walks or how she looks extra-small being led by Greyson who is muscled and over six feet tall; I'm not sure. But, the notion of her being gone like Aunt Lyrica suddenly terrifies me and I want to do everything I can to give her as much quality time as possible.

I want time for me, for my sisters, and I want Greyson to have it, too. I want Aunt Mimi to get more time with Greyson. He'd be the closest thing to a grandson she'd have.

"Where are we setting up?" I ask, to drive the negativity out of my head.

Aviva looks over her shoulder. "Not far past where the field of flowers is."

"It's not there," I say.

"It should be there," she insists.

Instead of arguing, I lead the way and am prepared to explain that where the field of flowers was is now a forest, but after a few minutes of walking, I see it. It's dark outside, but that's definitely a field of flowers.

"It was gone," I say. "I was here... not long ago."

"It's back," Lucinda says. "I'll leave it until tomorrow so you can visit it in the day if you like."

I frown.

She eyes me searchingly. "A little gift to you."

She can create illusions.

Memories wash over me of that day, gaily prancing in the flowers, singing my heart out, feeling high on life. I was high on the spelled wine, but it felt so good. And now I'm reflecting, because if she intervened in a way to keep me there, blissed out over a field of flowers, then it was likely intended that Riley find me that day. As if I was put there on purpose. By fate or design, though? The fact that she created a field of flowers temporarily and then does it again today sits like a brick in my throat.

"I like flowers, too," she says with a disarming smile.

But though I'm not fully disarmed, I hide it. I would normally want to explore that large field, but something tells me to stay out of it. Greyson's eyes meet mine and we communicate nonverbally. I know he agrees.

"This way, everyone," I say.

"We must ask that you leave us, Greyson Blackwood," Lucinda requests. "This is a circle for trained witches. Women. Not a mixed witch and warlock circle."

"Oh, really?" Greyson asks, sounding disappointed. "Thought I could just watch."

Lucinda remarks, "No observers."

Greyson shrugs. "Maybe next time. I'll take you all where you're going and then I'll take off. How long do you need, and I'll come back?"

"Three hours should do," Aviva tells him.

"Maybe just two," Lucinda counters.

"Give us three to be safe," Aviva says with a sweet smile.

"Fine," he agrees, "I'll grab a beer and a basket of wings at the tavern. If you need me back early, just call." He kisses Aunt Mimi's cheek before he turns and leaves.

Though we agreed to do this, Riley doesn't entirely trust it and I can tell Greyson feels the same.

I'm a little disappointed that there might be reasons for mistrust, though I'm hiding it. The idea of pooling magic across three covens to provide healing to Aunt Mimi, to get an idea of my abilities? It's exciting and I'm suddenly wishing we were all going into this completely open-hearted. Because I want this for her. I want to see my new magic, too, in this format, with guidance that can help me learn to manage and wield it in the right ways.

Each of us carries a bag, tote, or basket of the preferred tools of our individual practices.

Aviva abruptly stops and turns her face skyward. "This is perfect. Right here, ladies."

"Here?" I check.

We're almost right where Riley and I jumped earlier today.

"Here," Aviva confirms. "Spread out, ladies and let's define our circle."

I'VE GOT AVIVA ON MY right, Aunt Mimi on my left. Lucinda sits directly across from me, and my sisters fill out our circle.

The moon is directly above us, the eclipse lighting the space up well.

The cliff is at my back, about fifty feet behind us, and it strikes me as odd that our surroundings are so quiet. Eerily quiet. I dig my toes into the grass, feeling a lot of the energy around me. All of it available to me if I need it. I send intention to my surroundings, wanting tonight to go well, wanting Aunt Mimi to have whatever she needs to help her stay with us for a long, long time. Wanting this to be good, right, devoid of bad intentions.

Lucinda lights a bundle, smudging a perfect pentacle between us with glowing chalk. Each of us lays our practice tools in front of ourselves. Sage fills the air as some of us have already lit our own bundles. We want to first cleanse our implements and then charge them with the moon.

I unbag my crystals, my altar, and the willow wand Aunt Lyrica and Aunt Mimi made for me. I'm choosing to focus on positivity as Aviva circles us with a bag of salt.

"Lovely altar," Aviva leans over and caresses Jessica's altar, then looks to me and observes, watching me sweep mine with my small hand broom. Aviva sets a stone cauldron down in the middle of our circle and pours a bottle of water into it.

"We had them made from a three-hundred-year-old local tulip tree that was lost," Jessie shares, giving one more sweep across hers before setting her little broom to the side.

Aviva sets quartz crystals around the perimeter of the cauldron, carefully balancing each crystal on the rim before she opens a small vial and dumps clear oil into the cauldron.

"The one that made it into the newspapers when it fell on Halloween?" Aviva asks.

"Yes," Jessie states.

"The same tree I cast the Riley love spell under," I say.

"Ah yes," Aviva says softly.

Ronnie, Jess, and Dani came out here after it happened with a saw and their implements. We had some of the sawdust added to her remains when Aunt Lyrica was cremated. That tree was very special and is now the site of a rather large pumpkin patch each autumn. Now that I live nearby I'll be sure to harvest some this year.

Lucinda sees me looking at the bejeweled knife in her hand.

"My wand," she explains. "My spouse is a vampire. It doubles as a tool that can prevent supernatural attacks."

"Oh my," I reply. Some witches use wands, others use a knife; it's all preference. "Handy."

My wand is a simple willow one.

"I've had a few run-ins," Lucinda adds. "Not everyone is thrilled with the idea of a witch being mated to a vampire."

I resist the urge to ask questions. "People should mind their own business," I say instead.

Aviva laughs. "You would know."

I tip my head to the side and say nothing.

"Too soon," Aviva adds.

Aviva's wand is a tapered dark spindle with crystals embedded in the leatherbound hilt. It looks old.

She sees me looking at it but says nothing. Wands are very personal for some witches.

"Begin when you're each ready," Aviva suggests. "Meditate with intention while the moon cleanses our tools, and then when it feels right, is it agreeable if I speak?" She removes her clothes and carefully folds them, setting them in a pile behind herself.

"Agreeable to me," Lucinda advises, "though we're all skilled enough here, I doubt you need to give us this level of direction."

Lucinda is already set up and cross-legged, in a meditative pose, wearing a more casual white linen suit now. She left her Louboutins behind and wore cream ballet flats, which are now outside our circle with the shoes of everyone else, save me who left my flipflops on the bus.

Some witches prefer to practice magic in the nude. Lucinda likely chose her white outfit with intent, white chosen to symbolize openness and willingness in the circle tonight. I chose to wear the earthtone patchwork dress that I wore the day they spirited me out of here, feeling like things are coming full circle. I wore a tank top underneath tonight, and behind it is where my protection charm is hidden. Jessica has hers wrapped inside her headband. Ronnie's is in her pocket while Dani has hers wrapped around her ankle with several other anklets. Vivi wears a tangle of charm bracelets and necklaces so hers is either on her wrist or around her neck.

"Habit from teaching," Aviva explains cheerily.

"Do you have a large coven?" Ronnie asks.

Aunt Mimi leans over Danica, speaking into Jessica's ear.

"Everything okay?" Lucinda asks.

"Yes, fine," Jessie replies. "Low blood sugar." She pulls a wrapped mint from her pocket, opens the wrapper and pops it into her mouth.

She looks pale.

"Sure you're all right, Jess?" I ask.

She nods. "Think so."

"Would you like a bottle of water?" Aviva asks. "I have several. They've just come out of a cooler." She gestures behind herself.

"Yes, please. Thank you," Jessie nods.

"And yes, I do have a large coven, Veronica," Aviva says, opening a water and passing it to my sister. "I lead my coven, which has members on four continents. But teaching has always come naturally. I hold workshops to teach inexperienced witches of other covens. I teach lone witches as well. Also those who would like to level up. I felt the call to teach even before I felt the call to our craft."

"You teach in Albania?" I ask. "Where you invited me? Because I'm interested."

"That's right," Aviva says. "We can discuss that later."

"Maybe we could all go," Vivica suggests.

"That would be lovely," Aviva replies, though she's still looking at me. "Shall we begin?"

"Of course," I reply as we all move into our preferred meditation poses, which come from personal preferences. I gather the length of my dress, bunching it between my legs to cover my underwear. I bend my knees, planting my fingers and toes into the grass. I focus on my surroundings, feeling the energy of the environment. Listening for nature sounds, which I still do not hear. Welcoming positivity.

Other than the lack of sounds, almost everything feels harmonious right now. My eyes find Jessie's. She's feeling something, and I don't know what. But I know she'd tell us if it didn't feel like we should perform this circle. Jessica wouldn't just let it go and I'm certain neither would Aunt Mimi.

Energy begins to rise around me, and I can feel the energy of the others joining mine. Now... it all feels right. The combined energy of the seven of them lift my own energy and I'm guessing they feel the same.

I gaze at the sky. The moon is full, high, the ring around it bright. The sky is a velvet black, studded with stars. A soft breeze tickles my skin. Each of us has lit a candle as well and the air smells sweet with herbs, spices, and promise.

Aviva lifts three ropes from the bag behind herself and passes one end to Lucinda, keeps one, and passes the third to Aunt Mimi. The opposite ends are fastened into a knot.

She closes her eyes.

"Focus first on me, my face, my presence, and my energy. Give me all your positivity. And then I will pass my end on, and we'll send positive energy to Erica. When that end gets to you, Mimi, please fold it over and pass two strands along until it gets to Lucinda who will fold the third in. I'll do a braid when it gets to me, and each of you follow that motion when it comes to you. We'll keep going until it's a full braid. We'll weave it together with purposeful intention and when we come to the end, we'll have one rope instead of three, filled with the combined energy from three covens. Then we can move to the next step. Agreed?"

She gets nods from each of us, and we begin.

The three strands are soon formed into a rope and the space around us is eerily quiet, as if on bated breath. When the completed braid is in Aviva's hands, she anoints the ends oil from a jar.

She carefully wraps the braided rope around the base of the water cauldron, careful not to move any of the crystals resting on the bowl's edge.

"I'd like us all to send as much positive energy as possible to the bowl of water. We would normally allow it to charge overnight, and in the morning

Mimi would take it with her, then drink a mouthful each morning until it's empty. Because of the specialness of this evening and with our three covens coming together, I've prepared a mixture to augment the process and allow it to be consumed tonight. Each of us should have a small taste and then Mimi should finish it. We can then move on to getting an illustration of Erica's newfound abilities."

"Would it not be better to-" Lucinda begins to speak, but then stops mid-sentence and seems to change her mind.

Jessie makes a gagging noise, and all eyes move to her.

"There's a presence here. I don't know it," Jessie says.

"Does it feel positive?" I ask.

Jessie shakes her head.

"We're safe in this circle," Aviva says. "There's a lot of magic within it. Have you been in one of these before?"

Jessie shakes her head, hand covering her mouth.

"Would you like to stop?" Lucinda asks.

Jessie's eyes roll a little and she shakes her head. "No. Let's keep going."

"Sometimes mediums feel nausea in these circles. I've seen it," Aviva tells her. "If you need to step out, we'll have to start again, and we will miss out on your contributions. That would be a shame."

"I'll push through," Jessie says.

My eyes hit Aunt Mimi and I'm a little surprised she's so quiet.

Aviva smiles and looks to Lucinda, who nods.

Aviva opens a vial and pours the contents into the bowl and then she carefully removes each crystal from the edge, setting them into the grass.

"Are you all right, Jessica?" Aviva asks.

Jessie nods. "My apologies. Please continue."

"No need to apologize. A lot of energy through three covens flows within our circle and it stands to reason a medium might feel it more acutely than most. Are you able to continue?"

"I... yes."

"Good," Aviva says with a smile, "In a moment, I'll give you all the next directive. I just need to..."

Letting that hang, Aviva dips her wand into the bowl and then tastes the wet end. Immediately, there's noise, the noise feels like the earth is an egg and it's just been cracked against the side of a bowl. The sky appears to split, rented by a white streak. Lucinda gasps, eyes on Aviva with horror. Aviva simultaneously points her wand at Lucinda while grabbing my ankle.

And now I hear nature as if at full volume. It's nearly deafening.

I watch Lucinda drop like a sack of bones and before I can react, a gust of air sweeps up from the center of the circle and I feel frozen, rooted to the spot as I watch Aviva point her wand at Jess, who collapses. My eyes move to Aunt Mimi with horror as I realize I'm a hundred percent frozen in place, limbs feeling paralyzed. My hair blows everywhere but the rest of me is stone still. All sensation in my body is concentrated on the place Aviva's hand grips. My ankle. Aviva points the wand to her right, to Vivi who collapses, and then she points it directly ahead to Ronnie, then Dani, who do the same. They flop forward. And I'm here with my hair blowing, eyes moving, and the rest of me frozen. Even my mouth. I can't speak, can't scream; all I can do is watch. But as Aviva's wand points to Aunt Mimi, I notice something protruding from my great aunt's stomach. A jeweled knife. Lucinda's wand. My mind races as I take it in, and I can't wrap my brain around it fast enough.

Aunt Mimi collapses, face-first. My sisters are all fallen like dominoes and I'm frozen, the freezing cold grip Aviva has on my ankle vice-like. Her other hand dips the tip of the wand in the water again and now it bubbles. Bubbles rise higher in the water as something is pulled from me. Not just me. My sisters. My aunt. And Lucinda. Not just us, our tools as well. It sounds like fire crackling as I see I'm surrounded by the same blue sparks I saw when I realized something had changed with my abilities. She's taking energy from me. I'm being tapped, powers tapped like sap from a maple tree. So is everyone else here. Our energy is going into that bowl, and I know Aviva Starling wants it. This isn't a plan to enrich all three covens and buy Aunt Mimi more good years. That's not her plan at all.

She looks at me with a demented expression. "You swore all you wanted was your wolf. You didn't care about your magic. You have your wolf. All you've ever wanted, according to you." She shrugs.

I want to scream for her to stop because I know my power in her hands would be awful, terrible, horrifying. This woman is power-thirsty and evil. I can feel it in the grip she's got on me. But I can't speak. I'm frozen. I can't feel energy, can't summon anything. Candles flicker and everything else is still. How did Aunt Mimi wind up with a knife in her gut? Is she dead? Are my sisters dead?

I catch movement from my periphery. A large, silver wolf runs toward us, skidding to a halt behind Aviva. He transforms into my cousin Greyson and as he does, I see him drop something on Aviva. A necklace now rests on her collarbone. She jolts and turns, not letting go of my ankle. Red light swirls between Greyson and Mimi's forms as Greyson eyes the circle.

He grabs Aviva's wrist.

I read his lips as he aggressively tells her to "Let go!"

Suddenly, noise rushes in again as I hear the cracking of her wrist bones as he makes her let go of my ankle. He drags her away from me, outside the circle and suddenly things feel different. The circle is broken, so whatever she was doing halts. The water in the cauldron has stopped bubbling and the candles have all go out.

Riley's here, he's touching me, holding my face, but I'm in shock, I think.

Everything is loud. Too loud. Deafening. Like the entire environment around us is protesting. Did she do something to prevent me from hearing it before? Do something to prevent me from feeling that things here are all wrong?

"Auntie!" I pull away from Riley to grab for Aunt Mimi, searching for her pulse. "I can't find her pulse! Dani!" I grab my sister, who is still on the grass, but her eyes are twitching as if she's having a dream. She whimpers.

"Dani! Vivi! Ronnie, Jessie, you guys, please... please help!"

Greyson has Aviva by the throat and he's hauling her away from us. She's grappling with him physically, but seems disoriented, weak, and she's not striking back with magic.

Though the moon is high and the ring around it bright, the light sparking from Greyson's body is what lights the space the most.

Suddenly, Riley is a wolf. And he's growling, snarling, and looks even angrier than the night I saw him rip apart that guy that abducted me.

Greyson drops Aviva and she lands on the ground while Riley snarls in her face. She cowers, trying to crawl backwards, but her wrist is definitely broken so she collapses on her back.

He shifts and rises to two feet, looming over her. "You fuckin' bitch," he says, voice guttural. "Again. You tried to fuck us over again."

She pulls on the necklace Greyson had dropped around her neck but smoke curls from her fingers as she shrieks, pulling her hands away like they're burning.

"Won't come off unless I take it off," Greyson clips. She cowers some more, smoking hands shaking.

"Your bullshit fucked us for seven years," Riley shouts, "And it's pretty clear to me that you did it for your own gain. And now you try and fuck us again. Well, bitch, I'm about to fuck *back*."

"No. No," Aviva cries. "Not at all. I initially did it because it was the right thing to do. Because it was the necessary thing to do."

"Bullshit," he shouts.

I stare at my aunt and tears stream down my cheeks. "Auntie, please wake up." I try to summon energy, but I feel so weak.

"You're wrong," Aviva denies, "It wasn't until I dug into my own family history because of learning that my ancestral line had a witch who had been what Erica Young would become that I started to look at the possibilities. It was rather intoxicating." She smiles that demented smile I saw inside the circle.

"Aunt Mimi," I weep.

She's dead. She's gone. Gone. No, no, no, no. I rise to my feet shakily, feeling lost. Absolutely lost.

"She wakes up screaming, imagining this river," Riley shouts in Aviva's face, "is swallowing her because of the guilt she felt about disappearing on me," Riley says, "She dreams of drowning over and over. You cunts made her hide for all that time when I could've had her. When she could've had me." He thumps his fist on his chest then transforms to wolf again and lunges.

Aviva scrambles backwards as Riley's wolf closes in, growling, teeth bared. He nips at her. She screams, trying to back away from him. I see her look over the edge and then she scrambles off the cliff to escape him. He stops growling and looks over the edge, then shifts back to human form.

46

RILEY

Thunderous noise fills the air and I watch as the water below goes from still and calm to working into a frenzy, swirling fast when she lands in it. It's gone from zero to a hundred, like Class 5 rapids. She disappears into a vortex that I hope will take her to a reckoning for her bullshit.

I would've laid money on odds between the two SCC witches that it wouldn't be Aviva Starling that fucked things over. My money would've been on the stylish one with the resting bitch face. And I'm pissed because if we hadn't gotten here in time, if Greyson hadn't had the ability to break that witch circle and stop that cunt, my mate could've been lost to me.

Grey told me his aunt talked to him last night and again today about contingency plans, had given each of the Young girls a protective charm as well as given Greyson two other necklaces that would work to disable Lucinda and Aviva if need be. Another witch or a warlock from one of the three covens present would be able to breach that circle no matter which spell was underway. Grey had a conversation with Mimi today before we got here, giving him the rundown of how these circles work.

And at that old wood lot I was called out to do an early morning quote on the day I knew she was mine and thought I lost her forever, I noted there were several hunting tree stands. Seven years on, they were still there so we made use of a few of them. We planted them at strategic locations so we could get a look at what was happening in that clearing. It didn't take long for Grey to get tweaked and take off in the direction of the circle like his ass was on fire. He was shifting from the stand directly running, not climbing down the fifteen feet to the ground. And the fucker was fast. Faster than he's ever been. And me and the others were hot on his heels.

"Looks like the river's pretty angry right *now*, Rikki," I call over to my mate. "Never angry at you. Angry at her bullshit."

She's horror stricken. These women are all in this circle and my mate is the only one upright. She's looking at me but it's like she doesn't see me.

"Here," Greyson lifts her out of the circle and sets her down on the grass. "Get them out, too. You'll all feel better."

"I think she's dead, Greyson," she cries out brokenly.

Fuck, I feel her pain now that she's outside that circle. That's another thing. I couldn't feel anything once shit started to go south, so that bitch did something that fucked with our connection. Right now, her pain is enormous. I make my way to her and put my hands on her face. "Baby," I whisper.

Her chin trembles.

"Maybe not dead," Grey says. "I feel her." He taps his temple. "Don't give up."

Immediately, Rikki perks up just a little. "I feel the difference, feel my strength returning."

Grey gently lays Mimi on the grass outside the circle.

"Get 'em all out, boys," he tells us.

I move to Dani and pull her out. Rikki starts pulling her sister Ronnie out, but Linc takes over, so she rushes back to Mimi. Mase has Vivica and Tyson has Jessica.

"You feel stronger, baby?" I ask my mate, but I'm eyeballing the other witch, Lucinda, who is still face down in the circle.

She drops her head, still squatting over her aunt, "I think she's dead. I think she sacrificed herself so Greyson could have her power and use it to save us. Is that what those swirls were between you?"

"I don't think she's dead," Grey says. "Her power is here – " He taps his temple with his index finger – but I still feel like she's connected to it. How do these links work?"

"I… I don't know. Maybe it's not too late? Wake up, Dani!" she pleads, shaking her sister, blue light pulsing from her fingers. "Vivi, Ronnie, Jessie!" she shouts.

Danica jolts and springs into action, as if she was frozen in animation and those blue lights woke her. She moves like she knows just what she should be doing. She grabs her aunt.

"I need my medicine bag," she whispers, horror in her eyes. "Like... now."

"It's on my bus," my mate says. "Fuck!"

"Getting it!" Linc shouts and sprints into wolf form, running fast.

"Oh God, Aunt Mimi. Oh God!" Dani cries, rocking with her aunt's torso in an embrace.

"Rikki, it's gonna be okay," I tell her.

"Is it?" she looks at me and looks destroyed. I feel utterly helpless. And I fuckin' hate it.

"Let's break the circle up," Vivica shouts. "Come help. Maybe Lucinda will wake up and can help us. Can you wake her, Erica? Do whatever you did with us?"

Jessica and Veronica jump in and start moving the crystals, brooms, candles, and wooden slabs out of the way.

Blue light pulses from my mate and her eyes are on Lucinda Alexander. The other witch lifts her head and looks around with alarm.

47

ERICA

I feel like I'm in the middle of a wind tunnel, the force of the wind pushing me, shoving hard as I harness everything I have permission to use around me. I feel it coming through me from the sky, the trees, even the river. Like all this energy wants to help. I hope I'm reading it right and not harming anything. I pushed that energy at my sisters, and it woke them. At Lucinda. And now at Dani who's laid hands on Auntie, trying to help her reverse what's happened. I'm so thankful Grey broke that circle before whatever Aviva wanted to do was entirely done. My energy and Dani's healing powers, together, maybe...

"She's still not breathing," Dani cries. "I can't find a pulse."

Ronnie moves in and puts her hands on Aunt Mimi while Dani performs CPR.

"Aunt Mimi gave her power to Greyson?" Ronnie says like it's a question as she's processing whatever she's picking up through touch. "To help us?"

Vivica crawls over on her knees, crying.

"Yeah," Grey says. "Hers and Lyrica's. She... told me stuff last night about the powers, gave me some advice. I knew what to do tonight because she linked it in here." He taps his head. "We've got a link right now and she called to me and told me what to do and... I know she's not dead, but it's quiet now, it's... I don't get it."

My eyes dart to Lucinda and I wonder if she can help, if she can give us any information. She was shocked when she saw what Aviva was doing. She was the first one Aviva attacked.

I stop pushing energy through Dani and redirect it to Lucinda, hoping she'll snap out of the daze it looks like she's in and tell us what we can do to help Aunt Mimi. The circle was broken rather than opened and closed, so the water is useless now.

I look at Greyson, who stares at Aunt Mimi with confusion. Because he can't compute feeling a link to her and seeing her without a pulse.

Aunt Lyrica's powers went to Aunt Mimi upon Aunt Lyrica's death. It was how we knew she died. Aunt Mimi got violently ill, was overpowered by the rush of it.

That doesn't seem to be happening with Greyson here. Instead, he's emanating power and energy. I can feel it; there's a lot of it. Ronnie scrambles to put her hands on Aviva's implements. She lifts something from the ground and then drops it. It's Aviva's wand.

"That's her ancestor's wand. The witch who had powers like Erica. Wrapped pieces of her broom around it, too, under this leather. I think there's something in the salt. She paralyzed us all. My god, it's so fucking dark… the shit her ancestor did, the shit she was being pulled into. Like dark, black, evil quicksand. We could be dead if it weren't for these charms around our necks. If Erica didn't have unlimited energy to share with us. If Grey didn't break the circle and stop her. What did she give Jessie? She opened the bottle of water. She touched Jessie's altar."

You're not ever supposed to fuck with a witch's broom. I found that out the hard way, too. After the fact when on trial and getting lectured about pulling straw from Aunt Lyrica's broom. That piece of straw was believed to be pivotal in my spell to make Riley identify me as his fated mate because it had the essence of Aunt Lyrica's strengths and powers in it.

Lucinda is slowly moving toward us on her hands and knees.

"Are you part of this?" I demand.

"No," she rasps. "Where is she?"

"The river," I point. "Are you part of this? Tell me or I swear I will hurt you."

I'm gathering more energy now. It's rising in me. I can do damage. I can feel so much power rising with my fury, I'm almost afraid of it.

"No, I swear," she says. "I couldn't read her intentions, or I'd have stopped her myself. She must have cast a spell on me or found a way to cloak it in herself."

"She was using her ancestor's wand and strands from her broom," Ronnie tells her.

"The ancestor who owned that wand was trying to come through," Jessie says. "She..." She shakes her head, "Didn't want this. Didn't want it at all. It's like I'm getting a belated message. She was trying to communicate with me. As soon as I was in the circle I knew there was something trying to breach it. I know now it was her."

"Why isn't there any blood?" Dani asks, still holding Aunt Mimi. "There's like... no blood."

"She's not dead," Lucinda announces, suddenly leaning over Aunt Mimi. "My wand put her into a state of pause. She pulled it as I was collapsing, I saw her eyes flash, saw it move to her and knew she did it. She knew it would help. Before I pull it, I don't know how it'll affect what she gave to Greyson. We need to figure that out first or it could hurt him to abruptly break the link."

"How long is she okay like this?" Dani asks.

"She knew what she was doing, girls. She knows how that dagger works," Lucinda assures. "We were spelled still by Aviva, but your aunt magicked this to herself, knowing what it would do so she could pass the torch to Greyson who was outside the circle. He was close enough to breach it and we all know only a member of one of these three covens could breach it."

Greyson clears his throat. "She initiated me into the coven last night at Rye's. She told me she needed to spell her power to come to me in the event of her death. She told me last night she wanted contingencies in place before meeting with the SCC. She told me what the necklaces in my pocket would do, incapacitate witches. She told me earlier today that if anything went sideways, I should step in and break the circle, and that she'd get a message to me to let me know to help. She also told me she was wearing a partial cloak so she'd appear weak if either of the SCC witches were reading her abilities tonight."

"She's definitely not dead?" Dani checks again, looking as distraught as the rest of us feel.

"She's not dead. I promise," Lucinda assures. "And that was smart. She incapacitated me first, as the perceived strongest in the circle beyond Erica.

Mimi had more time to do what she needed to do as she was an afterthought to Aviva."

"Definitely not dead? Because she feels like she is," Dani adds.

"She doesn't," Greyson corrects. "I feel her through this link. She's just... at rest."

"Huh" Dani asks.

"She's not dead," Lucinda insists. "We need to keep her like this while we assess the link and figure out how to keep both her and Greyson safe. I've never linked like this through this wand, but I know someone who might know. Sergei. I'll call him and get guidance.

"Why should we trust you?" Greyson asks.

"Lay your hands on me, Veronica," Lucinda states.

Ronnie crawls to her and grasps her hands. And then she shakes her head, crying harder.

My sister feels what she touches. She feels it deeply and I can see she's feeling it right now.

Lucinda stares at the sky with a hollow look on her face as Ronnie weeps and then pries her hands out of Lucinda's, shaking her head.

"She's not lying," Ronnie croaks out, then dashes tears off her face.

Grey clears his throat. "Let's get you all out of here. Get her home while we figure this out." He lifts Aunt Mimi into his arms and begins walking back the way we came. My sisters, Lucinda, and I quickly gather all our implements. Riley picks up Aviva's wand and hucks it into the river with disgust on his face. He does the same with her cauldron.

"Damn it! You shouldn't have done that!" Lucinda yells. "That needs to be carefully-"

"I give no fucks," he hollers.

"It needs to be carefully handled. Not only is it an artifact, it's evidence."

"Ask me if I give a shit!"

"What if Aviva finds it? Or someone else gets their hands on it, Riley?" Jessie asks.

"It's gonna come back to us. I see it," Vivica softly says, eyes glassy with tears.

"In a bad way?" Dani asks.

"I don't… I don't know. I see it coming back though."

"Is Aviva dead?" I ask.

"I think so," Vivi says.

"I think so, too," Jessie echoes.

"Don't know. The water sucked her in and then the rapids took her downstream mighty fast. We'll organize a search party in the morning, I suppose," Riley says, wrapping an arm around me.

"Maybe a couple of us oughta look tonight, in case she made it," Joel suggests.

Lincoln is back with the medicine bag. I hear Mason filling him in on the side.

"Good thinking," Tyson says. "Could the necklace have come off in the water and allowed her use of her powers?"

"Don't know," Grey says. "New to all this."

"Not likely," Lucinda puts in. "That necklace would need to be removed by either the person who put it on, or one of their descendants."

I didn't realize they were all here. But they all are. All Riley's council co-alphas other than Jason. They're here for him. For Greyson. For me, too. For my family.

"Go on home and look after your mate and her family, bro," Mason says. "We'll keep you in the loop."

48

RILEY

I've got eight women in my house. Mimi, in a state of 'pause' with a dagger in her gut, is on the bed in my guest room with three cats and two nieces.

My mate is in the kitchen with the other supernatural council witch, two other sisters as well as my mother, who rushed over, bringing inflatable camping beds to put one on in the living room. The other is taking the couch. They're drinking tea.

Mitch is on his way here to pick up Lucinda and take her back to the rented cottage. We're all meeting in the morning to discuss this. It's already well after two in the morning and though I want to be out there looking for that cunt who tried to take my mate's powers, who tried to kill her family, I'm not leaving Rikki's side tonight. My link with my council co-alphas is strong and I know the rest of them are on this. I'm not taking chances there's not more I don't know about. Not leaving her until I know this shit is over.

I'm infuriated at the notion of what could've happened. If Mimi hadn't had a plan with Grey. I don't want my mate out of my sight any time soon. I want these SCC people fuckin' gone, out of our lives, so we don't have to worry about shit like this again.

SHE'S SLEEPING ON ME, holding me tight like she's afraid she's going to lose me. She's traumatized. I've stayed awake all night purring for her because every time I start to drift and the purring stops, she's jolting awake and gasping.

Not long after five in the morning, I realize I must've drifted too because my phone rings. Not only must I have drifted with my woman on me, at some stage all three of her cats piled on me, too. I've got one stretched across my ankles, one has its head tucked under my jaw, and the other is on my woman's back and she's on me.

I grab my phone from the table.

"Linc?"

"Found her. Washed up on the shore by Savage House. Dead. Her wand was beside her. Necklace still around her throat. We're bringing her to the town hall, and we'll stick her in a basement cell. No sign of that cauldron so far."

"Thank you, brother."

My little witch is awake, eyes on me, looking relieved.

"She's dead."

"I heard." She snuggles in further. "My cats are cuddling with you."

"Yeah. Weird."

"Nope. Not weird."

"One's technically on you. The one that hates me most. They'll cuddle with anybody?" I ask.

"Nope," she advises, and I feel her smile against my throat.

"Hey," she whispers.

"Yeah, babe?"

"It's my birthday," she says.

"Happy birthday, beautiful." I kiss her forehead. "How you feelin' this morning?"

"Like I'm thrice my age," she whispers. "Aunt Lyrica was talking to me, though."

"Yeah?"

"Yeah. Through the kaleidoscope like she sometimes does. She told me that I already know that sometimes you pay tolls for what you've got. She said some of us pay our tolls at the beginning, so we'll always know what's at stake."

"A wise lady."

"I need to go check on Aunt Mimi."

"Go ahead," I say, squeezing her ass. "I'll put some coffee on."

"Going for a run?" she asks, getting out of bed. The three cats jump down, too, undoubtedly sure she's up for the sole purpose of feeding them.

"Nope. I'm here where my mate needs me. We'll go to the town hall at nine. Close the book on all this."

"Okay," she whispers.

"Do they need to worry about that cauldron? The wand washed up but no sign of that so far."

"I don't know, but I don't think so. Our cauldrons aren't as personal as our brooms and wands. I'm not sure why, but they don't seem to hold the same energy."

"I'll let 'em know to keep an eye out. Better if we find it."

"Good thinking."

"What do you want for your birthday?" I ask.

"You," she replies. "Wished for you on my birthday candles every year since I was nineteen."

"You've got me, little witch. What else you want?"

"The greenhouse out back or a balcony out there." She points to the bay window. "When you can get to it." She kisses me again and then she pulls a short blue housecoat on over her slinky little white nightie which I'd somehow missed last night.

My dick goes hard at the shape of her peach-shaped ass. Too many women in my house and too few hours between them and the trauma they endured last night for me to have what I want.

As if reading my mind, she looks over her shoulder at me and gives me a once-over. She's about to take a step back in my direction when I hear female whispers down the hall.

"I'll get on both when this is done. Jessie and Vivi are up," I tell her.

She turns and heads that way. I talk my morning wood down, throw on a pair of trackpants and head downstairs to make coffee. My mother also dropped off two of her breakfast bakes last night, ready to go in the oven, so I turn it on and pull two packs of bacon from the fridge.

"LORD, HAVE MERCY," I hear.

I look over my shoulder from where I stand, frying bacon at the stove and see two sleepy-looking Young sisters approach and both of them are looking at me like I'm a slab of cake and they're half-starved.

"Eyes off my man meat," my mate commands, coming in and giving them both ass slaps as she passes them.

"What a wakeup call," Ronnie says. "The smell of coffee, bacon, and that sight? How do I get me one of these?"

"Wish upon some stars, cast a spell, fall off a cliff into nothing before you suffer for seven years," Rikki says, opening a cupboard and pulling out three cans of cat food. "And wish for it several years in a row over your birthday candles."

I smile at my mate's back.

I don't know when cat food got integrated into my kitchen, but there are now three cats circling my mate's ankles.

"Canned this morning, my babies," she coos, reaching into the next cupboard for a stack of bowls. "I'll make you the good stuff soon." She kisses my shoulder before passing me to get a spoon out.

"Good stuff?" I ask.

"I make cat food from scratch and freeze it once a month," she says.

I look at the three overweight cats who are waiting for their breakfast and shake my head with a smirk.

The black and white female hisses at me. Then the tabby hisses. The male cat meows at my mate.

"Be nice, girls," my mate says. "Riley's your daddy now, so you better get used to it."

My lip curls.

She smiles at me. "Cat daddy," and then she cackles with glee. "Maybe that'll stick instead of pooky."

"Unless you want your ass bared and spanked right here in front of your sisters, you best watch your p's and q's little witch," I warn.

She smiles.

I look to the sisters who are crowded around my island, smiling wide.

"Help yourselves to coffees, ladies. Rik, I already poured you one." I gesture with my chin.

My mate rises on her tiptoes and puckers, so I plant a kiss on her mouth. "Thanks, Mr. Wolf," she whispers.

I tug on her hair band to get it out of the ponytail she put it in.

"Why do you keep doing that?" she mutters.

"Pretty corkscrew curls like that deserve to be free."

She rolls her eyes.

"All good with your aunt?" I ask.

"So it seems. No change."

The blonde sister appears. "Mornin'. Oh my." She's also blatantly staring at my naked upper body.

"My eyes are up here," I tell her, pointing to my face with the bacon tongs.

"Might wanna wear a shirt if you don't wanna be objectified, there lover," Rikki says with an eyebrow wiggle as she dumps cat food into a bowl.

Ronnie reaches up beside me for coffee mugs while blatantly staring at me. "Sorry, Erica, but he made coffee and he's cooking bacon. Plus he looks like that? The shirt won't take the hot factor down, so he might as well forget about the shirt. So he should probably just go shirtless all the time."

"Good idea!" the now entering and smiling Vivica says.

All five are in my kitchen, all are checking me out.

I hear a hiss. I look down. The other female cat is putting her two cents in. "Bullshit," I tell the cat. "You were sleepin' on her who was on me last night so don't keep pretendin' that you don't dig me, too."

"Oscar is a cuddler," Rikki says.

"Yeah, he was sleepin' on my neck," I mutter.

Rikki smiles at me. "Petunia is bitchy by day, snuggly by night. Penny is shy and sweet and hisses only when Petunia hisses first. She doesn't mean it. If you pet her after a hiss, she'll just melt. Try it."

"I'll pass," I mutter.

"Lucinda sent me a text message," Vivica announces. "It's safe to pull the dagger out of Aunt Mimi, so I called Grey and told him. He's coming over. Can I get some java? One for Auntie too? Then shall we?"

I answer. "Help yourself. Make yourselves at home, sisters-in-law," I invite. "Breakfast'll be ready in ten minutes and then we'll head over to the town hall for nine, yeah?"

"Sounds good, cat daddy," Rikki kisses me and then sets the cat food bowls up in a line on the floor. She then pulls three more bowls down from the cupboard and turns the tap on.

I swat her ass.

She gives me a beaming smile. "Can you put their water down? I'm gonna run up and be there when they pull it."

"Yeah. Do that, baby," I kiss her and watch her jog upstairs.

As I'm nearly finished frying the second package of bacon, Jessica is back with a big smile.

"Everything good?" I ask.

"All good," she replies happily. "She looks fifteen or twenty years younger. It was like she opened her eyes and years just melted off. Says she feels great. She's hungry. I came to help you with the rest of this. What can I do?"

"Toast?" I suggest.

"On it," she declares.

Danica comes into the kitchen smiling. "That's why Lucinda is in her nineties and looks forty. Looks like we got more years out of that ordeal for Auntie so it wasn't a total loss. I need one of those daggers."

"Nineties?" I ask.

"Yup," Danica nods.

"Well, shit. We should get hooked up with one for all of us then. It'll work on any supernatural?"

"Yep. And no kidding," Jessica replies. "Though, I'm glad Vivi took out that dagger. Ronnie didn't even wanna set hands on it after touching Lucinda. Says that woman has a story and a half."

Danica steps up beside me and reaches into the kitchen cupboard. "I'll set the... oh... there's no table. I'll set up here for now." She pulls plates down and sets them on the island, then starts hunting through my fridge.

"You need a dining room table," Danica informs me. "But I do approve of your jam selection." She carries an armful of jam jars to the counter.

"My mother stocked the fridge in time for us to come back the other day. And yeah, I do need a table," I agree. "Once your sister finds homes for all these plants I'll make sure we get a table for twelve. I sense there could be a lot of these family meals in the future."

"You sense correctly," Jessica says, nabbing a piece of bacon from the paper towel-lined plate. "But, hear this: life with Erica Young? You will always have too many plants in your house from now on. Get used to it." She bites the end of the bacon strip and gives me an extreme expression.

"I'll deal. If I can deal with her three cats, I can deal with some plants," I mutter. "Cats in a fuckin' wolf shifter village." My eyes roll.

"She almost always has way more than three," Jessica advises. "The three she brought were only half of her current menagerie. But she wasn't about to take them all and leave our house without any. Erica's mantra is that a house isn't a home without housecats."

"Fuck sakes," I mutter, moving the last of the cooked bacon onto the plate. "One of you wanna put on another pot of coffee?"

49

ERICA

It's a parade of witches led by my wolf shifter toward the town hall from Riley's house and I can't get over the spring in Aunt Mimi's step. She didn't want to be driven. She wanted to walk, so we walked.

She woke hungry and full of energy after Lucinda's wand was pulled from her belly and not only was there no blood, the wound vanished instantly. Not even a scar. Over breakfast, she was talkative. She teased that we should've left her daggered another twenty-four hours, so she'd wind up looking our age.

She then told us that she didn't expect her power would revert to her when she woke, but thinks because of all the energy I sent, they've both got it. She also told us that Greyson is now an official coven member and as the eldest of our generation, he'll be the new leader of our coven after she's gone.

And now maybe we'll have twenty more years with her instead of just a couple.

Vivi didn't seem miffed about Greyson leading at all. We've never talked succession, have operated as a family unit always, and nobody ever told us about the eldest of a coven taking over as a general rule. I assumed it'd be Vivi as she was the first of us to join the coven, the most experienced of our generation.

Greyson is technically the eldest of our generation as he's a year older than Vivi and he's willing to be listed as the head of our coven, but Aunt Mimi says that with his life here, his pack responsibilities, his work, and his new mate, he doesn't know how involved he can be so wants to start out as a figurehead and see how it goes. He stopped by during breakfast to check on us all, stayed for a quick coffee, and then said he'd see us at the town hall.

The two of them seem to still have a psychic link, too, because of the power share of last night, which Aunt Mimi says also comes as a surprise.

Although Grey plans to defer to the rest of us, he's willing to do whatever he can to help when necessary, though doesn't want to be involved day-to-day. She's counting on all of us to guide him, particularly me since we'll be living in the same village. She then said she'll go back and forth between Marblehead and Drowsy Hollow to be present for all of us, particularly me as I'll need help learning to manage and wield my new powers. Being the fountain of information she is, she says she has connections that can help me. Connections that aren't part of the SCC. And I plan to study witch history the way she does. Supernatural history in general, because her experience and deep knowledge saved us last night.

Greyson has what he was born with, what she gave him from herself and he has what Aunt Lyrica had. And she told us while heaping seconds onto her breakfast plate that since at his mating he inherited his mother's original powers before hers were stripped, that meant he also gained the powers of his grandmother, Mimi's twin. He's a very powerful warlock. I don't know exactly what this means for us going forward, but I'm sure it contributed to things working out last night.

WHEN WE GET TO THE town hall, Lucinda and Mitchell are here along with the rest of the council alphas. But standing beside Greyson is a woman I don't recognize. She looks nervously at the group of us coming in.

"Aunt Mimi, everybody, this is my mate, Stacy," Grey confirms my suspicions, bringing her to Auntie. "Stace, my cousins: Vivi, Ronnie, Jess, Dani, and Erica. And this knucklehead is Riley Savage."

She's attractive. Wavy dark hair. Dark, pretty eyes. Thick lashes. Dressed in jean shorts, a t-shirt, and sandals. She's nervous. Very nervous. Her eyes lock on mine and I go directly to her, hoping to put her at ease. I have a pretty good idea how she must feel being here after how it all came about.

"I'm Erica. The other newbie around here. Great to meet you." I give her a quick hug, adding softly, "Let's exchange numbers. I thought they'd all hate my guts after what I did to Riley, but I promise you, these people are awesome."

She looks relieved as I pull back. And Greyson is looking at me with approval.

"Nice to meet you, Erica. Everyone. How are you feeling, Mrs. Young?" Stacy asks, nervously.

"Never married so nix the missus. I say, why cook and clean up after a pig year-round when you just get the craving for sausage occasionally?"

Riley barks out a laugh.

Greyson's face goes sour.

The rest of us are gobsmacked. Completely. She's been our mother figure for sixteen years and has never once told a dirty joke around us.

"Who are you and what have you done with Aunt Mimi?" Jessie gasps.

Aunt Mimi ignores her and keeps speaking to Stacy. "Since you're part of this crew now, you can call me Aunt Mimi or Auntie like the rest of these brats. Welcome to the family."

Stacy startles and then as her eyes bounce to the shock on all of our faces, she slowly smiles a dazzling smile.

"She's surly, but we wouldn't trade her for anything," I tell her.

Ronnie adds, "She's usually the quiet, observing type but she's had a harrowing twelve hours."

"I heard," Stacy says with wide eyes.

My sisters take turns hugging Stacy. When Ronnie does, her body goes rod-straight and she gives Greyson a look of alarm for a split second before she hides it. Ronnie felt something when she touched her, and we all know her well enough to know when we see her hide a reaction it means there's something extreme there.

"Can we get started here?" Mitch asks. "Sorry to rush you folks along, but Lucinda has a flight to catch and it's a long drive to the airport."

The circle is still set up from yesterday's meeting, but this time there are no refreshments. We all move in. The women sit and I note the men all remain standing. Riley is at my back, hand on my shoulder. His thumb grazes the mark on my neck briefly and I lean into his touch.

I love this man more and more every day.

"Right," Lucinda begins, "There needs to be an accounting for the events of the night for the SCC. I'll forward a copy of my report to Vivica to show you all before I file it so you can check it for accuracy and let me know if I missed anything important or if you want anything changed or added." Lucinda gestures to Mitch beside herself. "Mitchell is taking me to the airport, then coming back and staying until tomorrow before he goes back to Scotland. He's arranging to transport Aviva to her next of kin."

Riley says, "We'll arrange round-the-clock security to watch the building."

"That's not likely necessary. She's not going anywhere," Lucinda replies, but then adds, "Although that wand needs to go to our archives in Bucharest, so a separate transport needs to be arranged for it and I wanted to ask for assistance with that."

"You can't take it with you?" Tyson asks.

Lucinda shakes her head sharply. "I don't want it anywhere near me, especially after last night. I want no waters clouded because Aviva and I traveled here together and worked together seven years ago on Erica's case."

"If you never have it in your possession, you've got no shadow of suspicion on you," Greyson guesses.

"Yes. But not just that. Power is intoxicating. Especially dark magic. I go out of my way to avoid temptation. I don't even want to set eyes on it again. My advice to any witch in this room is to stay away from it as well."

"Don't wanna go all Gollum from Lord of the Rings?" Mitch jokes.

Lucinda looks at him like he's an ass for a brief moment before replying, "Something like that." And then she turns back to us. "It's a serious responsibility to make sure it gets there, and I recommend at least two escorts. Perhaps one from the coven and one from the pack. I also recommend a spell to protect it in a lock box. I can do it if the coven prefers not to."

"I'm taking a vacation in Greece next month. I don't mind doing a detour to Bucharest on the way," Danica offers.

"I'll go with her," Jase states. "We'll keep it under guard here until then."

"Fuckin' Jase," Riley mutters under his breath.

"Unless you're mated by then," Tyson adds.

"Yeah... uh... unless that," Jase mutters, looking pale.

"We'll make sure Danica has a shifter escort," Riley offers.

"I'll leave that with this group giving you the responsibility for it. You're willing to take that on? To be personally responsible for it until it's handed over?"

"Yes," Dani confirms.

"Mimi, would you be able to put a lock on it? Or would you like me to do it?"

"I'll do that," Aunt Mimi replies.

"Right. I have to say this is preferable to sending it via courier. We do use a service that transports important artifacts, but there's a familial connection to Aviva at that organization, so I'd rather not use it. That wand has the potential to be dangerous, particularly if another Starling coven witch gets their hands on it. Other than all that, I might need testimony if I'm called to answer for last night's events. If I do, I'll be in touch, or you'll get a subpoena. If any of you need me, please reach out." She moistens her lips and then her eyes are on me. "Erica?"

Riley wraps his arm around me protectively.

"Yes?" I reply.

"On behalf of the SCC, I apologize to you and to all of you for what Aviva tried to do last night. If I had any idea whatsoever, I would've stopped it. I've known her thirty-five years. I know her well. I would never, in a million years, have expected this."

"I believe you," I say.

"And that said, my door is open to you or anyone here. Please don't hesitate to reach out if you need help with anything. I know the SCC will not hesitate to reach out to you for help and that goes both ways. Don't be afraid to utilize us. We have a large team of experts on all things supernatural. I hope you'll all look on us favorably despite last night's events. That was definitely out of the norm."

Riley scoffs and I know he's still holding a grudge. I squeeze his hand.

"We always do what we can to help," Aunt Mimi replies. "And we appreciate the offer of help in return. But the SCC will need to put effort in to cultivate a relationship with Greyson and my nieces if they want a reciprocal relationship."

"We intend to," Lucinda says. "We have resources at your disposal if you need them. I've been advised to issue a stern warning to you, Erica, about conducting yourself within the guidelines of our treaties. But I already know I don't have to deliver that warning to you."

"No, you don't," I confirm, looking into her eyes.

"Good," she says softly, then she hands Greyson a business card and extends one to me. "Call any time. Erica, or any of you. Young family: there is an alternative to Aviva's witch retreat held in Ireland every year for Samhain. I can arrange invitations since the Albania option is now off the table."

"We've got an assignment at that point," Vivi advises, "Perhaps next year."

"Can I see the body?" Ronnie asks.

The room goes quiet.

"Why?" Mitch asks.

"I just want to ascertain that this is over," my sister replies softly. "Psychopically. I need to touch her. For peace of mind."

"Very well," Mitch replies. "Follow me downstairs. If you're quick. I need to get Lucinda to the airport."

"I'll wait in your car. I need to make a few calls," Lucinda says.

"I'll come," Aunt Mimi gets to her feet. "Goodbye for now, Lucinda. I might reach out in ten years for another night spent with your wand."

Lucinda smiles. "You'd be welcome to spend a weekend with me at my home. Do not share information about the function of my wand and I'll extend that invite to the rest of you, too. Best wishes, Mimi."

"Meet you outside," I say to Aunt Mimi and Ronnie, then get up. "Until we meet again, Lucinda."

"Accurate," she replies with a warm smile. "I have the feeling you will make an excellent council addition when the time comes."

"I want to make up for lost time with Riley. Have a family. Start a business. Heal. Flourish." I shrug.

"When you're ready, contact us. Though we might reach out before then."

"Try and wait at least eighteen to twenty years," Riley speaks up. "We have a family to make and raise."

Lucinda smiles and it seems genuine. "Until next time. Farewell." She waves and walks out.

"What are we doing now?" I ask. "Head back to our place?"

Vivi, Dani, and Jessie rise.

"We have a few errands," Vivi says. "Can we catch up a little later?"

"Oh. Okay," I say.

"I'll call you in a bit," Vivi says and hugs me.

"It's over," I whisper.

"I hope so," she replies.

"Do you have doubts?"

"Not doubts," she says carefully. "But something is brewing. I don't know if it's about you, about Grey and the problems he's having, or something else. But something's in the air."

"Might just be residual energy from last night," Jessica offers.

"Maybe," Vivi says warily. "Talk to you in a bit."

I hug Jessica and Dani and head for the door, seeing Riley standing outside talking to Tyson.

Once I get outside, Greyson's mate Stacy is behind me. "Erica?"

I turn.

"I have to tell you something."

"What is it?"

She looks worried.

"The witch my brother Wyatt was using to help him… she ran away. That's one of the reasons he tried to have you taken."

"Yes," I say, waiting for her to elaborate.

"Her name is Aphra Starling."

My eyes widen.

"You know her?" Riley asks. He and Tyson are both facing us now.

"No," I say.

"I do. She didn't want to help us, but Wyatt held her hostage. Forced her. She ran away," Stacy tells us, "but in case he finds her and because of what that woman said in there about the Starling coven, I wanted you to know."

"Thank you, Stacy. I'm glad we know that. Be back, Riley," I rush back inside to go down to Aunt Mimi and Ronnie. I want us to put a protective lock spell on that wand right now. Just in case.

50

ERICA

I'm so relieved that we're past things with the SCC. I'm finding it strange that I'm now someone they want to work *with* instead of being someone they want to punish.

I'm doing some more organizing of my stuff while Riley is in his office in the garage with Mason, talking about their work. It's going to be interesting getting into a routine. Him working. Me doing my thing. Starting that business if I can make it happen.

I have lived lean in Marblehead with my family and between helping with the family businesses between Drowsy Hollow and Marblehead along with selling some of my art here and there, I've saved myself a nice little nest egg.

It could very well get me started with my garden center idea. Me and my new mother-in-law will be talking about it in a couple days. She says she's got some money aside to seed into it too and she's trying to make it clear it's my baby, I'm in charge and she just wants to be part of it in whichever way makes me happy. And that thought makes me smile.

It's odd being here in Riley's house by myself. Partly because reality is still penetrating that this is my home, too. But also because it's my birthday and there hasn't been any fanfare. At all.

I have all I've ever wanted – Riley. And Aunt Mimi is healthier than she's been in years, so that's another plus after the fears we had last night. So, I'm feeling a bit guilty that I also feel a teensy bit pouty about it being almost three o'clock in the afternoon without getting a happy birthday from any members of my family.

I haven't heard from them since the town hall five or six hours ago and none of them even wished me a happy birthday this morning. Granted, our focus was Aunt Mimi, and we were all still shaken up from the events of the night before, so I didn't even think about it again until we got back after the town hall meeting, but it's been hours and... *crickets*. Either I remind them it's my birthday or let them fail at my birthday and then they all feel guilty about it later.

I need to let them off the hook.

I send a group text.

So... not to be pouty after all we have to be thankful for but it's actually my birthday today – don't worry I'm not mad you guys forgot – but how about we do dinner tonight? All I really want is a nice meal with my family. And of course for you all to sing to me with your terrible singing voices. LOL.

I wait. And... nothing.

It's approaching four o'clock, so I hang one more dress in the closet that Riley promised to upgrade later on (it's a little tight with his stuff and mine in there so I offered to put my stuff in one of the spare rooms, but it was important to him that I hang most of my dresses beside all his jeans and shirts). I wander outside over to the garage, knock on the side door and open it. He's at one of three desks, eyes pointed at his computer screen.

I don't want to show how disappointed I am that my family forgot my birthday, but I also know he can read me like a book so there's no point trying to hide it.

He holds his finger up to ask me to wait.

"Okay, yeah, say no more," Riley says. "It's got my thumbs up. Bye for now." He clicks something, then closes his laptop lid and beckons me forward with a crook of that raised finger.

As I move that way, the crooked finger adjusts to become a flattened palm. He raises a flat palm in the air and commands, "Stop."

I freeze.

"What's wrong?"

I'm panicked now, feeling like something might be wrong. Like my dream might be about to fall apart.

He gives a sharp shake of his head, like he wants me to halt that way of thinking. "Hello little witch. Here to ask me what time it is?"

My insides go liquid.

He jerks his chin up.

"Um… hello, Mr. Wolf."

He epitomizes the term wolfish grin as he eyes me up and down.

I continue, "I was coming out here to tell you it's about four o'clock, so I was going to suggest we meet up with my family for dinner in town, maybe. But maybe I'm wrong about what time it is."

"Before we talk about all that, how about you *ask* me what time it is?"

"Even though I just told you I think it's about four o'clock?" I ask, sassily.

"You're very bad at this game, woman."

"Thankfully it seems that you are not," I volley and then I ask the question in my best over-performing, melodramatic, bad actor voice. "Gee… wonder what time it is?" I press my index finger to my chin.

Riley shakes his head with fake dismay. "Ask the right way, little witch."

I hold back laughter and then ask, in my sultriest voice, "What time is it Mr. Wolf?"

"It's four o'clock," he replies, gaze heated, eyes drinking me in.

I take a step. "One." And then I take another. "Two."

"This gonna take all day?" he asks," Gonna be twenty-five o'clock before you ask me for the time again?"

I laugh.

"Hey! This is a serious timekeeping matter, Mrs. Savage."

I shrug.

He growls.

Ooh. I feel that in a *very* private place. I bite my lip as my belly dips.

His nostrils flare and his eyes coast over me.

"Three- four," I say taking two steps quickly, resisting the urge to run to him. "How was that, Mr. Savage Wolf?"

He leans back in his chair and waits, looking at me expectantly.

"What time is it now, Mr. Wolf?" I ask. I'm still about six or seven feet away.

"Dinner time," he says, and he rises, pushing his chair back.

I take off running. I'm out the door and halfway up the driveway when I'm caught.

I squeal with glee as he scoops me up into his arms. "I caught you, now what?"

"Now it's my turn to be the wolf," I tell him.

He laughs against my neck. "Denied. I'm always Mr. Wolf."

I giggle.

"Early dinner and then we'll talk about regular dinner." He carries me into the house.

He might be the one who caught me, but I'm the one who attacks first, lunging for his fly as soon as we're inside.

We're tumbling onto the couch and he's helping me free him from his jeans.

"Get this dress up, little witch."

I lift it high.

"Fuck. No panties again," he says, then growls and gives me a dangerous look. And my body reacts the way it always does whenever my man growls.

"Been like this all day?" he demands, smacking my ass with fire in his gaze.

I squeal as I shake my head. "Of course not. I took them off when we got home. I hoped we'd have some together time, but you had to go and work." I scrunch up my nose. "On my birthday no less."

Riley moves me to my back and sinks inside, staring into my eyes while he does it. "Love you, baby. No more work. The rest of the day is all about you."

God, that feels good. What he's doing and hearing him say that while he does it.

"I love you so much." I grab his hair with both hands and pull his mouth to mine.

IT'S A LITTLE WHILE later, after frenzied action that means we've wound up on the living room floor, me on my hands and knees on the carpet and Riley's knot buzzing against the inside of me, making me whimper hard. He's got a handful of my hair and he's not being gentle. I love it.

"That feels so, so good, little witch. This is where I'm meant to be – inside you." His free hand cups mine and then our fingers weave together as the buzzing revs up and we both groan out the rest of our release together.

While I'm catching my breath, he's dragging a blanket from the couch and throwing it over us, rolling over so that we're on our sides, facing one another. And then he kisses my throat directly on my claiming bite. I shudder. I love that he put that there. That people can see it. That when he touches it, the sensations drive me half-feral. I can't get enough of this man. I will never, ever complain about doing this with him.

"I love sex," I tell him.

He throws his head back and laughs.

"This is... like... the best drug there is. Being fucked by Riley Savage? Better than magic. And magic used to be my favorite thing."

His smile drops and he growls against my throat, kissing it again.

I let out a happy sigh.

"I'd go through it again to get here with you," he tells me, fingertips tucking my hair behind my ear. "It really fuckin' hurt. Fuck, did it cut deep. But Erica, I'd go through it again if it was what I had to do. I'm gonna be so happy with you that I'll never question what we went through to be together. I hate that they did this to us, but I'd let 'em do it again if it was the only way."

God, he's amazing.

"Thank you, baby," he continues. "For waiting to be mine. For not giving what's mine to anyone else. For waiting on that corner here in the village even though I wasn't givin' you time or respect. Thank you for protecting your body and your heart, saving it for me. You've already shown me it's not too broken to be fixed. I'm gonna make that seven years up to you."

I snuggle in and hang on tight. "You've already more than made up for it. I don't wanna ever go through it again, not because it wasn't worth it – it is – but because it sucked so bad to wonder if you were okay, to imagine you might never want to see me again after you found out the truth. Thank you, Riley, for being everything I knew you'd be the first day I saw you. I'm in awe of the fact that the reality of you is even better than the promise. Thank you, too, Mr. Wolf, for making seven years' wait worth it."

He's trying to kiss me, but I touch his lips with my fingertips and continue talking. "I knew you'd be a hundred per cent perfect for me. I knew we could have the most beautiful life together. It's just barely gotten started, and I love when I'm right. It feels like it barely happens – me being right – so when it does, I bask in it. I fucking *love* when I'm right. I was right about you. And I know how amazing it's gonna be. I'm *so* happy."

He dots kisses all over my face and then stares into my eyes again, while cradling my jaw in one hand.

He's so amazing. My beautiful, strong, fierce man.

I hear an angry meow, then a hiss.

We both look up and see Petunia about ten feet away, her ire directed at Riley.

"Toonie, be nice," I call out.

She hisses again and then starts the warning growl she makes when she's ready to attack.

"Oh no, Rye. She's gonna attack."

"Huh?" he asks.

"She makes that noise when she's about to attack."

Petunia crouches low and takes a step. And then another. She's stalking Riley, most likely because we're on the floor so they're at eye level and she thinks she can take him. She's ready to inflict damage.

Riley throws the blanket off.

"You want a piece of me, pussy?"

I laugh. "She gets pretty nasty. Be careful, honey."

She answers with her low, angry, *you're about to get fucked-up by claws and teeth* meow again.

"Toonie," I warn. "No!"

She looks at me like she gives no fucks.

Riley gets on all fours on the rug. "Come at me, bro."

I giggle. "She's got really sharp claws, Scooby Dooby. You better be careful, especially with what's dangling there right now."

I playfully slap his bare bottom.

He abruptly shifts, turning into his beautiful, huge wolf and he lets out a single, deep, loud bark.

Petunia, my bitchy fat cat with the attitude…she looks like she's going to piss herself. Her back arches straight up into a perfect semicircle and her hair rises like she's been electrocuted before her ears pin back and she runs like her ass is on fire, tearing up the stairs.

Riley shifts back to human form and he collapses to his back on the floor beside me; he's laughing his ass off.

"IT'S WELL AFTER SIX and everyone's phones are going straight to voicemail. Nobody's answering their texts," I mutter. "I hope nothing's wrong."

I'm dressed up. I ironed my hair straight, which startled Riley and I could tell he also liked it. He keeps coming into the bathroom and touching it, flirting with me, trying to sweettalk me into skipping dinner.

And he looks good, too. Damn good. He's wearing a navy button-down dress shirt, dark trousers, and glossy polished brown dress shoes. He looks and smells like a million bucks.

He shaved, too, doing it beside me at the double sink in his bathroom while I flat ironed my hair and though it was hot to watch, though his smooth face feels and looks really nice, I'm kind of partial to the beard. I told him that and he laughed, telling me that he's generally clean shaven but that the last few weeks he's had other things on his mind. I gave him a look of apology and he spanked my bottom once for it, admonishing me for feeling any sort of guilt.

"No more shrinking, baby. You hear me?" He rubs my bottom soothingly after the slap.

He then tells me he's happy to forego the morning shaving ritual most of the time if it floats my boat.

And I clearly float *his* boat tonight. I'm wearing a short, tight, lacy dress and my highest high heels that still make me feel like I'm a miniature person in the land of the giants with Riley's towering height, and I'm in makeup and perfume. I'm wearing dangling Celtic knot earrings and the protection necklace Aunt Mimi made for me. I started getting ready while multitasking by calling my family (who still hadn't answered my group message) to try to wrangle up a plan to meet up for dinner. Riley said there's a nice steak joint in Drowsy Hollow, so I thought we'd meet them all there, but nobody's answering phones. And I'm concerned.

Maybe birthdays aren't a big deal in shifter culture and if so, that's a bummer. Because in my family, another trip around the sun is a big deal to us, but I really don't like that nobody's been in touch for hours.

"What's going on?" I ask aloud to no one.

"We'll head down to their apartment and wrangle 'em?" Riley pops his head in the bathroom.

Aviva is definitely dead. And we put an extra-strong lock on the box containing that old wand. Both a physical lock and a spell. Jase and Linc took it and hid it in a little niche in the back of the cave under Arcana Falls. They confirmed that it was done. Maybe I should've put a protection spell on the cave, too. I sure hope everything and everyone are okay.

"YOU'RE QUIET," RILEY observes as we get into his truck.

"I'm just... hope they're okay."

"I'm sure they are, babe."

I force a smile.

"I feel your anxiety, little witch, and it's not necessary. Trust me. Okay?"

"Trust you? What do you mean?"

"Fuck. Gotta let you off the hook, but act surprised so your sisters don't take turns kickin' me in the nuts."

I stare at him for a minute before what he just said penetrates. *Wait. What? Wait. No...*

"Act surprised? Are they punking me right now?"

His phone makes noise.

He glances at the screen and says in an uber-fake bad actor voice, "Oh look! I have a text. I know I shouldn't text while driving, but I have a feeling I need to see this." He pauses for dramatic effect, lifts his phone, and his eyes scan the screen.

"We aren't even out of the driveway yet," I say, unable to stop grinning at him.

"Even still. Precious cargo." He leans forward with an exaggerated pucker.

I lean in and our lips touch.

"Mm," he says under his breath, then looking me over, gives me the sexiest growl I've ever heard. In. My. Life.

His eyes move back to his screen as I fan myself. "Tell my sister you need to stop by the town hall for something... come up with an excuse." He winks and then pulls out onto the road.

I'm flat-out laughing as we drive the short distance to the town hall.

"I thought maybe birthdays weren't a big deal around here and my family usually makes a big deal, but I figured they forgot what with everything happening."

"Birthdays are a big deal around here, too, darlin'," he says. "This pack would throw a party to celebrate a two-for-one sale on chocolate bars at Cicely's store if they could."

I laugh.

"Not jokin'," he says.

"That's amazing. Would you attend that party?" I ask.

"Absolutely. Love chocolate bars."

I laugh. "Yet another shining example of you and this place being the perfect man in the perfect place for me."

He has a gorgeous smile on his face as he parks.

My mood fades just slightly for a bit because *eesh*... this town hall has been a source of anxiety for me the past few days.

Riley turns the truck off.

"They've been running around cobbling this together today. But they asked yesterday mornin' if they could. So they didn't forget your birthday, Rikki. It's just that we've had shit happening, so they rushed to make it all happen after the meeting this morning. Sorry to ruin the surprise, but I couldn't stand another minute of watching you worry. It was fuckin' gutting me."

He leans in and kisses my neck. "You mad at me?" he asks.

"Not at all," I tell him and then kiss him, holding his neck while I do. "Let's go in. I'll act surprised."

When we get inside, I'm not remotely prepared for what happens.

I expected a little surprise shindig with my sisters, Riley's pack mates, pretty much the same people who were at his house for dinner the other night. But I'm greeted with many more faces than that.

Young faces. Old faces. And balloons. So. Many. Balloons.

"Surprise!" is a collective loud greeting.

I squeal and jump up and down with glee.

51

ERICA

There was not a better way for me to meet Riley's pack than this. I thought they'd hate me. I thought it'd be awkward for the first few months while they warily moved out of the way whenever they saw me coming. I figured I'd have to work for it, and I was fully prepared to put in the work.

But I've been genuinely surprised by many, many open, happy, welcoming new faces. Dozens and dozens of them. And I feel nothing but positive energy coming at me.

"Is this the whole pack?" I ask Riley.

"Good chunk of it, but not all of 'em. I'm impressed at these numbers though, considering the short notice. This is the bulk of the twenty-five-year-olds through sixty-year-olds. There are a few seniors here, too. Mostly my relatives."

A female voice calls out, "Happy..."

And then the rest of them join in to sing *Happy Birthday* to me while Riley's mom carries a large, pink candle-lit cake toward me while singing.

IT'S A PARTY FOR A few hundred. And it's amazing. My sisters and Aunt Mimi are being treated like VIPs. I was immediately outfitted with a golden tiara, a white and gold birthday girl pageant sash, and put on a chair festooned to look like a throne. There are giant, beautiful, colorful bouquets on either side of my 'throne', and I've been greeted by a seemingly endless reception line of people who want to welcome me to the pack and wish me a happy birthday.

When I remarked that my man wasn't given a king's throne, he took my throne himself, and planted me on his lap.

Mitch from the SCC is back from taking Lucinda to the airport and is enjoying the party. Riley told me he's not very happy that Mitch is here, but he is here until tomorrow and since he's a doctor who specializes in shifter illnesses, he has a collaborative relationship with Cat Savage. I guess my man decided it was impractical to ban him from my party.

Mitch is within the first dozen of the long line-up of people looking to wish me a happy birthday. When it's his turn, he hands me a birthday card.

"Little local spa trip on me and my missus. Happy birthday and sorry for all you've been through, lass. Truly."

I stand and give him a hug. "Thank you so much."

"Enough of that," Riley says and pulls me back onto his lap. He only seems like he's half-joking, either being possessive, holding a grudge, or maybe both.

Mitch laughs it off.

I'm greeted by some with handshakes. Some with waves. Some people bring me cards and others set gifts on the table beside us. Some are just here to meet me and extend best wishes and I'm overwhelmed by the kindness I'm getting.

I get hugs from Riley's parents. Riley's mom tells me softly that Carrie and Graydon couldn't make it. And then Bailey tells me her parents can't make it but that her mom sent a gift, which is set on the table. I notice she didn't say it's from her mom and her dad but figure I'll work on Graydon Blackwood later on.

After Cicely sets down a bottle of ice wine as my gift, I tell her we're going to drink it together one night soon. And then Lincoln steps up.

"Happy birthday, Erica," he says with a smile, reaching to shake my hand.

I get up and hug him, feeling like he's an unofficial brother-in-law. Riley growls and Lincoln takes a step back and laughs nervously, giving Riley a look as if to say it wasn't his fault.

"No more hugging boys," I remark when I sit back down on Riley's lap. "Got it." I smooth my skirt out and dare to look at his face. His eyes are fiery, and his hand grips my hip with purpose.

"I'm kind of a hugger," I explain.

"Oh yeah? Well I'm kind of a spanker," he volleys.

"Save 'em up for later. You owe me two, right? One for Mitch and one for Linc? Poppa Ace doesn't count since he's your dad."

He eyes me with a dangerous look that I find frankly thrilling.

"Hey, happy birthday, Erica."

I look back to the line. Mason's mom Skye is standing in front of us holding a big basket of goodies.

"That basket is from me and several other women. There's a card with all our names. You'd have gotten it anyway as a welcome to our pack, so we packed extra goodies in here since it's also your birthday."

"How sweet!" I exclaim. "I can't wait to dig into it. Is there more of that honey wine in there?" I take the basket from her and set it on the table.

"Sure is," she remarks.

"Happy birthday, Erica," Mason's father Andrew says.

"Hi." I say and as I'm reaching to shake Andrew's hand, he pulls me into a hug and lifts me off the floor.

"Uh oh," I whisper.

He sets me on my feet.

I can see the mischief in his eyes.

"Oh, aren't you a pot-stirrer," I observe while laughing.

Skye rolls her eyes. "Like you wouldn't believe."

I look over my shoulder at Riley. "That's three!"

"Not your fault, little witch, I'll let you off the hook," he grumbles, looking aggravated.

"No, no. Three it is. Let's see how high we can go."

He leans forward in his seat. "Don't push it, woman, or you'll find yourself pleading for me to stop."

"Hugs for everyone," I tease.

And people are laughing.

"Sorry. Don't mind me. Saved it for Riley all my life so feeling like I've got a new toy and I'm not likely to ever get bored with it."

I hear a lot of laughter. And my man's eyes are lit with so much light I want to cry happy tears. I lean over and kiss him. "I love you," I whisper.

My joke was for the people up close, which were Mason's parents and my man. And Amie, Mason, Tyson, and Ivy who are directly behind them. But when I turn back to the crowd I realize my voice either carried much further than that or the vast majority of these people all have extra-sharp hearing.

Duh. Shifter hearing.

I cover my face with embarrassment. "Shit."

"Around these parts, we have really, really good hearing in case you haven't figured it out, little lady," An older man calls from way at the back.

"I'll try to remember that," I reply, blushing. "Who's that?" I ask Riley.

"That's my grandfather."

"Oh shit. I'm gonna crawl under this gift table and hide," I say.

There's more laughter and then I meet more people, get more gifts, and the whole "meeting the pack" thing is absolutely amazing.

THERE'S BEEN FOOD, music, booze, and laughter. I've met so many people I know it'll take forever to remember names. And I got so many nice gifts. At least as many gifts as I am years old. Cards. Gift cards. A big, homemade card from the kids of the pack. None of them have come to the party, but I'm told I'll meet them all at the next pack event and Lucy-Mom told me to be prepared for a barrage of questions about being a witch.

I've eaten a slice of a giant coffee cake like the one Riley's aunt made for our time together in Tyson's cabin.

But it's layered, about two feet high and is frosted with baby pink cream cheese frosting – my favorite. Riley told me he asked his aunt to make it since I made a request that the coffee cake be my birthday cake every year from now on. And I'm all squishy because he remembered despite that being not long after he got trapped in his wolf's mind.

He also told me because it was short notice and lots had to be done, his aunt actually got several women to each bake two and it was several cakes that went into the building of it.

Riley and I took turns feeding cake to one another and I've whispered in his ear that we should take some home and reenact that original coffee cake scene for breakfast tomorrow... that I might be on his lap now, but I'd rather be connected when we eat some more.

"Better get that coffee cake recipe from my aunt, mate. I think we'll be eating it often," he says.

I shake my head and scoop a bit of frosting onto my finger. He sucks on it, staring into my eyes with intent. My belly dips, but I manage to say, "Nuh uh. I'm not a baker. I suggest you get your aunt to give *you* the recipe."

He smiles and whispers, "I can do that."

"Happily ever after is gonna be so happy," I tell him. "Especially if you do most of the cooking."

"We'll have everyone else do most of the cooking, babe," he offers an alternative. "Pack's all half in love with you already. All you gotta do is plant the seed that you can't cook, and they'll drop meals off left, right, and center."

"Awesome," I tell him. "But I'm not a freeloader. I'll trade vegetables, fruits, and flowers for meal prep instead."

He looks like he approves.

"Open this one right now," Vivi demands, handing me a heavy box.

"Okay…"

I rip the wrapping paper and unearth absolutely gorgeous stationery as well as a set of personalized ledgers and grimoires along with two monogramed sketchbooks. The stationery says Riley and Erica Savage. The grimoires and sketchbooks have Erica Savage in beautiful script.

"How did you pull this off?" I asked. "This is good stationery. It probably should've taken weeks to get with Erica Savage on it."

"I ordered it eight weeks ago," Vivi admits.

"Because you had high hopes or you knew?" Riley asks.

She smirks.

My mouth drops open. "And you didn't let me off the hook?"

She rolls her eyes. "I told you it was gonna work out. You didn't believe me."

"That's true," I say. "I love it. Thank you." I give her a hug.

Some pack members have given me candles, bubble bath, and other cute little trinkets. But my favorite gift of them all is a hand-carved stone wolf sculpture that Riley's grandfather gave me.

He informed me he wants to work part time in my garden center. He doesn't want wages, but he wants to make his own hours. He plans to water my plants and says he'll take care of the shopping carts. I wholeheartedly agreed to these terms as he presented me with the sculpture of about eight inches tall, hand carved from a chunk of stone from the Arcana Falls cave. It's painted brown with green eyes. And he's got amazing detail in it that really does look like Riley's wolf. It's beautiful and feels like there's energy inside it. Amazing energy. I almost cried when I was holding it, feeling super-emotional at the welcome. At how perfect it all is.

I got to meet both of Riley's grandmothers, too, and they were both very friendly. There's been no animosity today from anyone. No one!

Aunt Mimi has been up dancing with Amie and Ivy's mom, Kathleen. Auntie is like I've never seen her. Having a blast.

After eating a plate of food from the big, potluck spread and sharing my slice of cake with Riley, it occurs to me that we're celebrating above Aviva Starling's body, which is in a locked jail cell in the basement. But what also occurs to me is how much I can learn from that experience.

Aviva had a good reputation. She had a large coven, a large family. She was a respected member of the witch community and the overall supernatural community, too. She got lured with the promise of black magic. And that's beyond sad. I'm taking that as more than a stern warning to be very careful in my practice of magic. I'm not perfect. I might screw up sometimes, but I certainly do take warning signs very seriously and Aviva Starling's story is a cautionary tale to remember - experienced witch with a good support system seduced by the promise of unlimited power. This happens after she works to ensure a young witch who would come into a lot of gifts is ready to handle them without falling victim to the temptation of dark magic.

Seven years after she goes out of her way to make sure I come into my magic when I'm more prepared to handle it, she's pulled into temptation and darkness and loses everything because of it.

A SLOW SONG COMES ON and finally, we have a minute without people looking to talk to us. I've been so busy talking to people that I've been missing out on the dancing. Before seven years ago, I was always the first and last on any dance floor. And I didn't think that was me anymore. But it's feeling like it might be me again.

For the first few bars of this song, I've stared into his eyes with a big smile, hoping he can take a hint. Thankfully, he can. As he moves me off his lap, takes my hand and leads me to the dance floor, I take in Greyson and Stacy.

She's glued to his side at a nearby table. I feel like Grey probably promised to not leave her alone for a second in order to get her to come. To his credit, he hasn't.

I've seen people approaching them, heard people welcome her to the pack throughout the evening. Greyson is being very protective and word traveled a while after we got here for people to tone it down and give her some space. She did come over and wish me *Happy Birthday* after the line-up cleared.

"Hi Stacy. How are you?" I asked.

"Happy Birthday, Erica. I didn't have time to shop for a gift…"

"That's okay. Your presence is more than present enough."

"Well," she said, "I was going to bake you something. Baking is kind of my thing. But then I figured people in the pack might worry I'd poisoned you, so I… I'm here empty-handed."

"Parties are for partying. That's my favorite part," I assured, waving my hand. "Handmade gifts are my favorite kinds of gifts as they're from the heart, so maybe I can consider myself in the possession of an IOU for a cupcake or other baked treat made by my new friend Stacy?"

"Definitely," she said, giving me a beaming smile.

Grey gave me a big hug.

Riley didn't growl that time. Instead, he kissed my throat and told me with his eyes that he loved me.

"FINALLY, A DANCE WITH my foxy little mate," Riley says, hand grazing my ass as he pulls me close.

The song abruptly changes a few bars in from *Crazy Love* by Aaron Neville to *Truly, Madly, Deeply* by Savage Garden. And I know it's probably my sister Jessie that put this on. She often takes control of the music and I'd bet she put it on when she saw us get up. She knows how much I love this song. Though *Crazy Love* would've been nice to dance to, too, and I'm going to ask her to play it later.

"Truly, madly, and deeply. I am so, so in love with you, Riley Savage," I tell him.

His eyes ooze love as they travel my face.

"We're so sappy and disgustingly cute, aren't we?" I laugh.

I can't believe I have everything I want after being so certain that there was nothing on my horizon other than heartache and a gaping void the size of a giant brown wolf. But here I am. And his family, his pack, they're incredible.

"You fit right in. Like this is where you belong," he says, warmth oozing from his pores. He's read my mind again. "I'm madly and deeply in love with you too, Erica Savage."

His hand tightens in the length of my hair, and he bends to kiss me again.

It's a moment of perfection. I'm going to give myself a toothache – it's *that* sweet.

We sway and I feel the music, feel my feelings, fully feel this beautiful moment.

Riley feels good, right, real.

I get to have these arms around me. I get to have his lips on me. I get to spend the rest of my life pulling out all the stops to make him happy the way I know he's going to make me happy. I am so excited about our future.

"Happy birthday, little witch," he says against my lips as the song ends.

After we're back to the throne, a few are waiting to say goodnight, including Amie and Mason as well as Ty and Ivy who are calling it a night. Amie apologizes that they're cutting out early.

"The vibe is tipsy and party-like and it's after eleven o'clock so it's not cutting out early when you're pregnant and you last in this environment until after eleven o'clock," I assure her.

But I know that they both had difficult nights here in this space in this kind of environment while there was dancing, so I'm wondering if they want to leave early partly because we're at that part of the night.

She laughs and hugs me goodnight. I get a hug from Ivy, too, and they leave after the three of us make plans to meet for breakfast the day after tomorrow (since we'll be seeing my family off tomorrow).

Riley gets me another drink and Riley's cousin Leona along with Joel's sister Audrey invite me to dance with them. My sisters Jessie and Ronnie join us on the dance floor, and I know Riley's watching, taking a pull of his beer with a carnal expression, sitting on that throne looking like every little witch's fantasy come to life.

"Everyone here is so awesome so far," I tell Leona and Audrey. "I can't believe how amazing it is. How well everyone seems to get along."

"Oh, there are beefs here 'n there," Audrey leans in to say.

"Yup," Leona twirls. "Like any small town there are cliques, there are problematic people, busybodies, judgmental people, and bullies."

"Way to sell it," I hold both thumbs up.

They both laugh.

"Overall it's pretty awesome, though. Pack life is *the life*," Audrey says.

"Good thing she didn't meet Sherry Creed when she first came into town. Her opinion of our pack would be so different," Leona adds.

They laugh.

Riley's still watching me, so I shake my ass a little more.

And it earns me a very wolfish grin.

Joel approaches Riley so his eyes move away from mine and the song is ending, so my eyes scan the perimeter of the large, farmhouse chic decorated barn to see if I can find Bailey and Cicely. Last time I saw them, they were with some of the other ladies by the long dessert table.

I spot Cicely by one of the exits. I've got a view of her back, but can see she has a fistful of Lincoln's t-shirt. I don't know if her expression is angry or sexual, but I'd guess the latter with the hungry look on his face.

Hm.

My eyes move along, and I see Jase has my sister Dani pinned against the wall by the bar. I see his hand on her hip and his mouth by her ear. There's a tipsy glow in Dani's eyes as she laughs at whatever he's saying to her. And about twenty or thirty feet away, leaning against the wall is Bailey. Watching Jase and Dani.

Jase tags my sister's hand and grabs a bottle of wine from the bar, then, carrying the wine by the neck, pulls her out the nearest exit. And the look on Bailey's face? It's like the very last baby panda bear in the whole world was just shot in his fluffy forehead right in front of her eyes.

Bailey spins away and storms to the back hall that I already know is where some restrooms are, so I excuse myself from the dance circle, rush back to the throne, and grab my sparkly little cat face-shaped clutch from the table.

I kiss Riley, saying, "Right back. Little sorceress's room is calling." I rush to catch up with her and find her at the sink staring at her reflection.

"Hey? You okay?"

"No. Definitely not," she says, adjusting her bra while blowing her hair out of her eyes. "Did you see who just left with your sister?"

"I did," I say softly, giving her a look of apology.

"I've been pining for Jason Creed since before I grew boobs. I'm so done with watching him wrack up bedpost notches."

"Shit. One sec." I reach into my clutch and pull out my phone, setting the clutch on the counter.

I'm dialing. Straight to voicemail.

"Shit." I begin to work on firing off a text.

I don't have time to write a spell, gather what I need, and try to make something happen to stop those two from hooking up, because I know for a fact it'd go nowhere and do nothing good, so I'll have to rely on technology.

"What's wrong?" Bailey asks.

"One sec," I say.

Dani, don't hook up with Jase. Birthday request.

I immediately send another text to her.

Don't refuse me. Say nothing but Bailey is head over heels and will be crushed if you do this. Thx. Xoxo.

I see an almost instant 'read' and know my sister lives on her phone and would ignore a phone call all day long but would never be able to resist checking a notification. A prime example of why I was a little stressed out earlier when everyone went quiet for so many hours.

"She won't," I say to Bailey. "Forget about it. Put it out of your mind. Let's go dance and have a good time. But first, nature calls. Excuse me." I hurry into the stall, lift my dress, haul down my underwear and sit. I'm realizing that I'm drunk all of a sudden, and feeling kind of proud of myself, like I saved the mood for Bailey at least a little.

When I come out of the stall, the bathroom is empty.

"Where'd she go?" I ask no one.

I wash my hands and then shake them dry before I dash out to go find her. I go the wrong way down the bathroom hall and see there's an exit door propped open. I hear a voice out there and see the back of a guy talking on his phone. I spin around to go back the way I came.

Bailey is pouring herself a drink at the bar, so I join her.

"I'm such a dummy," she mutters.

"Why?"

"I bought this pheromone perfume online and have gotten into his space every chance I've gotten tonight, but nothing. It did nothing."

"Aw honey…" I pout and lean forward. "But you do smell good."

"It's hopeless, Erica."

"Aw." I give her a hug. "Wanna dance?" I ask. "Let's cut up the proverbial rug out there. Shake your ass and see who notices." I pull back and wiggle my eyebrows.

Stacy passes us, heading toward the bathroom. "Come dance with us when you get back," I invite.

She smiles as she passes, but I'm pretty sure she's nowhere near ready to dance like nobody's watching.

"Bailey," an attractive blonde greets in a way I can tell is a jab. As if Bailey's name is a joke. Bailey's expression sours.

The woman smiles big at me. "Hello Erica. It's nice to meet you." She extends her hand. "I'm Sherry."

I shake. Her handshake is limp, and her smile looks fake.

"I heard you weren't invited to this," Bailey mutters grouchily before I can reply. "Your bruise is healing nicely. Be sure you do not give me a reason to give you another."

I'm shook. This doesn't seem like Bailey at all.

Sherry laughs like she's shocked at Bailey's comments.

"There's history here," Bailey explains. "Trust me, I'm not in the wrong."

Sherry laughs harder, fake, like she thinks Bailey is a joke and slow claps a few times. "Wow, Bailey. Growin' a pair, are ya? Okay, yeah, I probably had it coming... I'll give you that, though I do say it was a cheap shot. Tell you what: try and take a swing at me again and you won't catch me off guard."

"You're such a bitch," Bailey mutters. "No remorse for what you did to Amie that night."

Sherry laughs. "And I have a question for you, Bailey. Did you wear that little gold dress to try to catch my brother's eye? Because I saw him go outside with the hot blonde witch. As per usual, you're invisible to him. Just the best friend's pesky little sister. It's not a good look. I really think you should give it up and go find yourself a nice beta."

"I don't like you," I say to Sherry. "I usually prefer to draw my own conclusions about people, even though people warned me about you. You're living up to your bad reputation. It's not too late to turn that around, though."

Bailey straightens up; she knows I've got her back like real friends do.

Sherry rolls her eyes. "Whatever. I see they're all treating you like Queen Shit tonight, but don't think for a second people won't continue looking at you thinking about poor Riley, spending seven years alone, sad, wanting to die because he thinks you're dead. They might smile to your face, but believe you me, they'll be –"

"Bailey!" An angry male voice shouts.

Our heads all swing right. Jase is stalking over here with a look of murder on his face. He stops three feet away.

"What the fuck, Bailey? Not fuckin' cool." He gives her an acidic once-over that would make almost anyone cower. His eyes bounce to his sister. "Don't you fuck around in here, you hear me, Sher?"

Sherry raises her hands defensively.

Bailey looks absolutely crushed. And there are a lot of eyes on her.

My sister Dani is over by the bar with my other sisters and Aunt Mimi. And she's shooting me a look of apology. I know she wouldn't have allowed Jase to see that text on purpose.

"That was me, Jase, not Bailey," I say.

His eyes flash with irritation in my direction.

"I'm sorry to cause a problem," I add. "It was all me; nobody asked me to send Danica that text. For real, Jase. You weren't meant to see it."

Sherry laughs. "Witches will be bitches." And then she turns, and we watch her strut toward the bathrooms.

Bailey's face is beet-red.

Jase looks pissed.

"Jase," I try.

Riley is suddenly at my back. "Everything cool here?"

I lean into him. "I fucked up," I say. "It's my fault, Jase. Not Bailey's."

"Can I talk to you, Jase?" Bailey asks. "Outside?"

"Don't know what you could possibly have to talk to me about Bay. But this bullshit has to stop. You hear me?"

"This… bullshit?" she asks, looking on the verge of tears.

"It wasn't her; it was me," I repeat. "I'm sorry guys."

"You know what I'm talkin' about," he says to Bailey. He says it low and then his expression gentles a little. "Don't make me spell it out, kiddo." He thinks he's being kind to her here, but it's clear he's just stomped on her heart.

He looks at me. "Happy Birthday, Erica."

"Sorry, Jase… I…"

"Forget about it," he says. "I'm goin' for a run. Night Rye."

"Night, man," Riley says, wrapping an arm affectionately around my waist.

My eyes are on Bailey, who watches him weave through the crowd, looking absolutely crushed.

"Bailey, I'm sorry. Someone should take my phone from me when I've been drinking."

"Don't be sorry, Erica. You were trying to help. It's not your fault that I'm a dummy." She straightens her back and then takes a big gulp of her drink.

Dani takes a step in our direction, and I give her a shake of my head, so she halts and turns back toward Aunt Mimi, Ronnie, and Vivi.

Something changes in the air, and I feel a strange prickling on my scalp as well as tingling in my spine. Riley still has his arm around me, but every muscle has gone taut. He feels it, too.

Suddenly, there's ringing and buzzing permeating the air. Dozens are reaching into pockets and purses and pulling out phones. My phone is buzzing. Riley's phone is ringing. And everyone is looking at their screens. Someone turns the music down.

"Code red!" Greyson shouts. "Anyone not alpha, you're being secured."

What's going on?

"Orderly fashion!" Riley calls out. "Two lines. Line up in front of the door by Jase or Joel. Nobody trample anybody!"

Jase hadn't gotten out yet and I see him and Joel forming lines in front of them.

I look at my buzzing phone as Riley rushes me toward a lineup. My screen is all pixelated; it's pixelated and buzzing, and it seems like everyone else's phones have gone wonky, too.

"Where is everyone going?" I ask.

"Basement," Riley tells me.

"I can help. Me and my sisters and Aunt Mimi might be able to help with whatever this is."

Riley nods but doesn't look pleased. He pulls me toward the wall and I gesture at Aunt Mimi, Vivi, Ronnie, and Dani to come over.

"Jessie!" I gasp. She's not here. Our phones are all going nuts and she's the only person I know with the ability to do this.

She converts energy, too, but not from things that are growing and alive like I do. She taps into and uses energy from other realms and within this one - cellular lines, power lines, wind, and water. She wants us to know something is wrong. Somehow, I don't know how, Greyson must know it because he called out Code Red.

"Jessie!" I say to Aunt Mimi and see a dire expression on her face. She already knows. She probably gave him the heads up when the phones went nuts.

"Where's my wife?" Grey shouts. His nostrils flare.

"Bathroom!" I call out, but he's already rushing toward the bathrooms at the opposite end of the space. I'm suddenly remembering Sherry Creed went that way just after Stacy. I hope she's not put that girl through the ringer with her verbal venom.

Before Greyson is all the way there, there's a man pushing his way out with Stacy's throat in the crook of one arm, another arm around Sherry. There's a knife pointed at Stacy's neck. Behind him is the guy Cade from Roxy's, looking infuriated. I guess he stopped him from leaving through that exit.

The guy with the knife moves with his back along the wall toward us. Both women are crying.

"What the fuck?" Grey demands in a guttural shout.

"I'm takin' my sister and this woman!" the guy replies, and I realize he was the one talking on the phone when I walked the wrong way down that hall.

"If any of you try and stop me," he warns, "the girl we took dies. And possibly this one." He's got the tip of a knife at his sister's throat.

His own sister's throat!

Greyson's pupils blow and blood begins to stream down his cheeks from his eyes. His neck muscles are bulging.

Stacy's brother looks thrown an instant later because the knife flies out of his hand and lodges into rafters above.

Okay, so it appears that Greyson has unlocked telekinesis, which is a gift he might have gotten from Aunt Mimi – I'm not sure. But I'd never seen Aunt Mimi use it, only know that's how she got Lucinda's wand into her belly.

"Not only do you need to let my wife go," Grey snarls, "You need to send the woman you've nabbed back in here. Or... I end you."

The guy immediately lets Stacy go. She runs to Greyson and he catches her in his arms.

"And my sister, fuckwad," Jase shouts.

"No," the guy replies. "Got here to get my sister and caught her scent. Turns out she's mine."

The room goes silent.

"What?" Sherry asks, aghast.

"Yeah." The guy taps the side of his nose. "Who'da thunk it."

"Let her go, then call whoever you need to call to get the woman you kidnapped back in here," Grey demands.

"I need assurances I'm gonna be let go."

"You're not in a position to bargain, asshole," Grey snaps, holding Stacy protectively. "It's obvious you used a scent mask to get in here. What else have you pulled tonight?"

"Wouldn't you all like to know?" The guy smiles in a way that can only be described as sleazy.

"Send her in or suffer," Riley warns. "*And* let go of Sherry."

The guy bares his teeth, lifts his phone out of his front pocket and stares at his screen. He's still got ahold of Sherry, and she looks so horror-stricken I feel bad for her.

"My phone's still fucked," the guy says and then his eyes land on me and he looks confused.

"Wyatt, please let her go," Stacy cries.

"Can't," he says. "Let me go, let me take her, and I'll have my guys let the witch go. Fair trade. Who... who are you?" he asks me. "You're not the witch that was at that cabin, are you? You a twin?"

"Why the fuck do you think we'd let you trade?" Jase snaps.

"Caught her scent on the way in here tonight. She's gotta come with me. No ifs or buts about it. Unmated alpha here. This one's my mate. But who the fuck are you? Are you the one who tried to set me on fire?" he asks me. "Who fried two of my betas? Thought I knew your scent, but it was covered by his claiming scent." He gestures to Riley.

The room goes dead quiet.

Riley told me about this being the monster who forced Stacy to shoot Tyson. Who had her poisoning the alphas in the pack and who wants to kill all the council alphas here and take over this territory. He shot Riley, Mason, and Lincoln. He thought they had me. They've got me and Jessica mixed up.

"You fucking jerk," I shout. "You have my sister! You thought she was me? Maybe I'll melt you right now."

I'm seeking energy, figuring out where to take it from. I don't need to be outside, surprisingly. I feel the nearby energy from the trees, the plants outside. From the moon itself. I could blast this son of a bitch to smithereens. Or maybe I should just take it from inside him like I did his guys. Like I almost did from him the other day. I know I need to be careful, but this guy is likely full of nothing but bad energy. By using his own energy against him there could be zero fall-out from ending him.

Yeah. I'll do *that*.

I glare at him as I summon it.

Smoke curls from his skin and he looks panicked.

"Hurt me, witch, and your sister dies," he threatens, holding tighter to Sherry, who's crying. "And other bad shit happens, too. Really bad shit."

"No. No way," Sherry cries. "No fucking way." She tries to fight her way out of his grip.

I shake off my urges as I hear, "Erica, easy baby," Riley warns, hand running up and down my back.

"You okay, Erica?" Bailey asks.

I see a few sparks in front of me, sparks I generated. They burn to ash and float to the floor as I try to settle myself down. I need to think. He has Jessie. I need to think.

I look around the room. Most of the pack was already led downstairs. But my family, Riley's co-alphas and several other men are still here. So is Bailey. Mitch Blakely is eyeing me with alarm.

Several phones are still buzzing. Jessie is still sending things haywire. That means she's alive, at least.

Stacy's brother is big, built like these alphas. He's probably considered good-looking to most who don't know he's a bad guy. I know different.

"Get my sister here right fucking now," I tell him. "And let go of Sherry."

He holds his phone up. "My phone's fucked, so I can't. You all need to listen to me and listen good, otherwise shit will go south for everyone here in a big way."

"Wyatt, please don't do anything crazy," Stacy calls out. "Please. Just... let's end this. These aren't bad people. This pack isn't bad. And like I said in the bathroom, the thing that happened to our father... it's not what you think. The man who's really responsible is already dead."

"Shut up. Traitorous bitch," Wyatt snaps.

Greyson immediately moves in, grabs Wyatt's wrist and we hear bones crack as he releases Sherry, who runs to Jase. Jase pushes her behind himself protectively as Greyson punches Wyatt with a whole lot of force. He goes down to his back.

"If I don't phone or show up at our rendezvous point in ten more minutes, bad shit is gonna happen," Wyatt warns, glaring at Greyson with a bleeding nose.

Greyson's eyes are still bleeding as he bares teeth at Wyatt. He bares teeth that are larger. His face is morphing toward wolf but not getting there. It's like it's flickering between wolf and man and if this weren't my cousin, a good guy, I'd be absolutely terrified. Greyson looks furious and unhinged.

"If anything happens to my sister," I shout, "You will be very fucking sorry."

"You're gonna be sorry anyway," Greyson tells him. "After the shit you've pulled. After the shit you've put your sister through?"

"I'll melt you into a puddle of bad guy goo," I warn. "You're gonna look like a steaming pile of wolf shit if you or your goons have harmed a hair on my sister's head!"

"Shh, baby. Easy does it," Riley coos into my ear.

"He wanted me. He took my sister because she has red hair and they thought she was me, Riley. She probably smells like me being my sister, right?"

"I know, darlin'."

I've got my hair flat-ironed tonight. Jessica's typically straight hair is curly tonight. We always laugh that her pin-straight hair done curly is party hair for her and my curly hair flattened to straight is *my* party hair.

I can see the disappointment in Wyatt's expression. "I'll give her back. She's unharmed, just mostly disabled right now. Let me take my mate. Let me and my guys out of here. You hurt me, you'll never find them. I've got all their scents masked."

"No, no, no," Sherry cries.

"No," Jase practically snarls. "You give her back and then maybe we let you live."

"I'm an alpha and I've identified my mate. Alpha code of conduct states no other shifter fucks with that."

"Oh, you adhere to shifter codes of conduct, do ya?" Riley quips. "Really fuckin' funny."

"Walk me to my rendezvous point, give me my female, and I'll give you back the redhead," he says.

"No, please no," Sherry cries. "Jason! Dad!"

"Lads?"

We turn to Mitch, who is talking. He's moving forward from a group of men. "Technically, you should release him with his identified mate."

"What the fuck?" Jase growls.

"Wyatt Meadows of the Silver Hills wolf shifter pack?" Mitch addresses him, "I'm Dr. Mitchell Blakely of the Supernatural Council Collective."

"That's me," Wyatt says with a shit-eating grin. "Nice to meet you Dr. Blakely. I wanted to rescue my sister here. I filed a complaint about them kidnapping her."

"Here's the thing," Mitch says, eyes bouncing between Riley, Greyson, and Wyatt. "Wyatt Meadows filed a grievance against your pack with the SCC, stating you kidnapped his sister. I got the report a few days ago. Didn't act on it because I found out Greyson identified her as his mate. You need to extend the same courtesy. Let him leave with *his* mate."

"No. Fuck that," Jase states.

"It's the law," Mitch tells him.

"He kidnapped my sister!" I shriek. "He had me kidnapped and he tried to kill Riley, Mason, and Lincoln!"

Mitch looks at me. "He filed a complaint against Riley for murdering his cousin. We let that go because James Meadows abducted you and interfered with an alpha and his fated mate. You."

"What the fuck?" Riley snaps. "These assholes have been poisoning our pack. They shoot Ty and have the nerve to file complaints about us with the SCC? He just admitted to abducting my sister-in-law."

"Technically, it was Greyson's mate Stacy Meadows who poisoned several pack members before shooting Tyson. Correct?" Mitch asks.

Grey glares at him and says, "Blackwood. Stacy's name is now Blackwood. And what happened is a pack matter. We haven't asked for involvement from the SCC."

Stacy is staring at her feet, looking like she wants to hide.

"There are clearly several beefs ongoing between these two packs," Mitch says. "As a member of the SCC, my recommendation is that you allow Wyatt Meadows to take his identified mate. He should return the hostage. Any further beefs between the two packs can go before a tribunal to be worked out according to the law. This pack needs to file their complaints officially like any other pack."

"This is bullshit," Riley snaps. "He just abducted my mate's sister thinking she was my mate and you're suggesting we let him leave? So he can continue to plot against us and look for more ways to fuck with us? He wants to have a witch in his possession to help him take us out and then take our territory over."

"Mitch, for fuck's sake," Riley's father says from behind him.

"You folks aren't above the law," Mitch replies. "And you've got a lot of eyes on you lately what with recent happenings. The SCC isn't thrilled with some of the antics of this pack lately and with these newfound supernatural gifts, they're not going to be okay with those antics continuing despite the strength of Greyson and Erica. You all need to follow the same rules as everyone else. Nobody gets between an alpha and his mate. The grievances between these two packs can be addressed in arbitration after reports are filed. For tonight, Wyatt Meadows should be allowed to leave with his fated mate after he returns the hostage. We'll launch an investigation and then we'll-"

"I'm not his mate. He's lying," Sherry shrieks.

"I haven't had the opportunity to prove I'm not lying," Wyatt counters calmly, looking smug. "But I'm very much looking forward to proving I'm not lying."

Jase is flexing his fists over and over, looking ready to lose it.

"Gross," I mutter. He's talking about having sex with her. Knotting her. Biting her.

"Let me fry his insides, guys, please?" I ask sweetly. "My sister is quite capable of dealing with whatever predicament his men have her in."

I'm bullshitting, but this guy doesn't need to know this. This guy needs to be afraid.

Riley flashes a grin like he wants to knot and bite me. I flutter my eyelashes.

Greyson pipes up. "Me and my mate have grievances to file against her former pack. Let's do that now, too, then. You ready to file formal complaints, Stace?"

Stacy looks frozen with fear. She nods timidly.

"And us. Attempted murder times three, a count of kidnapping and an account of attempted kidnapping," I put in.

"We'll launch an investigation," Mitch assures, "but for tonight, let's stick to some basics."

Mason rushes in. So does Tyson.

"What the fuck is goin' on here?" Mason shouts.

Tyson glares at Wyatt. "I can't smell this fucker but I'm pretty sure he needs to die."

"We all want a piece of this guy," Riley states.

"Flip you for it?" Ty suggests.

Riley laughs.

Wyatt's eyes bounce between them like the whole thing is bizarre.

"This is Wyatt Meadows," Grey calls out. "Stacy's brother. And I think you're right, Ty, but Mitch disagrees."

"Update us," Ty demands, glaring at Wyatt.

Grey replies, "Tried to take my wife and says he's identified Sherry Creed as his. Thing is, he took Jessica Young somewhere. She's making the phones all go nuts, probably to alert us they've got her. Mitch here is suggesting we let him take Sherry and give Jessica back. Mitch says we've got grievances against Wyatt's pack, he's got some against ours. Wants us to settle those in arbitration."

Mason looks thrown. "Give us Jessica and take her, then. We'll sort the rest of this later."

"Fuck that. He's not taking my goddamn sister!" Jase shouts. "I know she pissed you off, bro, but come on!"

"He's lying. I'm not his mate!" Sherry cries. "Nobody's listening to me. This is my life here!"

"There's a solution," Tyson says. "Put Sherry and this assclown in a cell in the basement tonight. We find out tomorrow if he claimed her in a way that proves she's his."

"Wait. What? That's barbaric!" I say. "Women should not be treated this way."

Riley wraps his arms around me. "Erica," he says softly.

"Don't *Erica* me, there pooky. This is bull pucky."

"I agree!" Bailey calls out from where she stands by the door. "If a woman is repulsed by an alpha, if he's a psychopathic criminal, he should not automatically get to take her just because he identifies her as his. She should have a choice!"

Sherry looks at Bailey with shock.

Bailey keeps talking. "Don't mistake me, Sherry. I hate your guts. And that's on you. Because you're a shitty person. But that doesn't mean you shouldn't have rights. It doesn't mean that just because you're a girl you should be stuck with a psychopath."

"These are the rules. If you have a problem with them, there's protocol," Mitch says. "But as of right now, my recommendation is that we follow Tyson Savage's suggestion. Though instead of a cell, perhaps Tyson's cabin and have guards posted."

"No. Not my cabin," Ty denies. "That's for pack use only."

Mitch shrugs. "I was thinking this way, the lass is safe while it's determined whether this alpha does have a legitimate claim to her."

"The cells downstairs can be used for that," Riley puts in. "Grey was willing to stay there with his mate when he identified her."

"Jase, no," Sherry buries her face into Jase's chest and bawls.

"Sherry," a voice calls out and I look over at Robert Creed, who I met earlier. "You need to go with the man that says he's your mate. I like Tyson's idea. Then you're still here while we find out for certain."

"Dad-" Jase starts to say.

"No, son. You mate next. Would you want someone standing in the way of that? Would any alpha here allow anybody to get in between them and their mate? We don't know this guy. We don't know what led him to think we're their enemies."

"Tyson Savage killed my old man," Wyatt speaks up. "That's where all this started. I might be willing to talk it out. Look for resolution."

He's lying and everyone in the room has to know it. Maybe not about the death of his father, but about willingness for resolution.

"I don't know you, man," Tyson tells him. "I don't know who your father was. Your sister told Grey this, but I was in another life back then. My uncle used drugs to send me into the red haze for fights for money. I don't know any of these details. Whatever I did to your family, if it wasn't deserved, I apologize. But I apologize to your sister, not you, because what you've pulled is bullshit. Using a woman in your pack to enact your revenge? Treating your pack badly? She told Grey that you're a dictator, that you're abusive. You need to be usurped. Maybe one of our alphas should take over for you if you have nobody who-"

"Whoa whoa. Seems like there's been hurt on both sides," Mitch interrupts. "How about if we table all this until there's a tribunal? I'm trying to help you all find peaceful resolution tonight so that common sense will prevail."

"I don't want to be alone with him," Sherry pleads. "No. I'm not okay with going to a jail cell or anywhere else with him, especially not in a cell next to a dead witch. I want to go before a tribunal *before* I'm alone with this guy. What if he's lying? He gets to have sex with me even if he's lying?"

"Lass, you know that's not how it works when an alpha identifies his mate," Mitch tells her.

"He's lying! And this isn't fair!" Sherry cries out. "This is my home. He's not even in our pack! Daddy..."

"I'm sorry, Sher. You know this is our way," Robert replies.

"It's wrong!" Bailey says. "This stuff needs to change."

"Viva la revolution," I say, loudly.

"Yeah!" Ronnie chimes in.

Riley gives me a squeeze. "Don't, baby."

"It's true. This is the fucking twenty-first century, people."

I hear him sigh.

Wyatt speaks up, "If you want your witch sister, these people will let me be alone with my mate. Non-negotiable. I'll stay with her in that cabin if needed. But she's mine. I want what's mine. We'll sort the rest of this out later."

Sherry openly weeps. Jase hugs her tight, looking ready to rip Wyatt's head off.

"In fact, I'll show any who wants to watch that she's mine." He snickers. "Prove I'm telling the truth. But we have seven minutes to meet my rendezvous so... *tick tock*."

I look at Stacy. She's staring at her brother with true fear in her eyes.

Stacy says loud. "Wyatt has a thing for explosives."

Wyatt shoots Stacy a death glare.

I speak up. "We need to figure out where my sister is because our phones are still messed up but they're no longer buzzing or ringing and that better not mean she's hurt or so help me Wyatt, you'll be sorry."

"Is her sister hurt? Are we in danger here?" Riley demands.

Wyatt snickers. He says, "Tick tock. Take me to my rendezvous point, let me take my mate, and I'll give you the redhead and stop bad shit from happening."

"A lot of the pack is downstairs? Why?" Tyson asks. "I smell them."

Grey explains. "I called for code red when Mimi told me why the phones went nuts. We put all non-alphas downstairs to keep them safe. Gus, Andy, and six betas took off to go door-to-door to tell people not here to get secure. The Youngs are here as they might be able to help. Bailey, you shouldn't be up here."

Bailey folds her arms over her chest as if to say she's not going anywhere.

"This place doesn't feel safe," I say.

"No. It doesn't," Vivica agrees.

"Six minutes," Wyatt advises.

"Save this fight for another day," Mitch suggests. "You girls want to petition to have new rights, that's your choice to initiate and you can discuss that with your pack after this is over, or petition the SCC if you want new laws brought in for all shifter females, but..."

"Enough with the longwinded shit, Mitch," Riley snaps, then looks to Wyatt. "Why is the clock ticking, fucker? What did you do?"

Wyatt laughs like he's holding all the good cards.

Robert steps up. "Meadows, if you're telling me you're my daughter's mate, you're going to be connected to me and my pack. That's reason enough to cooperate and ensure nothing harms us."

"I didn't know your daughter was my mate until ten minutes ago. My phone's fucked so I can't call anything off. I need to meet my guys at the rendezvous point. *Like now.*"

"Everyone who doesn't need to be here, clear out," Tyson shouts. "Erica, do you have something of your sister's so we can track her scent?"

"I already memorized her scent," Linc answers. "I can tell from here it dead ends in our parking lot."

"I masked her scent. We need to go. Follow me to meet them. You can have the redhead. I'll talk my guys down and I'll go spend the night in that cabin this other witch was at with my mate. Tomorrow, when I've proven she's mine, I'll take her back to Silver Hills where there's a pack with one alpha. Me. Like it should be unlike this abomination here. And she'll be my queen. You'll be my queen, mate."

Sherry's and Wyatt's eyes lock for a second and then she says, "Um..."

"No," Jase growls.

"I don't want anything bad to happen to everyone. I'll... I'll go with him," Sherry says, eye-locked with him.

"No," Jase says. "Not likin' this at all."

"If it's meant to be, we'll know it by the morning," she says. "I want to help find resolution. This might be the resolution."

"More like she's in a place where everyone hates her and she wants to know what sort of queendom awaits," Bailey says.

I look at Stacy. She looks pale. Horror-stricken.

"Downstairs, Bailey. Girls," Greyson calls out. "Hurry."

"Go on downstairs, baby," Riley says, steering me toward the rest of the departing group.

"No," I deny, "I need to know Jessie's okay."

"Let go of your sister, Jason," Robert orders.

"Yeah. I will go," Sherry whispers, looking up at Jase. "I don't want to cause irreparable harm here tonight by being stubborn or scared. If this is fated, it's fated. We'll find out, I guess. Can I go pack a bag from home first?"

"No. I don't trust that," Wyatt states. "Let's walk to my rendezvous point now. You're in my grasp. Let's get there quick so I can call them off. But know this everyone, any bullshit flies, a bomb *will* go off and I happen to know that the house it's in has someone sleeping in it right now. All of you need to listen to me to make sure nobody dies tonight."

Tyson lunges forward, his pupils blow and he half-shifts, looming over Wyatt. "Did you fuck with my house?"

"I never said I did," Wyatt replies, and it's obvious he's trying hard not to shrink away. "They won't hit the button if I get there within the next five minutes, so let's fucking go then."

He's trying to act nonchalant, but he is definitely about to shit his pants.

Stacy is bawling, face buried in Greyson's shirt.

Sherry's eyes are dry now as she pulls away from Jase and moves in Wyatt's direction.

"Fuck," Jase cusses.

"I'm not gonna let anything bad happen to our pack if I can stop it," Sherry says. "Maybe we can work things out if our packs are connected this way." She gets to Wyatt, and he grabs her and pulls her close, nostrils flaring as he buries his nose in her throat.

And Bailey and I exchange looks like... what the fuck?

"Stay here," Riley orders, kissing me. "I need you to stay here and stay safe. I'll get your sister back here. Promise. I love you."

"I love you," I whisper," But Riley..."

"Stay here, Rikki," he says.

"No, baby," I deny.

"Mate," he looks into my eyes. "I love you and we're partners but in this, I'm taking the lead. Fuckin' please. Don't fight me on this."

"Look after Stace for me?" Grey asks me. "I'll get Jessica back. Promise."

Aunt Mimi steps up and puts her arms around Stacy. "I've got her. Go ahead." Aunt Mimi looks at me. "Let them go."

"Darlin'," Riley says, looking deep into my eyes. "Please stay here."

"Don't get hurt," I demand.

He kisses my neck and heads for the door.

I'm not happy about it but I watch Riley and several others move toward the back door.

Tyson turns to go out the front door instead. Running.

"With Ty," Linc calls out and Riley gives him a thumbs up.

"I'm goin' to Amie," Mase states, heading out behind Linc.

"I don't trust Wyatt at all," Vivi says as soon as the space has emptied of men. "I'm getting a bad feeling about Ivy."

"Nobody should trust Wyatt. Ever," Stacy says with such conviction that you can feel all our panic levels rise.

"Let's hurry," I shout, grabbing Dani's hand.

"Where are we going?" she asks.

"To make sure nothing goes wrong at Ivy's," I say.

"You'll stay and protect her and everyone here?" I ask Aunt Mimi, Ronnie, and Vivi.

"We will," Auntie vows.

"Keys, Vivica?" I request. "Shit. Who's sober?"

"Me," Ronnie advises. "And I was already coming."

Vivi tosses Ronnie her keys.

52

RILEY

Me, Grey, Jase, Joel, and Mitch walk with Wyatt Meadows and Sherry Creed out of the building. We follow for less than a one-minute walk before Meadows calls out, "Comin' in, soldiers, stand down."

We step through some thick woods into a small clearing.

There are four male shifters, armed with guns standing shoulder to shoulder. Machine guns.

My blood runs cold, and I can feel the chill in my connection with my pack. Fuckin' machine guns. This could go bad. Very bad.

I'm also aware of Ty's heightened state of fury through our pack connection, which is probably why he and Mase ran to us, feeling it from the other five of us.

I know he's run to make sure his mate is all right. I know if I were in his or Mase's shoes I'd have done the same.

"Where's Jessica?" I demand.

"Stand down, soldiers," Wyatt states again, obviously grandstanding. "Show 'em."

They move out of the way to reveal they were in front of her.

"Jessie!" I call.

She's breathing steadily but she's out. I can't smell her. I can't smell these four betas either. Jessie is blindfolded, gagged, and bound, and lying on the grass all dressed up and I'm pissed that my sister-in-law is lying on the ground like this.

"Fuckin' move," I snap as I close in. Two of the assholes lift their guns and point them at me.

"Down, men," Wyatt grinds out.

I lift Jessie up and glare at the fuckers as I move back to my group with her in my arms.

She's out, but looks unharmed.

I'm still not fuckin' happy. Not about any of this. I want to turn Wyatt Meadows into mincemeat. He ordered a hit on Tyson. Had his sister poison several alphas. He had my mate abducted and then attacked her and me at the cabin. He tried to kill three of us that day and wanted to take my mate. The list of this guy's crimes is long.

"Now, there's been the exchange," Mitch says carefully, "Anything else put in motion before our agreement, has it been disabled?"

"Yeah," Wyatt says. "I've just told my men to stand down."

"Smoke," I say.

"Lie," Grey says. "Absolute bullshit. What've you done?"

I see multiple sets of nostrils flare.

"No idea what you're talkin' about," Wyatt Meadows lies with a shit-eating grin on his face.

Grey takes a step forward, about to lunge for him, when he presses Sherry in front of him, holding onto her, using her as a shield. Her eyes fill with panic. My first thought is, yeah, this is the kind of mate you'd get fated to, Sherry Creed.

His four betas all point their weapons at us.

"Pull their weapons the way you pulled my knife and it'll be too late," Meadows threatens. "I've got one more man hidden where he can see all of us and he'll push the button if any of you move or if this dickhead pulls our weapons from us with magic. Stand there, keep your hands where I can see 'em, and there will be far less bloodshed. I'm also gonna need you to give me that witch there, Savage."

"Not a fuckin' chance," I snap.

And then Meadows starts belting out a long monologue about how packs should have one alpha, about how we're not real alphas if we're willing to share command. How Tyson killed his father and what a great man he was.

Suddenly, Meadows, Sherry, and three of the four Silver Hills guys are three inches off the ground, guns out of their grips and lifting up higher into the sky, floating out of their reach.

"What the fuck?" I hear Jase gasp as Sherry and Wyatt are lifted up higher.

"The fuck?" Wyatt shouts. "Get the guns. Get 'em!" The betas all look terrified. This guy is delusional thinking they can reach those guns. The guns are now twenty feet away from them.

Jase tries to grab his sister's ankle. She's screaming.

"Shoot 'em, Lucas!" Meadows demands to the one beta left standing.

A closer look at Lucas and I see he's just a kid. He can't be any older than sixteen or seventeen.

My eyes pivot around the space and none of the rest of us are moving. The smell of smoke is in the air and then there's a loud bang. Scents assault my nose while the sound fills my ears. Wyatt, three of his betas, and Sherry are lifting higher, then they're flying through the air as if they're leaves on the wind. Wyatt has a firm hold of Sherry and she's screaming at the top of her lungs. They're floating toward the village, where the explosion came from.

"What the hell?" Mitch calls out, staring at the group of people being pulled through the sky as if by strings.

"Gimme that," Jase demands, and the fourth beta immediately hands him the machine gun. "Where's the hidden guy?"

The kid shakes his head and shrugs.

"Where?" Jase grabs his throat.

"It's just us. There's no hidden guy."

Jase releases him and we all go running, everyone dropping clothes and shifting into wolf form except me and Jase. Me, because I've got Jessie in my arms, Jase because he's got the gun.

The only thought in my head is getting to my mate. She needs to be okay. Needs to be. Anything else is unfathomable.

53

ERICA

A Few Minutes Ago

As soon as Riley, Wyatt, Sherry, and the other guys are out of sight, me, Ronnie, and Dani rush to Vivi's Land Rover and Ronnie drives toward Roxy's bar. Fast.

"Swing left," I tell her, remembering how to get there because Amie and Ivy argued over whose house was closer for me to shower in that first morning I was here.

I see it. A big house surrounded by iron gates. And one small section of it is smoking. There's a fire!

"Oh no!" I gasp. "Fire!"

A compact SUV pulls up behind us. Bailey.

We park by the gates and get out of the vehicles. "Shit, what are you doing here?"

"I wanna help," she says. "I smell Ivy inside. And smoke. And Tyson and Lincoln." She stares at the house in horror. "And Ivy and Ty's baby."

"Baby?" Ronnie asks.

"Ivy's carrying Ty's baby. It's a baby girl, I think."

I'm feeling utterly panicked. And angry. Furious. I request energy from my surroundings as I hold the necklace Aunt Mimi gave me yesterday, chant a protection spell for Lincoln, Tyson, Ivy, and their baby. For all the citizens of the village of Arcana Falls as well as my family. I'm pushing the energy of the necklace toward all of them.

Ronnie touches the gates. "I feel their energy through these gates. Tyson's and Ivy's. They're okay so far."

"Linc?" Bailey asks.

"I don't know," Ronnie tells her.

Dani puts a small cauldron on the ground and fills it with a carrier oil from a jar she pulled from Vivi's truck kit. She then adds a sachet of herbs.

"What are you doing?" Bailey asks.

"Thank goodness she has her travel one." I know Dani's pulling unhealthy energy out of the air and sending it into the small pot placed between us. We'll work together to undo bad energy around here. It has to go somewhere.

My sisters and I hold hands and focus. I focus on everything harmful and negative in the village, anyone who's not a pack member or a member of my family. I add Mitchell Blakely to the equation. I work hard, feeling like I've got the ability to siphon bad energy like Danica can, though she focuses on physical and emotional health, I'm focusing on all negative energy around us. Anything that's a danger to this pack. And for the first time, I can sense the bad energy and differentiate it from the good. It all needs to go.

I've been through too much to not get my happily-ever-after. So have Tyson and Ivy. I can't let the evil energy take anything else from us. No!

While I focus, I see Tyson carrying Ivy out the front door and about ten seconds later I see Lincoln directly behind them and hear Bailey sigh with relief.

The pot begins bubbling hard and then something flies through the air, making us duck.

A box has landed in the pot, it's half hanging out.

"Shit," I say. "Aviva's wand."

It was pulled from the cave under the falls. That was covered by my intention. I was too panicked, too broad in my request.

Tyson is running in our direction with Ivy, and I focus my energy on the house. I see more smoke and an orange glow from one of the rooms.

I accept offered energy from the water behind the house as I see Ivy staring at the house with a devastated look in her eyes. As soon as they're outside the gates, a giant wave from behind the house crests over the rooftop and douses that section of the house.

"What the-" Tyson stares behind himself and then looks at me with shock.

Ivy bursts into tears. "Set me down, Ty," she requests.

And when he does, she comes closer, "Thank you, Erica, thank you for saving our house."

"Wait there, please," Ronnie calls out as we continue focusing with our hands joined.

Bailey pulls Ivy close. "They can't have their circle breached."

"Too much. Oh no," Dani screams as an explosion sounds from somewhere beyond us and we see what looks like a big cloud of debris flying in our direction.

"What the fuck?" Ty shouts.

There's a massive pile of stuff coming at us through the night sky.

I feel the earth, trees and the water imploring me to request help. It's the strangest sensation.

"It's coming for us. For the pot?" Dani shouts.

Did I do that? Did I fuck up this badly?

Danica wanted bad energy from Tyson's house to go into the pot, to make sure they could get out despite smoke or fire, to help them get to safety. We could've then carefully neutralized any supernaturally remaining negativity, but I focused on all the negativity around us, having no idea how much negative energy there really was. How much stuff would come at us. There's so much coming at us, aiming for that pot, that I need to find a way to direct it elsewhere. Where nobody will get hurt.

"What is all that?" Bailey asks, aghast.

I break our circle and lift my hands up and point into the sky as I do my best to quickly communicate, get permission, make sure I'm not about to cause more harm than good. But I don't know how long it'll take to get the answers I need so in my haste I make a decision and hope it'll somehow work.

54

RILEY

Now

I'm running for my mate and really do not fuckin' like what I'm seeing. The air feels wrong, thick, and the moon looks wrong. I don't know what the fuck is happening here.

I feel like I'm running underwater but that's because I'm chasing a field of debris that's moving across the night sky.

There was an explosion in the town hall. One corner of the barn was blown out, and Grey ran for the building, for his mate and the pack members we left there while I handed Jessie to Joel and asked him to check on Rikki's family. I kept running, knowing my mate's scent wasn't there, knowing she was deeper into the village, meaning she didn't listen, didn't stay put.

I'm suspecting the field of debris in the sky is heading to wherever she is. Suspecting she's the one that yanked those assholes up into the sky. To save us. My beautiful Rikki.

Jase is chasing to get to his sister while I follow my nose toward Erica. I know this wreckage is at least partly what was blown out of the town hall but also the people being carried through the sky who are ahead of it. And their weapons.

I see the woman I love in front of the open gates to Savage House with Ty, Linc, and some of the girls about twenty feet away from her. And what I'm seeing tweaks me even further because Rikki's hair is flying in multiple directions and she's holding her hands up, reaching for the sky. As I slow, shifting to human form, I see she's holding what looks like a tornado above herself, holding it in the sky. The rest of the debris is sucked into it. It's twirling slowly, directly above her. If she wasn't doing whatever she's doing right now, it'd fall all over the place. All over the people here, all over Savage House. On top of her.

"Fuck," I cuss, looking at barnboard pieces, men, guns, Wyatt still holding onto a screaming Sherry, and fuckin' Aviva Starling's nude corpse. They're all part of this slow-turning tornado in the sky above my mate.

"What are you doing, baby?" I shout.

"Stay back, Riley, please," she cries. "I don't know where to put it."

"What the fuck?" I croak out.

"It's everything negative in this town. It's all the bad energy. I wanted it gone. I wanted everyone safe. And I didn't realize it'd all come at me like this. We only had a small pot. I fucked up and I don't know what to do."

Blue sparks flit around her body as she holds her hands high, the cloud of negative shit churning in the sky above her.

"Send it into the water, baby. Behind Ty's house. Send it there," I tell her.

"But there are people up there," she cries.

"Bad guys that wanted to shoot us," I tell her. "It's okay, Rikki. Send it there."

"And my fucking sister!" Jase shouts.

"I didn't mean it, Jase," my woman cries. "I thought I protected her. She's part of the pack. In my spell I protected people in the pack."

"Then set everything into the water and Sherry'll be okay," I tell her.

She swallows hard.

"Set everything into the water, baby," I say.

Jase paces, still holding that machine gun. "I'm gonna shoot that fucker as soon as my sister is clear," he warns.

"Rikki, set it in the water," I repeat.

She nods, then moves her arms and points beyond Ty's yard and the funnel cloud moves slowly that way.

Everything in the sky then freefalls into a rain of debris, including screaming men who fall into the lake with a thunderous splash that sends a massive wave away from Ty's house.

We all watch, and it looks to me like Sherry and the asshole who is wrapped around her fall further away from the debris field. He pulled her into the mess because he had ahold of her and my woman's protection spell meant that because he was holding Sherry, he's likely gonna survive this.

My mate drops her hands and her lip trembles as I rush to her.

She falls into my arms.

"Jessie?" she asks.

"Got her. She's with Joel."

She bursts into tears.

I lower us to the grass and hold her in my arms, purring as she weeps.

"It's gonna be okay."

She nods with tears on her cheeks. I use the pads of my thumbs to wipe them away and kiss her softly.

"It's okay, Rikki," I say. "It's all gonna be okay."

"More purring," she whispers and tucks her head under my chin.

55

RILEY

I'm in my bed, holding my mate, purring for her. It's late. So late it's almost early.

Quite a night, and her family is once again camped out in my house. Jessie regained consciousness not long after I left her with Joel. She seems fine. She'd gone outside for air and the asshole came up behind her and chloroformed her.

Stacy and Grey tracked her little cousin not far from Drowsy Hollow. He's sixteen and he was recruited into Wyatt's army. He was scared. Clearly not a bad kid by the fact he wasn't carried off with all the bad shit. He spilled the beans on everything.

Meadows was running low on potions. He had enough of the magic potion to mask himself and the witch he planned to take so he had his boys wait outside of town and got them to eat catnip.

Tonight's plan came together after he kayaked across the lake after seeing Mason bringing people over on his boat from the cottages on the other side and made his plan from there. He landed at Ty's and skulked around in shadows, seeing a lot of the town heading to the town hall, so he was in communication with his lead beta on cell. Wyatt planted an explosive device at Ty's house with a timer. He did the same at the town hall, managing to avoid our cameras by coming in not via the four corners where we have cameras but through town because he snuck in via the back way. He bullshitted about having someone else hide, likely doing that on the fly after Grey was able to use magic to get his knife away from him.

My mate was distraught, thinking her negativity-gathering spell caused the explosion in the town hall because of pulling Aviva Starling's body. But when the explosion happened, which was started by Wyatt, it created a hole directly over the cell Aviva's body was in.

The reception hall was empty during the explosion. Most were downstairs. Right after my mate left, disobeying my order for her to stay, her aunt moved Grey's mate and the other sister into the library where they were performing a protection spell over the people in the town hall. We had no injuries on our end.

My mate pleaded with Jase and his father to believe that she included Sherry in her pack protection spell. We all knew that though Sherry was absolutely one of the most negative people around, that she was swept up into that field of negativity because Wyatt Meadows refused to let go of her when he got carried up into the sky.

With Jessie conscious, the phones started working and we called Mase who got his boat out on the lake with a light. Andy Quinn got out on another boat, and they retrieved two dead betas and one injured, who is now in one of the two undamaged cells under the town hall.

And they retrieved the corpse of Aviva Starling as well as her wand.

A few of the men tracked Sherry's scent and the faint scent of Wyatt Meadows in the Sleepy Cove resort. Lucas Meadows, who's at Grey's place now with Grey and Stacy, confirmed they all stayed in a cabin there last night and came from their village in two cars. Wyatt left with Sherry in one of them.

Jase and Linc took off to track them and will keep us in the loop.

Aviva's ancestor's wand is back in the niche under Arcana Falls. Aviva's body is back in the basement of the town hall.

We'll assess whether the barn can be fixed or if we'll tear it down and build something new.

Ty's house is damaged in the bedrooms section from the bomb that went off there. He and Ivy went to stay at Mason's place.

"My family is going home in the morning," my mate's voice pulls me from my thoughts.

"Yeah, baby. Get some sleep. It's nearly morning."

"You're gonna have to make up with Toonie in the morning, Mr. Wolf."

I snicker. Two of the cats are on the bed with us. The third hasn't come out. I know she's hiding under the bed in the spare room.

I've established dominance. She doesn't like it, but too bad.

"I think if you feed her a can of salmon, she'll forgive you," Rikki adds.

I scoff. "The minute your family is out of here, first thing that happens is you get a spanking for disregarding my directions tonight."

She stiffens. "You already said I saved the day."

Yeah, there's that. Because who knows how that shit would've gone down with us facing off with four men with machine guns who'd planted two bombs.

"I'm gonna talk to Lucinda and Aunt Mimi though about figuring out how to manage this extra magic. It's definitely easy to lose control of it. I thought I fucked up badly."

"You didn't," I assure. "Things could've really gone south in a lotta ways tonight, little witch. Damage was minimal considering what coulda happened. They could've turned on us with those machine guns. It felt like it might go south, but they were suddenly sucked up into the sky at the right moment. People could've been hurt in the town hall. All of Ty's house could've gone up in smoke. Ivy with it. It didn't."

"Yeah," she says softly, snuggling into me.

"But you're still getting punished," I tell her. "After your family leaves, I'll spank you and I'm gonna make you come over and over for the rest of the day to punish you for not listening to me."

"Poor me," she fake complains, walking her fingers up my chest.

"Poor you, indeed. "Cuz I'm gonna work hard, baby, hard."

"Work hard?" she asks. "Fixing the town hall and Ty's house? Guess my greenhouse might have to wait a little."

"Yeah. Maybe a little. Also gonna work hard to plant my first pup in your belly," I tell her. And then I growl.

"I love it when you growl," she tells me.

"Me, too," I say. "So I can catch my favorite scent. You... wet for me."

"It's my favorite scent, too, Riley," she says, throwing one leg over mine and sitting up, rubbing her hot, wet pussy over my hard cock. "Because when you growl, my body responds. And when my body responds, I know what's coming next."

Addicted to her own juices. *My* little witch.

"Time for my favorite taste," I say, flipping her to her back. Two cats jump out of the bed as I spread her thighs wide.

"The only thing that tastes better than you, Riley, is when I taste *me* on you," she tells me.

"Wicked little witch," I say, then while I taste her, I decide to try my newfound talent, the half-shift, because I know for a fact that my wolf's tongue is much longer and thicker than my human tongue.

My mate lets out a throaty sound that absolutely will wake the whole house, so I pull back to human and order, "Bite the pillow, baby, because you're about to feed your Mr. Wolf his dinner."

Epilogue

ERICA

I wave my family off after what felt like the second longest night of my life. The first longest? The night I knew how badly I fucked up by casting that love spell.

As soon as we know things are sorted here with the Silver Hills situation, I'll go visit my family. Bring Riley.

As soon as their SUV is out of sight, I find myself thrown over my mate's shoulder. I giggle as he carries me into the house.

I'm taken directly up the stairs and thrown on the bed. Thrown!

The look in his eyes as he does this is the hottest look I've ever seen.

He rips his t-shirt off, drops his jeans and flashes me a smile before he yanks my dress up over my head and tosses it.

"No panties. Good girl," he says.

I'm melting. Also smirking. Because I know what's coming. Me. Him. Me again. And again.

He grabs my ankles and tugs so I'm flat on my back, legs dangling off the edge of the bed.

And then he leans in like he's about to put his mouth on me. Before he gets there, he says, "But darlin'... disobey a serious order like that again, you won't get my mouth down here for a month."

My mouth drops open in shock and then I pout. "That's not fair."

"Listen to your mate and you'll be golden."

His head descends and I close my legs hard, my knees clapping his ears. His eyes meet mine.

"Most times excessive levels of shifter testosterone are hot, but not so much when it comes down to the difference between me sitting back and doing nothing and doing what I know I can do – help the people I love."

"Point taken," he says, then he quickly flips me to my belly. "You're still getting a spanking."

"Well, I'd be disappointed if I didn't."

"And then I'll decide if I'm gonna lick your cunt or make you wait."

He's totally going to lick it.

I'M LYING IN RILEY'S arms, drawing on his chest with my fingertip.

"Why you always draw eights on me?" he asks.

"They're not eights. They're eternity knots," I advise.

He drops a kiss on my head and holds me tighter.

"What's your superpower?" I ask him.

"Hm?" he sleepily replies.

"Your superpower. You know, the thing you're good at ... the thing you're known for. Non-supernatural, I mean."

"Hm." He's quiet for a moment. "Staircases."

"Staircases?"

"Yeah. For work. I build 'em, stain 'em, and always get big compliments on them."

"Ah. Cool, I say."

He yawns.

"Can you re-stain the staircase here sometime? I'd like to see what you can do."

"Sure. Been plannin' on that actually."

"Aren't you gonna ask me what my superpower is?" I ask, looking up at his sleepy face.

"Fishin' expedition, huh? You led me here so you could tell me your superpower, I take it?"

"Duh," I reply.

He smiles. "What's your superpower, little witch? Besides inspiring your man to fuck you for three hours, rendering him exhausted."

I smile big. "And you fucked me very well, thank you. My superpower is massages."

"Oh yeah?" he looks intrigued.

"Uh huh," I confirm. "Want one?"

"Fuck yeah, I do," he says. "I might fall asleep while you do it if you're good at it."

"Right back," I say and zip to the spare room where a lot of my craft implements are, sift through my stuff, and find the bottle I want. Sweet almond oil. Another of lavender oil. Not originally intended for massages, but they'll do. I grab a small mixing bowl.

I find him on his belly, his nakedness on display. My man is absolutely gorgeous. Hot, tanned, muscled skin for miles and miles. *Yum.*

I mix some of each oil into the bowl and drizzle some onto his spine. I work my way over his butt cheeks first. I slap them both playfully. He chuckles. I rub the oil around some more.

"Hey, baby?" he asks.

"Hm?"

"Spendin' an awful lot of time rubbing that oil on my ass, ain't cha?"

"Hm," I reply and then work my way up his back and then massage his shoulders for a minute before I run my slippery hands up and down his biceps.

"Turn to your back, please?" I request.

"You're done my back already? Didn't work out any knots. Didn't do much but rub oil on me gently. Ain't ya gonna work on my legs, too? Ain't you gonna put your back into it?"

"Please follow your masseuse's instructions, sir."

He rolls to his back and smiles at me.

I take more oil and drizzle it on his abs. *Fun.*

And then I rub my palms through the puddle of oil and work my way up over his chest to his throat and then back down. Riley's hard, beautiful magic wand is at attention.

I take it into both hands and squeeze, then work my slick palms up and down.

"Do you have any idea how to give a massage, Erica Savage?" he asks.

"Hm?" I ask, focused on what I'm doing.

He chuckles but it turns to a groan as I apply more pressure to my strokes.

"You haven't a fuckin' clue how to give a massage."

"Nope," I admit. "But it's fun to try."

"Fun does not equal superpower, woman."

I smile big.

My phone rings from the bedside table.

I don't recognize the number.

"My hands are all oily, Mr. Wolf. Could you answer that on speaker for me?"

He rolls and touches my screen.

I should've had him put a towel down. These sheets are likely ruined. Oops. Damn is it fun to massage him, though.

"Hello?" I call out.

"Erica Young?" comes a male voice.

"This is her."

"This is Sergei from the SCC. Is this a good time?"

Riley bares his teeth.

"Uh…" I feel a little lost for words.

Riley pipes up. "Not sure any time'd be a good time to hear from someone who decided to let some witches fuck with our lives seven years ago."

"That's fair," Sergei responds. "I've heard from Lucinda about the events of the last several days. I wanted to tell you that I wanted a much lighter sentence. We were deadlocked on that point. I fought their decision, requesting a review by a new panel. Because they won Mitch over, that was the end of it. I made a stink but in the end, I was overruled. I never agreed with it but was bound by nondisclosure agreement."

"I understand," I say. "We're trying to move on."

"I hope you can," Sergei responds.

"We can," I assure. "Thanks for calling."

"Before you go… there's something I'd like to ask of you."

Riley's expression darkens and I know he's about ready to blow his top.

"What's that?" I ask quickly.

"I'd like to ask you to help me with a problem. Not long ago, Aviva Starling contacted me to tell me of a vision she had. A friend and colleague's daughter will develop a fixation on me in about twenty years. It can't happen. It's dangerous, and… it can't happen. I need help ensuring it won't happen. I'm supposed to die. But her birth, which recently happened, has changed things. I need this matter to be handled quietly, which is why I'm calling you. I'd be very grateful and would be in your debt."

"Why aren't you dealing with Lucinda?" Riley asks.

He replies, "Because she's mated to a vampire. It's a conflict of interest to ask her and I won't put her in that position. My colleague is also vampire. It's a unique situation, not entirely unlike Erica's. This girl is special."

I frown. "One second, okay? I'm going to take down some details and I'll talk to my coven for you. See what I can find out. Find out if we can help."

"Are you fuckin' kidding me?" Riley snaps.

"I assure you, I'm not," he replies.

But Riley is looking at me. Of course I'm going to help if I can.

"One second, please." I dash to the ensuite bathroom to wipe my hands on a towel and then I'm digging through my purse for a pen and a notepad.

My hands are still sort of slippery.

"Okay," I say when I get back. "Sergei Voitenko and what's the colleague's daughter's name?"

"This is highly confidential, Ms. Young. I've already said more than I'm comfortable with."

"Savage," Riley corrects, sounding very grouchy.

"This is highly confidential, Mrs. Savage," Sergei amends, sounding bored.

"I assure you of confidentiality."

"A hundred per cent confidentiality," he presses.

"Fuck sakes," Riley mutters.

"A hundred per cent, Sergei. You have my word."

"I'd prefer to come see you."

"Oh," I say.

Riley's face is red.

"Okay," I say.

He looks at me like he wants to spank me. And not for the fun reasons.

"I'll make travel arrangements and contact you when I'm on my way. When I arrive, you'll need to compose something to avoid the hypnotic state humans usually go into when they come in contact with one of my kind."

"I'm aware. And okay," I say, ready to hang up.

"I hope you and your mate are very happy together," he says. "I'm sorry I wasn't able to help seven years back."

"Thank you for trying," I say softly.

"You're welcome."

"Speak to you soon," I say.

Riley ends the call with an annoyed look on his face.

"Well, that was .." I start to say, but my phone rings again.

"Answer?" Riley asks.

I grab the phone, answer, and put it to my ear. "Vivi?"

"I just got a vision," she says. "You're either going to get a phone call from Sergei Voitenko or-"

"Just did," I cut her off. "He wants us to stop a colleague's daughter from fixating on him twenty years from now."

"We can't. She's his second fated mate. His first one died, and he thought he was dying because he lost her. But his second mate is his second chance at immortality. He's going to try to do everything he can do to stop it from happening because his future mate is the daughter of a dangerous vampire."

"Yikes," I say.

"She's a baby. So it's gonna take a while, but we can't intervene," Vivi says. "He has to figure it out on his own. And he's not going to be real happy about it. In fact, it's kind of a disaster."

Greyson Blackwood

My phone rings. I grab it and leave the room since my mate is sound asleep in my bed. She sleeps on her belly. Nude. Beautiful. And all *mine*.

"Hello?"

"Hi Grey, it's Ronnie."

"Veronica," I greet my cousin.

"Do you have a minute?"

"I do," I say.

I've got nothing but minutes right now as I wait to hear from Jase and Linc who are looking for Wyatt and Sherry.

I'm wishing about now that I hadn't let them run off half-cocked like that. I'm wishing I'd had my cousins whip up some of whatever potion allowed Wyatt and his betas to get into our village without us picking up their scents.

If they don't have luck in the next twelve hours, I might ask Erica if she can help with that.

"When I met Stacy yesterday, I touched her," Veronica says. "And you know when I touch people or their things... I often get information about them."

"Yeah, I know," I say.

"I don't always want information. And I don't get all the information, just big things. Traumatic events or big secrets. Things that dominate their personalities."

"Okay."

"I'm sorry to tell you this, but she's been very badly abused, Grey. Badly."

I already know this. It's not only obvious, she's dropped a few facts that have pissed me off. But now my blood runs cold. Because my cousin's tone is severe.

"What does badly mean?"

"We have to find a way to stop them. I don't know how much Stacy has shared about her upbringing, but Greyson, it's bad. Like... really bad."

She's shared a little. Not a lot. She's timid. She's got hangups about sex that I've been working on with her. She's coming around with me but it's obvious to me she hasn't completely leveled with me about her old pack, the life there. I know she was forced to shoot Ty. I know she did what her brother said because she was absolutely terrified of him. The entire pack is. He's a tyrant. I've been working at helping her settle in. Working to build trust with her, figuring she'll open up more as time goes on.

"Thanks for telling me, Veronica."

"Ronnie," she corrects. "And call me if you need any help with anything, okay? We're so happy you're part of our coven, Grey. Part of our family."

"I am, too," I say. "Talk soon."

I end the call and stare out the window, trying to simmer the rage now boiling in my blood. I wanted to rip Wyatt Meadows apart last night. I really fucking did. If I weren't freshly mated I'd be on the road looking for him, relentless in my pursuit to stop him and his reign of terror.

My phone rings again, pulling me from my thoughts.

I don't recognize the number calling.

"Hello?" I answer.

Nothing.

I repeat, "Hello?"

A female clears her throat. "Greyson Blackwood?"

"Yeah. Who's this?"

"I... I'm Soleil Young. I... wonder if we could meet. And if you agree, I would just please ask... not that you owe me anything... but I would ask that you keep it just between us for now."

The End (for now)

(Greyson's story, Claimed, Savage Alpha Shifters Book 4, is coming next. Join my newsletter for information about it. AND: good news. At the time I publish this, I've already started to write this book.)

Join my newsletter and reader group to stay up to date on news of my sales, new releases, and freebies. Subscribe to my newsletter at http://ddprince.com/newsletter-signup/ so you can be notified when it's live. I'll be sharing teasers and further information in my reader group on Facebook – DD's Chickadees – http://facebook.com/groups/ddprince-fangroup.

Interested in the Holden and Isabella story related to the Young witches? I wrote two novellas a few years ago. You can read Hollow (Part 1) and Holden (Part 2) separately or buy the duet and read them together.

If you love paranormal romance, one of my earliest works was my Nectar Trilogy. This is a dark and taboo vampire trilogy about a very possessive vampire who is addicted to his fated mate's blood, which means danger for a lot of reasons. There's a little easter egg here with Sergei Voitenko who is in Essence, book three of The Nectar Trilogy. As you can tell, I have plans!

If you love hot alpha men in a non-paranormal world, you might want to check out my Beautiful Biker series, which starts with Detour.

I have contemporary enemies-to-lovers roommate romances too with my Alphahole Roommates Series.

I even have an alien matchmaking series called Hot Alpha Alien Husbands.

And I've got lots of dark romance, too. I started out as a dark romance author with The Dominator Series, my bestselling series.

And check out The Devious Games Duet, too, to meet my morally grey antihero Killian Coulter. Book one in the duet, Kill Game, has a jaw-dropping plot twist.

Huge thanks to my readers, my beta team, arc and street team, my designer and friend Hayley, and my author friends. You guys make this so much fun. And you make it so that I can do this for a living. Thank you, sincerely.

The Savage Alpha Shifters series order will be as follows:

1. Tyson (Wild)
2. Mason (Twisted)
3. Riley (Wicked)
4. Greyson (Claimed)

5. Jase (Jilted)
6. Lincoln (Hunted)
7. Joel (Knotted)

End of Book Notes:

THANK YOU SO MUCH FOR coming on this journey with me. Riley and Erica's story has been brewing in the cauldron for quite a while. I knew when I wrote Hollow that there was more to tell about the Young witch who met Isabella in that pumpkin patch. I wasn't sure if I'd link a witch series to that duet, if it'd tie into my shifter series, or both.

I hope you enjoyed Riley and Erica's story. I hope you're even further invested in the Savage Alpha Shifters. I know I am! As I wrap this up, I'm already working on Claimed and have lots of other stories in my cauldron, brewing for you, including a Nectar trilogy spin-off, as you can tell by the epilogue.

Thank you so much to everyone who helps me behind the scenes.

I appreciate my readers, my amazing street team, my wonderful beta team, my ARC team, my chickadees, and those who encourage me to keep writing.

If you love this book, leaving a review (even a short one) on Amazon is a humongous help to me. Recommending it on social media and in reader groups and book clubs also helps immensely.

Thank you for reading this story.

Hope life is filled with love, laughs, great people, good food, amazing orgasms, and lots + lots of delicious book boyfriends.

XOXO

DD Prince

I'm on social media and interact almost daily in my Facebook reader group. I'd love for you to join:

http://facebook.com/groups/ddprincefangroup

Fun, teasers, book chats, giveaways, the insider scoop, ARC/Beta reading opportunities, and most of all… shenanigans!

I've also got a free newsletter that goes out with new release info, sales, and freebies and I've got plans to cook up some exclusive content, so I hope you'll join- http://ddprince.com/newsletter-signup/

DD Prince's Books:

This list might have been updated since publishing so check my website ddprince.com for the latest information.

Alphahole, an enemies-to-lovers contemporary and roommates romance. Yes. It's all those things. And more. Carly is ready for a new job and a new start in a new city. But she has to share her corporate apartment with an absolute alphahole. He's also her boss. Aiden Carmichael is absolutely infuriating. You're going to fucking love him. Carly's not sure what the arrogant man-whore wants more – to ruin her career or get into her pants.

When you're done, there are books for Austin, Aiden's brother, and Ally, Carly's bestie.

The Beautiful Biker Series: MC Romance: Romantic suspense with comedy, angst, steamy scenes, and a little bit of gritty darkness.

This alpha-male is not an alpha-hole. You're going to FLOVE Deacon Valentine.

Detour (Beautiful Biker 1) Deacon and Ella

Joyride (Beautiful Biker 2) Rider and Jenna

Rider starts out as a little bit of an alpha-hole. Jenna resists, but resistance is futile when a Valentine brother has you in his sights.

Scenic Route (Beautiful Biker 3) Spencer and Pippa

Crossroads (Beautiful Biker 4) Fork and Jojo.

Jaded (Beautiful Biker 5) Jesse and Gianna

LOTS more biker books coming.

Dark Mafia Romance: dark romance with a debt flesh payment plot.

This one DD's most popular book, but it is dark. Non-consensual / rough sex. Tommy Ferrano is an anti-hero you may love to hate and hate to love.

The Dominator

The Dominator 2. Truth or Dare (Sex slave rescue romance with dark themes. Dario Ferrano's story).

The Dominator 3. Unbound (More Tommy, More Dare; More Domination!)

Saved (Spin off Dark Romance (maybe DD's darkest romance book yet). Lex isn't the hero in this story. Holly is.)

TNT – 4th Anniversary Novella – (Timeline is book 1.5 but best experienced after book 3.)

The Devious Games Duet – Kill Game and Dirty Stack (connected to the Dominator series but can be read as standalone).

Nectar Trilogy (Includes Nectar, Ambrosia, and Essence)

Dark Paranormal Romance: Vampire dark romance / kidnapping. Capture romance with dark and taboo elements.

Dirty / fun / insta-love alien romance

Hot Alpha Alien Husbands: Book 1 – Daxx and Jetta

Hot Alpha Alien Husbands: Book 2 – Zane and Tanya

Book 3 coming!

The Hollow Duet: (Hollow and Holden)

A dark and erotic fairytale retelling. Erotic thriller/horror.

There's a quick list of all currently available books with universal links at http://ddprince.com/about-dd_prince/quick-info-buy-links-for-all-dd-prince-books/ .

Please note: book retailers and subscription program participation may change without notice.

Thanks for reading! If you enjoy my books a huge help is posting a review where you purchased it. Thank you!

www.ingramcontent.com/pod-product-compliance
Ingram Content Group UK Ltd.
Pitfield, Milton Keynes, MK11 3LW, UK
UKHW011339050825
7244UKWH000041B/41